Pink Sky & Mourning

Kim Scott

ISBN: 10: 1480004790
ISBN-13: 978-1480004795

DEDICATION

This book is dedicated to my mother, Georgia Jones.
Her encouragement, support and assistance is greatly appreciated.

Many thanks!

RUTH CHERNOCK SERIES

The books in this series are:
Regarding Ruth
In Ruth's Memory
On Grace's Shoulders
Pink Sky & Mourning

ACKNOWLEDGMENTS

Great thanks to my family and friends for
their patience and support!

Special thanks to Georgia Jones for her
tremendous assistance with editing.
To my family and friends for their support and encouragement.
I could fill pages with all of the additional acknowledgements.
To my family, friends, readers, fellow authors, and the myriad
of people who keep me going in the right direction, thank you!

For a better feel of the historical fiction in this series, go to
http://pinterest.com/kimscottwrites/

Look for Kim Scott on Facebook at
http://www.facebook.com/RegardingRuth

On her website at http://www.kimscottbooks.com/

Her Twitter ID is ttocs3mik

Or email her directly at KimScott@kimscottbooks.com

1

Sheriff Mitchell brushed the black crepe aside. He lifted the brass knocker, clacked it against the door and waited uneasily. Two yellow butterflies fluttered around the spindly blue flowers to his left. Growing impatient, he rapped the knocker more firmly and scuffed his boots against the fieldstone steps. As the lock snapped back and the latch clicked, he lifted his chin and rolled his shoulders back.

"Good morn, Dr. Wallace," he announced boldly as Luke swung the door open and stood looking down at him.

"Good morn, Sheriff Mitchell," Luke responded uneasily. "Tis unusual that you shall come to Burghill House."

"Tis a legal interest," Mitchell responded as he held out the warrant. Luke broke the wax seal on the envelope and shook out the crisp page. He read quickly and looked up in disbelief.

"Why should you think to pursue this thing?" he snapped, angrily.

"Twas not my doing, Dr. Wallace. A complaint was made and Judge Daniel Gage did sign it. Tis naught I might do but make the arrest," the sheriff replied, smiling smugly.

"You shant be welcomed as a guest of this house," the doctor announced. "Linger on the doorstep if you must. I shall require ten minutes to attend to this matter afore you shall see the end you seek."

"Tis reasonable, good Sir," he smirked. "I shall not linger at your door, but shall wander along the roadside as I do tarry."

Luke slammed the door shut and bounded up the stairs. He pounded urgently at the door and stepped back toward the window seat at the end of the large open hallway. The warm August sun streamed through the glass and he forced the sash up further. A slight breeze stirred the curtains but provided little relief from the summer heat.

Joseph strode out of the bedroom with little Teague following close behind him. He closed the door quietly and gave Luke a sideways glance as he raised his eyebrows quizzically. "What troubles you so, Uncle Luke?"

"Teague, Mrs. Whitley did prepare blueberry muffins this morn. Mayhap you shall run and ask for a cup of milk with it!" Luke heralded, cheerfully. Teague smiled and hurried down to the kitchen. "Joseph, Sheriff Mitchell has come for you this morn."

"Why should he think to seek me?" Joseph asked, confused and worried.

"Tis a warrant for your arrest. Judge Gage did endorse it," Luke told him and rubbed his forehead in frustration. "Tis stated that the new baby, Thea was conceived afore you did marry Colleen."

"Tis falsehood!" Joseph shouted. "Colleen did permit no liberties afore I did wed her!"

"The child did come but nine months from your wedding. Tis asserted that you did violate her and worse. The trouble with Naomi is avowed within the warrant."

"My son is six years-old! Why should this issue be broached now?"

"I know not, Joseph," Luke responded. "Surrender fairly to the sheriff. I shall ride for Judge Gage and he shall work to make it right. Timothy shall be sent for you swiftly."

"Speak naught of this to Colleen," Joseph charged. "I shall not have her worrying over this thing as she does mend from Thea's birthing."

"Tis fair and true," Luke nodded as he clapped Joseph on the back. He strode toward the stairs, while Joseph slipped back into the bed chamber.

After a quick farewell to Colleen, Joseph trudged down to the kitchen. Calmly, he kissed his mother and patted Teague's head before he walked out the back door. He saddled his horse and walked along the drive to the road, holding the leads. Sheriff Mitchell stood beside his mare, watching Joseph approach.

"Shall you yield freely, Joseph Grenier?"

"I shall," he answered and glanced up at the bedroom window, grateful that Colleen did not appear there.

"Let us ride," Sheriff Mitchell declared and mounted his gray horse.

2

"Judge Gage, might you speak with me this morn?" Luke pressed as he stood in the doorway of the judge's private library. The housekeeper waited nervously behind him, wringing her hands.

"Come!" he announced as he looked passed Luke to Mrs. Quinn. "Bring victuals and see that we are not disturbed!"

"Yes, Sir," she hurried anxiously back to the kitchen as Luke shut the door.

"Daniel, you did sign a warrant against Joseph!"

"That I did," he proclaimed and slammed the massive book closed on the heavily polished table.

"How should you think to do it? Twas near seven years ago that Joseph did err with Naomi Hughes. The midwife shall tell that Colleen did deliver a small babe at nine months after the marriage of Joseph and Colleen Sweeney. Tis no cause for this arrest!"

Mrs. Quinn tapped softly at the heavy door and entered with a tray of tea and fruited cakes. She placed it on the table and scurried back out of the room again. Daniel filled a cup and passed it to Luke, then filled his own. He drew a silver flask from his coat and added a dollop to each teacup then secreted it away again.

"Luke, why shall you think it rightful that Lily shall be punished so for her acts of adultery, yet Joseph shall not. Tis a wrongful air about Burghill House that shall be remedied. How do the children of that house think it rightful to sin so? Twas I who did swear to the warrant against Joseph Grenier. The wicked ways of the Grenier's shall be cleansed!"

"Tis spiteful that you shall see Joseph arrested. Twas reasonable that the child conceived of Lily's adultery be removed from your house and away from your son. Timothy should not be required to raise the progeny of his wife's lover. Yet Joseph and Colleen were blessed with a child but weeks ago and you shall deny him the site of the babe, if you persist."

"What of Naomi Hughes, Luke?"

"Twas wrongful that Joseph did lay with her afore they did wed. Still do you not believe that he has suffered well as he has grieved her death these long years?"

"I do not!" Daniel thundered. "The law shall be satisfied. If you do seek to serve his interests then you shall instruct that he confess his sins and beg for mercy from the court and God!"

"Mayhap you shall alter your thinking. Joseph is father to Teague and Thea. How shall he provide for his wife and children as he does linger in the jail?"

"Tis not my concern, Dr. Wallace. Let those of Burghill House who did foster the air of iniquity tend to his family now."

"Daniel, how have you been made such a condemnatory man?"

"My dear wife does lie in her bed weeping night and day. She is inconsolable after the departure of Albert! I do watch her decline and know not how I shall repair this thing. My son does resent me greatly and our rapport is gone from us. His wife, Lily does grieve for the son of her lover as she neglects Timothy's own children. You presume to speak of the inconvenience to Joseph Grenier as my house does agonize so? Take leave, Dr. Wallace. I shant talk with you again afore his trial."

Luke rose slowly and walked to the door. "Daniel, my family does mourn for Albert as well. Grace does weep often over his loss. The happiness of Lily and Timothy is principal for me and mine too. Twas a dreadful thing that we did seek to remove the baby from Lily and more tragic still if he had remained. Yet the punishing of Joseph shall not heal your house."

Dejectedly, Luke walked along the hall to the front door. He closed it softly behind him and stepped down onto the slate walkway. The great stallion waited for him at the hitching post near the road. He climbed up into the saddle and trotted unhurriedly back onto Kings Wood Road, bound for Burghill House.

3

Joseph followed closely behind Sheriff Mitchell as they entered the jail. The thick stone walls of the building kept it cooler through the heat of summer and far colder in the bitter winter. The keys jangled loudly in the narrow hall. Mitchell chose a large, iron key and forced it into the lock box on the cell door. It swung open with a loud, unnerving creaking sound.

"Have you a statement or confession afore I shall depart?" Mitchell asked as he ushered Joseph into the small, stone room with the straw bed in the corner.

"Tis naught I shall confess to the likes of you," Joseph responded.

The sheriff swung without warning, striking a glancing blow to Joseph's cheek bone and knocking him back into the wall. "There shall be respect shown in this place, Mr. Grenier."

"Tis respect for your office," Joseph uttered as he gripped the doorframe and pulled himself up. "Yet you shall not oblige that I shall esteem you as you do lock me away wrongfully. If I shall make confessions it shall not be unto your ears," Joseph said as he glared at him.

The sheriff clouted him again, connecting with Joseph's chin. Understanding his situation, Joseph simply stepped back from the door and wiped the blood from his lip. Mitchell kicked at the empty chamber pot and nodded, smiling complacently. "You shall receive sustenance twice daily," he announced as he banged the cell door closed and locked it.

Joseph gingerly touched the cut on his cheek bone that bled as it swelled further. His jaw ached and his head throbbed. He bunched the straw in a pile in the corner and sat there. With his long legs and his arms crossed, he leaned back against the cool stone and closed his eyes. He thought of Colleen and his children before his mind quickly wandered in search of Naomi. She was seldom far away and she always provided great comfort.

Late in the afternoon Luke visited the jail. The sheriff's brother, Adam Mitchell welcomed him and escorted him to Joseph's cell. He examined the bruise that had swelled, nearly closing Joseph's right eye and the nasty cut on the cheek bone. The mark on his jaw was less severe but had blossomed into a deep shade of plum.

"Did you provoke the man?" Luke asked worriedly.

"In his estimation, I did so," Joseph told him as he sat on the straw again.

"Tis naught to be gained as you do rouse a man with power over you," Luke cautioned.

"Tis fair and true."

"Judge Gage shall not bend," Luke declared. "Yet Timothy did consent to act for you afore the court. Tis no more I might do to remedy this trouble."

"What of Colleen?"

"She must be told, Joseph. Timothy did warn you shall linger for a time."

"Uncle Luke, how shall I remain in this jail?"

"You shall remain, as you have no option."

"Might you know when I shall be freed?"

"Timothy did state you shall prepare to linger over the coming months."

"The coming months!" Joseph bellowed. "Shall there be no bail?"

"Tis at Judge Gage's discretion. His ire has been raised and I know not if he shall acquiesce."

"Mayhap Lily shall plead it to him."

"Shall you have a woman speak for you to the man?" Luke asked and scowled.

"No, I shall not. Twas a desperate thought."

"Draw on your patient nature, mind your tongue and pray ceaselessly as you do linger. Trust that the matter shall come to a swift end."

4

More than a month passed before Judge Gage consented to a hearing. Timothy prodded gently but did not dare pursue other legal routes, given his father's foul mood. He knew he could resolve the matter and free Joseph, but there would be repercussions. While Timothy prepared and Joseph waited, summer submitted to fall. Moderate days and chilly nights prompted the change of the leaves from the lush green hues to the rich, warm yellows, oranges and reds. Too soon September passed into October.

"Mr. Grenier!" the deep, booming voice echoed in the small space.

Joseph gripped the rounded stones along the wall and scrambled to his feet. The bruises received on his first day in the jail had faded, but a thin scar remained on his cheek bone. He inhaled and coughed painfully. Grudgingly, he looked at the judge, who blocked most of the light from the narrow doorway.

"Good, Sir," Joseph nodded deferentially.

"This day you shall be liberated. You shall compensate the County for the outlay of board and repasts given you as you did remain within this jail. Additionally you shall make confession for your misdeeds and shall satisfy fines imposed against you. Shall you consent?"

"I shall," Joseph responded, anxious to be released.

"The jailer shall take your confession and accept your coinage. Shall you be trusted to go forth and sin no more?"

"'Tis my word and my bond, I shall transgress no further, Judge Gage," he answered and coughed harshly.

"See to it!" Daniel responded as he stepped back and watched as Adam Mitchell entered the cell. "Dr. Wallace shall be summoned to make good the fines. Good day, Mr. Grenier," he asserted and turned to walk away.

Joseph's confession was recorded and substantial fines were paid that afternoon. A hefty charge was added for the use of the cell and his meals during his detention there. Luke waited under the trees outside the jail. He greeted Joseph with a powerful handshake and led him to the horse cart, in the shade trees. He passed the reins to Joseph and the Morgan horses were quickly galloping through the town center from River Road onto Kings Wood.

Colleen's "lying-in" had ended weeks earlier. Through the afternoon she worked with Grace and Mrs. Whitley to prepare a great feast, to welcome Joseph home. The family gathered at Burghill House, excited over his return. Turkey, venison and wine stewed rabbit were laid out on ornate silver trays. Roasted vegetables, bread pudding, fried eggs, and fruit compote were set out in bowls and baskets. Wine and ale were poured and pitchers provided for refilling. While the family ate and talked, Mrs. Whitley loaded a variety of cakes, pastries and pies onto a solid oak cart and wheeled it along the hall to the dining room.

Before the dinner concluded, Timothy offered a toast to his wife Lily and announced that she would bless him with another child in the spring. Lily smiled adoringly up at her husband and sipped the sweet, dark wine. Luke raised his glass high and breathed a silent prayer for a healthy infant who might help to heal the rift between the Gage and Burghill households.

The autumn sun coaxed an array of enchanting, aromatic fragrances from the trees and the earth. In the woods the animals prepared for the coming of winter. Even the gentlest of breezes teased the colorful leaves from the trees. The ground was littered with decaying leaves that faded from their opulent colors to shades of brown. As they declined, they continued to scent the air with a delightful aroma.

After dinner, Joseph tended to the horses and returned to the house. Grace greeted him with a warm hug and encouraged him to slip out to the benches, under the tree in the back yard with Colleen. Joseph took Colleen's hand and pulled her toward the door as she quickly untied her apron and tossed it into the washtub. The door banged shut and she giggled, running to keep up with him. He dropped onto the bench and pulled her down beside him.

"I did miss you greatly, Colleen," he breathed and gently kissed her.

"And I you, Joseph," she told him as she blushed. "'Twas a frightful thing that you did go so quickly."

"I believed it best that you not be worried over it. Uncle Luke and I did think it would be done with swiftly. Yet Judge Gage did prevent the resolution. 'Tis done and I shant dwell upon it."

"Your uncle did forbid that Grace and I visit with you."

"'Tis no place for a woman of virtue, Colleen."

"Joseph, why should the good judge think to charge you with such improprieties? 'Twas naught between you and me afore we did marry."

"Must we speak of this thing, Colleen?"

"Your uncle did state that a confession was required of you."

"He should not have disclosed my business unto you."

"Joseph, did you tell lies of me? How should you confess to that which we did not do?"

"I did confess to the truth alone," he told her as he pondered his dusty boots.

"Husband, pray tell me your confession. If it was not of me you did speak, then what?"

"Tis but hours since I did return. Must you badger me so?" he snapped.

"Have I no right to know of the misdeeds of my husband? Joseph, did Naomi permit you liberties afore you did wed her?"

"Speak not of Naomi!" he shouted as he jumped up from the bench. "Her name shall not pass your lips!" Angrily he strode through the tall dry grass. Shocked into silence, Colleen watched as he strode out behind the barn. A single tear rolled down her cheek as she listened to the heavy thwack of the axe hitting the logs. She drew in a sharp breath and walked slowly across the backyard.

"Joseph," she called to him. He ignored her and set another log on the chopping block. He lifted the axe above his head and swung with all his strength. The two halves of the wood dropped to the ground and he grabbed another log. "Joseph," she repeated.

"Leave me be, Colleen," he exhaled as he hefted a fat log onto the block and quartered it.

"I should like to apologize. Twas wrongful that I did ask of your concerns," she pleaded.

"Go!" he bellowed as he swung the axe forcefully.

Colleen turned back toward the house. When she had gone, he sat heavily on the stump behind him. The wretched coughs rattled his chest and he dropped his head in his hands. Thoughts of Naomi rushed at him and he felt the sensation of drowning. He struggled to fill his lungs as an intense wave of guilt engulfed him. He stood as another coughing fit shook him and he moved toward the path into the woods. Slowly he made his way along the trail to the family cemetery.

The afternoon sun drooped low in the sky. As the temperature cooled and the breeze stilled, a low bank of fog blanketed the ground. Joseph sat on the fieldstone wall that bordered the graveyard, staring at Naomi's marker. He coughed again, painfully and looked up at the darkening sky.

"I must go, my love," he whispered as he stood and moved to touch the cold stone. He blew a kiss and walked slowly back to the gates. Sadly, he moved along the path, moving through the shadows, toward Burghill House.

5

The last of the guests had gone and a stillness settled over the house. Joseph stood alone in the hall staring out the window. High in the pine trees across the road an owl turned to look in his direction. He sighed and thought about Naomi. He recalled the feeling of holding her in his arms and the scent of lavender on her neck.

Quietly, he pressed the latch and opened the bedroom door. Only a faint glow remained in the fireplace and the shadows crept out from their corners. He pulled off his boots and crossed the room. Stirring the embers with a piece of kindling, he watched a low flame ignite. Scraps of wood touched the fire and it rolled over the surface. He placed a fat log gently atop the low fire and watched as it caught.

"Colleen," he whispered, looking through the orange blaze. "Colleen," he repeated, louder this time.

She lay still with her eyes closed. In the wooden cradle beside the bed their infant daughter slept soundly. Colleen listened to him moving near the fireplace. They had not spoken since he shouted at her behind the barn that afternoon. He coughed harshly and she fought the urge to comfort him. Several minutes passed and she waited for him to come to bed or leave the room again.

"Colleen, do not flout me this night," he murmured and coughed again. "I do need you this night," he breathed. He sat heavily, on the side of the bed and looked down at his hands.

Reluctantly she surrendered and turned over to face him. "Husband," she spoke softly as she looked up at his handsome face. Her heart melted as she studied the painful look in his eyes.

"My father did forbid that I court Naomi. Her father, Rev. Hughes and mine detested one another. I did respect Papa greatly, yet I could not resist her from the first. She did enchant me so. I travelled often to the orphan asylum for the mere sight of her. When Papa did prohibit my scheme I did effort to obey him.

Tis a lie! I did not submit to his will. Often I did hunt the woods behind the children's home to be near her. Boldly I went close to the house near every day. To catch sight of Naomi was my only desire. When the morning came that I did observe her pinning wet linens to dry, my heart thundered inside me.

Mindlessly I strode through the tall grass and called her to me behind a copse of thick pines.

Naomi smiled and all was forgotten. I did take her into my arms and the scent of lavender was on her skin. With not a care I did clutch her hand in mine and pulled her far from the path. A girl of virtue, she did protest my advances. Yet I heard her not. My mouth pressed hard against her lips and I did furiously work the buttons at her bodice.

When the deed was done I did turn from her in shame. I had taken her with no consent from her lips. Tis the most shameful act of my life. Humiliated, I turned away from her as she dressed and repaired her hair. I thought to run from her and end myself. Twas naught I might do to remedy my horrific actions. My heart ached and I listened, waiting for her to take leave of me.

I felt her hand on my shoulder yet I could not look upon her. Behind me she spoke softly as she told me twas wrongful that I did know her afore we did wed. Yet she did love me equally and could not condemn my doing. She bid me marry her and safeguard her virtue. I did yearn to make her my bride, still our fathers would not hear it." Another fit of coughing began and he paused, waiting for it to pass.

"We did congregate in the woods often. I did lay with her among the trees and did relish her every touch. Desperately, I did devise a plan to take her away with me to Boston or Philadelphia. Yet afore I might spirit her off she did conceive my son. Frightfully, I did go to Rev. Hughes and did beg that he should permit the marriage. He did refuse and turned her away unmercifully.

With Naomi, I did return to Burghill House to plead with Papa. He was enraged and did strike me forcefully afore Uncle Luke did bid him end it. Angrily, he did command me go. Shattered, I did depart the home of my family. Uncle Luke provided me coinage and instructed that I journey to New Anglesey. Terrified, she and I did travel in the night away from all we knew.

Many months later my Naomi lay at my side in our bed. She had become the core of my life and the love for her filled my heart. In the night, the baby kicked hard against her great round belly. She wept and pleaded for respite as the pains gripped her. At her behest I did journey to East Grantham for the midwife.

Naomi did pass in the morning. Papa, Uncle Luke and Joanna did tend her but none could save her. The surgeon did mind her and liberated my son. My heart did shatter as I held him and knew my beloved had gone from me. I did pray my life be ended that I might hold Naomi in my arms again. Yet Rev. Pender did caution against it for I should be denied her forever as I lingered in the fires of hell. I could not abide eternity without her.

As I did linger in the jail I did dwell painfully on my short life with Naomi. Twas a horrible time I did endure. Sleep did come to me with dreadful nightmares of her death and the agony I did know. She shall never depart from my heart or vacate my thoughts utterly. My son does remind me continually of the woman I did lose too soon." He began coughing again and raised his head, gasping for air.

"Colleen, I cannot abide the queries of Naomi as it brings the pain fresh again. The horror of her death and the shame in my misdeeds. Twas wrongful that I did confront you so, yet I cannot bear it. Shall you forgive me? I do need you desperately this night. I pray you shall not deny me your arms that they might hold me," he pleaded.

"I shall not rebuff you," she responded as she touched his arm. Frantically, he moved to her side and pulled her tight against him. She felt his warm tears against her neck as he clutched her to his chest.

"Colleen, I do love you greatly. I beseech you do not go from me," he begged and choked back sobs and coughed.

"I shant take leave of you, Joseph. Tis none I shall love over you," she replied gently as she struggled to breath in his constrictive embrace. She lay still as he drifted into a restless sleep. Through the night she woke often as he coughed beside her and moved continually. Worriedly, she considered waking Luke to care for Joseph but decided to wait for morning.

6

The bright orange moon darkened to a deep red. Luke stood in a clearing, surrounded by tall pine trees. A brisk wind tugged at his thin coat, chilling him. He shoved his right hand into his pocket and looked around, searching for the path. Behind him the spring bubbled with fresh, cold water. As he turned slowly, the clear water turned to blood and flowed over the edge of the small pool.

"Looking for someone?" a deep voice called from the dark pines.

"Who is there?" Luke responded, his words quivering anxiously.

"Tis I, old friend," Phillip chuckled as he jumped down from a great boulder and strode toward him.

"No, you are gone!" Luke felt the panic rising.

"Would that you had treated me months afore I did pass. You watched the signs of my heart worsening yet you did not heal me, physician. Did you will me away that you might wed my beloved Grace?"

"I did not! You did conceal your symptoms, Phillip."

"You knew, physician!"

"What of me, Uncle Luke?" a soft voice spoke from behind the cluster of birch trees. Cherish dragged herself slowly across the muddy ground toward him.

"Cherish!"

"I did choke to death as I lay before you. You did naught but to push the bread into my throat."

"Twas believed you did swallow the fish bone!" Luke pleaded.

"Physician, you had but to reach your fingers into my mouth and pull out the chunk of venison. You could have saved me. My life was only beginning and I was betrothed to Carter Fontaine. You did forsake me."

"No, Cherish," he appealed. "I did all that I might."

"You did relinquish me, Physician. Afore I did pass you did not acknowledge me as your daughter. Did you not love me?"

"Cherish, I did love you greatly," he called out as he dropped to his knees on the damp forest floor.

"What of me, Uncle Luke?" Reynolds shouted as he stepped forward. "The surgeon could have saved me yet your pride did prevent it. Why did you think to treat me wrongfully afore you did summon Ben Andrews?"

"Reynolds, I did think it a sound treatment."

"No, Dr. Wallace!" Reynolds replied. "You did question the method as you applied it. Twas wrongful yet you refused to call for the surgeon that night. My wife and son are denied my love. 'Tis a shameful thing, Physician."

"Luke Wallace!" a gruff angry man bellowed as he shuffled through the accumulation of dried leaves. "You shant deny my undoing!"

Luke shivered as he recognized the voice of Ross Eastman. Slowly he turned to look behind him. Ross stood near the spring holding the rock. His ruined face made him nearly unrecognizable. He angled his head and stared at Luke through his remaining eye. Warily he stepped forward and began tossing the round stone from hand to hand.

"Ross, I did act irrationally to save Julia and Reny from your attacks."

"Shall you think your reasoning did justify my murder, Physician?" Ross mocked him.

"I do not. Yet tis done with," Luke stated firmly. "'Tis naught I might do to remedy your deaths. Take leave of me and give me peace."

"You shall not have serenity, Luke Wallace!" Ross hollered as he threw the rock, striking Luke's shoulder. He winced at the pain and looked down as Cherish gripped his ankle. She pulled quickly, throwing him off-balance. He fell back, thumping his head hard against the ground. Ross stepped forward and placed his boot on Luke's chest, pressing firmly and forcing the air from his lungs. Luke gasped for air and struggled as Reynolds and Phillip moved forward.

A primal scream escaped his lips as he sat up quickly in the bed, gulping mouthfuls of air. Wildly he looked around the bedroom, desperately trying to shake off the nightmare. Grace sat beside him watching him worriedly in the dim light from the dwindling fire. He threw back the quilt and looked for a boot print on his chest. Gradually his drumming heartbeat slowed again and the feeling of horror subsided.

"Luke, shall I make tea for you?" Grace asked softly.

"No, no, sleep, Grace," he stammered as he slipped down off the bed and dressed quickly.

He strode across the hall to the sitting room and lit two lamps. Prodding the last of the burning logs in the fireplace he threw on two logs in the shape of an X. Warily he dropped into his chair behind the desk and rubbed his forehead.

"Luke, what troubles you so?" Grace asked from the doorway.

"Tis naught I shall discuss," he answered.

"The nightly dreams do fill me with worry."

"Grace, tis but an hour to sunrise. Sleep while you might."

"How shall I sleep while you do suffer so? Acknowledge your fretfulness to me and ease your head."

"Tis naught I should confess!" he roared, the panic filling him again. He threw the fireplace poker down on the slate hearth mat and stomped out to the kitchen. In the dark pantry he felt along the shelf for the whiskey jug and pulled it down. He removed the stopper and touched the salt glazed clay to his lips. He swallowed deeply and leaned back against the wall. After another long drink of it, he pushed the jug back up on the top shelf. He moved quietly to the table and sat. With his head resting on his arms he waited for daylight.

7

The sun broke over the horizon with a soft yellow glow against the deep blue of the fading night sky. Luke was startled awake as Mrs. Whitley shut her bedroom door and entered the kitchen. He rubbed his eyes and nodded politely to her. She smiled in return and began preparing breakfast for the family. Quietly, Luke rose from the table and wandered back toward the bedroom.

Grace sat dozing in the chair beside the fire, a quilt draped over her lap. She looked up as he stepped into the room. He frowned and stretched out across the width of the bed with his boots hanging over the edge.

"Luke, I am greatly worried," she spoke softly. As he lay with the left side of his face against the pillow, his scars were hidden completely. She bit her lip and sighed, admiring his striking good looks.

"Twas but a wicked dream in the night, Grace," he assured her and smiled.

"No, Luke. Tis more yet you shall not speak it."

"Nagging shall not draw it from me, woman. Come to my bed and lay with me, Wife!" he growled and held out his hand to her.

She stood and reached toward him. Quickly he pulled her onto the bed and opened her gown.

"Tis breakfast to be readied," she resisted, giggling as he kissed her face and neck.

"If it shall please the master of the house greatly, then Mrs. Whitley shall be only too happy to attend to it alone."

"Luke Wallace, you are shameless this morn!" she called out as she surrendered to him.

In the kitchen Colleen held Thea at her shoulder as she moved about, helping Mrs. Whitley. When the final preparations were done she carried the infant into the dining room and placed her in a cradle near the fire.

Joseph stood in the upstairs hallway, leaning against the balustrade as he waited for another coughing fit to pass. Mac climbed the stairs to the landing and stood watching him closely. Joseph only nodded to him and held his hand against his chest.

"Tis a violent hacking," Mac muttered.

"It shall pass," Joseph grumbled and frowned.

"Mayhap I might aid you."

"You are but fifteen years, Mackenzie. How shall you think to aid me?"

"If you shall indulge me, mayhap I shall," Mac offered as he turned and walked down to the kitchen.

Mildly amused by his younger cousin's persistence, he followed him. Watching him move about the kitchen, Joseph dropped into a chair at the end of the table. He reached for a corn muffin from the tray and ate it while Mac worked in front of the hearth.

"Tis work to be done, Mac. I shall soon depart for the Chernock's woodshop. Shall you be done with your women's work in short?" Joseph teased.

"Tis no women's work, Joseph!" Mac barked as he moved a steaming copper pot to the table. Carefully he placed it in front of Joseph and grabbed for a linen cloth from the mantle above the hearth. "Cover your head with the linen and breathe deep of the steaming liquid."

Skeptically Joseph looked up at Mac as he grabbed the towel from him and did as instructed. He coughed and choked briefly as he breathed in the vapors from the hot vinegar. For five minutes he sat hunched over the pot as Mac measured and mixed, beside him at the table.

At last Mac removed the linen towel and pushed the copper pot away. He held out a tankard to Joseph and stirred it well. "Drink the full of it," Mac advised and Joseph took a quick sip.

"Tis ghastly," Joseph protested.

"Drink!" Mac ordered.

When Joseph had drained the last of the murky brown liquid, he banged the pewter tankard against the table. "Tis done with," Joseph complained, and shivered with distaste.

"Swallow a full spoon of the wildflower honey and a bite of the honeycomb. Repeat this thing four times each today and breathe of the vinegar again afore you sleep this night."

Joseph chuckled and took the spoon from Mac. "Do you believe yourself to be a doctor now?"

"I think myself a doctor in training," Mac answered and pushed the honey pot at him. "If you shant follow my scheme then you shall suffer of your own."

Joseph sighed and tasted the delicious honey. He reached for another corn muffin and bit into it, smiling broadly. "I shall abide your remedy, Mac," he responded. "Yet if it shant heal me I shall taunt you mercilessly over it."

"Agreed," Mac replied as he sauntered along the hall to the dining room.

8

Joseph continued Mac's prescribed treatment for several days as his cough and the rattle in his chest improved quickly. Grudgingly, he acknowledged that the plan had worked and he thanked Mac for his assistance. Colleen happily baked an apple and raisin spice cake with sweet icing for Mac and presented it with her thanks as well.

As November arrived with unseasonably warm days and light breezes, winter preparations continued. Together Joseph and Mac split another full cord of wood and stored it beneath a lean-to. Grace hoped that the weather would remain mild and allow for a great Christmas ball. Yet in less than a week the temperatures began falling. A brief storm with freezing rain and a biting wind signaled the end of autumn.

A light snow fell only days before Christmas. Sub-zero conditions and strong gusts discouraged travel, yet friends, family, and neighbors filled Burghill House for Grace's great party. An impressive feast was laid out in the dining room. As he passed the dining room, Luke was completely unnerved. The unpleasant reminder of Cherish's party nearly two years earlier was too much for him to bear. He demanded that the food and drink be moved to the informal kitchen. The large dining room was cleared of all furniture and left for dancing alone.

Grace greeted her guests, dressed in a pale rose Indian muslin with silver embroidery. A dark rose sash belt, woven from silk thread, was tied just below the bust line of the empire waist. She swept across the room, with an elegant air, in silk party slippers embroidered with sequins. She smiled easily with Luke at her side.

Colleen tapped softly down the stairs with Joseph at her elbow. She dressed in her rust brown gown with diamond-shaped motif, embroidered with gold sequins and chenille. Small pleats in the back draped to form a sculptured bustle. Her lovely strawberry blonde hair was adorned with yellow and orange silk flowers and loops of gold thread in the center of each bloom.

Lily arrived with Timothy close behind her. She wore a rich blue silk gauze gown with silver stripes and dots woven throughout the fabric. Her matching petticoat was trimmed and appliquéd with shells made of silvered, embossed paper. Like her petticoat, her shawl matched her dress with delightful shells. Below her half sleeves, shimmery white gloves covered her arms and hands.

Emma followed Noah into the entryway, with a smile on her lips. She winked at Noah and he smiled in return as he strode into the sitting room and she moved back to the kitchen. Her gown was a rich burgundy silk taffeta gown, with an ivory underskirt visible in the front. A gold mesh French ribbon formed a great bow at her waist. Her infant son was bundle in a boiled wool blanket, sleeping against her shoulder.

Julia arrived late with her husband, Laurent Morgan, following behind her as she hurried in from the cold. She wore an icy blue polished cotton gown with white, silk embroidery edging the bodice, hem and sleeves. An organza drape covered her shoulders and was pinned with a simple silver pin at the center of her bodice. As she moved toward the kitchen where most of the women congregated, Laurent followed her. Gently she squeezed his hand

and smiled as she nodded toward the sitting room where the raucous voices of the men could be heard over the music.

The children were fed and quickly ushered up the stairs to the old nursery. Lily's Nanny and Mrs. Whitley settled in with the babies and toddlers left in their care. The string quartet, normally seated in the upper hallway had been moved down to the entryway. The music floated up the open stairwell, lulling the children to sleep.

Downstairs, the dancing had begun in the dining room. In the sitting room, cordials and fine cigars were offered as the older gentlemen settled in near the fireplace to talk of serious matters. In the kitchen, the guests sampled the delicious array of fine foods provided. A smaller table was placed in the hall with a variety of rich desserts to sample. Late in the evening several carolers gathered at the bottom of the stairs and began to sing. As the family and guests celebrated the holiday gregariously, the tragedies of the past few years were quickly forgotten.

Grace stood in the doorway to the dining room, smiling as she watched Joseph and Colleen dancing happily in the far corner of the room. Closer to the doorway, Laurent held Julia in his arms as he twirled her around with a broad smile on his handsome face. Julia's cheeks flushed bright pink. Grace raised a curious eyebrow and Julia mouthed the words new baby. Julia reached for her hand and Grace pulled her into an embrace.

"'Tis a fine thing you shall be blessed with a new baby," she murmured next to Julia's ear.

Lily stopped beside Grace, with a glass of mulled cider. She sipped from the goblet and nodded toward Julia. "You are to be blessed with another child as well?"

"I am," Julia affirmed as she moved to hug Lily. Laurent stood beside Julia, beaming over the news.

"Many blessings," Lily forced, as she turned to Laurent and leaned awkwardly toward the big man. His arm circled her slight waist and he pulled her toward him as he bent down, forgetting all social decorum in his moment of bliss.

"How shall you dare?" Timothy roared as he raced across the hallway from the sitting room. He swung wildly, grazing Laurent's chin and knocking Lily aside. "Was it not sufficient that you did bed my wife? You shall hold her publicly and move to take her from me as well?"

Drunkenly, Timothy threw another punch, aiming for Laurent's face. Laurent dodged it easily and landed a blow to the left side of Timothy's jaw. Laurent stood watching as Timothy crumpled to the floor in front of him.

The musicians and carolers fell silent and the room filled with gasps and whispers. Timothy lay still on the polished wood floor as the guests backed away from him. Luke, Joseph and Mac hurriedly picked him up and shuffled back through the sitting room to the bedroom with him. Luke carefully examined the jaw and advised him it appeared to be cracked. Mac slipped outside for several packed snowballs to ice it.

Laurent stared down at his shoes, his face bright red and beads of sweat glistened on his forehead.

"Mayhap we shall take leave, Julia," he mumbled and reached for her hand.

"Did Timothy speak the truth?" she asked as she looked from her husband to Lily and back again.

"Come," he urged and tugged her back toward the kitchen.

Lily looked to Grace, fighting the tears that threatened to flow. She closed her eyes and chewed her lower lip. Grace sighed heavily and grasped Lily's hand, rushing up the stairs as she announced they should check on the sleeping babies.

Noah strode out from the sitting room with a flint glass of amber liquid in his hand. He looked around the open hall at the shocked faces, as the murmur of gossip rose. Emma stood in the doorway to the dining room cringing.

"Tis a shameful thing that the good Esquire, Timothy Gage did overindulge this night," Noah announced. "It does appear a foolish imagining did overtake him! Let the pain and illness he shall suffer in the morn be his punishment," he laughed heartily.

The guests relaxed visibly and the musicians began to play again. The carolers followed their lead and resumed their singing. Gradually the chatter diminished and the dancers in the dining room moved in time to the music again. Noah held out his hand and pulled Emma close as they turned and swayed under the great twinkling chandeliers.

Laurent led Julia out the back door and into the barn beyond. With two lamps lit they stood in the dim light of the large open space. Behind Julia the horses brayed and the great draft horse stomped his feet in irritation at being disturbed. A number of mice scurried in the loft above and scraps of hay drifted down to the floor. Julia inhaled deeply, taking comfort from the familiar scents of the hay, the animals and the old wood.

"Did you know Lily Gage?" she asked bluntly.

"Twas afore I did court you, Julia," he responded as he studied the worn floor.

"You did commit adultery with a married woman, Husband," she snapped.

"I did sin and repented."

"Shall all be forgotten as you did repent? Is the child Lily carries of you?"

"No! No, twas near on two years past!"

"What of Albert?" she shouted. "Laurent, what of Albert?"

"Julia, it cannot be so," he pleaded as he swept his hand over his thick, dark hair. "No, it cannot be."

Julia turned away and ran for the house. In the kitchen she saw Mrs. Whitley at the hearth. "Where shall Lily be found?" she asked angrily.

"Mrs. Gage is in the nursery minding the children with Mrs. Wallace," she replied, watching Julia warily.

The revelers celebrated loudly throughout the first floor as Julia moved through the hallway. She maneuvered passed the carolers and rushed up to the landing. She gripped the newel post and rounded the stairs to the door of the nursery. Without warning, she yanked the door open and stalked into the room. Grace sat in the rocker with Thea in her arms while Lily stood beside the crib at the far side of the room.

"Julia," Lily declared as she looked to the doorway.

"Lily Gage, you disgraceful sinner!" Julia pronounced.

"Shhh!" Grace hushed them. "Julia, close the door and speak softly. I shall not have the children roused."

"Was Albert the child of my husband?" Julia demanded.

Lily stood frozen in place with her eyes wide and her jaw hanging open. Shocked, she turned to Grace to rescue her. Grace only looked down at the baby and rocked a little bit faster.

"My child is dead and you shall accuse me so?" Lily entreated.

"Lily Grenier Gage, did you birth a child by my husband?" Julia persisted with her jaw clenched tight.

"Twas a grave mistake and I do regret it daily. Albert is buried and this shall be talked of no more."

"Tell me true, Lily! How many of your children are blood to Timothy?"

"'Tis naught to you, Julia!"

"No more," Grace stated flatly. "Julia, Lily has been punished more than you could know. I beg you, speak of this no more."

"Aunt Grace, how many do know of this truth? My husband is known to be an adulterer and I was not told of it."

"Lily, take leave and attend to your husband," Grace instructed as two of the toddlers fussed in the cribs.

Quietly, Lily slipped out the door and hurried down the stairs. The carolers had gone and many of the guests as well. She walked through the sitting room and tapped at the bedroom door. Mac opened the door and stepped back as she moved close to the bed. Timothy sat staring into the fireplace. He held a bloody bundle of linen filled with snow to his face. He moved the cloth to reveal dark bruising and a small cut on the right side of his jaw.

"Yo veejez," he mumbled as he glared in her direction.

"'Tis no place for a woman, Lily," Luke advised as he gripped her shoulders and steered her back toward the door. As he opened it, Ben Andrews stood ready to knock.

"Uncle Luke, the surgeon?" Lily protested.

"Ben shall make it right," Luke assured her as he pushed her out into the hall and closed the door. She walked quietly passed the door to Azaria's nursery and sat on the small bench by the window at the end of the hall. She lifted her apron to her face and wept softly.

The door opened again and Luke stepped out into the dark hallway. He walked quietly toward Lily, knelt in front of her and grasped her hand. Over the sound of the music and the chatter of the guests in the sitting room, they heard the shriek. Lily tensed and looked up into Luke's face.

"The jaw bone is broken, Lily. Ben must manipulate it to correct it," he reassured her. Gently he squeezed her hand and forced a smile.

"Uncle Luke, shall I ever be done with my misdeed? Shall it haunt me always?"

"I cannot say," he responded, and pulled her against his shoulder. He kissed her forehead and leaned back again.

"'Tis my fear that Albert shall be among us always. I shall be punished evermore by the specter of the boy."

"Mayhap you shall take a dose of Laudanum and sleep. Tis rightful Timothy shall remain this night that I might watch over him."

"Shall Mr. Andrews cut him?" she asked, cringing.

"He did right the bones and shall bind his head tight with oil cloth strips. Mac and Joseph shall aid him in securing the jaw correctly."

"Shall his mouth be bound as well?"

"He shall consume naught but watery solutions for a time. He shant move to bite or speak afore it shall be healed."

"Uncle Luke, Julia is greatly angered. Shall you talk for me? Twas done and all has been drawn to sight yet again."

"Mayhap twas wrong to secret it from family. On the morrow the air shall be cleared and naught but truths shall be spoken. You shall confess unto Joseph, Emma, Julia and Mac and all shall be forgiven."

"I cannot," she whispered.

"You shall, Lily," he told her as he released her hand and stood. "If you shant, the family will be dishonored. You shall speak it and your family will mend this thing. It shall be done and forgotten, Lily."

"If I shall be punished with such penance then tis rightful that Albert be returned to me," Lily brooded.

"No, Lily," he admonished. "Albert shall not come to you again. A fitting mother was found and she shall raise him well. You must think your Albert does rest in his grave and let it be."

Lily turned away and stared out at the dark outline of the trees. Luke shook his head and walked out to the sitting room. He poured a glass of whiskey and wandered through the house to the back door. The snow had begun falling and a brisk wind swirled the small flakes in white eddies. He shuddered in the frigid air and ran toward the glow of the light in the barn.

"Dr. Wallace," Laurent called out, startled as the door swung open. He stood inside the first stall brushing the tall draft horse soothingly.

"I do not come to you with malice," Luke told him as he pulled the heavy door closed.

"Twas wrongful that I did strike Timothy so, yet he meant to harm me."

"Timothy Gage is not likely to render great pain against you, Laurent," Luke chuckled.

"Was he terribly injured?"

"The bones at the right of his jaw are fissured. Ben Andrews did state it shall mend."

"Shall my Julia forgive me? I shant bear it if I might lose her heart for the misdeed."

"Tis likely she shall."

"I did drink the mulled wine with Lily. She took my hand in hers and made to tug me onto the ladder to the loft. In the afternoon sun she did appear as an angel and I did succumb. Twas wrongful and I know not how I might be forgiven for my sins."

"Did you know of the child, Laurent?"

"I did not. When he did pass I stood with my Julia in the cemetery. I did not grieve him as a father. Dr. Wallace, I knew nothing of my son. I beg you, forgive me, Sir."

"Tis not for me to absolve you, Laurent. On the morrow Lily shall confess afore the family in Burghill House. You shall profess your wrongs as well. Tis rightful you shall ask the pardons of all present. Mayhap you shall walk to the cemetery and pray there as well. I cannot think what more you might do to repent."

"How shall I sway Julia? I shant sin against her, Dr. Wallace. None shall come into my heart but Julia."

"You shall assure her with naught but the truth, Laurent," Luke advised him. "Come closer that I might examine your hand."

9

As Luke strode back into the house he noted that the music had stopped. The chatter of the guests was gone as well. Laurent sat near the hearth and welcomed the warmth while Luke rinsed his knuckles with vinegar. He soaked away the dried blood and cleaned the cut. A thick poultice was pasted over his hand to reduce the swelling and fresh linen applied over it. Luke advised him to leave it on overnight.

Laurent sat at the table, quietly contemplating his situation while Luke made his way through the empty hall. The dining room was dark and deserted. He sighed heavily and stepped into the sitting room. He refilled his glass with whiskey and sat in the chair behind the desk.

"Dr. Wallace," Ben declared from the doorway, where he stood watching him. "Joseph and Mac walked Timothy up to an empty bedroom and secured him there in a lounge chair."

"Thank you, Ben. I think it likely that he shall remain at Burghill House as he does mend."

Ben untied his leather apron and picked up his surgical box from the floor. He nodded to Luke and shrugged into his coat. Quietly, he strolled out to the front door and shut it quietly behind him. Grace ambled down to the first floor and stopped in the doorway to the sitting room. She brushed the loose curls from her forehead and forced a smile for Luke.

"Timothy shall remain as he does convalesce," he told her as he lifted the glass and swallowed the amber liquor.

"Tis rightful. Where shall Lily be found?"

"I know not," he replied as he peered into the hallway at the empty bench where Lily had been. "Mayhap she did climb the stairs with Joseph and Mac as they moved Timothy up."

"Julia is sleeping in a chair in the nursery with Reny in her arms."

"Her fearful husband is warming at the hearth in the kitchen," Luke told her.

"Mayhap you shall bid him take leave," Grace suggested.

"On the morrow Lily and Laurent shall confess their sins afore the family."

"They shall not, Luke Wallace!" Grace snapped as she closed the sitting room doors. "I did plead that they be told when you did think to bury a casket and be done with Albert. My child shall not suffer more humiliation, when she did grieve so for the boy you thought to take from her."

"Grace, tis right that they shall speak the truth of their sins. They must be forgiven."

"You did tell Lily she would be punished no more if she might permit you to take her baby from her. She did relent, Luke Wallace. You can reprimand her no more!"

"Twas divulged publicly, Grace. If they shall confess it all we might resolve this thing."

"Why, Luke? Why shall you hurt Lily so?"

"Tis not to hurt Lily! Tis to offer repentance for their sins alone."

"What of our sins, Luke? Shall you confess that you did bed me and fathered each of my babies as well? Shall you repent and make right our transgressions? Will you publicly declare me an immoral woman as well?"

"Grace, you shall not speak so!" he shouted as he moved toward her.

"Mama?" Lily whispered as she stepped around the corner into the room. "Uncle Luke…"

"Oh, Lily, no…" Grace uttered and her hand covered her mouth.

"Lily, twas not… no…." Luke stammered as he grasped her hand. Angrily she jerked it away from him.

"Do not handle me!" she shrieked as she ran to open the doors and rushed into the kitchen. Laurent stood and watched her warily. "Timothy!" she shouted and backed into the hallway again. "Timothy!"

"Lily, no," Grace pleaded as she stopped beside Luke at the bottom of the stairs. "Come into the sitting room."

"My Papa," Lily asserted. "Timothy!"

"Lily, stop this!" Joseph called down as he leaned over the balustrade. "Timothy did drink to excess and Mr. Andrews did dose him with Laudanum."

"She shall wake the children," Julia snapped from the other end of the hall and pulled the nursery door closed.

"Joseph, I need you!" Lily called out as she pushed passed Luke and rushed up to the landing. "Mama… Uncle Luke… Joseph how could they? What of Papa?"

"Lily, shhh!" Joseph insisted as he hurried to the landing. He grasped her shoulders and shook her firmly. "Why do you ask of Papa?"

"Oh Joseph," she cried as she threw her arms around his neck and hugged him tight. "Uncle Luke… Papa… oh Joseph she did…"

Joseph grasped her arm and led her down the stairs again. Grace and Luke stepped aside as he walked her into the sitting room and poured a cordial for her. He held the small glass while she sipped then lowered her into a chair. Laurent, Julia and Colleen stood behind Grace watching curiously. Luke advanced into the room and refilled his own glass of whiskey. He sat at the desk and waited for Lily's revelation. He wiped the sweat from his forehead and felt his stomach tighten.

"What of Papa, Lily?" Joseph prodded gently.

"Mama did tell it, Joseph. She did sin against Papa. Uncle Luke did…"

Grace closed her eyes and shuddered as they all looked to her. Trembling she walked to the chair beside Lily and sat slowly. She looked down at her hands and drew in a deep breath. Without looking up she spoke softly. "Tis naught you should hear of. Yet I fear for Lily if I do not speak it."

"Grace…" Luke protested.

"No, Luke, I shall tell the truth of it. Twas my blunder that Lily did hear my words."

Julia, Laurent, Colleen and Mac sat near the door of the room and waited quietly. Luke hung his head, with his right arm resting on his leg. The log on the fire shifted as the charred wood beneath it crumpled. The only sound in the room came from the fireplace and the eerie wind outside. Joseph turned to Grace and took her hand. Slowly she looked up into his eyes.

They listened intently as Grace told the story of the pale green Chrysoberyl pendant she wore for Phillip. He was fourteen years older than she was when Teague Johnes agreed to their courting. Quietly she told the tale of their wedding and the happy days that followed. Tears rolled down her cheeks as she thought of lying in his arms. As she spoke her heart ached for him. Her tears rapidly worsened and she sat sobbing, unable to speak.

"No more!" Luke thundered as his fist slammed down against the desk top. "I shant see her tortured so!"

The windows rattled and the boughs of a pine tree brushed against the side of the house as the wind blew harder. In the stillness Grace's sobs distressed them all. Uncomfortably they watched as Luke approached her and offered his handkerchief. Lily covered her mouth and choked back fresh tears. Near the door Laurent reached for Julia's hand and she leaned back against him.

"Tis no tale I take pride in, yet I shant agree twas wrongful," Luke spoke softly as he regarded the darkness beyond the window. "I was but seventeen years when I did come to East Grantham. Phillip did choose me to apprentice for him. Twas required that he travel and many a time I was left behind. Twas confided that Phillip was injured and there would be no children for his poor wife. It did trouble him greatly.

As he did travel I plied his young wife with liquor and did entice her to my bed in the night. She did conceive and they were exceedingly happy with the birth of a son. In time I did bless Grace with three children. When Cherish did come Phillip meant to send me away. I did relent yet afore I might go twas a fire that nearly took Cherish and Emma as they slept in their cradles."

Joseph recalled the night that he had come home to Burghill House to tell Phillip of Naomi's pregnancy. Phillip had been enraged by the news and lashed out at him. Yet Luke had been quick to intervene and press Phillip back. Luke and Grace had been there in the small church when Joseph and Naomi were married. Phillip had been a good and loving father but clearly Luke had loved the children as well.

Luke removed his coat and pulled off his shirt. Colleen and Julia gasped at the terrible burn scars that marred his shoulder and arm above the amputation point. He turned slightly to reveal more disfigurement and discoloring on his back and up his neck. He exhaled slowly and worked into his shirt again. Soundlessly, he moved to the desk again and refilled his glass.

"I shant bid you forgive me for twas a great sin I did commit. Yet twas no trace of malice in my heart as I did so. I pray only that you shall find mercy for Grace. Tis no fault in this for her," he stated, as he left the room and slowly climbed the stairs. At the end of the hall he opened the door to the room where Timothy slept and stepped inside.

"I prayed you might never know of this thing," Grace whispered, her breath hitching as the sobbing gradually ceased. She pressed her hand to her forehead and studied the handkerchief in her hand. "I did love Phillip Grenier greatly. He did treasure you all so. Pray forgive me, twas naught but to be blessed with children that I did seek. Teague's wife Selah did end herself when she was denied a living child. Twas my wickedest fear that I should meet her end."

"Mama, was this thing known to Papa?" Joseph asked gently.

"Twas known yet he could not love you more if his blood did flow within you. He did name you, each of you. To you, he did freely grant his family name. To see me blessed with the children of my heart did satisfy him."

"Phillip Grenier shall ever be my father. I shall accept none other," Joseph stated firmly. "None shall speak this tale again. If Papa were among us he would bid us be done with this and disclose it not beyond the doors of Burghill House."

"Joseph, what of Timothy and of Emma?" Lily swallowed hard.

"No, Lily, tis done. We shall speak no more of this thing. Our father is Phillip Grenier. The misdeeds of your past shall be laid to rest as well. Albert is gone from us and we shant save him if we shall speak of it. Naomi is no more and though my heart does ache, it shant be undone. We cannot relive the past daily. Shall each of you accede?"

"Shall we know the truth of it afore it shall be secreted?" Julia asked as she glared at Lily.

"Will it yet benefit our children if the truth be told?" Joseph retorted. "It shall not. Twas a sinful thing yet Lily did lose her infant son for it. My Naomi is gone from me. There shall be no more punishment for wrongs of the past. Tis done, Julia. Shall you relent?"

"I shall speak of it no more," Julia replied. "Laurent, I beseech you bring my son to me and let us take leave." Silently Laurent bounded up the stairs to the nursery.

"It shant be related to Timothy," Lily agreed.

"Tis beyond me to think of this iniquity. I pray end this thing," Colleen declared as her shoulders hunched forward and she moved back toward the stairs.

"No reference to such transgressions shall pass my lips," Mac stated, and followed Colleen up to the dark hallway.

"Mama, none shall fault you for these offenses. If Papa did accept this and made Luke Wallace a brother unto him…"

"I can hear no more, Joseph," Grace breathed.

From the nursery beside Grace's bedroom she heard the cries of Azaria. Exhausted, she rose from the chair. She patted Lily's hand and kissed Joseph's cheek before she walked despairingly passed the fireplace.

"Lily, take respite in the bedroom with Timothy this night," Joseph instructed as he grasped her hands and pulled her up from her seat. She lowered her head as she slipped passed Julia in the doorway.

"Twas afore Laurent did know you, Julia," she whispered.

Julia slapped Lily's face and stepped back as Lily continued on to the bottom step of the staircase. Julia wiped away angry tears and declared, "I shall not hear of this again."

Lily stopped on the stairs and looked up at Laurent on the landing, holding the sleepy child in his arms. She thought of Albert again and pressed her back against the wall. He noted the dark handprint on her cheek as he hurried passed her to the entryway.

"All shall be righted," Joseph told Julia as he hugged her briefly. She followed Laurent out into the bitter cold night and Joseph secured the door behind them.

Joseph dropped into the chair behind the desk and placed his head on his arms. Colleen would still be awake if he went up to her now. But he could not endure more of her judgments after the grueling evening. He thought of sleeping on the sweet scented hay in the loft but recalled the chill at the front door and dismissed the idea.

"Joseph," Luke's low voice surprised him. Reluctantly, he raised his head and looked to the doorway. "Shall you bid me take leave from this house?"

"I shall not. You are of my blood, I shant see you put out. Yet I cannot know you as more than my uncle. Phillip Grenier shall ever be my father."

"Tis rightful," Luke agreed.

"This thing shant be spoken of ever more. Tis an affront to my Papa that we should do so."

"Tis fair and true," Luke nodded.

"I shall not see my father dishonored. Nor my family name."

"What of Grace?"

"Grace is my mother and she shall ever be the virtuous Grace Grenier in my heart and mind. I shall hear nothing less."

"Lily does lie in Timothy's arms on the lounge chair. If it be your wish I shall sleep on the bed in that room this night."

"I shall not ask it of you, Luke Wallace. It would be unkind to deny my mother comfort this night. Go to her now."

Luke nodded slowly and strode toward the bedroom door. In the hall he heard Grace's voice in the nursery. She murmured soothingly to their young daughter by the dim light of the candle. In her words he heard her tears and felt a sharp pain in his chest.

A single tear rolled down his cheek as he slipped quietly into the bedroom.

Startled awake, Luke rolled over to face his beautiful wife. She clutched at him desperately and he quickly folded her against his strong chest. In the dark she pressed her face to his neck and breathed slowly.

"I feared you would not return this night," she whispered.

"'Tis with Joseph's blessing that I shall remain," he responded.

Gently she moved down to lay her head against his chest. She listened to the steady beat of his heart and felt the stirring of a distant memory. So many nights she had been comforted by her father in the great rocker in the sitting room. With her ear to his chest she heard the strong thumping of his heartbeat. She smelled the strong scent of the whiskey on his breath as he spoke soothingly with his deep voice nearly a low growl. It was the place where she felt safe and secure. No one and nothing could harm her as she rested in his arms.

Grace smiled and closed her eyes. She faintly recalled her father's attractive face and his enchanting smile. Laying there in the night she was certain she smelled lilacs. She remembered walking along the drive with her tiny hand lost in his. He laughed heartily as she raked her hand over the blooms and inhaled the sweet perfume. With a smile touching her lips she drifted into a restful sleep.

10

Luke walked along the path through the woods and out through the copse of birch. Ahead of him he saw the family cemetery under the glow of the moon. A strange stillness fell over the woods. Not a bird or animal stirred as he approached the gates. The wind died away and in the silence he could hear nothing but the blood surging through his veins and his rapid heartbeat. He called out but not even an echo responded.

Anxiously, he entered the graveyard and stopped. The gates swung closed behind him. Above the cemetery a large black bird began circling. It was soon joined by another and quickly there were three. The largest of them soared higher then fell fast down toward the gravestones. Swiftly it rose again and glided gracefully with the other birds.

A massive gray wolf walked out of the woods and eyed him curiously. Casually, it sauntered along the outer wall and stopped periodically to sniff the air. At the back wall the wolf paused and sat considering him again, then chuckled and moved on. When it reached the closed gates the animal halted as a fat brown rabbit came to sit beside him.

One of the birds fell from the sky and landed beside Luke's muddy boot. He stepped back in revulsion as blood flowed over the black feathers. The single eye that was visible, stared blindly up at him. In the quiet of the night he heard the familiar squeak as the gates swung open and the dead thing rolled out before they slammed shut again.

"Dr. Wallace," the wolf called in a deep, husky voice.

Luke looked around, feeling a panic rising inside. He saw no one and at last looked to the wolf and the rabbit.

"Twas I who did speak, Dr. Wallace," the wolf continued. "Why have you come to the graves in the dark of night?"

"Tis to pay respects to my good friend that I did come."

"That is a laughable thing!" the wolf retorted and howled. "Your good friend did pass as you watched unbidden. Why should you think to tend his grave now, oh kindly medicus?"

"I did what Phillip would allow in his last days. I did love him as a brother and do miss him greatly."

"Ah, yes, you did love him as your brother. And did hold his wife as your lover."

"Twas right that Grace should be blessed with children. She is a loving woman who should not be denied that right."

"Do you think yourself a God that you shall determine who shall be blessed?"

"Tis not my meaning!" Luke shouted and the rabbit trembled beside the wolf.

"You did gift children to her, Luke Wallace, yet twas not your right. If Phillip could not, then God did not will it. Such a sinful thing, that you did think it rightful to judge it."

"No, twas not my thinking! I did love Grace and did wish only to see her happy."

"A verity at last! You shall confess that you did take Grace to your bed to love her as your own. To see her happy in your arms was your greater wish, Physician. And your friendship with Phillip Grenier be damned!"

"No..."

"Deny it no more, Dr. Wallace. Tis truthful that you did love Grace and coveted her. You did see symptoms of Phillip's failing heart, yet you did not intervene. Twas not in you to make him well, if it would end with your loss of the lovely Grace Grenier. He did pass and Grace was made yourn."

"I beg of you, no more."

"You have failed as a friend, deceived your brother, coveted his bride, and fathered the babies who shall be ever known by his name. You did forsake your mother in her hour of need and neglected the old woman who did take you into her home. Cherish Grenier, Reynolds Luciern and others did die of your mistreatment. Luke Wallace, you are a sinner and a regret of the Lord."

"No, no, say no more!" Luke called out as he backed away, stumbling over a rock, he nearly fell to the ground. Quickly he turned and ran toward the tombstones. As he rushed toward Phillip's grave marker, he tripped again, thumping his head against the fieldstone wall. Looking toward the gate, he watched in horror as the wolf jumped into the graveyard and rushed toward him.

"Tis rightful you shall end as well, Dr. Wallace!" the wolf called out and howled as it pounced on Luke. A blinding rain fell and lightning flashed across the sky as the wolf tore at his flesh.

Luke shrieked in terror as he fought with the blankets. Flailing and kicking wildly on the bed, he fell and landed on the cold floor. Shocked and terrified, he scrambled back against the wall and pulled his knees up to his chest.

"Luke!" Grace shouted. She jumped down and hurried around to sit beside him. He gulped in air, sweating as his heart thundered in his chest. She slipped an arm around his neck and felt him shivering. In the next room she heard Azaria crying and stood anxiously, afraid to leave Luke alone in his state.

As she opened the door, she nearly ran into Joseph in the hall. "Joseph!"

"Mama, I heard yells from your bed chamber!"

"Tis Luke," she explained nervously. "Tis a terror that has overcome him. Tend to him, Joseph."

"I am a carpenter, I know not of minding the sick. Sit with him as I fetch Mac."

"Azaria does cry for me."

"She will keep. If he is unwell, he shant be left to himself. Wait for Mac," Joseph ordered and she moved back into the bedroom. She sat on the floor and gently pulled Luke's head to her shoulder. She whispered soothingly and waited for Joseph and Mac.

"Pa," Mac murmured as he knelt in front of him. Joseph stood in the doorway, holding Azaria at his shoulder and patting her back as she calmed. Grace remained beside Luke as Mac lowered the lamp and looked into his eyes.

"He did awaken greatly frightened and screamed so. The fear was such that he did thrash about and fell from the bed," Grace advised him.

Mac placed the lamp on the small table and hurried out of the room. A few minutes later he ran back into the room. "Aunt Grace, move away from him," he instructed confidently.

Grace stepped toward the door and stood beside Joseph. Mac walked around the end of the bed to the other side and looked at Luke. He lifted his arm and lobbed a loosely packed snowball, striking Luke's cheek. The snow sprayed over him, leaving a scrape and bright blush where it struck his face.

"Mackenzie Wallace!" Grace shouted, indignantly.

"Twas required," Mac declared, apologetically, as he rushed back to Luke.

Luke shook off the snow and grabbed for Mac. "You are not too grown for a whipping boy!"

"Pa!" Mac announced excitedly and moved to hug him. "Twas a great fight that did addle your brain. I meant only to startle you right."

Luke accepted the hug then pushed Mac away and struggled to stand. He brushed away the melting snow and looked to Joseph and Grace. Silently he moved to the fireplace to warm himself. He thought of the horrifying dream and shuddered.

"All is well," he lied convincingly. "My greatest apologies for the waking of the household. Return to your beds and rest well."

Joseph eyed him warily as he passed Azaria to his mother. She carried the sleeping toddler back to the nursery and tucked her into the crib. Mac watched him closely, studying his slow movement and the haunted look in his eyes.

"Pa, if I'm to be a respected physician one day I shall practice the keeping of confidences. If a troubled mind does plague you then I shall listen well to your unburdening."

"Tis too great a thing to tell, Mac."

"No, Pa. Speak it to me afore you rest your head. Mayhap we shall slip out to the barn," Mac pressed.

Luke sighed heavily and turned as Grace entered the room. He carefully considered Mac's words and nodded slowly. "Go for your boots and coat," he mumbled. Eagerly, Mac left the room, closing the door behind him. "Rest, Grace. Tis a concern I must tend to." He kissed her quickly and stomped his feet into his boots. She held his coat as he slipped into it. Worriedly, she hugged him tight before he hurried out.

Mac sat on the milking stool in the barn with three lamps burning. He rubbed together the deer skin palms of his rabbit fur mittens and exhaled a plume of warm air. As Luke entered he nodded politely, but did not stand. Luke closed the door and barred it. Stamping the snow from his boots, he moved toward the ladder to the loft. He sat on one of the lower steps and his shoulders slumped forward.

"Pa, the shrieks in the night are heard more often now. Tis over many months that you have been plagued so. Your words shall not leave this barn. Many a secret of this house is known to me and I shant share them. What vexes you?"

"My son, you are not yet a man. How shall I burden you with the troubles of my conscience?"

"Tis rightful you shall trust your son as your noblest friend did pass from you. Speak the verity of your soul and if it be a strain unto me I shall end it."

"Mac, how shall you reason as an aged man when you are but a few years from your boyhood?"

Mac chuckled and shook his head slowly. "Tis thought I cannot govern, Pa."

"As a small boy I did witness the beating of my mother with a riding crop and walking stick at my father's hand. She did move about in great pain with stripes upon her back and bruises at her face and neck. He did not spare me from his kicks and brutal whippings. A cruel man at his best, none did find him to be likable.

He did end her viciously and left her in a sticky pool of blood on the wood planks of the kitchen floor. The night did pass as I sat frightened at her side. She was buried in a pauper's grave and I travelled with strangers to live with an old woman I did not know. Her name was Azaria and she was my grandmother. She did keep me in her home for ten years and did love me well. When I was but seventeen years I deserted her and left her behind as I began my apprenticeship with Dr. Grenier. I know not when she did die or where she might rest. I did forsake her unconscionably.

In the home of Phillip Grenier he did treat me as his brother and did train me up to be a doctor. Twas a remarkable healing gift that he did possess. I dwelt beneath his roof and did covet his beautiful bride. I coerced her and drew her to my bed. She did birth three children unto me. As Phillip did present them as his own, I felt a great anger and resentment for him. When he did suffer as his heart did weaken, I paid no heed.

At the party to celebrate her birthday I did fail poor Cherish. Twas the first such party that she did see in her honor alone. She beamed as she sat aside Carter Fontaine and did feel his great love for her. Cherish did suffer a tortured life yet she smiled always and offered naught but good cheer to all. She did cough and choke with a bite of venison in her throat. I was but to force my hand deep and extract the impasse. Yet I pressed the bread into her mouth and waited as she lay dying in my arms.

Reynolds came in the night, delivered unto me by Dutch Sailors. He did trust that I would save him. But I did lack the skill and gift of Phillip. Reynolds did suffer greatly. I did botch him so that even Ben Andrews could not aid him. The man did die for my failings!

Worst was my greatest sin as I did seek to end Ross Eastman for his heartless abuses of Julia and little Reny. I did entice the man into the wood as we did seek a rogue wolf. Alone in a clearing I did strike his head with a rock and did finish him with his own weapon. I did murder the man! The mar he put upon Julia and Reny was more than I could bear. Such bruising and lacerations I have not witnessed from the days I lived in terror from my father's deeds.

As Eastman did lie in a puddle of his own blood I did look to him and felt my mother had been avenged at last. I did murder a cruel man yet my heart was not pure. Twas not to safeguard Julia and her child that I did bash his head. I did fail Mama in that cold kitchen. Behind the table I hid when father did crush her throat.

Secreted by the broken chair, I watched and did naught. Ross did pay the penalty for my father's horrors."

Luke held his face in his hands and shivered. He felt a weight on his chest and his head began to pound. He drew in shallow breaths of the frigid air. At last he looked up at his young son. Mac sat with his legs apart, his elbows resting on his knees and fingers steepled. His index fingers rested against his lower lip and he considered Luke carefully.

"Pa, do you mean to end yourself?" he asked gently.

"Tis a great fear in me, I cannot lie," Luke responded.

"You do have the look of a man who shall seek comfort in death."

"My heart aches," Luke whispered. "I have failed those I do love most. The secrets within me are too much to bear. Tis likely I shall confess to all and it shall ruin me. When all is done I shall be remembered for such misdeeds. My name shall be spoilt and my family disgraced."

"Pa, tis wrongful thinking that does muddle your head. Twas naught you might have done to save your mother. To effort such a thing meant your sure death as well. Do you think a small child the match of a man such as your father? Tis folly."

"Tis but one of my actions I do greatly regret, Mac."

"Only one of your misthoughts," Mac declared. "Uncle Phillip was a man of fortitude. Twas not in him to be directed. He did live and die by his own choosings. Twas naught for you to save him by means he did not desire.

As you did covet his wife, twas not unknown to him. He did bid you stay and Aunt Grace was blessed with the children they desired. Twas wrongful that you did desire her in a sinful manner yet twas made right to him. That he did propose the marriage of you and Grace when he was gone does uphold that he forgave your wrongful thoughts and deeds. Twas enough that you did gift the children to him and his wife.

The night that Cherish was taken from us I did stand at your side. She was a slight girl, Pa. Raise your hand and study it well. Shall you believe that your great hand might be inserted passed her tiny mouth? It could not be done. All did state that she choked with fish bones in her throat. You could not know of the venison. Afore you did hold the forceps in hand twas naught you might do. No neglect by you did take the life of Cherish.

Mayhap you did mistake as you treated Reynolds. In the night if you did err twas no malice in your heart. The damage was done and likely Mr. Andrews could not repair it if he had come earlier. You did repay the debt, if it be owed, when you sought to end Ross Eastman. With thoughts of your mother in your head you did kill the man. Twas a sinful act, yet Julia and her child were spared."

"But for my folly, Reynolds would be alive and Ross Eastman would have posed no threat unto them."

"Pa, you cannot say tis so. You cannot know what might have been. Tis not in you to change the past, or to envisage the future."

"Mac..." Luke hesitated.

"No, I can hear no more, Pa. You have rescued the lives of many as the years did pass. You have not a wasted life. As you did covet Grace Grenier, three good lives were made. Phillip Grenier did teach you the means to tend the sick and dying. When fire did threaten Cherish and Emma you endangered your own life and lost a hand that they might live. Phillip did beg you walk with him on the day he did pass. Shall you not see the love and indebtedness that dwelt in his heart?

As you acted wrongfully, you did seek to make right it again. Tis no malevolence in you. You do worship the Lord properly and seek to harm none without purpose. Confess your sins to God alone and speak no more of your comprehended misdeeds. To think your life wasted, you shall believe the lives of Joseph, Lily, Cherish and me to be of no consequence. Tis an untruth and I shant hear it."

"Tis fair and true, Mac. Twas a great determination that I did choose to wed your mother and you were given unto me."

"Mama did love you greatly?"

"As Isannah did pass, I thought myself faulted for her undoing. Yet Phillip did counsel me, and in time, I did not grieve so. Mayhap tis yet another deed I shall answer for at the end of my days, yet I cannot think it my burden that Ren did go at my hand. He did raise his gun and did shoot at me twice afore I did aim in return. Twas naught I might do but fire or surrender unto my death."

"You are accepted rightfully as a decent man, respectable husband, and father and a sound physician as well. Shall you think a man must be thought to be more?"

"I shall seek to right my stupefied head. We can linger now in this icy place no more. Extinguish the lamps and let us realize the comfort of the hearth."

Mac nodded and stood quickly. Luke stepped toward him and realized for the first time that his son was nearly his height already. Mac would likely be a man of 6' 4" or more like the Chernock men. Luke smiled, and thought that it would be a great thing if his son followed that bloodline. They were tall, strong, industrious men of good moral character. He reached for Mac's large hand and pulled him into an embrace. Quickly he released him and they moved toward the doorway.

"Pa, what you did relate unto me this night cannot be spoken of beyond," Mac hesitated as they neared the back door to the house.

"'Tis known," Luke responded as he lifted the latch and pushed the door open.

"It must remain between you, me and your God," Mac pressed as he touched Luke's sleeve. Luke sighed, and strode through the hall to the sitting room. Mac stood by the doorframe for a moment, watching as his father dropped heavily into the chair behind the desk. Reluctantly, he turned away and climbed the stairs.

In the sitting room, Luke filled his glass again and unlocked the bottom drawer of the desk. Feeling blindly in the dim light from the fire, he pushed a small leather book aside and located the journal he sought. He placed it on the desk and opened it. Quietly, he lit the lamp and removed the cover from the ink well. He dabbed his quill into the ink, and the scratching of the pen against the paper could be heard over the crackle of the logs in the fireplace.

Cursing the cold night, he moved to put more wood on the fire. Agitated, he jabbed at the embers underneath and watched a spray of sparks drift up the chimney. The ends of the biggest log smoked as it sizzled and popped. He uttered a prayer and sat again at his desk. Sitting alone in the sleeping house, he penned his meticulous confession.

11

The morning sun crept over the icy horizon. Weak rays shivered against a cold blue sky. Cottony clouds had drifted south, leaving the heavens naked while the biting wind whipped cruelly through the trees. Judge Daniel Gage looked out the window at the bleak gray and brown of the woods behind the house. The occasional drab green of the slumbering pines did little to soften the look of it.

"Papa, Mrs. Quinn did summon me," Timothy stated as he peeked into the library.

"Come," Daniel replied. He waved his arm, indicating that Timothy should sit at the table.

Timothy had remained at Burghill House for more than a month before Ben Andrews agreed to remove the tight bindings from his head. A week later Dr. Wallace had agreed that his jaw had healed well and he returned to the Gage family home with Lily. In their absence, the children had remained in the care of Sarina Gage and the governess who tended to them. Through the six weeks, as the gossip continued, Judge Gage expressed his great disapproval of the situation daily.

"Tis rightful that you and Lily have come home at last," Daniel commented as he pushed aside the law books and sat across from Timothy.

Mrs. Quinn carried in a large tray with a pot of black tea, cups, a vessel of whiskey and a plate of pastries and fruit. She placed it on the table in the space the judge had cleared. Quietly, she hurried out of the room and closed the doors securely.

"Papa, twas not of my own choosing that I did remain at Burghill House."

"Tis agreed, Timothy," Daniel observed as he poured the tea and added a splash of liquor to each cup. He pushed a cup toward his son and sipped from his own. "As you did linger, did you know of the chinwagging throughout East Grantham?"

"No, Sir," Timothy mumbled and looked down at the steam rising from his tea.

"Tis a disgraceful thing that you did provoke an act of violence in Burghill House. How should you think to do so?" Daniel demanded as his fist struck the heavily polished wood, rattling the cups.

"As the party did progress I did overindulge. Tis a great regret."

"You are a Gage!" the judge bellowed.

"Papa, I pray you shall accept my apology and assurances that it shall not be repeated."

"Shall you think that sufficient to quell the chatter? You did stir talk of an affair between your wife and Morgan!"

"What might I do to allay such talk? Lily has been penalized exceedingly. Tis no more she might do to correct her botch."

"Your wife did not stir this foul brew, Timothy! Twas you who did act so afore a full room of neighbors. You know not who shall be friend or enemy to you when your back shall be turned and the knife placed in his hand. To quash the gossipmongering you shall make your declarations afore the church on the morrow."

"Papa…"

"You shall make your declarations afore the church on the morrow!" Daniel roared. "At the podium you shall affirm that you did drink to excess and did mistakenly accuse your dear wife. You shall make apology unto Laurent Morgan as well."

"I cannot!" Timothy cried as he jumped up from his seat. His cup rolled to the side, spilling tea across the table. "The man did know my wife!"

"Twas put to bed when Albert was removed. Your mother did grieve dreadfully for the boy. Yet all was done with. Your word and deed did draw it up again. Tis to you to remedy this thing. I shant talk of it further," Daniel proclaimed as he gestured for Timothy to leave the room. "Prepare your words for on the morrow you shall speak."

He pulled the books closer again and began flipping through a massive, leather bound volume. Timothy stepped outside the door and closed it firmly. Angrily, he strode up the stairs.

12

Sunday arrived with a vibrant blue sky, partially obscured by streaming clouds. The sun appeared for short periods and the wind blew in gusts. At Judge Gage's request, the residents from Burghill House travelled to the First Parish Congregational Church of East

Grantham on Sunday morning. Rev. Michael Pender shuttered his church and escorted his family there as well.

The pews filled quickly and the majority of the men shuffled to the back of the church to stand. As the parishioners waited for Rev. Tomas Murray to enter, they chattered noisily. Curiosity created by the judge's unusual request fueled the prattle.

The back door to the stairs opened and Rev. Murray strode across the floor toward the altar. A rainbow of colors flashed across his face as the pale February sun shone briefly through the tall stained glass windows. The minister stepped up to the pulpit and raised his hands high. He lowered them slowly and the volume in the room dropped with them.

"Brothers and sisters I shall ask that you join me in our opening prayer this morn."

With the prayer concluded, an echoing of amen rang through the large space. Along the pews, the congregation sat again and the men at the back of the room leaned back against the wall. Rev. Murray nodded politely to the judge and moved to sit to the right of the altar. Judge Gage and his son stood and walked to the pulpit.

"From the eve of Christmas forward, many among us have been guilty of gossipmongering. I have not come before you this day to level accusations. Yet tis known to be a prosecutable corruption!" Judge Gage announced. "Yet the chinwagging, begun as a falsehood was uttered, shall cease this day."

Daniel stepped down and moved to stand beside the minister as Timothy climbed up behind the podium. With his jaw clenched he struggled to pull folded pages from the pocket of his coat. He smoothed them against the bookrest and looked out over the room. He choked down his anger and cleared his throat.

"A number of you did revel at Burghill House afore Christmas day," he read then paused to inhale again. "Twas an evening of great celebration and none but the finest spirits were offered unto the guests. As I did imbibe, my lack of restraint was wrongful. In my inebriated state, I did improperly accuse Laurent Morgan falsely. Tis reprehensible that I did act so afore my beloved wife. I am grateful that she did forgive my transgression. Mr. Morgan did pardon my absurdity as well."

At the back of the room Luke shook his head slowly as he listened to Timothy's degradation. He looked to Judge Gage where he stood stoically with his hands clasped behind his back. To Luke's right, Laurent Morgan stared down at the weathered oak floor. His cheeks glowed with shame as Timothy's words echoed throughout the room. From the far corner Mac watched Timothy, then turned to study his father and Laurent, curiously.

Timothy crumpled the thick pages and shoved them back into his pocket. He stepped down and waited as the judge climbed up yet again. He slapped a hand against the thick slab of pine and nodded slowly. "'Tis a forgivable offense that a man shall nip more than he should reasonably on occasion. Still to natter of it and speak of his drunken speech is un-Godly! I shall have no more of it in our town. If it be talked of hereafter I shall see the offender locked in the pillory."

Daniel walked toward Rev. Murray and shook his hand firmly. With Timothy at his side he returned to the family pew and settled in beside Sarina. Daniel closed his eyes as Sarina sniffled and dabbed at her eyes with a lavishly embroidered handkerchief. He patted her hand and pulled his shoulders back as he waited for the minister to begin his sermon.

Seated on the other side of Sarina, Timothy kept his clenched fists in his pockets and his right foot waggled anxiously. His jaw clenched again and he ignored the reverend. Slowly, his rage grew as he thought of the humiliation he had endured. Laurent Morgan had lain with his wife and he had forgiven the deed. Yet for a moment of weakness, as he saw the man touch Lily, he was forced to utter untruths before his family, friends and neighbors. A respected esquire, he would be thought a drunkard. His jaw ached as he tensed it and he was forced to relax it.

Beside him, Lily felt the vibration of the bench as his foot twitched restlessly. Butterflies fluttered around in her stomach while she thought of the words Timothy had spoken. It was so unfair that he had suffered the broken jaw and been forced to take responsibility for the gossip as well. He had been wronged by her affair with Laurent yet Timothy suffered most for it. She fantasized of moving to Portsmouth but they could not go before the new baby arrived in summer.

"And James did tell us: Go to now, ye that say, Today or tomorrow we will go into such a city, and continue there a year and buy and sell, and get gain. Whereas ye know not what shall be on the morrow. For what is your life? It is even a vapor, that

PINK SKY & MOURNING

appeareth for a little time, and then vanisheth away. For that ye
ought to say, If the Lord will, we shall live, and do this, or that. But
now ye rejoice in your boastings: all such rejoicing is evil.
Therefore to him that knoweth to do good, and doeth it not, to
him it is sin" Rev. Murray sermonized.

13

The wind stilled at last and a bright moon illuminated the sky.
Timothy threw another log on the fire and slipped under the heavy
quilt again. He moved quickly to press his body against Lily. He
smiled at the delightful warmth she radiated and draped his arm
over her waist. She pressed back against him and smiled.

"You do enchant me, Lily," he breathed close to her neck.

"Hmmm," she murmured.

"Mayhap we shall take leave of this place," he whispered.

She rolled quickly to scrutinize his face in the glow from the fire.
"Might we live in Portsmouth or Boston in a home all our own?"

"Far from East Grantham we shall not feel the shadow of my
father. Where we are known to none, there shall be no wrongful
scandalmongering. The past shall be washed away."

"Timothy, when shall we depart?"

"When the child is born I shall travel to Boston alone. We will
begin anew, Lily," he told her and pressed his lips to hers.

"Shall I be mistress of the home at last?"

"It shall be a fine house," he added as he bared her shoulder and
pulled her into his arms.

"Mayhap we shall retrieve Albert as we do go?"

"If it shall please you, my love," he smiled. "In Boston he shall
be rightfully thought my son. His name shall be corrected to
Albert Gage again."

Lily nodded and melted against him.

The following Sunday, after the church service, they travelled to
Burghill House. The family gathered in the dining room and
shared the large tom turkey that Mac shot the day before. At the
head of the table, Luke comforted Azaria and spooned in a

47

mouthful of honey to soothe her cough. Across the room Joanna and Michael worried over the coughs of their little girls as well.

Before Mrs. Whitley could bring in the bowl of chocolate pudding and apple spice cake, Molly suggested that they depart. She asked Luke's advice regarding her ailing granddaughters, as she and Joanna tugged little arms into coats in the hall. Mrs. Whitley hurriedly packed a box of cake and pumpkin muffins and handed it to Rev. Pender.

When they were gone, the men moved to the sitting room to enjoy the desserts, cordials and cigars. The women carried plates and platters back to the kitchen and visited while the dishes were washed. Grace sat near the hearth with Azaria at her shoulder. She patted her back and talked soothingly as the toddler stirred feverishly.

In the sitting room, Timothy stood and grabbed the fireplace poker from the post beside the wood rack. He tapped the glowing embers that had dropped beneath the grate. Distractedly, he tossed in a few more strips of kindling and topped them with a fat chunk of hard wood.

Luke, Joseph, Mac and Noah sat discussing the relocating of the State House from Philadelphia to Trenton, New Jersey due to the yellow fever outbreaks. Laurent listened as he enjoyed a large piece of cake sprinkled with sugar and ground cinnamon. He refilled the glasses and took another slice of cake.

"Philadelphia is greatly plagued by the yellow fever epidemic, yet Boston is a fine city," Timothy commented.

"Boston is agreeable, still I shant abide life in a city," Luke observed.

"When Lily's child does come I mean to travel to Boston. I shall acquire a fine house there for my dear wife."

"You propose to take Lily and the children away?" Luke asked surprised at the suggestion.

"Tis rightful that she shall oversee her own home."

"Mayhap you shall build such a house in East Grantham."

"My father shall object and will intercede," Timothy sighed and looked back to the fire.

"I pray you shall ponder this idea," Luke responded. "Boston is a great distance and we shall sadly miss the children as they do grow quickly. Might you walk with me, Timothy?"

Luke tugged his heavy cloak over his shoulders and opened the front door. Timothy pulled his boiled wool cape down from the peg and followed. Outside they circled the house, and wandered out behind the barn. Luke sat on the chopping block and looked up at the gathering clouds.

"Why shall you think to take Lily and the children away?" Luke asked.

"Uncle Luke, tis rightful that Lily be taken away from the chinwagging in this town. I should like to be free of my father's domination as well. It shall be for the best."

"Tis understood, yet I shant state that I shall be pleased."

"Mayhap you shall think to disclose the place where Albert is tended? As we do dwell in Boston, the boy might be returned to us."

"Timothy, tis done," Luke responded as he looked disbelievingly up at him.

"Journey to the woman who does mind him and make clear that he shall be delivered rightfully unto his mother."

"No, he shall not be removed from her to Lily," Luke protested. "Tis a child born of the liaison between your wife and Morgan. He cannot be made your son. It shall destroy your union if you think to bring the boy to Lily again. Be done with it, Timothy!"

"I cannot see her suffer."

"Tis to you to end this thing. You cannot forfeit to gratify her. Timothy, I shall not disclose the family or home of Albert and I shant speak of this again," Luke declared as he stood and walked back toward the barn.

"Uncle Luke, I cannot bear her tears."

"No more!" Luke shouted as he whirled to face him. "Comfort her if it be required, yet she shall not be granted her every desire."

Timothy remained behind the barn as Luke walked quickly along the drive. Irritated, he strode back into the sitting room and poured a glass of whiskey. He listened to the discussion of the covered bridge to be constructed over the Scaffel River in the spring. With the toe of his boot, he kicked the chair sideways and sat behind the desk.

Eventually Timothy strolled back inside. He dropped into a chair near the open doors and sat brooding as the other men chatted.

14

Late in the day, Grace first noticed that Azaria was sweating. She moved the girl from her shoulder to her arms and brushed damp curls from her forehead. Worriedly, she kissed her forehead and felt the heat. Hurriedly, she carried her through the sitting from the kitchen. She passed the girl to Luke and he walked into the nursery with her.

Concerned about Azaria and anxious for their own children, the rest of the family gathered their children and left the house. Colleen rushed down the stairs to announce that seven month old Thea was suffering with a high fever as well. She followed Joseph into Azaria's nursery and held Thea out to Luke.

Azaria was settled into her crib and blankets were tucked around her. Thea was placed in the cradle across the room and snuggled in with a folded quilt. Luke requested corn mush diluted with boiled wine for the sick babies. The mothers were advised to bathe the feet of their little ones with warm water to reduce their fevers. Luke warned them that he might need to bleed them or induce vomiting if their fevers did not pass quickly.

While Grace and Colleen remained in the nursery, Luke and Joseph returned to the sitting room. They talked and waited for word of improvement. Late in the evening Joseph suggested bleeding the girls to rid them of the fever, but Luke refused. He explained that a fever would be better relieved through purging of the stomach first before bleeding. Mac only watched and listened.

As Luke began blending a foul brown liquid to induce vomiting the door knocker echoed in the hall. Joseph walked to the door and welcomed Michael Pender into the house. He announced that his daughters had been put to bed with raging fevers and were vomiting continually. His mother-in-law, Molly Andrews, had asked that the doctor come quickly. Luke understood that Molly would not summon him if the children were not in mortal danger.

"Have you a carriage or your horse alone?" Luke asked the minister.

"Tis my sleigh, Dr. Wallace."

"Linger as I do concoct medications for them. I shant tarry," Luke assured him.

"Many thanks, good Sir," Michael nodded as he stood anxiously by the door.

"Mac, if the purging shall be required I trust you to do it," Luke declared. "If their conditions shall worsen Joseph must come for me."

"Yes, Sir," Mac responded.

Luke quickly prepared the needed blends and packed his bag. In ten minutes he and Rev. Pender were moving south along Kings Wood Road toward the Pender home.

Mac walked quietly into the nursery where the mothers worried over Azaria and Thea. He placed his hand against Azaria's cheek and frowned. Her fever had increased and her hair was wet with sweat. Carefully he considered Luke's instructions.

"Shall I wash her feet again?" Grace asked.

"Might you bring a fresh basin of cool water?" he asked. She grabbed the pitcher and basin and hurried out of the room. While Colleen rocked the cradle slowly, he pulled back the blankets and lifted Azaria from her crib. He noted her flushed cheeks and lethargic manner. Gently, he undressed her and examined her carefully. He opened her mouth and looked at her tongue and throat as well. Reluctantly, he placed her on top of the blanket and left her uncovered there.

Grace returned with the basin of cool water and he slowly wiped the damp cloth over her chest and stomach. He rinsed the linen rag again and mopped it over her hair. Slowly he washed her face and watched her staring up at him.

"I shall require a drink made from a measure of apple cider, a dollop of dark wine and a drizzle of honey. It shant be warmed," he cautioned. "Bring it in a cup quickly if you might."

In a few minutes Grace was back again with a tea cup in her hands. She held it out to him, watching warily.

Mac picked up Azaria, dressed only in her diaper, and touched the cup to her lips. He allowed a trickle of liquid into her mouth and waited. She swallowed and he permitted more of it to flow. When she had emptied the cup he put her back in the crib again. He waited for nearly a half hour as her cheeks gradually changed from bright red to a deep pink. Slowly he repeated the process with Thea.

Mrs. Whitley was instructed to prepare a drink with marshmallow roots, linseed, apple-tree buds and mashed carrots. The dark wine was added to thin the blend and the girls were fed small sips of it. They were wiped down again with witch hazel and cool water.

Soon after midnight their fevers diminished visibly. Mac suggested that the baby girls be nursed and dressed in summer night dresses before they were put to bed. Through the night he remained in the sitting room where he dozed and checked on girls hourly.

Luke did not return through the night. In the morning, Mac examined Azaria and Thea again and was satisfied that the danger had passed. The family gathered in the dining room for breakfast as they waited for news from the Pender household.

Tired after the sleepless night, Luke opened the front door, stamped his feet and removed his cloak. He kicked off his boots and lurched into the dining room. He poured a cup of black tea and sat in his chair.

"Have Azaria and Thea worsened?" he asked, looking from Grace to Mac.

"Both are well this morn," Grace declared. "Mac did mind them well through the night."

Luke nodded and lowered his cup. The china cup rattled against the saucer as his hand shook. Grace looked at the dark circles under his eyes and the troubled look he tried to conceal.

"What of the Pender girls?" she asked.

"Althena and Dorcas did pass in the night. The fever of Margaretha and Cora did end in this morn. Molly and Joanna shall tend to them this day," he responded sadly. His voice had an eerie tone that Grace found unnerving. She felt a shiver travel down her spine and she looked away from him.

Grace stood and walked slowly back to the kitchen. She and Mrs. Whitley began preparing food to be delivered to the Pender's home. Grace thought of Azaria, lying in her arms the night before with her damp hair and flushed cheeks. She lowered herself into a chair and lifted her apron to her face. She remembered the pain of burying Cherish and understood the horror that Joanna would endure in the days to come.

Colleen placed her hand on Grace's shoulder, reassuringly. "Mayhap you shall sit with Uncle Luke as Mrs. Whitley and I attend to the kitchen."

"Thank you, Colleen," Grace responded.

Grace glanced into the dining room but found only dirty dishes on the table. She paced through to the bedroom but Luke was not there. She heard a sound and moved along the hall to the nursery door. Gently she pushed at the door and it opened slowly.

Luke sat on the floor near the cradle with his back against the wall. His eighteen month-old daughter sat on his lap with his right arm wrapped around her. The stump of his left arm rested against his forehead and tears ran down his face. Grace felt her heart breaking for him as she watched. She raised her apron again to her eyes.

"A pa, a pa," Azaria muttered and yawned.

Grace stepped over the thresh-hold into the room. Tenderly, she lifted the child from his lap and settled her in the crib. She sat beside Luke on the floor and reached for his hand. With her head against his shoulder, she touched his wet face.

15

February progressed with dreary skies and light snowfall daily. Althena and Dorcas Pender waited for spring in simple caskets in the stone tomb behind Botts' Tavern. Alongside them Lemuel Botts, Malcolm Grantham, and Ollie Litchfield lingered in their own coffins. Before the month ended four more children and several adults passed away from the fever. It would be a grim spring with many funerals.

Luke's nightmares continued with less savagery and less frequency than before. But following the deaths of Althena and Dorcas, a new component was added. The wolf and rabbit continued to visit him in his dreams, with the wolf sitting quietly as the rabbit taunted him. After each night terror, he woke in the morning feeling intense guilt and sorrow.

March blew in with a snowstorm out of the Northeast. The first morning began with brisk winds and a mix of snow and ice.

Through the day, the weather changed over to freezing rain and eventually a chilly drizzle. Into the evening, the temperature fell rapidly and the snow began accumulating. The days rain quickly froze, leaving a slick layer beneath the fresh snow. The following day the storm passed, leaving nearly 36 inches of snow behind.

Frigid days and bitter nights persisted through March and into April. At last the winds shifted and began blowing from the south. The snow and ice melted, leaving slushy paths throughout the town. Soon the first green buds appeared and spring flowers sprouted. Gradually the ground thawed and Jacob Frawley began digging graves. Penn Cooper was hired to assist with the numerous burials.

Two years earlier Penn's wife and three of his children had died of pneumonia in their small house in Coningsborough. A year later, heavy snow had collapsed the roof of his house and his remaining son had been killed. He salvaged the few belongings from the home and began travelling the region with all he owned in a wagon that he pulled behind him. When there was work to be done, he worked hard. Yet when the work was done he took the coins earned and sought out the nearest tavern. Laurent Morgan offered him a room and meals with a few coins now and then for his efforts and Penn gratefully accepted.

In mid-April a simple funeral service was planned for Althena and Dorcas Pender. Family and friends travelled to the East Grantham Cemetery. Joanna wept uncontrollably as she climbed the hill with Michael at her side. He stopped periodically to pull her into his arms and hold her tight. At last they passed a cluster of maple trees and saw the two white coffins side by side under the morning sun. Overcome by the sight, Joanna collapsed in Michael's arms.

Rev. Murray cleared his throat, choking back tears, as he began the service for the children. With his wife Aileen and daughter Norah at his side he struggled through the prayers. He offered words intended to provide comfort, but they sounded hollow and insincere in his ears. He could think of nothing that could genuinely console the grief-stricken parents.

As the funeral concluded, Joanna knelt beside the coffins and Michael carefully removed the lids. Gently, Joanna leaned forward to place a new doll and a Bible in each of the coffins. She told them how much she loved them and would miss them until they were together again. Tenderly, Michael helped her up to her feet again. He replaced the coffin lids and stepped back. Behind him, not a dry eye remained. Rev. Murray coughed and wiped his eyes as well.

Michael put an arm around Joanna's shoulders and led her down the hill again. Molly followed closely behind, holding the hands of her two remaining granddaughters, Margaretha and Cora. The breeze stirred the branches of the trees and clouds drifted lazily across the morning sky.

Luke hung his head and walked slowly behind Grace. Mac moved beside him, with Azaria in his arms. She babbled softly and pressed her cheek against his. Two brown squirrels ran in circles around the gravestones. Luke stamped a foot in their direction and they scurried toward the maple trees.

Near the bottom of the hill, Lily tripped over a thick tree root that poked up through the dirt on the path. She stumbled forward with her arms pin-wheeling as she fought to regain her balance. She landed on the rocky trail and her forehead thunked hard against a rounded stone. Dazed, she rolled to her side and cried out as she clutched her belly.

Luke and Joseph ran back to find Lily lying on the path with Timothy kneeling beside her. Luke brushed her hair back and wiped the blood from her forehead. Timothy lifted her carefully in his arms and hurried along the trail to the carriages outside the cemetery gates. There Luke looked at the wound again.

"Deliver her to Burghill House and be quick!" he demanded.

On the road in front of the house, Joseph rushed to Timothy's carriage and carefully lifted his sister down. He carried her inside and up the stairs. In the vacant front bedroom, he placed her on the big bed and stepped back. Luke wiped more blood from her face and Mac opened Luke's bag. Grace brought in a basin of warm water and waited.

"Tis but a bump," Lily protested, as Luke examined her head.

"It shall be to me to determine if all is well," Luke snapped.

"Luke!" Grace cried and grabbed for his arm. He turned, to look at her worried face. She nodded toward Joseph and Luke turned quickly. The sleeve of Joseph's coat was stained with blood from the back of Lily's dress. Luke looked back to Lily and saw the smudge of blood that had soaked through her skirt.

"Go for the midwife!" Luke ordered and Joseph ran for the stairs.

Grace and Colleen dressed Lily in a simple nightgown and settled her into the bed. Molly arrived quickly and examined her. Reassuringly, she patted Lily's hand and left the room.

Luke, Timothy and Mac waited in the hallway. Molly sat heavily on the bench in front of the window. She wiped her forehead with the back of her hand and exhaled. Timothy stepped back to the balustrade and gripped the railing.

"The bleeding did slow, yet her travails have begun. I fear greatly for the little one. I shall give penny royal to progress her labor, for Lily's welfare. I pray it shall be done swiftly," Molly explained gloomily. "'Tis rightful she shall have mulled wine to dull the pain and render her unawares."

Mac walked to the steps and down to the kitchen for a flagon. He stopped to utter a simple prayer before plodding back up to the hall. Grimly he passed the bottle and cup to Molly and moved to stand in the corner near Timothy.

As her contractions increased, Lily realized that her labor had begun. She accepted the mulled wine and cried softly. Grace sat on the bed beside her, holding her hand. Colleen left to tend to Azaria and Thea and aid Mrs. Whitley in the kitchen.

Emma and Julia soon arrived and hurried upstairs to sit with Lily. Molly blended herbs and brewed them into a strong tea. She provided a cup of the steaming liquid for Lily and gave her leaves to chew. Into the afternoon, Lily drank more of the emmanogogue and asked for still more of the robust wine.

"'Tis a strange pain in me, Midwife," Lily stammered. "The pain does not upsurge as with my babies afore. Shall this child tarry?"

"The travails do progress," Molly responded.

"It shall be another healthy son," Lily spoke dreamily and sipped still more of the wine. "Shall he come this day?"

"Dear Lily, worry not," Grace spoke soothingly.

"Mama," Lily breathed. "'Tis to be a baby boy."

"Shhh," Grace comforted as she smoothed back Lily's hair.

"Mama, bring Timothy!" she moaned. "Please, Mama I do need Timothy."

Discretely Emma stepped out into the hall and closed the door firmly. She looked from Timothy to Luke and back again. "Lily does plead for Timothy."

"Tis not reasonable," Luke responded.

"Shall you come?" she asked, looking into Timothy's eyes.

Frightened, he looked at Luke pleadingly. "I cannot see her suffer."

"Emma, tell the midwife to come out," Luke stated as he looked out at the sky beyond the window.

Molly agreed to permit Timothy to enter the room. He was instructed to go to the far side of the bed and sit close to the headboard. He could hold Lily's hand and reassure her, but would not be permitted to interfere with the midwife's duties. If the situation worsened, he would be expected to leave quickly for Lily's safety. He agreed and followed Molly into the dimly lit room.

"Timothy!" Lily cried as she gripped his hand anxiously. "The child shall come this day!"

"Shhh, my love," Timothy spoke gently and brushed his fingers over her cheek.

Gradually, Lily calmed as Timothy leaned close and whispered to her. She sipped more of the wine while he talked of the fine house they would have in Boston. Timothy stroked her hair and talked of an enchanted future far away from Judge Gage and her past. He promised that she would bless him with many strong sons. She would not know a moment of unhappiness throughout her life.

Lily turned her head to look at Timothy and smiled distantly as she welcomed the wine induced sleep. Timothy slid down lower to rest beside her on the bed. Lying at her side, he continued to utter fantastic promises, long after she had drifted away into a dreamless slumber.

The strong herbs and wine worked quickly through the afternoon as Lily slept. Emma led Timothy down to the sitting room to wait with Luke, Joseph, and Mac, while the midwife managed the final stage of the birth. Lily woke again as the pains increased and she lay quietly waiting. Early in the evening the feet of the baby appeared first. Gently Molly worked to remove him as quickly as possible. As his head appeared she saw the cord, snugged tight at his throat. Silently she wrapped the boy in linens and passed him to Grace.

Emma provided more of the strong wine and Lily accepted it gratefully. In her languorous state she waited for the cry of her new baby. Molly delivered the afterbirth and breathed a sigh of relief as the heavy bleeding diminished. She made her way down to the kitchen to prepare a special brew to induce a deep sleep and speed Lily's recovery.

Grace wiped away tears as she tenderly bathed the infant's body and swaddled him in fresh linens. She shrouded him in a rabbit fur bunting. For a short time she sat holding him as she prayed for him. Hesitantly she carried him into the sitting room.

Gently, Mac lifted the still bundle from Grace's arms and walked outside with him. He carried him along Kings Wood Road to Botts' Tavern. In the stable, he found Jacob Frawley and Laurent Morgan working. Jacob accepted the child from Mac and offered his sincerest sympathies. Mac assured him that Timothy would pay well for a fine casket. Jacob nodded, and strode toward the scullery behind the tavern.

Late in the evening, Lily woke to find Timothy lying beside her again. Molly and Grace sat near the door talking softly. Two lamps had been lighted and a low fire burned in the Franklin stove across the room. Lily felt Timothy squeeze her hand and looked up at him.

"When shall my baby come?" Lily asked.

Anxiously, Timothy looked toward Molly and Grace as the women interrupted their conversation. Molly stood and moved toward the bed. "Lily twas naught to be done for the child."

"Timothy, no!" she shrieked. "I cannot lose another son! I cannot!"

"Twas no son," Timothy lied and closed his eyes tight. When he opened them again the midwife stared at him in disbelief. "Twas no son, Lily. The girl was small and sickly and could not endure."

"A sickly girl child?" Lily asked as she watched his face.

"Tis so," he answered. "You shall yet be blessed with another healthy son. Worry not."

"A sickly girl," she repeated softly and turned to look at Molly.

"Tis so," Molly stammered and bit her lip. She glanced back at Grace and frowned. "Mayhap we shall take leave that you might speak in seclusion."

"Shall you depart for Boston on the morrow?" Lily asked him as she yawned.

"Why should you think it so?"

"You did tell it," she whined as he eyes fluttered closed. "When the child did come you were to find a stately home for me there."

"Lily, I cannot go afore I shall know you are well. Mayhap you shall permit me to tarry through the week."

She nodded slowly, and surrendered to sleep again.

16

Lily refused to see anyone outside her family as she remained at Burghill House "lying-in". Timothy left daily to work and returned at the end of the day to sit through the evening with her. Daily, Sarina Gage and the governess arrived with Lily's children, Eddie and Faith. They sat with her for a short time each day before she complained that they exhausted her and should go.

Timothy named the baby Francesca Leigh Gage to prevent Lily from learning that the child had been a boy. A simple service was held at the family cemetery. The small casket was lowered into the ground beside the empty grave of Albert. When the service was done Timothy tossed in a big handful of dirt and apologized to the boy for the name he had been given. He continued to pray quietly as he walked along the trail back to Burghill House.

"Timothy, must we go to your father's home this day?" Lily pressed as she slowly packed her trunk. She had remained in Burghill House for six weeks and Timothy urged her return to his father's house.

"Tis our rightful home, dear heart," he coaxed.

"When shall you travel to Boston?"

"Lily, father is not well. Tis likely he shall pass soon and the house shall be made mine. You shall be the lady of the manor at last," he teased. With his hands on her shoulders, he leaned to kiss her forehead.

"Did Uncle Luke warn that Judge Gage shall expire quickly?" she asked as her fingers traced the front of his vest.

"Father shant talk with Dr. Wallace of his ailments. Trust in my judgment, dear wife. He shall not be long for this world."

"Then I shall travel to the Gage house this day," she yielded. "Would it be wrongful that I do pray he shall take leave of us soon?"

"You shant speak of it," Timothy cautioned.

"No, I shall smile as I do greet him and conceal my thoughts."

Timothy closed the trunk and buckled the leather straps to secure it. He carried it out through the bedroom door, following close behind her. The carriage waited in front of the house and he quickly loaded the chest on the back. Lily accepted a cinnamon cake from Mrs. Whitley and hugged Grace before she hurried down the front steps.

In the evening, the Gage family sat quietly at the dining room table. Lily watched the judge as he ate heartily. Timothy kept his head down and only picked at the roast lamb on his plate. Beside Daniel, Sarina remained lost in her thoughts as she sipped her tea between tiny bites.

In the kitchen the governess fed the children. When they had finished with supper, she walked them up the stairs and put them to bed. Silently, she padded along the hallway to the small room at the end. Unless one of the children cried out, she would remain there until morning.

The windows remained open throughout the house on the warm June night. A slight breeze ruffled the curtains. In the dark bedroom, Lily laid awake thinking about Timothy's promises. She had listened to the judge speak and watched him closely as he ate well. Clearly the man was well and Timothy could not bring himself to leave. She recalled the bitter humiliation that Timothy had endured in the church as he confessed unfairly. It would be wrong to force Timothy to act now. Yet she could not bear to see him unhappy, living under his father's tyranny. She felt compelled to resolve the problem on her own.

In the dim light from the moon and stars, Lily studied Timothy's strong back. She reached to trace her fingers across his shoulders and down his well-muscled arm. A smile touched her lips as she moved to kiss his smooth skin. He muttered in his sleep and she moved closer. Her hand touched his side and brushed over his stomach to his chest. He placed his hand over hers and lifted it to his lips.

"You should sleep," he whispered as he kissed her fingers.

"Hold me," she told him.

Timothy rolled over and pulled her into his arms. He held her tight against his bare chest. "I do love you so."

"And I you," she answered softly. "Bless me with another son and all shall be well," she told him and smiled wickedly in the dark.

17

Lily rose early and hurried down to the kitchen. Eagerly, she blended the batter and added plump blueberries that Mrs. Quinn had gathered. She gently folded them into the muffin batter and tasted it. She smiled and added another small scoop of sugar. The cook watched curiously as she stirred the corn mush bubbling in the cast iron pot. She was not accustomed to seeing Lily in the kitchen.

"Judge Gage does fancy blueberries," Lily commented as she pushed the baking pan into the brick oven beside the hearth.

"That he does," Mrs. Quinn agreed, still watching her curiously.

"Mayhap I shall prepare the vessel of coffee for him this morn as well," Lily giggled nervously. "Oh, I did err. The sugar crock has been emptied. Have you a sack in the storage cellar beneath the pantry?"

"'Tis so," Mrs. Quinn responded as she grabbed for the hook at the side of the hearth and lifted the pot from the fire. She placed it gently on the slate hearth mat and hung the hook back on the rack. "I shall fetch it, Ma'am."

"No, Mrs. Quinn," Lily declared. "You do toil endlessly. I shall retrieve it."

Lily wiped her hands on her apron and hurried toward the pantry. She grasped the iron ring on the floor and raised the heavy wooden trap door. She let the hatch rest against the cupboards and moved carefully down the stone steps. In the dimly lit space, she squinted at the thick pine shelves.

Quickly, she bent low and looked under the lowest shelf. She pulled the sugar scoop out from her pocket and scraped up grey powder from the edge between the wall and the floor. She poured it into the pocket of her dress and dug out more of it. Carefully she maneuvered her pocket deeper into the folds of her skirt and stood again. Swiftly she pushed aside a tin of ships biscuits and grasped the sack of sugar. Her mouth twitched in amusement as she rushed back up to the kitchen.

Breakfast was served in the dining room as usual. Daniel and Timothy discussed legal issues and made plans for the day. Timothy planned to visit with Victor Windham at the jail to discuss his upcoming trial. The man had been charged with cutting down a tree in the town square and faced the death penalty, if convicted. Daniel would be seated at the Court of General Sessions, presiding over hearings through most of the day.

"Might you return for lunch?" Lily asked sweetly.

"When I have done with my meeting in the jail this day, I shall travel to Georges Falls," Timothy told her, "I shant return afore supper is laid upon the table."

"Good Judge Gage, shall you grace us with your presence as we do dine?" Lily prompted.

"Tis likely I shall," he responded, looking over the top of his bifocals at her.

"Eddie and Faith shall be seated for lunch if you shall oblige. They do miss their Grandfather of late."

"Yes, tis likely I shall come," Daniel announced, pleased by her manner. He rolled his shoulders back and puffed out his chest, reaching for his cup of coffee. He swallowed the last of it and stood to go.

18

The windows in the kitchen stood open. Sheer fabric had been stretched across the opening to keep out the vile flies from the livery. Not even the slightest breeze moved the air under the intense July sun. Emma filled a pitcher with hot water from the kettle and carried it into the bedroom. She placed it beside the basin on the bedside table and stepped back.

Grace wrung out the cloth and gently patted at Julia's face with it. Julia forced a smile and nodded. "Mayhap you shall fetch a pitcher of frigid water and pour it upon my head."

"It would shock you, dear child," Molly protested as she dug through the pockets of her bag for select herbs, leaves, and seeds.

Julia's travails had begun the day before but had progressed only slightly through the night and into the second day. In the oppressive heat, the women waited impatiently for the infant to arrive at last. As the sun finally made its way down behind the trees and dropped beneath to the horizon, night settled in at last.

Laurent sat outside on the fieldstone steps hoping for some relief from the hot weather. He strode toward the corner of the house and began pumping cold water into the wooden bucket there. He dipped his hands in and splashed water into his face.

"Reny!" he called to the small boy. Reny left his toy soldiers in the shade under the hemlock tree and ran to stand beside Laurent.

"Da?" he responded as Laurent splashed him with the cool water. Reny giggled and moved close to the barrel to splash his step-father in return. The two laughed as they emptied the bucket and Laurent quickly refilled it.

The back door opened and Grace stepped outside. Surprised, she looked from Laurent to Reny, as they stood dripping wet in the tall, dry grass.

"Laurent!" she called apprehensively. "The child has come."

Laurent grabbed Reny and boosted him up onto his shoulders. Excitedly, he followed Grace, ducking low before he stepped through the doorway.

"Laurent, all is well," Molly assured him as he entered the bedroom.

"What is the child?" he asked, raising an eyebrow.

"'Tis a healthy girl," she told him as she noted the water puddling at his feet.

"'Tis a daughter, Julia!" he shouted, beaming with pride.

"Yes, husband," she told him, smiling. "Shall you give a name to her?"

Laurent lowered Reny onto the bed. Julia patted his back and frowned at the wet spot spreading on the bed clothes. Laurent moved closer to Molly as she held out the new baby, swaddled in a thin layer of linen. Anxiously he held her, waiting for her to break in his huge hands. When she started to cry he pressed closer to Molly and implored her to take the infant from him.

"She is fragile as a rose in full bloom," he whispered as he touched her cheek. "She shall be called Rose Mary Morgan."

"'Tis a fine name for her," Julia smiled.

Laurent snatched Reny up from the bed and held him close to his new baby sister. "Your sister, Rose," he uttered as Reny touched her thick, dark hair. Reny leaned to kiss her nose before Laurent carried him out of the room and closed the door quietly.

"I am greatly relieved that I did birth a girl," Julia whispered to Grace. "I did worry for Lily if twas a healthy son."

Grace hugged her awkwardly as Julia lay flat in the bed. She turned to help Molly clean the room and put it back in proper order while Julia dozed.

19

Over the long, hot and humid summer, Thea Grenier and Moses Taylor celebrated their first birthdays. Azaria enjoyed a special party for her second birthday in August. In the oppressive heat, the celebration was held in the shade of the trees behind Burghill House. Mrs. Whitley served delicious fresh strawberry ice cream and chocolate cake.

Late in the day the toddlers and babies slept on blankets in the grass, close to the benches. The older children wandered into the woods as the women visited near their sleeping little ones. Gradually the men moved into the cooler shade of the barn, where they passed a jug of whiskey and talked.

By early evening the guests had gone and Mrs. Whitley set out a cold supper in the dining room. The windows stood wide open, but the heat and humidity still hung in the air. Not even a hint of a breeze moved to provide respite. Lazily, they ate and wandered outside again.

Luke took Grace by the hand and led her behind the barn. Her back pressed against the worn wooden plank siding as Luke leaned close. His lips moved slowly over her cheek to her soft lips. He kissed her passionately and inhaled the floral scent of her perfume.

"Mayhap you shall come to Norwich Pond with me this night, Mrs. Wallace," he teased as he bent to kiss her neck.

"Dr. Wallace, tis a fine idea. Yet near the edge of the water we shall be greatly tempted to enter in."

"Might you shed your lovely gown and linger under the moon with me?"

"Good sir!" she feigned shock at his suggestion. "What shall people think of such a thing?"

"I shant tell of it, dear lady," he whispered as he pressed his mouth over hers.

Luke mounted his horse and held his hand out to Grace. In the dark she lifted her skirt and swung up behind him. She wrapped her arms around his waist as they rode leisurely on through the town center and onto Killock Road. Luke tied the dark animal to the hitching post at the head of Somner Trail.

He slipped an arm around Grace's waist and steered her onto the path. Listening to the music of crickets, they walked languidly in the moonlight. Fireflies blinked as they flitted around the low branches of the trees. In the cloudless sky a million stars sparkled.

"The blackberries are delightfully fragrant," she murmured as she stopped to pick several from the tall bushes. She fed him a few and they moved on.

At the edge of the pond he smiled and raised an eyebrow before he began removing his clothes. He placed them on the slate outcropping with his pistol on top of the pile and looked to Grace. She blushed as she watched his naked body moving in the moonlight. Slowly she began removing the layers until she stood nude before him as well. He touched her hand and lured her down over the smooth rocks into the water.

"Hold fast to my neck," he told her as he moved out into deeper water.

"Luke, I cannot swim," she warned.

"Nor I, my love," he responded and chuckled warmly. "My feet do reach the bottom and I shant move beyond this depth."

With her arms around his neck and her legs around his hips she held tight. He kissed her tenderly and recited her favorite sonnet. "Let me not to the marriage of true minds admit impediments. Love is not love which alters when it alteration finds, or bends with the remover to remove: O no! It is an ever-fixed mark that looks on tempests and is never shaken; It is the star to every wandering bark, whose worth's unknown, although his height be taken. Love's not Time's fool, though rosy lips and cheeks within his bending sickle's compass come: Love alters not with his brief hours and weeks, but bears it out even to the edge of doom. If this be error and upon me proved, I never writ, nor no man ever loved."

"I do love you so, Luke Wallace," she whispered and hugged him tighter.

"Your greatest love for me cannot compare to my love and desire for you, Grace," he replied and rested his forehead against hers.

20

"Joseph," Colleen voiced as she slowly fanned her face with her hand. She sat on the cool stone steps in front of the house with a glass of wine beside her.

"I am here," he answered. In the dark he stood leaning against a large tree, staring up into the night sky.

"'Tis my greatest wish that you shall permit me to call upon my family. I shall take Thea and linger among my people for a month."

"You are needed here, Colleen," he stated as he looked at the owl, seated high in the pine across the road.

"Joseph, if you shall approve it, I shall be grateful. My mother is not well and I do fear that she shall pass afore I do sight her again."

"I shall allow it," he sighed at last. "In one month you shall return to Burghill House."

"Yes, husband," she told him and sipped from the glass.

"Penn Cooper shall accompany you on the morrow," he advised her, before he strolled into the trees.

In the morning Penn Cooper arrived with a closed carriage, as a light rain fell. Earlier Joseph had visited the tavern to pay for the Landau and a driver. At home, Colleen packed a trunk and readied Thea for the trip. She placed a berry pie with cornmeal crust into a box, to take to her mother. A sack with bread, wine and apples would provide food and drink for the journey.

Through the day Joseph worked and worried about his wife and daughter. He deeply regretted consenting to their travel. When the long day was done, he rode to the tavern and waited there for the return of Penn Cooper. Near ten in the evening Penn finally rolled up the drive to the livery. He tended to the horses and strode inside for a mug of beer and plate of supper.

"Greetings, Penn," Joseph called as the man stepped inside and banged the door closed.

"Mr. Grenier!" Penn responded as he reached to shake his hand. "Your wife and child are secure in the home of her father."

"I am greatly reassured."

"Might you sup with me?" Penn suggested.

"Many thanks. I would enjoy a bowl of Julia's fine stew and a tankard," Joseph declared as he tossed two coins on the table. Penn nodded thankfully and slid into the chair across from Joseph. Laurent and Jacob soon joined them at the table. They ate and drank as they talked of the covered bridge being constructed over the Scaffel River.

21

Lily crept out the back door and hurried to the barn. The thick white clouds hid the moon and stars in the sky above. She stumbled in the dark and caught herself before landing on the rocky drive. She lifted the latch and pulled the heavy barn door open. Field mice scurried out of sight and the cat in the loft meowed.

"Shhhh!" she hushed.

Once inside, she tugged the door closed and marveled at the solid darkness. She dug in her pocket for the small brass tinderbox and a dipped candle. Nearly ten minutes passed as she struggled in the dark before she finally lit the candle. She held it high and looked around the large, cluttered space. Carefully, she made her way to the far wall and knelt there. She brushed away the loose straw and searched the area where the stones at the lower half of the wall met the rough wooden plank floor.

"Ahhh," she sighed, happily as she spotted the first trace of the gray arsenic powder. She moved to the left and brushed away more of the straw. She dug in her pocket for the large spoon and began scooping the powder into a small silk pouch. When she had filled it, she moved along the wall and pulled out another little sack and stuffed it too. Satisfied, she tied it tight and tucked it all back into her pockets.

Warily, she extinguished the candle and waited for the wax to cool. The darkness quickly swallowed the shadows and she dropped the candle into the pocket of her apron. Smiling shrewdly she worked her way through to the doors and pushed them closed behind her. She snapped the latch securely and danced along the drive toward the back door.

"Lily?" Timothy called out.

Her blood ran cold and she stood frozen in place. She held her breath and waited, fighting a rising panic.

"Lily, I can smell your perfume in the night air."

"Tis, I," she uttered as her heart thundered in her chest.

"Why have you come out into the dark?"

"The heat within did overtake me," she cringed, hoping he would accept her lie.

"Tis not a fitting place for a woman alone," he said as he walked down from the steps. He peered into the gloom and moved toward her shadowy outline. Uneasily she rubbed her hands against her apron to remove the traces of the powder. He touched her arm and trailed down to her wrist. Gently he pulled her into his arms and lifted her chin to kiss her. "Might you come up to the bedroom? The wind has shifted to blow from the east and tis likely the night shall cool."

"That shall be a welcome thing," she proclaimed as she followed him into the dark kitchen.

Through the night, thundershowers passed over the region and the heat diminished at last. In the morning the temperatures climbed slowly under the late August sun. A steady breeze provided some relief but the humidity remained. Lily entered the kitchen early and hurriedly prepared a dozen blueberry muffins. The last two poured into the pan were heavily laced with the arsenic powder.

At the kitchen table she sprinkled sugar on top of the warm muffins. She put the two tainted muffins on a pewter plate then placed it on the large silver tray. Quickly she filled the coffee carafe and poured a single cup. She added more of the arsenic to the cup, then tucked the silk pouch back into her pocket.

Smiling cheerily, she grasped the handles of the heavy tray and hurried into the dining room. The judge sat at the head of the table with a leather sheath of papers to his left. He looked up as she entered and scowled.

"I shant abide coffee this morn," he grumbled. "Mayhap weak tea shall aid me this day."

"Shall I summon Dr. Wallace?" Lily offered sympathetically.

"Tis no physician required. The slight ailment shall pass," he mumbled stubbornly as he reached for one of the blueberry muffins.

Quickly Lily rushed back to the kitchen. She licked her lips and considered the situation. Finally she opened the door and emptied the cup on the ground. She refilled it with tea and diluted it with a pale wine.

"This shall surely mend what ails you," she told Daniel as she placed the cup in front of him. He sipped and nodded to her then turned his attention back to the papers he had been reading. As he pulled several documents from the pile, he took a big bite from the second muffin. Lily smirked and hurried up the stairs to wake Timothy.

22

In early September Judge Gage relented and asked for Dr. Wallace. He had remained in his bedroom for two days as he suffered with vomiting, diarrhea, dreadful cramps in his muscles and blood in his urine. As the sun rose that morning he experienced the first convulsions. Worriedly, Sarina fed him weak tea and Timothy rode to Burghill House.

An hour later, Luke stood beside Daniel's bed, examining him carefully. He prepared an herbal blend that would work to resolve the symptoms. It was quickly steeped and the dark, minty scented tea was provided to the judge. Hesitantly he drank it and lay back on the pillows.

Luke opened his box and removed the lancet case. He removed the lid on one of the 10 oz jars and stretched a small sheet of oil cloth under Daniel's arm. With the largest of the lancets he made a clean cut over the man's vein. The blood flowed into the jar sitting below it as Judge Gage fussed and complained. When the jar had been filled he bandaged the incision and put the cover on the jar again.

"Continue to sip the brew," Luke advised him.

"Mayhap you shall eat a bite," Lily offered. She stood in the doorway holding out a china plate with a blueberry muffin on it.

"Breakfast shall do you good," Luke agreed. Daniel accepted the plate from her and nibbled at the muffin. "If you shant improve afore nightfall, I shall think to bleed you again."

"Uncle Luke, he did suffer so in the heat of summer. I am greatly fearful," Lily murmured sympathetically.

"Judge Gage, I cannot cure you if you shant summon me as your ailment does progress," Luke chastised.

Daniel waved him away and swallowed another bite of the muffin. Luke shook his head and collected his tools. With the box tucked securely under his arm, he left the bedroom. In the hall he kissed Lily's cheek and thanked her for attending so lovingly to her father-in-law.

Near midnight Luke returned to assess Judge Gage again. He prepared a stronger brew for him and urged him to sip it. The man had grown weaker through the day and more convulsions began as Dr. Wallace debated more bleeding. When the seizure passed, he vomited again and dropped back against the pillows in exhaustion.

Luke walked back down the stairs to blend another brew. Worriedly, he stood beside the table as he carefully ground the leaves with mortar and pestle. The kettle hung inside the hearth with the bright orange flames licking along the bottom of it.

"Dr. Wallace!" Timothy called from the top of the stairs. "Come quickly!"

Luke ran up the steps and into the bedroom. He moved close to the bed and studied Daniel's face. The right side drooped while the left side of his mouth moved continually. A foamy substance flowed from the corner of his mouth and his words were slurred and impossible to understand.

"He did stiffen and strained greatly as pains did grip his middle," Sarina explained, as she rung her hands and winced.

"'Tis apoplexy," Luke proclaimed as he exhaled slowly. "'Tis naught I might do to cure him of this thing."

"Dr. Wallace, he cannot perish," Sarina whined as she backed away from the bed.

"Might you prepare tea?" he asked, hoping to distract her.

"Assuredly," she prattled on as she hurried out of the room.

For several days Judge Daniel Gage lay still in his bed. The 17th century Friesian, oak, four-poster bedstead had belonged to his grandfather, Eiditch Gage. Ornate carvings adorned the head and footboards and the four posts appeared to be made of braided and twisted saplings. Lily stood at the end of the bed and watched the judge as he stared up at the engraved oak canopy. She smiled and circled around to the side near the windows.

"Shall I bake you more of the blueberry muffins?" she asked and giggled. "Mayhap you have swallowed plenty. We shant see you growing plumper with the sweets."

Lazily, she looked out the window and watched several chickadees hopping on the pine boughs. She eased the window up and slapped her hands flat against the window sill. Startled, the small birds fluttered away. Calmly she forced it back down again and turned to look at the still figure lying on the bed.

"Shant you speak to me?" she prodded cheerfully. "I do come to divert your head as Uncle Luke instructed, yet tis no gratitude. As with the muffins and coffee I did prepare. No gratitude."

Distantly, she stroked the smooth carved word of the bedposts. She recalled the stories her father told her when she was a small child. There were wonderful tales of kings and queens and remarkable castles. She looked around the room at the incredible furniture that fit beautifully in the massive space. It would provide a delightful bedroom for her and for Timothy. Sarina would need to be moved to a smaller space when the judge had passed.

"Timothy was a fine prince yet you did not value him, Sir. You were exceedingly harsh with my handsome gentleman. A cruel and uncaring man you have been. You shall be dead and buried quickly, Judge Gage. Timothy shall be made king and he shall revel in this fine house at last. You shall condemn me no more," she proclaimed laughed casually.

His left eye twitched rapidly and the left side of his mouth moved as he struggled to speak. As the afternoon light filled the room, his face grew paler. Bored, she looked around a last time and dropped into the richly embroidered Bergère chair between the windows. She picked up a copy of, *The Arabian Nights* from the small table and opened it.

"Shall I read aloud to amuse you?" she asked and waited for his reply. She listened to the strange noises he made and nodded as she began reading silently.

23

Judge Gage passed away late in the afternoon. Sarina and Timothy took comfort from the knowledge that Lily had been with him in the end. They marveled at how close Daniel and Lily had become as he suffered with his ailment. Lily told them that the change in their relationship had given her great joy as well. She assured them that the special attention she had shown him was the very least that she could do for him.

A tremendous funeral was conducted in the East Grantham Cemetery. Dignitaries travelled from as far away as Massachusetts to show their respects for the honorable man. He was laid to rest in a lavishly carved casket. Two weeks after the burial a spectacular granite headstone was set in place to mark the head of his grave. A small footstone with his initials and the year of his death, 1798 were noted.

Sarina sobbed inconsolably throughout the funeral and the placement of the markers at his grave. Dr. Wallace provided Laudanum to calm her and advised Lily to dose her whenever she felt the poor woman needed it.

In the days that followed Sarina insisted that Timothy and Lily accept the larger bedroom filled with the magnificent furniture. She maintained that she would be happier in a smaller room with far less grandeur. Contentedly, Sarina sat alone in the parlor daily, sipping brandy tempered with tea, in her fine bone china cups.

24

After lunch Joseph stood and Mac wandered out behind the barn. The early October day was comfortably cool and colorful leaves littered the ground. Their axes remained wedged in the chopping blocks where they'd finished with them earlier. Joseph pried his loose and lifted it to his shoulder. Mac smiled and pulled the second one free. At sixteen Mac was already four inches taller than the man he called his cousin. He admired Joseph, but with broader shoulders and a stronger back, Mac could split the big logs nearly twice as fast if he chose to.

Joseph smiled as he felt the spirit of competition hanging heavy in air. He lifted a fat chunk of oak and set it level on his block. Mac tilted his head and eyed it, then selected a slightly larger section of maple. He flashed his charming smile and placed an additional chunk of pine on top of it.

A fat squirrel sat on a branch in one of the elm trees behind them. He watched them and chattered as he held up a warped horse chestnut. Joseph chuckled and gripped the handle of his finely sharpened axe. He lifted it high and with a whoosh and thwack the wood split down the center.

Mac bobbed his head and tapped the pate of his axe against his boot. He raised it slowly and swept his arms back until his hands were behind his head. Smoothly, his arms flew in a sweeping arc. With a loud cracking sound, the blade ripped through both logs and stuck into the chopping block. He let go of the handle and stepped back, shaking his arms painfully.

"Did it best you, Mac?" Joseph laughed and kicked back several split pieces.

"It did recoil," Mac responded, laughing as he continued rubbing his arms. "I shant repeat that error."

Late in the afternoon Grace carried out a pitcher of mulled cider and apple cake. She placed it on a nearby stump and stopped to brush loose tendrils back from her face.

"Joseph," Grace called to him. "Have you a thought of when Colleen might return to us? Tis a great deal to be done afore the first snow shall fly."

Joseph glanced at his mother than studied the block of pine that stood in front of him. Finally he looked back at her, "She shall come on the morrow."

"On the morrow?" she questioned, surprised by his answer.

"I shall depart when the church service is done with," he told her and lifted his axe again.

She turned away and strode back to the house as she worried about troubles between Joseph and Colleen. Still, she did miss Colleen and Thea and looked forward to their return. Her skirt rustled in the tall grass as she crossed the yard to the clothes line where Mrs. Whitley stood folding dry quilts.

25

Joseph sat in the family pew with little Teague beside him. They both fidgeted, waiting impatiently for the service to conclude. Teague thought of his tin soldiers and playtime with his cousins Eddie and Reny. Joseph's mind wandered to the night that Colleen suggested the trip with Thea. He had reluctantly agreed but had stressed that she return after a month there. Well over a month had passed and she had not come home. No message had been received from her. Through the morning he wavered between worry and irritation.

With the closing prayer spoken, Joseph rose quickly and grabbed Teague's small hand. He rushed toward the front doors, nearly crashing into Rev. Pender there.

"Good day to you, Joseph," Michael smiled as he offered his hand. Joseph shook it firmly and ran down the steps.

"Mama, shall you mind Teague this day?" Joseph called back to Grace as he halted on the slate stones of the walkway.

"Certainly, Joseph," she responded and waved. "Go with God."

"And with you also," he answered as he rushed to carriage.

Dull dry leaves littered the roadside as the horse trotted along. Joseph pressed him to gallop for a distance before he took pity and slowed the fine animal again. He stopped at a spring filled trough before the Talloway Covered Bridge and let the stallion drink his fill. Impatiently, Joseph sipped whiskey from his father's silver flask and thought of Colleen.

The October sun moved across the clear blue sky. A flock of wild turkeys hurried to cross the road, as the horse moved along towards them. Joseph debated stopping to shoot one or more but it was already well into the afternoon. He shook his head and continued on.

Halting in front of the small house, he jumped down and stepped to the back of the carriage. He pulled down a clump of hay and tossed it in the grass in front of the animal. He tied him loosely to the ring mounted on the side of the hitching post at the side of the road. Hastily, he moved through the opening in the low stone wall and sauntered up to the front door.

The door swung back and an old man stood squinting up at him. With a pair of pince nez resting on the man's broad nose, he studied Joseph. He drew an arthritic hand over the remains of his white hair.

"Grenier?" he barked in his gravelly voice.

"Tis I, Mr. Sweeney," Joseph answered and offered his hand.

"Have you come for the girl?"

"I have," Joseph declared.

"Tis rightful," Walter Sweeney agreed as he swung the door wide and welcomed Joseph inside. "A man shall claim what is his own."

Joseph stepped inside the shadowy entryway and followed Sweeney into the shabby little parlor. He sat in the chair offered and accepted the flint glass filled with Irish whiskey. An old woman tottered into the room, carrying a simple pewter tray with plates of bread and cheese. She bobbed her head quickly toward Joseph and left the room.

"Tis the widow Bailey who does aid my wife," Sweeney gestured toward the doorway.

"Where shall Colleen be found?"

"Behind the house she and my Maddy are fussing over the wash."

"Might I speak to her?"

"Rest your head young man. Sip the whiskey and fill your belly. No man should face a willful wife unwarily."

"Have you an opine to relate?" Joseph asked, narrowing his eyes as he watched his father-in-law lighting his pipe.

"Grenier, you did undertake to wed my child when none other should consider her. Yet she does not treasure the blessings granted her. Colleen is a willful woman plagued with discernments that are distasteful in a woman."

"Does my wife judge me unworthy?"

"She does think the house of Burghill morally intolerable of her highness."

Joseph clenched his jaw and thought of Colleen's past comments regarding his family.

"And how shall I resolve this trouble?" Joseph asked as his irritation progressed into anger.

"Tis your wife, Sir. You shall determine the remedy of her delinquency."

"I cannot abide her improper appraisals of my family. A wife shall not speak against her husband. Tis wrongful!" Joseph snapped.

"You shant find a quarrel with me, Joseph. Afore Colleen did come, my Maddy was a headstrong woman with wayward thoughts. She did think herself o'er by dear mother. Maddy did learn at the end of the leather strap."

Joseph cringed and looked away from the old man. "I shall clarify my thinking and trust that Colleen shall correct her mind."

"My razor strap does hang in the hall if it be needed to right her," Sweeney added and swallowed another gulp of the whiskey.

"I should like to speak unto Colleen," Joseph announced as he devoured the bread and cheese and drained his glass.

Mr. Sweeney stood and hobbled back out into the hall. Joseph walked along behind him as they passed a bedroom on the left and the kitchen on the right. Sweeney pushed the back door open and stumbled down the uneven wooden steps.

Across the yard Colleen stood in the dry tall grass with her back to them. She and her mother were folding a heavy wool blanket under the afternoon sun. Not far from them, Thea sat in a large wicker basket, playing with a carved bone teether.

"Colleen!" Sweeney shouted. Colleen and Maddy both turned to face him. Colleen saw Joseph standing behind her father and she bit her lower lip. "Come here, girl!"

Colleen released her end of the blanket and strode toward the men. Her skirt brushed against the dry grass as she moved. She felt her heart race as she glanced from her father to her husband.

"Wife," Joseph uttered as he watched her approach.

"Why have you come?" she asked cagily.

"I did consent to the journey yet did instruct that you return at the end of a month. Too much time has passed, Colleen."

"Husband, I do mean to remain another month. Tis much to be done afore winter shall come."

"No, Colleen," Joseph stated flatly. "You shall depart with me this day."

"Mother does require my aid," Colleen protested.

"I shall not abide a public quarrel," Joseph told her as he looked down at her father.

"Might we talk in seclusion?" she pressed.

"We shall not. Pack your trunk and ready for the journey home."

Colleen sighed heavily and folded her arms. "Joseph Grenier, I shant abide the iniquity of your family and shall not depart on this day!"

Walter Sweeney backhanded Colleen and she stumbled backward as her hand flew to the side of her face.

"Sir!" Joseph shouted as he grabbed Sweeney's arm.

"Tis my daughter, Grenier! You did grant her take leave of you. Do not think to determine how she shall be managed in my house!" Walter commanded. "Colleen, you shall not defy your husband! Take up your baby girl and make to go."

Colleen swallowed hard and walked back to the basket where Thea played. She walked to her mother and hugged her tight. She pursed her lips and strode back toward the house. The men stepped aside and she stomped up the steps.

"Do not flaunt your temper, Girl or you shall meet my razor strap!" Sweeney called after her.

Joseph scowled and followed Colleen into the bedroom closest to the kitchen. He took Thea from her arms and feathered kisses over the baby's cheeks. He left Colleen to pack her trunk and carried the baby outside, as he watered his horse.

While Colleen packed a small sack of food and drink for the trip, Joseph loaded her trunk on the back of the carriage. At last she lifted Thea from her mother's arms and tearfully hugged her good-bye. Hesitantly, she approached her father and gave him a half-hearted hug. Sadly, she plodded down the steps and out to the road.

Joseph offered his hand but she refused and climbed up on her own. He shook his head and handed Thea up to her. Dolefully, he shook hands with Walter Sweeney and nodded politely to Maddy. He climbed up onto the bench and grabbed for the reins. He uttered a series of clicking sounds and snapped the leads. The horse stepped forward and the carriage rolled along the road.

Joseph and Colleen sat in silence for an hour as the animal trotted on. The sun eased across the sky and hovered above the trees in the distance. A chilly breeze had begun to stir the air. Colleen bundled Thea and turned her to face her chest as the toddler slept. Joseph stared down at the road between the legs of the horse and tugged the flask out from his pocket.

"Colleen," he uttered as they rolled over a narrow wood bridge.

"Husband?" she responded.

"I did miss you greatly. Why should you think to depart from me?"

"Twas but to aid my mother," she murmured and twitched her foot agitatedly.

"No, Colleen, you did not," he disputed.

"You cannot know what might be thought in my head."

"Colleen, I fear you cannot state a love for me," Joseph whispered sadly. "From the days of my arrest a change did overtake you. Your heart has grown cold."

"If it be so, tis naught I might do to change it."

"Shall you not dispute my words?"

"If you bid me lie unto you then I shall do it."

"Colleen, have you no love that shall remain within you?"

"I cannot say that I do," she answered and turned away as her tears flowed. She cleared her throat and swallowed hard. "If you did know it true. Why should you take me from my mother?"

"I did pray that my thinking was wrongful. Twas my hope that you might desire me still."

"Joseph, what shall become of me? Do you mean to take my child from me afore you shall cast me out?"

"I shant bid you go," he sighed. "Thea does require her mother."

Colleen breathed a great sigh of relief as she watched the shadowy trees pass by. The sun had slipped below the horizon and she began spotting eyes among the low branches alongside the road. They rolled by a family cemetery and she could smell the scent of the soil over a fresh grave. She shuddered and turned to look at Joseph. Even in the dim light she could not deny he was a remarkably handsome man.

As the darkness thickened, a wolf howled deep in the woods. Another wolf answered the call. A buck and two does leapt out of the trees and bounded to the left, as they darted between a pair of massive maple trees on the other side of the road.

Joseph halted the carriage and reached beneath the bench for his rifle. He primed it and rested it between his legs. From his pocket he withdrew his pistol and readied it as well. He secured the pistol in a leather pocket at the side of the carriage and rested his outer thigh against it. Anxiously, Colleen slid closer to him and held Thea tighter.

A heavy bank of clouds blew across the sky, veiling the sliver of moon above them. Joseph's visibility diminished further and he slowed the horse to a walk. He noted that Colleen had settled closer beside him. A fisher screamed in the woods and he felt her press closer still.

"Halt!" A voice called on the road ahead. Joseph heard the scuffle of feet and low voices that were distinctly male. With his heart thumping hard he raised his pistol and fired high. He grabbed for Colleen's arm as the horse bolted.

The carriage rattled and bumped over the roadway as two voices shouted curses behind them. Joseph peered into the murky blackness struggling to see the road ahead. At last he calmed the horse and it slowed. When the stallion walked at a leisurely gait again he reloaded his pistol and placed it back in the leather pocket at his side. He listened intently for more signs of highwaymen or flowing water warning of bridges, as either would pose a great danger in the night.

A short time later they crossed a covered bridge and Joseph stopped at the edge of the woods on the other side of it. He jumped down with his rifle and walked the horse to the bubbling spring that he knew would be filling the stone trough there. The horse dropped his head to drink greedily. Joseph waited beside him, peering into the shadows and listening intently.

He climbed up onto the bench again and coaxed the animal back onto the road. Hesitantly, the horse walked, then trotted along into the night. Seated in the top of a tall pine, an owl hooted as they rolled by. A raccoon ran along the top of a low stone wall until it ended abruptly against an oak tree. It scurried behind the tree and disappeared in the deep shadows.

At last Joseph spotted the lamps burning in the town square of Georges Falls. He relaxed further as the wheels bumped over the uneven path. Reassured by the familiar surroundings, he snapped the reins and they sped on to East Grantham.

On the drive beside Burghill House, Joseph halted and secured his weapons. He quickly rounded the carriage and extended his hand to Colleen. She accepted it gratefully and stepped down with Thea snuggled tight against her. She drew in a deep breath and walked to the front door, while Joseph led the horse to the barn.

Colleen tested the latch at the front door and it moved freely. With a loud clicking noise she tripped it and pushed the door open. She slipped inside and tapped quietly to the stairs.

"Colleen," Grace cried as she rushed toward her from the kitchen. She hugged her and quickly apologized as Thea lifted her head and looked around. "Might I take her from you?"

"Certainly," Colleen agreed, grateful for the dim light as she flushed brightly.

Grace hurried into the sitting room, unbundling Thea's blanket as she moved. Luke sat at his desk and Grace held up the sleepy child. Thea smiled and held out her arms to Luke and Grace passed the toddler to him. Colleen sat in the rocking chair, watching as Thea patted Luke's face and chattered happily.

In the kitchen, Grace threw another log on the fire and began preparing a simple meal for Joseph and Colleen. When he carried Colleen's trunk in through the back door, Grace was hanging another pot over the fire. She crinkled her nose at him and scurried into the pantry for fresh bread and apples.

Joseph stopped at the bottom of the stairs and looked into the sitting room. Luke raised his eyebrows and Joseph shook his head slightly in return. Sadly, he hefted the trunk again and carried it up to the bedroom. He placed it on the floor at the end of the bed and hurried back down to the kitchen.

He sat at the table and grabbed a wedge of apple from the plate. Grace sliced into the bread and glanced sideways at him. She poured him a cup of black tea and pushed it to him. He sipped it and popped another piece of apple into his mouth.

"Shall Colleen remain," she asked at last.

"I pray she will," he replied.

"If she shall bid you release her?"

"I shant hold her to me if it shall pain her to stay."

"With patience, your love shall soften her heart, Joseph."

"Mama, she does state there is no more in her."

"Time did harden her heart to you and time shall temper it," Grace assured him.

He stood and kissed her cheek, then wandered back to the sitting room with a handful of apple slices.

26

Joseph waited in the hallway outside the bedroom door while Colleen undressed and slipped into a nightgown. He rested his back against the cool wall. Quiet had settled over the house and dark enveloped it fully. Tentatively, he tapped at the door and waited. Her silk slippers whispered over the wood floor and she opened the door to him.

A single candle burned on the table beside the bed and the fire glowed as it warmed the room. He watched her move as she walked to the dressing table to remove the pins and combs from her hair. He stared as her fingers worked deftly through the strawberry blonde curls. Slowly he stepped forward and pondered how long it had been since he had last noted her unpretentious beauty.

As she turned quickly her robe swirled out around her and he saw the pale blue gown underneath. His mouth gaped open when he realized that the garment was sheer. She glanced up at him, looking into his dark eyes. With his eyes locked on hers, he took another great step forward. Emboldened, he reached to brush his knuckles over her cheek. She closed her eyes and stood still.

His hand opened and his palm brushed over her smooth cheek. He pressed forward, sweeping her hair back to reveal her neck. His breathing quickened as he bent to touch his lips to her warm skin. She gasped as his lips parted slightly and trailed up to her ear lobe. Hungrily, his mouth found hers and she melted against him. With a swift movement he lifted her in his arms and carried her to the bed.

Gently he laid her on the counterpane and tenderly peeled back her robe. He moved quickly to blow out the candle and stretched out alongside her, on the bed. His kisses teased along her jaw and down her throat as his fingers tugged at the ribbons that tied her bodice closed.

"Forgive me, Colleen," he whispered close to her ear.

"Twas a failing by me as well," she spoke as her fingertips touched his closely trimmed beard.

"As I did linger in the jail I did think only of Naomi. Twas wrongful."

"I did know of it and the pain did anger me. Twas a bitter thing that I did envy the woman, as she does lie in her grave."

"Tis forgivable, my beloved wife."

"Do you love me truly, Joseph?"

"More than I did realize." He breathed as he covered her mouth with his and pulled her into his arms.

27

Lily was delighted at having become the mistress of one of the finest homes in the region. Although it did not surpass Burghill House, it did equal it. During the busy days in the fall she hired two women to work in her home. Sarina protested weakly but relented as Lily insisted that the ladies of Gage house should not be working with lye soap.

Timothy noted the glow in Lily as she took over the management of the great house. In November she began preparations for a tremendous Christmas party. It would be the first grand celebration in the home in more than twenty years.

Lily coaxed and prodded until Grace, Colleen, Julia, Emma and Sarina all went with her to be measured for new gowns. Their dresses would be fashioned from heavy velvets and rich silks in feminine pastels. The stylish empire dress with puffed cap sleeves would require a jacket for warmth. Lily insisted they wear the voguish pelisse style with the empire line that stopped at the hip or knee. Lastly she cajoled until they surrendered and purchased new flesh toned pantaloons to be worn underneath.

The ladies travelled in the new closed Landau coach that Timothy had procured for Lily. The coachman managed the two fine white horses and steered them onto the drive beside Burghill

House. The driver offered a hand to each woman and helped them down before he moved on to the barn to wait.

Mrs. Whitley served a fine lunch in the dining room and the women talked about the fabrics they had chosen. Lily announced that she planned to have matching heavy white velvet garments made for Eddie and Faith as well. She planned to invite the governess to attend too. Grace glanced at Sarina and shook her head slowly. Sarina nodded slightly and looked away.

When the mid-day meal was done Grace, Sarina, and Colleen moved to the kitchen to help Mrs. Whitley with the clean-up and preparations for supper. Julia and Emma left to tend to supper for their own husbands and children. Lily strode into the sitting room and sat at Luke's desk. She flipped through both the ledger and journal stacked at the far left corner. Curiously, she opened the drawers and looked through them. She found the bottom door locked securely and frowned. Quietly she searched for a key but found none.

Bored, she stood and turned to face her father's book case behind the desk. She pulled down several of his beloved books. She turned the pages and remembered sitting in the rocking chair with him as he read to her. Swiftly, she pushed them back up on the shelf and grasped a small brass box from the top shelf. She rattled it and snapped it open. Inside she found a key with filigree work at the head. She raised her eyebrows and tapped a finger on the shelf.

Quickly she spun around and inserted the key in the lock. She turned it and heard a faint click inside. She pulled the drawer open and flipped through the papers inside. At the very bottom she found a thick old leather journal. She placed it on the desk top and sat back in the chair with the loose papers on her lap.

"Lord, tis rightful that I shall make confession of my transgressions unto you this night," she read. With curiosity nibbling at her, she turned the pile over and lifted the last page. It was signed, "Luke Wallace", in his flowing script. She giggled and moved back to the first page again.

Lost in her thoughts, she sat facing the fireplace as she studied the page. Luke and Joseph strode in through the front door and stopped in the doorway to the sitting room. Joseph tip-toed forward and inched along the wall to stand behind her. Quietly he rested his arms on the sweeping wings of the shepherdess chair. Swiftly he snatched the papers from her.

Startled, she shrieked and jumped up. She turned to face Joseph and Luke and the color drained from her face as she began stammering and babbling.

Luke recognized his handwriting on the papers Joseph held and reached for them. Joseph handed them over and smiled at his younger sister.

"Lily, how did you acquire my private letters?" Luke asked angrily.

"In, I, no..." she struggled incoherently.

"The drawer that held them is ever locked," he declared, tilting his head as he glared at her.

"Tis a key on the desk," Joseph observed and folded his arms.

"You did unlock the drawer!" Luke shouted. Grace appeared in the doorway behind him. "Shall you deny it?" he roared.

"Luke, why shall you speak so?" Grace asked as she touched his arm.

"She is a sneak thief!"

"Luke Wallace!" Grace yelled, tugging at his hand to turn toward her. He yanked his arm away and stalked toward the desk. "Private papers and documents were stored within my desk. The drawer remained locked and the key placed out of reach. Yet she did search out the key and opened it. When the papers were withdrawn she did undertake to read them!"

"No, I could not," Lily protested.

"The letters were found in your hands and you did peruse them closely afore I did seize them," Joseph argued.

"Mama, you shant believe them! I did never see such papers afore!"

"Lily, did Joseph take them from your hands?" Grace asked, puzzled by Lily's response.

"He did not!" she vowed as she folded her arms and stomped one foot.

Grace looked from Joseph to Luke then back to Lily. She frowned and moved toward the desk. "Lily, there was no key upon the desk this morn."

"Mayhap Mrs. Whitley did pull out the key. Assuredly she did take the papers from the drawer as well. Why shall you think to declare me culpable? Are you judges? You are not judges! The judge did pass! I did naught to the man and yet he did pass! Bother me no more!" she demanded as she waved them away.

"Come into the kitchen and share tea with me," Grace urged as she took Lily's hand and led her through the doorway and out into the hall.

Luke walked to the desk and shoved the papers back into the bottom drawer. He locked it and dropped the key into his pocket.

"Uncle Luke, I do recall such jabbering from Auntie Sannah," Joseph spoke as he sat in the rocker.

"I am greatly worried for her," Luke expressed and lowered himself into the chair behind the desk.

"What is to be done?"

"This day I shall speak with Timothy. If her head is muddled surely he must know of the trouble."

Joseph sighed loudly and shook his head. "Might you cure her? I cannot bear to see her end as Aunt Sannah did."

"No, she shall not meet the fate of Isannah. I shall seek out a remedy." He stood and reached to the shelf behind him. On the top shelf there were many journals from Dr. Bell and Phillip. Both men had struggled to cure Ruth Burghill. Phillip and Luke had tried unsuccessfully to treat Isannah. When he had studied their notes extensively he would plan a trip to Boston for more current medical literature. Worriedly, he opened the first tome and placed it on the desk.

28

The Gage household was a veritable beehive as preparations for the Christmas ball continued. The servants managed the last details throughout the first floor. Upstairs the family dressed in their finest. Lily whirred excitedly while Timothy pretended to listen. She sat at the dressing table tucking sprigs of bayberry into her dark hair.

"None shall present a greater merrymaking," she declared as she stood and reached for her pelisse, laid out on the bed.

Timothy rose from his chair and moved to hold the jacket behind her as she slipped her arms into the sleeves. She kissed his cheek and adjusted the deep azure blue pelisse. She tugged at the front of his coat, smoothing it. Admiring the sheen of the fabric, she rubbed away a smudge on one of the polished silver buttons.

"Shall you accompany me, Mr. Gage?" she asked, looking up into his blue eyes. He smiled and nodded as he offered his arm to her.

In less than an hour the house was full of cheerful guests. In the dining room the long table had been pushed back to the wall. A delightful array of food and drink was presented on the finest china and silver. Guests sampled the foods and filled their glasses repeatedly.

The great open hall in the center of the house had been cleared of all but the side chairs. The floor had been hand rubbed with bees wax until it glowed. Tremendous brass chandeliers had been raised up close to the high ceiling to light the room with more than 100 candles. The effect was a romantic glow that the guests enjoyed.

In an alcove near the hall, the musicians were seated. They had begun with melodies to accompany the carolers. When the house was full and guests moved to the dance floor, the carolers were dismissed and the musicians switched to a baroque style. Quickly the majority of the revelers moved to the hall to dance or sit and watch.

Lily was delighted with the spectacular party. Her guests ate, drank, danced, and laughed enthusiastically. Timothy took her hand and pulled her through the crowd, into the dining room. On the dance floor he twirled her around, with the other young couples pirouetting.

The music halted briefly before they began Handel's Water Music Suite. Throughout the room the gentlemen grasped their scented handkerchiefs and held them high. Ladies grasped the tail of the cloth and followed as the men turned slowly with the music. Gradually the strain built and the speed of the dance increased. As the pace grew, the excitement in the room swelled with it.

Servants stoked the fires to chase away the bitter cold December wind. Two maids meandered throughout the first floor with silver trays of wine. Bowls of sugared grapes and spiced cakes were left in the parlor. On a table near them, wine and cordials were offered as well.

Lily had spared no expense in the presentation. As Timothy wandered through the rooms he began worrying at the great expenditures. He decided to put it aside for the night and enjoy the wonderful party but he would need to review the household expenses and counsel his dear wife. He accepted another glass of wine from the passing maid and considered the bill that might be due from the millinery.

Late in the evening the first revelers prepared to leave as they thanked Timothy and Lily for the impressive ball. The governess excused herself and led Eddie and Faith up to bed. Sarina quietly thanked Grace and Luke for attending, before she climbed the stairs as well.

Lily stood beside the table of sweets in the dining room as she took a piece of chocolate cake and put it on a plate. She tasted it and smiled as she turned around. Her guests were filling dishes with food and moving back out to sit in the hall. As the room cleared, she noted Laurent Morgan standing at the far side of the room with a heaping plate in his hands. She watched the happy dancers as she strolled casually toward him.

"Tis a fine thing that you and Julia did come this night," she declared.

"Many thanks, Mrs. Gage," he responded.

"Tis no such formality required, Laurent," she teased. He nodded politely, but appeared uncomfortable as she moved closer. "Tis a concern I wish to speak of."

"Do you mean to talk of it to me?" he asked nervously and inched away from her.

"I do," she murmured. "Shall you hear my words?"

"Mayhap I shall bring Julia here afore you might tell it."

"No, Laurent," Lily told him coldly as she looked up into his dark, seductive eyes. "Tis a matter of our child and naught that she might know."

"Tis told the child did pass," he told her as he eyed her warily. "What more have you to talk of?"

"Our son is not dead," she breathed and a smile touched the corners of her mouth.

"Lily, he was buried. I did attend the funeral of the boy."

"Twas but a casket of rocks they did place in the ground. Our child did not pass."

"No, Lily," he protested.

"'Tis truthful," she insisted. "Ask of Uncle Luke and he shall tell it. Judge Gage did see the boy removed from me to punish my transgression. Yet the judge did pass and tis rightful that our son shall come home to us now. Judge Daniel Gage is buried yet there are no rocks within his casket. He did pass yet I did naught to the man! I did not!"

"Where shall the child be found?" Laurent demanded, as he set the plate firmly on the table and grasped her shoulders.

"I know not," she stated. "Uncle Luke did wrench Albert from me and spirited him away in the night. Command that he shall tell it to you, Laurent!"

Laurent stepped back and blinked unbelievingly. Her words whirled in his head and he looked down at her again. Stunned by her revelation he moved passed her and strode across the dance floor. In the sitting room he saw Luke standing behind the tete-à-tete where Grace was seated.

"Might you come to speak with me?" Laurent asked and turned to rush out to the kitchen. Luke followed, scowling at Laurent's unusual behavior. "Shall you speak freely afore the servants or might we move to the barn?"

"If it shall require seclusion then let us be removed from this house," Luke replied, watching Laurent curiously.

Laurent hurried out the door and stomped over the thin layer of packed snow. He yanked the heavy door open and quickly lit a lamp. Luke felt uncomfortable as he stood with his back against the barn door.

"Luke Wallace, where shall my son be found?" Laurent challenged.

"'Tis a grave in the cemetery for him," Luke muttered and looked away from the big man.

"Lily did state that the child is not dead."

Luke exhaled loudly and rubbed his forehead. He felt a great anger rising as he thought of Lily's revelation of the truth to Laurent. Looking into the poor man's distraught face he considered insisting that the child had been buried.

"Laurent, the families did determine that the child should be removed from this place. The boy was given over to a loving mother of great wealth. She shall tend him well and ensure a good future for him. Lily could not love him as this woman shall. Judge

Gage and I did believe it should be done with. I pray you shall let it be disremembered."

"Dr. Wallace, he is blood of my blood."

"The child was conceived in great sin. 'Tis wrongful that he shall be known to be a bastard. A father of means and social standing shall serve him well."

Laurent nodded slowly and studied his snow covered shoes. "'Tis fair and true. He would bear the label of bastard in this town."

"Put this thing from your head, Laurent. Go to Julia and speak no more of this thing. I shall tend to Lily," Luke advised him and extinguished the lamp. "Revel in the news that your child shall be spared a wrongful future and shall live well."

"Thank you," Laurent responded as he grasped Luke's hand and shook it firmly.

Angrily, Luke marched through the door into the kitchen with Laurent close behind him. He stopped when he heard sobbing and looked to the cook. She shook her head and gestured toward the pantry where the trap door to the storage room beneath stood open.

"Who?" Luke asked.

"'Tis Mrs. Gage," the cook uttered apologetically. "Mr. Dobbs did go for Mr. Gage. I did near the stairs yet she cast me away."

Luke hurried across the room and ducked, as he moved down the stairs. He maneuvered around Lily where she sat on the bottom step.

"Be gone from me!" she shrieked.

"Lily!" he shouted and lifted her chin to look into her eyes.

"I cannot find my Papa!" she cried and jumped up to throw her arms around him. She dropped the doll from her lap and the face shattered against the stone floor.

"Shhhh, Lily," he spoke softly as he hugged her close and stroked her hair. "Walk at my side."

Holding her tight at his side, he helped her up into the pantry. Laurent waited beside the table with Timothy. Slowly, Luke walked her through the kitchen and up the stairs to her bedroom. Timothy brought Grace up with him.

Luke and Timothy waited in the upstairs hall while Grace helped her into a nightgown. She settled under the covers and laid there crying quietly as she continually asked for her father. Luke sent Timothy for the bottle of Laudanum and a glass of wine.

"She does weep ceaselessly and pleads only for Phillip," Grace advised Luke as she stepped out into the hall and closed the door behind her.

"I am vexed by her comportment of late," Timothy asserted.

"Mayhap the loss of her baby and the judge did disorder her head," Luke suggested.

"Twas the death of the infant when Albert had been removed from her," Timothy disputed. "What shall be done?"

"She shall be dosed with Laudanum for a time and we shall pray for her," Luke answered. "I shall see to her afore we do take leave. On the morrow she shall be distracted by the Christmas festivities at Burghill House. When you do depart you must instruct your mother and housekeeper that she shall be watched over."

"Shall it be required?" Timothy questioned.

"Tis rightful that she shall be tended well as I do seek a remedy," Luke responded woefully.

Grace and Timothy waited beside the balustrade as Luke opened the door to the bedroom. He felt a sharp blast of cold air from the dim room as he closed the door. Puzzled, he looked to the fireplace before he realized one of the windows had been opened. In the gloom Lily sat on the windowsill, staring out into the night and catching snowflakes in her open hands.

"Lily," he spoke gently as he hurried toward her.

She turned to look at him then tilted her head up to peer at the sky again. Luke realized that her legs hung outside the window. He slowed his approach, worried that she might fall and land on the small trees and rocks below. Cautiously, he moved closer and touched the wooden ledge that protruded inside.

"Lily, take my hand," he offered and reached guardedly.

"Tis enchantment in the wind as the snow does fall," she whispered dreamily. "Papa did not like the snow."

"Lily, your papa did state that you should remain within this bed chamber!" he stated firmly as he laid his hand on hers.

Surprised by his touch, she yanked her hand away and nearly fell forward. She caught herself and gripped the edge as she began swinging her legs. He could hear the heels of her shoes tapping against the side of the house and he cringed. She lifted her arms and giggled as the snowflakes melted on her tongue. He considered slipping his arm around her waist and pulling her backwards but feared she might pull away again.

"Lily Grenier Gage, you know I am your blood father. I shall not abide your insolence!" he snapped. "Come inside afore I shall take you to my knee!"

She glanced back at him and frowned. Hesitantly, she twisted and pulled her legs back over the ledge. She pouted as she stood and looked up at him. Quickly he closed the window. He took her hand and led her back to the bed. He slipped off her shoes and covered her with the bed clothes and a heavy quilt.

"You are not my father," she uttered conspiratorially and wrinkled her nose.

"Lily tis known to you that I am your father," he told her sadly.

"Could you love me as my Papa did?"

"I shall ever love you as deeply. As you were born I did deliver you unto your mother. I did hold you in my hands and tears did come to my eyes. I shall remain your Uncle Luke, yet I could not love you more, Lily."

"My head is cluttered and does pain me to think."

"Tis not of your doing," he assured her as he pulled the bottle of Laudanum from his pocket. "I bid you swear unto me that you shall not open the window again."

"I shant," she responded and sipped the tincture of opium. "Laurent Morgan did tell that Albert is not in his grave."

"Lily, mayhap you did speak it."

"I could not," she objected. "Judge Gage did forbid that I talk of the boy. The judge did pass yet he hears me still. He shall know it if I shall speak the name and he shall be wrathful."

"Daniel Gage did pass and was buried. He shall come no more unto you."

"I am weary," she told him and her eyes closed slowly.

"Tis rightful you shall sleep now. Do not open the windows, Lily," he repeated as he leaned to kiss her forehead.

"I love you, Uncle Luke," she mumbled.

"I love you as well my beautiful daughter," he stepped back and added another log to the fire. Dismally, he walked to the door and noiselessly passed out into the hallway again.

Diffidently, he related most of the details of his encounter with Lily as he looked from Grace to Timothy. He warned Timothy that he would need to mind her well. He explained how Isannah had progressed and told him about the troubles that he had endured with her. Timothy cocked his head and stared into the corner with a defeated look in his eyes.

Quietly, they walked down to the great hall again. Most of the guests had gone and the musicians were preparing to leave. The household staff busily collected dirty plates and glasses throughout the first floor. The remaining food was moved into the kitchen. Luke helped Timothy to amiably encourage the lingerers to go.

"She shall require great patience," Luke told Timothy as they stood at the front door. "We shall speak on the morrow if you have a mind to."

"Many thanks," Timothy replied as he hugged Grace and watched them move carefully along the snowy front path to the drive. He closed the door and barred it before he climbed the stairs again.

29

Through the long, bitter winter Luke tried a number of potential cures for Lily. None appeared to improve her condition, yet she did not seem to worsen either. Timothy worried over her and prayed that a remedy would be found soon. He was encouraged by her lucid days yet Luke reminded him often that he could not be overly optimistic.

As spring faded into summer, the weather warmed. Under the pleasant June sun Mac and Joseph moved the copper bath tub out into the back yard. Ropes crisscrossed the area and quilts were hung to conceal a space near the house. An ice bath was prepared and Lily was lowered into it. Following the notes from Dr. Bell's journal, Luke carefully watched for the signs that would indicate that Lily had been shocked sufficiently.

"Raise her up, Mac!" Luke shouted and Mac reached into the frigid water. Her white gown clung to her as he lifted her out. Luke draped a quilt over her body and he led the way to a blanket on the grass near the back of the barn. She was laid out in the late morning sun as she warmed slowly.

When the shocking failed, Luke resorted to bleeding her again. Lily accepted a variety of herbs, tonics, brews and other remedies. She swallowed the vile brown syrup that cramped her stomach and triggered severe bouts of vomiting. The purging was followed by increased doses of Laudanum and mulled wine and the bleeding was repeated. Yet month after month Luke's best efforts failed.

The first week of August Emma delivered a second son. The new baby provided a wonderful distraction for the family. Noah named him Jessup Abraham Taylor. Daily, Grace travelled to assist with the chores in Emma's home and sit with the new baby. She forced herself to go on to Lily's home to talk with Lily and see her grandchildren before she returned to Burghill House.

On Lily's best days Grace found her perfectly coiffed and reading to her children or sipping tea with Sarina. Yet there were other days when she sat in the storage room beneath the pantry crying with the broken doll in her arms. On more than one occasion she had been found in the loft of the barn, dressed in nothing but her pantaloons and a corset as she talked with the barn cat. The greater concern was not that she spoke to the cat but that she claimed that the animal chatted with her as well. She believed that the cat wandered throughout the town daily and returned with wicked gossip to share with her.

Grace and Luke both feared that Lily would eventually be confined to the attic. Grace worried most that Lily could not endure the confinement, as Isannah had. In early September, Luke travelled to Boston to meet with a number of doctors there. Each provided details of treatments they had heard of. Yet none offered much hope for a cure. The only point that they all agreed upon was the recommendation that Lily be placed in an insane asylum as her condition worsened.

In October Colleen announced that she was expecting another baby in the spring. Joseph was delighted with the prospect of another son. After Colleen's return, the couple had settled back into the comfortable, loving relationship that they had enjoyed earlier in their marriage. Joseph enjoyed his work with the Chernock's and had become a skilled carpenter. Colleen was content to tend to Teague and Thea while she managed her daily chores. Gradually, she had put aside her judgments of the family.

On a brilliant sunlit Sunday in November, the family gathered at Burghill House for dinner. Lily was enjoying one of her better days. The children ran and played in the hallways as the adults appreciated Mrs. Whitley's chocolate cake with boiled icing and coffee laced with brandy. Apprehensively, Grace proposed that a Christmas party be held in the house.

"Grace, tis a perilous venture that you do suggest," Luke cautioned.

"Mayhap we shall invite family alone," Joseph offered.

"How shall we exclude friends and neighbors?" Grace countered.

"Might we entertain in the Gage house?" Lily asked Timothy.

"Tis better that we shall attend your mother's celebration," he answered worriedly.

"Luke, a new century shall begin at the first day of January," Grace reminded him. "Tis rightful that we do revel as the holidays come upon us."

Luke considered her argument and looked around the table. The men shook their heads or frowned as they pondered the idea. Disregarding the reservations, the women appeared excited about the prospect. Lastly, Luke turned to Grace again. She smiled sweetly and mouthed the word, "Please."

"If it be your wish I shant deny you," he conceded at last.

"As the men do retire to the sitting room, we shall make plans in the kitchen," Grace announced in a bubbly tone. She stood quickly and began collecting dirty dishes. The discussion began with a number of party ideas as Lily, Emma, Julia, Colleen, Molly, and Joanna gathered platters, dishes, and trays. Carefully each woman picked her way through the maze of children in the hall, and moved into the kitchen beyond. Luke refilled his glass of red wine and crossed the hall to the sitting room with the other men close behind him.

30

Many of the guests arrived early, eager to attend a grand Christmas party at Burghill House. As they stepped into the entryway, they smelled the rich aromas of gingerbread, roast turkey, and warm apple cider. The heat from the fireplaces coaxed the appealing scents from the pine cones and boughs that had been placed on the mantles. Hand dipped tapers made of bayberry wax added to the enchanting fragrances.

The brass chandeliers had been polished and fat bees wax candles were inserted. Sparkling rock crystals and pearls hung gracefully underneath each of the elaborate lighting fixtures. The heavy Chippendale furnishings from the dining room had been moved out to the barn and covered with oil cloth. The floor was hand rubbed to a rich sheen and chairs were placed around the sides of the dining room.

In the upper hallway the musicians were seated and had begun to play as the first guests entered the house. Rich notes floated along the stairwell and flowed leisurely throughout the first floor. Over the sound of the music and the chatter of the guests, the delightful voices of the carolers rang out.

Grace plated the last of the desserts and carried them to the narrow table along the wall in the hallway. In the doorway to the sitting room, she saw Luke and moved quickly toward him. She reached to grasp his hand and waited as he finished his conversation with Ben Andrews. Gently, she tugged his arm and he followed her through the sitting room and hall beyond to their bedroom.

"This shall be a great celebration," she announced excitedly.

"I am weary of troubles," he declared as he put his arm around her waist and pulled her close. "Pray that we shall enjoy an uneventful evening."

"The night shall end well and I shall relish the sound of your heartbeat as we do sleep."

He bent and pressed his lips to hers. Passionately, she kissed him in return. His hand moved to her bodice and she quickly brushed it away.

"Shall you deny me?" he asked playfully.

"I cannot deny you, yet I shall implore you wait. Many guests do await us beyond the door."

Smiling devilishly, he released her and followed as she strode back out to the sitting room. He sat in a chair beside Patrick Carmody as Grace continued on to greet more guests in the entryway. By early evening the first floor of the house was crowded. Mrs. Whitley put out more food and it was quickly devoured. Joseph carried in another wooden keg of ale and various cordials decanters were refilled.

The revelry continued well into the night. Near three in the morning the last visitants left the house. Luke locked and barred the door. At last the lamps and candles were extinguished. He stoked the fires on the first floor while Joseph fueled those upstairs. A comfortable silence fell over the house as they fell into bed and slept fitfully.

Early in the morning Grace, Colleen and Mrs. Whitley finished cleaning up from the grand party. Joseph and Mac moved the furniture back into the dining room. Hurriedly, they prepared to leave for church to attend the Christmas Day service.

Only two hours later they returned to the house and the women were busy again in the kitchen. The family assembled at Burghill House. In the sitting room the men talked over goblets of red wine. The children were sent upstairs where they played noisily in the hallway.

Great platters, trays, dishes, and bowls were eventually carried into the dining room. Mac circled the table, filling the glasses of wine before he placed a remaining flagon at the head of the table. When everyone had been seated, Rev. Pender led them in a special prayer of thanks. A modest man, he quickly acknowledged that the words he had spoken were credited to Rev. Cotton Mather.

Timothy and Lily arrived late. The family had already begun passing the food around the table. The governess quickly settled Eddie and Faith into high chairs before she retreated to the kitchen to dine with Mrs. Whitley. Timothy helped Lily out of her heavy cloak and hung it in the hall. She remained standing in the doorway to the dining room until he returned and led her to a chair at the table.

"Is all well this day?" Grace asked as she looked at Lily.

"All is tolerable," Timothy answered as he began filling plates for Lily and the children. Lily sat silently studying the decorative pattern on the china plates.

"Lily?" Grace persisted. But Lily did not raise her head and spoke not a word.

"Laurent, my carriage is in need of repair yet the blacksmith did state tis greatly flawed," Molly declared, in hopes of distracting attention from Lily.

"'Tis a timeworn thing you do possess," he chuckled and Molly smiled in return. "Mayhap you shall think to take one of my Landaus?" he suggested.

"If it be an agreeable price you shall state, then I shall ponder it."

Gradually, other conversations were sparked. Mac asked Joseph about the recent completion of the covered bridge at the Scaffel River. Luke and Noah discussed the news that Napoleon meant to take back the Louisiana Territories from the Spaniards. As they ate, there were random glances toward Lily but no one addressed her directly. Timothy dipped her spoon into the spiced pumpkin soup and jabbed her fork into small bites of turkey and pheasant. She accepted the various utensils from him and put the food into her mouth, chewing distractedly.

When the meal was done Molly, Joanna, and Emma remained in the dining room with Lily. Molly coaxed tenderly but Lily refused to speak. She sipped the wine when it was offered but would not reach for the glass on her own. Emma placed a small dish of chocolate pudding in front of her and handed her a spoonful. Lily took it and pushed it into her mouth.

Anxiously, Luke and Grace drew Timothy back to their bedroom to speak privately. Timothy recounted his family's trip to the First Parish Congregational Church of East Grantham that morning. Seated in the Gage family's pew with Sarina and the governess, they listened intently as Rev. Murray preached a thought provoking sermon. The church was full of parishioners who had come to listen to one of the minister's marvelous Christmas homilies.

"And Joseph also went up from Galilee, out of the city of Nazareth, into Judaea, unto the city of David, which is called Bethlehem…" Rev. Murray sermonized from the pulpit as the congregation listened intently.

Suddenly, Lily removed a small orange kitten from her pocket and began to stroke the fur. Surprised by it, Timothy leaned close and whispered, "Lily the animal should not be in the church. Place it into my hand and I shall remove it to the paddock."

"I cannot," she responded. "He has much to tell me this morn."

"…so it was, that, while they were there, the days were accomplished that she should be delivered," the minister continued.

"Lily tis wrongful. Give the thing to me," Timothy insisted.

"I cannot," she protested. Her volume had increased and the people seated around her turned to look at her with irritation.

"...she brought forth her firstborn son, and wrapped him in swaddling clothes, and laid him in a manger; as there was no room for them at the inn," Rev. Murray read on.

Timothy reached for the kitten and Lily slipped it inside her cloak. She looked up at him and scowled. Frustrated with her stubborn behavior, he tried to ignore her and faced the front of the church again. Slowly, their neighbors focused on the minister again.

Suddenly, Lily stood and pulled the kitten from her cloak again. She inhaled deeply and began to sing the Christmas Carol, *O Come All Ye Faithful*, in Latin as she had learned it from her father. "Adeste fideles laeti triumphantes, venite, venite in Bethlehem. Natum videte Regem angelorum, venite..." Timothy grabbed her arm and pulled her along as he stumbled over legs and feet to the end of the pew. In the fracas, Lily dropped the cat. Timothy snatched it up and stalked toward the front doors with Lily scuffling along behind him.

They waited on the front steps for a short time. Timothy handed the kitten back to her but would not release her wrist from his grip. Exasperated, he stared out at the deserted road as she continued to sing softly beside him. Quietly, Sarina and the governess slipped out of the church with Eddie and Faith in tow.

"Timothy, I shall share Christmas dinner with the good reverend and his dear wife this day," Sarina advised him.

"Shall I come for you in the evening?" he asked.

"Tis likely it shall be a fit night for a serene walk," she replied.

"I shant abide that you stroll alone in the night. I shall come for you at 7:00," he advised her.

"Thank you," she responded and moved quietly back into the church.

Timothy rounded the corner onto Killock Road and steered his team up onto the drive. Impatiently, he helped Lily and the children into the house and left the governess to mind them as he hurried back out to tend to the horses.

He remained in the barn until his anger had diminished. Finally, he strode up the back steps and into the kitchen. The fire in the hearth had been built up as Mrs. Quinn prepared the Christmas dinner for the household staff. Sarina had instructed her to prepare a tremendous meal. The remains were to be boxed and delivered to the orphan asylum late in the day. Sarina had also packed a large basket of candies, sweets, and other treats for the orphans.

Timothy found Lily in the bedroom watching a bird hopping on a branch outside the window. She stepped back and began undressing. She pulled the kitten from her pocket again and placed it on the bed.

"Tis the kitten of a barn cat, Lily. This thing shant remain in this house!" he snapped and picked it up. "The mother cannot enter the house and her kittens shant either."

He left her pouting in the bedroom as he ran down the stairs and outside. As the animal cried and meowed, a big cat jogged out from between the big barn doors. Timothy put the kitten down in the snow and left it to the mother. He stomped back inside and walked into the library for a dram of fine whiskey.

When he entered the bedroom again, Lily was seated in a podgy arm chair, reading. He shut the door and looked at her in shock as her realized she was completely naked. The beautiful dress she had worn to church lay in a heap on the floor. The layers of undergarments and her shoes had been tossed around the room. It looked as if she had removed them as she waltzed throughout the space.

"Lily!" he shouted. "Dress yourself! We must travel to Burghill House this day."

"Tis oppressively warm this day," she declared. "Uncle Luke did state that I shant open the window. Twas naught I might do but to remove my wrappings."

Drained, Timothy sat on the chest at the end of the bed. He rubbed his hands against his face and moaned, exasperated by her reasoning. At last, he opened her armoire and withdrew a lovely black velvet gown with silk piping and a perfect white sash tied in a large bow under the bodice.

"Come," he ordered and held out his hand. Watching her approach, he fought temptation and handed her undergarments to her. He felt the first stirrings as she leaned back against the bed and pulled on the flesh toned pantaloons. Without a word, he lifted her onto the bed and removed the garment again.

He nuzzled her neck and kissed his way up to her soft lips. Smiling, he jumped back and shed his own clothing. She lay giggling on the bed as he tripped and nearly fell in his rush to get to her. Furiously, he pulled her body against his and forgot the problems of the morning.

As Timothy communicated the tale to his in-laws he excluded his seduction of Lily. In the version he told, the story began again when he was dressed and seated at the end of the bed. He waited patiently as Lily dressed in layer upon layer until she wiggled into the attractive black velvet empire waist gown. He left her to slip on her shoes as he went down to ready the carriage again.

With the horses hitched to the post near the walkway, Timothy marched in through the front door and called to Lily and the governess. Eddie and Faith hurried down the sweeping staircase with the governess close behind them. Timothy told her to settle them in his carriage then he yelled to Lily again.

At last he stomped up the stairs again and threw the door open. He found the bedroom empty. Quickly he checked the other rooms upstairs, then ran down to the kitchen. The cook was just coming up from the storage room beneath the pantry. She assured him that she had not seen Lily in hours. Growing anxious, he went outside and instructed the governess to take the children back into the house to wait.

For an hour he and the handyman, Mr. Dobbs searched every inch of the house from the storage room up to the attic. Becoming desperate, he directed the Mr. Dobbs to begin searching the land around the house. Timothy checked the stables, smokehouse, wood shed, and barn. Dobbs moved on to the spring house at the bottom of the slope at the back of the property.

Timothy opened the barn doors and saddled his favorite horse. He planned to expand the search beyond his land. While he worked to secure the tack under the horses belly he heard giggling. He stopped and listened carefully. Quietly he walked to the ladder and climbed up to the hay loft. There, seated in the far corner, he found Lily sitting with the mother cat on her lap.

"Lily Grenier Gage!" he roared as he stared at her in disbelief. "I have searched an hour for you!"

"The cat told me not to speak to you," she replied, lifted her chin haughtily and turned away from him.

He stepped over the top rung and bounded across the floor. He grabbed her arm roughly and pulled her to her feet as the cat scurried away. Furiously, he hurried back to the ladder with her.

Swiftly, he scrambled down to the barn floor again then motioned for her to follow. Still four rungs from the bottom he snatched her from it and threw her over his shoulder.

While she shrieked and kicked her feet wildly he plodded back through the snow to the back door. "Dobbs!" he bellowed before he stepped inside. "Mrs. Quinn, see that Mr. Dobbs ends his meaningless search promptly. Advise him that Mrs. Gage has been found and all is well."

Mrs. Quinn nodded and looked anxiously at Lily as the young woman continued to struggle. He trooped into the parlor and ordered the governess to follow him with the children. He traipsed outside and deposited Lily in the Landau. The governess rushed after him and lifted Eddie and Faith up to sit beside their mother. Angrily, Timothy climbed up onto the driver's bench and snapped the reins.

"I know not what I might do!" Timothy declared as he looked from Luke to Grace. "She grows more frustrating with each passing day. "A cat did tell her she shant speak? Tis madness!"

"Mayhap you shall see her secured in your attic," Luke suggested. "Twas a painful thing that my wife Isannah did dwell in the attic of this house. Yet twas naught to make her well. She did wander in the rain and cold of night. Tis a distressing thing that I do understand well, Timothy."

"Surely we shant resign her to the attic," Grace disagreed. "She shall be lonely and unhappy in such a space. Mayhap a governess shall be retained to mind her."

"I fear she is fixated on the barn cat," Timothy observed. "She does make claim that the thing speaks to her and does relate gossip and secrets. It is greatly unsettling."

"If she shant be managed, her condition shall soon be known publicly. It shall be a humiliation for poor Lily," Grace implored.

"Fairly a governess for Lily shall resolve the trouble," Luke advised.

"I shall seek a suitable woman. Mayhap she could be convinced that the woman is but a friend for her. If she is a woman of Boston, with breeding, that shall satisfy Lily," Timothy agreed.

Desolately, Luke opened the door and they wandered back out to the sitting room. Grace refilled glasses and passed goblets to Luke and Timothy before she strode back to the kitchen.

31

The long winter brought less snow than usual but the bitter cold was punishing. With weeks of temperatures at or below zero, even the fast moving waterways quickly froze. The unusual depth of the ice permitted sleighs and carriages outfitted with runners to travel across them. Still the arctic weather made travel dangerous. Timothy's plans for a governess for Lily would be postponed until spring.

In early March, Colleen delivered another healthy baby girl. Joseph named her Clarinda Colleen Grenier. Thea was born with her mother's strawberry blonde hair, but the new baby arrived with thick dark hair like Joseph's. Happy and proud, he carried the infant downstairs to show her off. He settled into the rocking chair in the sitting room with Thea on his lap and Clarinda at his shoulder.

The first week of April the spring thaw began at last. Timothy sent a missive to Boston asking that the new governess, Miss Jane Appleton, travel to East Grantham as soon as possible. As the last of the winter weather passed, Lily showed no improvement, yet her mental state had not worsened. With the assistance from his household staff, Timothy had managed to monitor Lily sufficiently.

Easter Sunday the families attended church services in the morning before returning to Burghill House for dinner. While the women worked in the kitchen, Lily sat near the hearth slicing warm bread. Suddenly she stood and hurried out the back door. Grace and Molly followed quickly and found Lily behind the barn. Kneeling in the snow there she vomited.

"Lily," Grace bent beside her and touched her warm cheek. "Molly, please go for Luke."

Molly hurried back to the house and returned with Luke and Timothy. Gently, they helped her to her feet and walked her back into the house. Timothy carried her up to one of the front bedrooms on the second floor. Lying on the bed, she turned on her side and dozed as the meal was served in the dining room below.

Late in the afternoon Luke went up to assess her again. He woke her and began his examination. Her face was flushed yet she did not have a fever. He suggested that she sample the rabbit stew and she turned away clutching her stomach. Worriedly, he strode down to the kitchen for a pot of weak tea and ships biscuits for her. Quietly, he asked Molly to aid him.

Luke waited outside the bedroom door while Molly examined Lily. In a short time she opened the door and advised him that Lily was indeed pregnant again. She estimated that the child would be due in September. When Lily had finished the tea and crackers, she moved slowly down to sit in the dining room. She could not bear the aromas of the food in the kitchen or the cigars and alcohol in the sitting room.

"Timothy!" she called out and lowered her head to the smooth, cool surface of the table. He stepped into the room and pulled out a chair. She cringed at the scraping sound on the floor and squeezed her eyes shut.

"Let us take leave," he offered sympathetically.

"Timothy, tis another baby to come," she told him without lifting her head.

He let his head drop back and stared up at the ceiling. Uneasily, he thought of Lily's mental state and the problems they had experienced over the past year. He sighed heavily and looked down at her. Resignedly, he leaned forward and placed his hand on her back.

"Tis a fine thing we shall be blessed," he uttered reassuringly.

"I only desire sleep," she breathed.

Quickly he advised the governess that they would be leaving. He readied the carriage and made apologies to the family for their sudden departure. Grace handed him a folded linen napkin filled with ships biscuits for the short journey. He thanked her and escorted Lily outside.

Through April into May, Lily rarely left her bedroom and ate only when coerced. She slept soundly during the night and napped off and on, through the day. When Eddie and Faith returned from school daily, they hurried up to the bed chamber to sit with their mother. Six year-old Eddie read to Lily as she snuggled in the big bed with them.

In mid-May the new governess arrived by ship at the East Grantham docks. Seated in the library with the young woman,

Timothy confided that there would be little work for her with the unexpected changes. With the children attending school daily, the current governess, Alice Ramsey, had little to do with her time. As Lily refused to leave her bedroom, she required no monitoring. Timothy agreed to pay the promised wages yet Miss Appleton would reside at the orphan asylum until the situation varied in the Gage household.

32

"Mac, might you linger?" Luke asked, as Grace and Colleen cleared away the last of the supper dishes. Joseph lifted Thea from her high chair. He gestured to nine year-old Teague and the boy followed him, out through the kitchen to the back yard.

The heat from the summer day remained, but a delightfully cool breeze lifted the curtains, at the sides of the dining room windows. Luke refilled his wine glass and passed the flagon to Mac. He stood slowly and closed the doors to the room. Mac watched him uneasily as Luke sat again.

"Mac, you have completed your schooling and tis rightful you shall progress to a college now."

"Pa, I did mean to apprentice under you here," Mac protested.

"Tis reasonable that you shall. Yet afore you might begin your medical study, you shall conclude the course of a respected college."

"You and Uncle Phillip did practice well, yet did not attend any college."

"Mac, I shall hear no argument from you. You shall depart for Boston in the month to come. Tis a fine school at Cambridge, by the name of Harvard and it shall serve you well. It shall require four years afore you are done and shall then begin a year of medical lectures."

"Tis a great distance to Boston, Pa. I shall greatly miss my home."

"Your time there shall pass swiftly," Luke reassured.

"Shall this thing be required of me?" Mac tested.

"It shall," Luke replied. "I will arrange for your passage, on one of the ships bound for Boston. Worry not, tis rightful that you do this thing."

"Yes, Pa," Mac agreed half-heartedly.

As the weeks passed, Mac struggled to prepare for the trip and the beginning of his college education. He visited with friends and enjoyed time with his family. Outwardly he appeared confident and excited, yet inside he felt increasingly anxious and worried.

The Sunday before Mac's departure date, Grace and Luke hosted a delightful party. Family and friends gathered behind the house, to eat, drink and dance. Musicians were seated near the back of the barn. Mac had hoped to begin courting Annie Stanton soon, but his plans would now be postponed.

When Annie stepped through the gate with her parents and many siblings, he watched her closely. Several times, he caught her looking his way as well. A few couples had begun dancing in the area where the ground had been cleared, back behind the great oak tree. Mac worked up his nerve and approached Annie.

"Annie Stanton, might you favor me with a dance?" he asked and his cheeks flushed bright red.

"Thank you, good sir," she replied, as she accepted his hand.

When the music stopped briefly, he led her toward the table of beverages. He poured a glass of mulled cider and handed it to her. The musicians started to play again and they watched as more of the people began dancing.

Mac noticed that several couples had wandered onto the path through the trees, trusted to chaperone each other. Apprehensively, he touched Annie's elbow and encouraged her to move in that direction. Timidly, she stepped between the pine trees and he followed closely behind her.

As the others walked on ahead of them, Annie slowed. When the sound of the music diminished behind them Mac reached for her hand and stopped. Shyly, she looked up at him. Standing a foot taller than she was, at 6'5" he looked down into her bright blue eyes. Gingerly, he brushed blonde curls back from her forehead.

"Annie Stanton, I did mean to ask that your father permit me to court you. Yet afore I might, I must depart," his deep voice rumbled as he tried to speak quietly.

"I shant fault you, Mac," she responded kindly.

"My pa shant permit a delay, yet I cannot declare my intentions to all afore I do court you."

"My father is fond of you."

"Annie, might you think to await my return? Tis unjust that I shall ask this of you, yet I cannot bear to think you shall wed another."

"Tis no burden, Mac," she whispered and smiled. "I shant accept another suitor."

Excited and relieved he lifted her up and hugged her tight. He kissed her quickly and nearly dropped her, as he realized that he had gone too far. Swiftly, he set her down again and stepped back.

"Forgive me!" he implored.

"Tis naught to worry over. You are to be my husband one day, Mackenzie Wallace. I shant fault you such a botch," she told him and giggled.

He knelt in front of her and looked up into her pretty face. Her tiny hand disappeared as he folded his fingers around hers. "Miss Annie Stanton, when your father shall consent to our courtship and the man shall accept my offer of marriage, then might you consent to be my wife?"

She bent forward and touched her lips to his as she breathed, "I shall." Boldly she sat on his leg and wrapped her arms around his neck. "I shall sew fine articles for our home as I do await your return."

"Annie, I am so greatly comforted by your words," he told her. Awkwardly, he encouraged her to stand again and he rose beside her. Holding her hand, he led her along the trail. Walking out between the birches, he saw the cemetery ahead. Walking around the low stone wall, he stopped at the far corner. "Tis my Mother's grave."

She nodded sadly and looked at the gravestone. "Shall I take leave as you do linger within?"

"No, you are welcome," he assured her. He sat on the wall and helped Annie up beside him. "I was but a small child when she did pass."

"Tis a sad thing."

"She was sickly and I did not know her well. Aunt Grace did tend to me."

"Shall we be blessed with children to love, Mac?"

"Annie, we shall live in a grand house and shall be blessed with many healthy babies."

Annie smiled and blushed again.

"Mayhap we shall revisit the gathering," he announced. Quietly, they strode back to the path, walking hand in hand.

Nearly a week passed before Mac left for Cambridge. Luke rode to the docks with him. His trunk was loaded onto the ship, *Querida Dama Olivetta*. He felt his stomach rolling and churning as he stepped aboard. Luke sat on the dock and waited for an hour until the ship was navigated out into the deeper waters of the river. He sighed and watched as the great sails unfurled and the magnificent vessel moved swiftly to the south.

33

The third week of September Lily began sleeping in her favorite chair beside the bedroom window. With her legs folded up and her head resting against the arm of the chair, she dozed off and on through the night. When Molly visited, she encouraged Lily to move to the bed, insisting that she could not possibly be comfortable sleeping there. Eventually she coaxed her to the bed long enough to examine her.

Settled back into her preferred seat, Lily laid her head back again and closed her eyes. Molly watched her and worried over Lily's condition. She had become painfully thin as the pregnancy progressed. Dark circles under her eyes stood out against her pale skin. Quietly, Molly stepped forward and placed her hand on Lily's swollen belly. She felt a strong kick from inside.

"Tis likely the child shall come in no more than two weeks," Molly advised her.

"I should like to remove it of my own this day and see it gone away from me."

Molly gasped and pulled her hand back. "Lily tis your baby within."

"Tis a pixie who does fly about kicking and striking me continually. He loves me not and thus I shall not favor him.

Mayhap you shall take him to the wood and release him in the night."

Speechless, Molly stared down at her. Shocked and confused, she collected her bag and left the room. She entered the kitchen and asked for Timothy. The cook directed her to the library and she hurried to his door.

Seated at the great table in the library, she repeated her conversation with Lily. He dropped back in his chair with his hand pressed to his forehead. Slowly he began shaking his head.

"I know not what I might do," he told her.

"The child shall come in but a few weeks."

"There shall be a governess to mind the infant and a woman to tend to Lily. Yet I do fear for the well-being of the infant," he looked down, feeling intense shame at his disclosure.

"Timothy, I was but a child when Ruth Burghill did suffer so. She was not a strong person and could not endure the trials she struggled through. Her daughter Isannah did agonize so as her mind became muddled as well. None did think it would come unto Lily too."

"Shall this dreadful happening curse my daughter thereafter?" he asked.

"No, surely it shall not," she offered hollow reassurances. "Worry not, Timothy. As the child does come, Grace and I shall be with her."

Timothy thanked her as she stood to leave.

That night, as Lily slept in her chair, Timothy tossed and turned in their bed. He rose several times to check on her. When he woke near 4:00 in the morning he pushed another arm chair across the room and placed it beside hers. He settled in and leaned to kiss her hair. With his head resting next to hers, he finally fell asleep again.

He woke as the sun climbed above the horizon. Feeling stiffness in his neck and back, he stood and stretched painfully. He knelt in front of her and brushed his lips against hers. She opened her eyes and reached to place her hand against his face.

"I love you," he sighed.

"My love, I beg you remove this imp from within me," she pleaded.

"Lily, no," he frowned sadly. "This shall be the boy we did pray for."

"No, this is not my son," she replied as she pressed her hand against her belly.

"As you do look upon the child you shall feel a mothers love."

"Tis a goblin, Timothy. I do feel the claws and great teeth. I beseech you take the thing into the wood and be done with it. Tis a dreadful fear that it shall end me as it does fight to be born."

"Lily, it shall not. I promise it shall not. Your mother and the midwife shall not permit it."

She sat up and put her arms around his neck. He lifted her from the chair and frowned at how light she had become. He sat again in the chair beside hers and held her against his chest. He brushed her hair back from her face and wiped away her tears as she wept. Sorrowfully, he kissed her forehead and whispered comforting words to her.

Later in the morning, he carried her to the bed and begged her to stay there until he returned. He planned to travel to the jail, the courthouse and the customs house and would return by early afternoon. Lying on her side, curled around his pillow, she agreed.

The children sat in the dining room with the governess as they ate their breakfast. Timothy sipped coffee and nibbled on a muffin while they talked. Before he left he instructed the cook to take a tray up to Lily and sit with her as she coaxed her to eat it. He charged Mr. Dobbs with travelling to the orphan asylum to advise the governess that she would be needed again in two weeks. He urged the children out the door and walked them down the road to the school house before riding on to the jail house.

Lily picked at the apple bread and finally ate most of a slice with honey spread on it. She kept the hot tea and sipped it slowly, but refused the corn meal mush and sent the cook away with the tray. As the morning passed, she clutched Timothy's pillow and tried to sleep. She imagined the horrible monster scratching and clawing inside. She considered bringing up a knife from the kitchen to quickly remove the thing from her belly. Instead, she lay on the bed alone and sobbed.

Lily slept for a short time and woke in agony. She knew that the imp had finally begun clawing its way out of her and weakly she cried out. She felt her wet gown and was certain that the thing had begun to tear through her flesh and that she was bleeding. Convinced that she would soon be dead and the monster would be freed, she screamed into the pillow.

Repeatedly, she cried out but her voice did not carry to the first floor. Alone in the sunny room, she trembled in fear and closed her eyes tight. Twisting in pain, she drew her knees up and held her breath. The torture increased until she felt an intense burning sensation.

"Help me!" she shrieked. She rocked forward and grabbed at the head of the demon between her legs. Desperately she felt for the horns on its head or something else she could grasp. Under her fingers she felt the wet fur on the creature's smooth pate.

She screamed as the thing twisted and slipped forward. The pain diminished and she reached for the horrible thing again. Terrified, she grasped it and lifted it up to look at the vile beast. She stared into the tiny face, distorted as it began to cry. Curiously she pulled it closer and forced the mouth open to look at the creature's razor sharp teeth but found none. She checked the hands and feet but found no claws. Amazed, she studied the crying thing and realized that it was a human baby.

Hot tears rolled down her cheeks as the relief washed over her. She clutched at the counterpane and covered the squirming baby. Exhausted, she dropped back against the pillow. She drew in a deep breath and screamed one more time.

She heard footsteps on the stairs and tried to call out again. Outside the door Sarina knocked and waited. She inched the door open and peeked inside. In the sunny room she saw the bright red stain against the pale yellow and cornflower blue bedding. She ran back to the balustrade and shouted to the governess and the cook downstairs.

"Send Mr. Dobbs for the midwife. Tis frightfully urgent! Be quick!" she shrieked.

Sarina rushed back into the room and pulled away the quilt. She was startled by the baby lying against Lily's arm. Quickly, she realized that the umbilical cord was still attached. Nervously, she assessed Lily and hastily removed a hairpin from her own hair. She crimped the cord and delivered the afterbirth.

"Lily," Sarina spoke softly as she leaned close. Lily's face was ashen and her eyes remained closed. Afraid to leave Lily alone she covered them again and sat on the bed to wait for Molly.

Worriedly, she began pacing and looked out the windows repeatedly. She pulled the quilt away and studied the infant, then covered it and paced from the door to the windows. Some time passed before she heard the footfalls on the stairs.

Molly ran in with her bag and ripped the quilt away. She examined Lily and ordered Sarina to go to the kitchen for a pot of hot water and steeping ball.

"And tell the governess to bring a basin with fresh linens!" she called after Sarina.

When Sarina returned with the tea pot, Molly passed her a handful of herbs to be suffused. She finished swaddling the new baby and placed her gently in Sarina's arms.

"Is she well?"

"Lily and the child shall both endure," Molly answered and smiled. "Mayhap you shall send for Timothy and Grace."

Before Timothy returned, Lily had been dressed in a fresh gown and she lay comfortably on clean sheets. The infant slept quietly beside her. He sat on the bed and caressed her face.

"I did cry out to you, yet you did not come to me," Lily whispered hoarsely.

"Forgive me, I knew not of the birth," he apologized.

"Mama and Molly were not with me," she told him.

"Forgive me, Lily. I could not know that the child would come this morn."

"Lay with me," she murmured and closed her eyes again. He turned on his side and stretched out behind her as she slept.

"Have you a name for her?" Grace asked, speaking softly from the end of the bed.

"Hephzibah," Lily spoke weakly.

"Lily, you cannot!" Timothy argued as he pulled himself up on his elbow.

"I did promise," she mumbled with an edge of irritation in her voice.

"No, Lily."

"Timothy, I did promise her," and she began to cry.

He felt his heart break as he watched her, so frail and deteriorated over the past months. He looked at the baby as she stirred and down at Lily again. "I shall relent," he conceded. He turned to face Grace. "She shall be Hephzibah Jane Gage," he declared.

Puzzled Grace raised her eyebrows and waited for an explanation but Timothy lay back down again. He took Lily's hand

and interlaced his fingers with hers. He lifted it to his lips and kissed tenderly.

Molly, Sarina, and Grace left the room to give the young couple privacy for a while. In the kitchen, they sat sipping tea and talking.

"Lily must be encouraged to eat and drink if she is to nurse the new baby," Molly declared.

"The cook is preparing her favorite supper and desserts," Sarina announced proudly.

"Sarina, is Hephzibah a distinguished woman of the Gage family?" Grace asked.

"She is not," Sarina responded as she stared into the tea cup. "She is the barn cat."

They sat in silence and sipped the tea.

34

As Lily began her lying-in, she refused to allow anyone else to care for the new baby. The cradle was moved into the room and placed beside the bed. The new governess tried repeatedly to tend to the child but Lily refused to permit her to touch the infant. Timothy worried over her uncharacteristic behavior but could not argue with her desire to mind her own baby.

In late October, Molly assessed Lily and determined that the lying-in period should end. Lily was eating well and her condition had greatly improved. The family marveled at the improvement in Lily after the birth of Hephzebah. Timothy started to feel hopeful about her condition.

Lily began dressing in her finest and travelling to visit family and friends again. With the infant close at her side, she smiled easily again. In the afternoons she returned to her home to greet Eddie and Faith as they returned from the school house. The governess was banned from the parlor, as Lily sat in there with her children. She read to them and related the amazing stories Isannah had told her years earlier.

With great reservations, Timothy sent Jane Appleton back to Boston. Alice Ramsey remained to care for Eddie and Faith alone.

The family settled into a comfortable routine and Timothy enjoyed his life with Lily again.

In Cambridge, Massachusetts Mac began his college education at Harvard. He made friends easily and was well liked by his instructors. He studied hard and looked forward to the end of it all when he would return to marry Annie Stanton.

Weekly, Annie wrote long letters to Mac and he sent starry-eyed responses in return. Annie's family did not attend the church where Mac's family worshipped. Their fathers were neighbors but did not socialize. She desperately wanted to go to Burghill House and introduce herself and to work in the kitchen with Mac's Aunt Grace. A relationship with them would make her feel closer to Mac. Yet such a thing would be improper before any courtship had begun.

Annie confided in her sister Megan alone. Together they began sewing a quilt and other items for Annie's trousseau. Annie's mother overheard some of their conversations. She kept their words secret and hoped for Annie's sake that Mackenzie Wallace would eventually return to court her.

The preparations for winter progressed in Burghill House. With Mac away, Joseph worked hard to split the logs that would be needed to heat the house and fuel the hearth and ovens. Nine year-old Teague stacked the wood and struggled to chop some himself. Joseph smiled, watching his son's efforts.

At four years old, Azaria treasured Thea and Clarinda. She had begun calling Clarinda, Clara, and the nickname quickly stuck. While Grace, Colleen, and Mrs. Whitley managed the canning and preserving of foods, Azaria happily tended to Thea and Clara.

In early December, Timothy returned from a long day at the courthouse to find Lily sitting alone in the parlor, reading. He was pleased to see that at last she had permitted the new baby to be out of her sight for a time. Happily, he greeted Eddie and Faith and moved to sit beside Lily. She chattered on about plans for a Christmas party and he listened patiently while his children climbed on him.

The delightful aroma of turkey roasting, spilled out of the kitchen. In the dining room, the cook prepared the table for the evening meal. Timothy walked up the stairs to stoke the fires on the second floor before supper.

He rapped at Sarina's door and entered quietly. She was seated near the fire studying her Bible. He talked with her for a few minutes as he tended to her fireplace. After reminding her that supper would be served soon, he left and moved on to his own room. He rounded the end of the bed to see the sleeping baby. Puzzled, he looked down at the empty cradle.

"Lily!" he shouted as he leaned over the balustrade in the hall.

He heard the tapping of her shoes on the floor below and waited. She stood on the bottom step and tilted her head back to look up at him. "Husband?" she called back.

"Where is the baby?" he asked anxiously. She stared blankly and turned away. He ran down the stairs and grabbed her shoulders. "Lily where is child?" he demanded and shook her furiously.

"Hephzibah does tend her well," she responded and scowled.

"Your infant is Hephz..." Timothy released her and ran through the kitchen and out the back door. In the barn he scrambled up the ladder to the loft. Startled, the barn cat ran along the edge of the outer wall and down to the floor below. He heard the infant's weak cry as he rushed to the far corner. He lifted her gently and removed the hay from her blanket.

Carefully, he climbed down the ladder again. Mr. Dobbs stood in the doorway watching curiously. Timothy stepped outside and Dobbs followed, closing the doors securely behind him.

"Be done with the cat!" Timothy ordered as he marched back into the house.

In the parlor he pulled back the blanket and examined the baby. Her diaper had saturated her gown and she appeared to be hungry but she was still warm. He watched closely as Lily changed her diaper and nursed her. His anger rose and he fought the strong urge to strike his wife for her neglect of the baby.

"Why?" Lily, he demanded.

With a confused look on her face, she shrugged and held the infant to her shoulder as she patted her back. "I cannot think what you mean to ask of me."

"Lily, why did you leave your child in the barn?" he demanded, angrily.

"The cat did require it," she responded, as if it were the most reasonable explanation.

"Wife, you shall not remove the infant from this house without my mother at your side. Am I well understood?" he shouted.

"You do frighten me, Timothy," she responded, annoyed.

"I shant abide any more of your talk of that cat! Tis done, Lily!" he ordered, as he took the baby from her and strode toward the dining room.

The family ate in silence as Timothy simmered over Lily's actions. He kept the cradle close to his chair and watched his wife as she took small bites of the turkey and dipped it in the pumpkin soup before eating it. Frustrated, he shook his head and turned away.

"Mother, on the morrow Lily shall travel to the millinery and Burghill House. Might you accompany her?" he asked, struggling to control his irritation.

"If it shall please her, I should be happy to enjoy her company," Sarina responded.

"Lily shant depart from this house if you do not escort her," he insisted.

"Yes, Timothy," Sarina agreed as she looked down at the food on her plate.

"Lily, the barn cat shall be removed on the morrow," he advised her.

"No!" she shrieked, pounding her fists on the table as she jumped up, knocking her chair over backwards.

"I shall endure no more of this mania! No more!" he ordered and thumped his fist against the polished wood. "Be seated, Lily!"

She drew in a sharp breath and huffed it out as she picked up the chair. She sat again and lifted her fork as she glared at Timothy. "Hephzibah is mine and you shant bother her," she declared, defiantly.

"Speak no more!" he spoke through clenched teeth. She shifted her gaze to the chandelier that hung over the table. The flames above the rolled beeswax candles flickered and danced. Her thoughts drifted to memories of the glass lamp that sat on the table beside her father's favorite chair. She could hear his deep voice as he read to her in the sitting room at Burghill House.

"*Can pleasing sight misfortune ever bring? Can firm desire a painful torment try? Can winning eyes prove to the heart a sting? Or can sweet lips in treason hidden lie?*" she mumbled softly.

"Lily?" Timothy eyed her curiously.

"Tis *Pamphillia to Amphilanthus* from the works of Mary Wroth. My father did recite to me in my childhood," she explained, and smiled sweetly.

Not willing to forgive her so quickly, he excused himself from the table before she enchanted him further.

35

In early December, the first snowfall of the season began. The wind stilled, as snow continued falling through the night. Into the next day, the flakes were smaller and the accumulation slowed. For days it amassed gradually and was easily brushed away from walkways. On roads, the travel of horses and carriages was enough to clear the path appreciably.

After several days of the wintry weather, the morning sun burned through the cloud cover and shone brilliantly. Luke stood at the window looking out at the blinding reflection of the sun on the fresh blanket of snow in front of the house. He blinked a few times and stepped back. On the bed behind him Grace sat up and stretched.

"Yesterday, on the waterfront I did hear the tale of a great storm on the wind," Luke told her as he reached for the fireplace poker.

"Shall the weather hinder the Christmas revelry?" she asked.

"Grace, mayhap it shall be a slight gathering of family alone at this celebration."

"A fine holiday ball shall be greatly enjoyed," she asserted.

"Tis so, yet I do worry over Lily."

"We cannot regulate our lives by thoughts of but one child. As we did worry over Isannah and Cherish we did appreciate the company of friends and neighbors. Tis likely it shall be a good thing for Lily as well," she suggested as she stood behind him and slipped her arms around his waist.

"I shall not forbid it," he replied as he turned slowly and pulled her against him. He kissed the top of her head and closed his eyes as he pondered a silent prayer.

The spectacular Christmas party was enjoyed without any unpleasant incidents. Burghill House was filled with happy guests late into the night. The weather remained calm and the temperature was moderate.

Christmas morning the families made their way to the local churches. Both Rev. Murray and Rev. Pender preached strong sermons to appreciative congregations. Cheerfully, the family returned to Burghill House to enjoy a fine feast.

As December waned, the New Year of 1801 was observed as a severe winter storm hit the region. Early in the afternoon it increased to blizzard conditions. Through the night, the wind howled and pushed the snow into great drifts. By morning many of the roads were impassable. For another three more days the stormy weather continued.

Throughout the month of January a wave of winter storms continued. In early February a week of warmer temperatures and southern breezes began melting the accumulated snow. But that brief respite ended with freezing rain sweeping in ahead of another massive snowstorm.

Spring arrived early at the end March. After the long winter, with too many days confined to the house, Timothy was exhilarated by the chance to travel. He planned to journey to Portsmouth for several days on his own. Dutifully, he made arrangements for the care of his family and the house in his absence.

Lily's mental state appeared to have stabilized at last. She seemed to be managing reasonably well with less supervision. Sarina remained close to Lily and watched the baby carefully. While Timothy was away Sarina and the governess would both be tasked with monitoring Lily day and night.

The day before Timothy planned to leave, he rose early to work out the final details of the trip. When breakfast was served he noted that Sarina had not yet come downstairs for her morning tea and toast. Uneasily he ate with Lily and the children, but his eyes continued to wander back to the empty place setting.

Resignedly, he climbed the stairs and rapped at her door. He found her lying on her side in the bed. Her eyes were open but she could not move to speak. He called for the governess to sit with her while he rode to Burghill House for Dr. Wallace. In only fifteen minutes they returned and Luke hurried up to her room.

"Tis apoplexy," Luke explained gently, when he had examined her. "Tis little I might do for her. Do all that you might to make her comfortable, as her end does draw near."

"Does she suffer from a painful condition?" Timothy asked.

"No, she does not," Luke speculated. "Mayhap the governess shall see that she does eat this morn."

"Assuredly," Timothy responded. "Shall it be a lingering death?"

"I cannot know with certainty."

Timothy cancelled his plans to travel and remained at home with Lily. Grace quickly suggested that Timothy deliver Lily and the baby to Burghill House each morning where she could be watched over. Gratefully, Timothy agreed to the arrangement.

"Luke, tis rightful we shall enlarge this house," Grace suggested as she lay beside him in bed that night.

"Why should you think so?" he asked.

"There are more children to come and shall require more rooms to offer accommodations," she explained.

"Grace, the children shall grow and will make their own way. They shant linger ever more under this roof."

"Mayhap you shall consider it," she prodded.

"If you will permit me sleep, I shall contemplate it on the morrow," he teased.

"Tis rightful you shall come to me in agreement in the morn," she replied with a smile and closed her eyes.

36

Sarina Gage survived through the spring and into summer. Luke was pleased with her progress through June, under the watchful eye of the governess. By the end of the month, Sarina was able to sit on her own in her bed and feed herself with a spoon. Her speech was still slurred but Timothy remained hopeful that she would recover fully.

In mid-July, Julia went into labor late in the evening. It had been an extremely hot day, but a gentle breeze provided relief as night fell. She progressed through the night and delivered a son for Laurent. He was named Bradford Charles Morgan. Laurent beamed with pride as he showed off the new baby boy to Reny and

Rose. Hurriedly, he crossed the yard to present the infant to the morning diners at Botts' Tavern.

The following month Emma gave birth to her third baby boy. She struggled for nearly two days before she heard the strong cry of the infant. "Tis a remarkably large child," Molly announced as she held him.

"He is a vigorous boy," Grace agreed.

Proudly, Noah lifted the infant from his mother's arms. "His name shall be, Byron Micajah Taylor," he announced cheerfully. "This boy is big as a fat tom turkey!"

Too soon, the fresh green leaves that adorned the trees were splashed with bright yellows, oranges and reds. Sarina's condition had improved greatly and she required less care. With the tremendous patience of the governess, she walked down to the dining room table at mealtime.

The household staff in the Gage home had become relaxed and complacent with Lily. She enjoyed more freedom as the daily chores and winter preparations preoccupied them. While they were busy working on a warm fall day, she quietly slipped out the front door. Happily she strode out to the barn and hurried inside. Humming softly, she climbed up the ladder to the loft. She worked her way passed the hay to the corner where the cat had made her bed. Surprised, she found the space empty.

Growing more anxious, she searched the loft but found no trace of the cat or her kittens. She scrabbled down to the floor again and began searching in and around the entire barn. Crossly, she slammed the heavy door and stood looking back into the woods. She heard a banging sound behind the stables and ran toward it.

Mr. Dobbs held a heavy wooden mallet in his hand and he carefully banged a peg into the underside of a chair to repair it. He glanced up, alarmed as she approached.

"Mrs. Gage, you should not be out here," he stammered.

"Where is my cat?" she demanded.

"Might I walk with you as you do return to the house?" he encouraged.

"You shall not!" she shouted with her hands on her hips. "Where is my cat?"

"The cat is gone from this place," he mumbled, looking down at the wooden mallet.

"Where is my cat?" she screamed.

"Mrs. Gage, twas not my doing. Mr. Gage did bid me remove the cat," he pleaded.

"You shall return it to me this day!"

"I cannot," he implored. "The animal was left upon the docks and did board a ship."

Furiously, Lily stomped back along the side of the barn to the back door of the house. She banged the back door open and slammed it shut again. The cook looked out through the pantry door and her eyes grew wide as she saw the rage on Lily's face. Quietly, she stepped back and stood still, waiting for Lily to move on.

Lily flew up the stairs to the attic door. In the dim light of late day she began searching the large open space. She opened trunks and chests and threw the contents out on the floor. She called to the cat as she continued her rummaging. With dirt smudged on her face and her hair coming undone, she finally gave up the hunt.

Discouraged and angry, she stamped down to her room and kicked the door shut behind her. She searched around the furniture but found no sign of the feline. Standing in front of the window, she considered opening it to call out to it, but remembered Luke's instructions. She strode back to her armoire and yanked the doors open. Swiftly, she dragged out her gowns and dresses and threw them across the room. When she had emptied the drawers as well she stood back and looked down on the great pile.

Suddenly, she moved to the tallboy and withdrew Timothy's clothing as well. She hurried to her dressing table and emptied the contents there onto the floor as well. With a quick swipe of her arm she cleared the top of the dresser. She reached for one of the oil lamps but remembered a caution from her father in her childhood and she pulled her hands back.

Standing in front of the windows, she ripped down the heavy drapes and added them to the pile. The pillows and bedding were mounded there as well. Magnificent portraits of long-dead ancestors of her husband were snatched from the walls and hurled at the splendid bed.

She opened the door and trooped down the stairs, grabbing at paintings on the walls as she moved. From the parlor she heard Timothy's voice and ran across the heavily polished floor. In the doorway to the parlor, she stopped and glared at him. Slowly he turned to face her, quickly noticing her torn dress, messy hair and dirty face.

"Lily?"

"Where is my cat?" she demanded.

"Go to the kitchen, I must speak with your mama," Timothy instructed Eddie and Faith. Respectfully, they hurried through the great hall to the kitchen.

"Timothy, where is my cat?" she insisted, glowering at him.

"Lily, the cat is gone. I did tell of it afore yet you would not hear my words," he snapped and turned away from her. Near the fireplace he stopped to pour a glass of rum before she could continue her tirade.

"Twas wrongful that you did remove her! You shall return her this day, Timothy."

"Lily, twas near a year ago that she did go. Tis done with."

"You did hold me prisoner that I would not know of this cruelty!"

"I shall not suffer more of your rant this night!" he responded and swallowed the rum. He refilled his glass and moved to sit in a chair.

"Tis not your opine that I do seek!" she shouted. Swiftly she grabbed for the heavy mercury demijohn vase from the table beside her. She threw it straight at the Flemish, tortoiseshell framed mirror above the mantle. As the vessel struck the mirror and shattered it, glass and debris sprayed out from the wall. Shocked, Timothy jumped up and moved back away from the fireplace.

As he touched his hand to his hair he felt pieces of glass from the mirror and vase both there. He touched the side of his face and found a number of small cuts that were bleeding. Stunned by the incident, he turned toward Lily in time to duck before she released a tray of crystal cordial decanters in his direction. He bent low and moved closer to her as she hurled cordial goblets and books across the room.

Before he could grab for her, she ran to the dining room. At the end of the large room she worked her arm in between the wall and the back of a mahogany cupboard full of bone china. Wiggling feverishly she pushed it off balance and jumped back as it crashed down on the end of the formal dining room table. At the other end of the room she quickly upset the tall glass front cabinet that held the heirloom crystal and silver.

With Timothy close behind her, she darted into his library and grabbed for the first barrister cabinet. The glass doors exploded as it hit the floor and blocked Timothy from entering the room. He clambered over the broken furniture as a second tall cabinet of rare books smashed against the wood floor. She could not move the heavy walnut desk, so she swept her arm across the surface. The glass inkwell shattered against the wall, splattering ink up the wall and across the upper shelves of the bookshelf closest to it.

She was throwing books from the shelves when Timothy finally grabbed her arm. He yanked her toward him and shook her violently.

"Sir?" Mr. Dobbs called from the doorway as Timothy drew back his hand to strike her. He lifted her and sat her roughly on the top of the desk before he turned around.

"Bring me rope from the barn, Dobbs," Timothy called, struggling to catch his breath. "Lily, do you see what you have done?"

"I want my cat," she announced angrily.

"I can endure no more of this," he told her as hot tears stung his eyes. "I cannot."

When Dobbs returned with the rope, Timothy tied her wrists loosely and looped it around her waist. He and Mr. Dobbs moved the barrister bookshelf that blocked the doorway. He lifted Lily and carried her into the parlor. Surprisingly, gently, he lowered her into a chair well away from the glass and other debris.

"Mr. Dobbs, ride for Dr. Wallace and Joseph Grenier. Return with them as quickly as you might," he told him.

"Yes sir," Dobbs responded and hurried back through the kitchen.

37

Luke walked through the front door with Joseph close behind him. They looked into the parlor at the scattered fragments. Lily remained seated, bound by the rope. Luke rushed into the room and began untying her. He wiped the tears from her cheeks and pulled her up from the chair.

"No!" Timothy shouted as he ran down the stairs and saw her standing in the hall. He held the baby in his arms and stopped across the room from Lily.

"What have you done?" Luke roared angrily at Timothy.

"No, Sir, not I. Lily did lay waste to my house!"

Luke and Joseph looked to Lily and she shrugged innocently. "Lily, did you do this?"

"Why shall you think to believe him? Mayhap I did not," she stated coyly.

"Why?" Luke asked as he turned back to Timothy.

"Shall you tell it?" he asked Lily.

"I want my cat," Lily declared and folded her arms.

"I bid you go to the dining room, library and the bedroom upstairs."

Reluctantly they followed Timothy across the great hall. Joseph grasped Lily's wrist and pulled her along with him. They looked into the library then crossed the hall to the dining room. Dazed by the extent of the damage, they climbed the stairs and looked into the bedroom.

Luke exhaled slowly and fell back against the bedroom wall. "Lily, what has become of you?"

"I can endure no more," Timothy spoke sorrowfully. "Shall she harm my children as she storms next?"

"Tis reasonable that you should think so," Luke acknowledged.

"Lily, my heart shall shatter without you. I do love you exceedingly. Yet I cannot endure it. My children do tremble in the arms of their grandmother this night. Tis wrongful!"

"Timothy, shall you bid me take leave?" she asked, shocked by his words.

"Tis naught I might do."

"Your face does bleed," she whispered as she stepped forward and touched his cheek.

"Twas the glass from the mirror."

"I could not harm you, Husband. No, twas not my act that did shatter the mirror. I could not."

"Lily, why must you break my heart?" he asked, choking back tears. He pulled away from her. "I must bid you go."

"What of the little one?" Luke asked gently.

"She is but a year old now and does nurse at her mother's breast. Mayhap Grace shall tend her and permit Lily to suckle her still."

"Assuredly, Grace shall mind her well," Luke responded. "Shall you manage Eddie and Faith?"

"'Tis a governess to worry over them. If it be agreeable, I shall deliver them unto your house often that they might enjoy time with their mother." Timothy coughed and cleared his throat again.

"Joseph, walk Lily to the kitchen and wait with her there," Luke instructed him. Joseph nodded and tugged at her arm as he moved down the stairs. "Timothy, I beseech you do not do this thing. Not this night."

"I can endure no more of this. Have you not seen the wreckage of my household? Luke, my child does carry the name of a barn cat!"

"Bring the children and your mother. You shall all be made welcome at Burghill House. 'Tis my word and my bond, she shall not act against you and yours there. The children shall rest securely this night."

In the early months after Hephzibah was born, her sister, Faith had begun calling her Bonbon, the French word for *sweets*. Timothy gratefully accepted the nickname for her. She was soon referred to simply as Bon. He patted Bon's back as she rested against his shoulder. He kissed her head and considered Luke's proposal. "How shall you grant surety that she shall be calmed?"

"She shall be dosed with Laudanum. Herbs steeped in boiling wine shall slow her thinking and she shall be made unflappable."

"What of my mother?"

"'Tis a fine bed for Sarina as well. Timothy, she shall be greatly strained if she shall rise in the morn to the ruins of this house that she does love so."

"'Tis fair and true," Timothy agreed. "I bid you restrain Lily and I shall prepare a trunk."

Luke reached to take the sleepy child from him. Timothy walked back into the bedroom and picked through the pile in the middle of the floor.

Near midnight the family was finally settled in at Burghill House. Eddie and Faith slept in Azaria's bedroom next to Luke and Grace's room on the first floor. Bon was placed in a crib in the nursery upstairs with Thea and Clara. Sarina and the governess were given the front bedroom. The last empty bedroom at the back corner, over the kitchen, was for Timothy and Lily.

Luke gave Lily a heavy dose of the Laudanum with a cup of wine. He watched her as she sipped and the drugs took effect. In the kitchen, Grace carefully combed the glass and other fragments from Timothy's hair as he leaned over the wash basin.

Luke passed a medicine bottle to Timothy and advised him to give Lily more if she woke and showed agitation in the night. Timothy lifted her from the chair in the sitting room. Her head lolled back against his chest as he carried her up to the waiting bed.

38

On a cold, rainy night in October, Sarina passed away in her sleep. The governess moved to wake her in the morning and quickly summoned Luke. She was laid out in the sitting room at Burghill House for two days before her casket was transported to the cemetery.

Under a cloudless blue sky, the graveside service was conducted by Rev. Murray. The rich scent of fall hung heavy in the air. Colorful leaves danced gracefully around the gravestones. Timothy studied his father's stone and thought of his mother. He drew comfort from his belief that his mother was at his father's side again at last.

Luke and Grace marveled at Lily's strength following Sarina's death. Lily consoled Timothy and reassured him as he mourned. There were periods when she acted strangely but that did not detract from her devoted manner.

The repairs and renovations at the Gage house continued as the first snow fell in early December. Luke encouraged Timothy to remain through the winter months for Lily's sake. She seemed to be more stable and far less volatile during their stay at Burghill House. Timothy considered the idea carefully and finally agreed. Timothy's family home was shuttered for the winter.

Spring arrived at last with heavy rains and blooming flowers. Timothy made plans to travel to Boston and purchase large pieces to replace the furniture that Lily had destroyed. Lily would remain at Burghill House with the children until he returned. Repairs on the house had begun again. Timothy hoped to leave in mid-May and return by ship in a month.

The full moon bathed the back yard in a soft bluish haze. The day had been unusually warm for the first week of May. There was a chill in the night air but the second floor windows were left open a few inches. The fog hugged the ground, undisturbed by the breeze that sang through the highest branches of the tall pines.

Lily woke and sat up in the bed. Timothy lay on his side facing toward her but he did not stir. She listened keenly for the sound that woke her. Somewhere outside a cat meowed again. She climbed down from the bed and tapped across the floor to the window. With a faint squeak of the sash against the wooden window frame, she inched it up further.

The cat cried and stalked across the yard to the barn. Lily leaned out over the window sill and watched the animal twitch its tail as it moved. She smiled and hurried toward the door. Quietly, she slipped out into the hall and down the stairs. She banged her palms against the wooden plank twice before it moved. She lifted it and placed it in the corner then unlocked the door and walked out onto the top step.

Under her bare feet she felt the damp, cold stone. She wrinkled her nose and closed the door behind her. She ran to the barn and gripped the heavy door firmly. Struggling, she pried it open at last and stepped inside. The moonlight did not penetrate the great open space. She extended her arms and felt ahead as she walked forward cautiously. Twice she stumbled and nearly fell but caught herself.

Finally she found the ladder to the loft and climbed blindly. Moving upward she felt around above each rung before rising higher. She reached the top and felt the platform. Lifting the bottom of her night gown she made it up onto the floor of the loft. She heard something scurry close in the dark but saw nothing.

To her left she heard a soft mewling sound. She shuffled her feet and kicked away low piles of hay. Following the sound of the kittens, she tripped on a warped board and fell against the railing. The dry wood barrier cracked and she pushed away from it, landing on her bare knees. She stood again and crept closer.

With one hand she felt in the dark and touched the warm fur. Gently, she lifted a kitten and touched it to her cheek. She kissed the tiny nose and put it back down with the other kittens. Boldly, she patted the hay around the kittens until she found the mother cat.

"Hephzibah!" she cried, excitedly. She stroked the cat's fur and talked softly to her. "Come with me," she told her and started to pick her up. The cat uttered a low growl and swiped at her face. Startled and frightened, Lily screamed as the feline attacked.

Timothy woke with a start when he heard Lily's scream. He felt the bed beside him and jumped up. He ran down the stairs and back through the kitchen. In the dark he rushed to the open door of the barn.

"Lily!" he shouted from the doorway. Her cries came from the loft above and he climbed hurriedly. "Lily!"

"Timothy!" she cried. He found her sitting on the floor of the loft, crying. Carefully, he maneuvered her back to the ladder. He started down and helped her onto the rungs above him. Slowly, he helped her along until she reached the barn floor.

He walked her outside and secured the heavy doors again. She stood sobbing and babbling incoherently as he scooped her up in his arms and carried her back inside. He pushed the back door closed with his foot and set her on the kitchen table. He lit a candle from the low fire in the hearth. When he realized that she was bleeding from several deep scratches and bites, he darted through the house to wake Luke.

While Luke washed the scratches with vinegar and removed numerous splinters from her palms and knees, Grace held her hand and talked soothingly. Timothy sat across the table from her, sipping whiskey from a small glass. Lily calmed at last and her sobs faded into short gasps.

"She did sleep aside me," Timothy mumbled and swallowed more of the drink. "I cannot assure she shall be safe through the night as she does slumber in the same bed."

"'Tis alike the troubles with Isannah," Luke agreed. "She did flee in the night afore she did wed Ren Luciern. I did search in the dark, with Teague and Mica Johnes, and Phillip. I did find her scarcely clothed in the wood. 'Twas unsettling that she did behave so."

"Shall we build a pillory within the bed chamber to secure her?" Timothy posed and swallowed the last of the whiskey in his glass.

127

Luke chuckled, "No, we shall not bind her so. Mayhap you shall lock the door nightly and withdraw the key."

"You believe it rightful that I shall imprison her nightly?"

"Timothy, you shall undertake to uphold her safety. Look upon her face! Shall you see her wounded again?"

"I shall not!"

"She shall be confined in the bed chamber through the night or removed to the attic. Tis rightful, Timothy."

While Luke finished dressing the deepest scratches along the side of her face and neck, Grace washed the dirt from her feet. When they were finally done, Timothy carried her upstairs to the bedroom again. He pushed the bed across the floor to block the door then lay down with her again.

"You shall not leave this room again afore morning," he ordered. "Am I well understood?"

"Twas Hephzibah in the barn," she implored. "She does believe that I did abandon her and is angry at me."

"Lily, that cat is gone away from this place. Sleep now and do not leave this bed afore the sun does come again."

39

On a chilly morning in May, Timothy boarded the Dutch ship, *Onze Godin Holda.* The cold drizzle continued as the ship sailed south along the Coningsby River. He stood on deck watching the docks of East Grantham shrink in the distance. It would be at least a month before he would return. An unnerving sense of foreboding stole over him and he gripped the railing.

At Burghill House the day progressed with the usual routine. Grace kept Lily close as she baked and cleaned. She felt encouraged by Lily's calm demeanor through the morning. Into the afternoon they settled in the sitting room with the smaller children. Lily sat in the rocking chair and read from one of her father's books with Bon on her lap.

Late in the day as the babies napped, Grace, Colleen, Mrs. Whitley, and Lily chatted in the kitchen and prepared supper. Grace suggested that they begin repairing the old patchwork quilts in the morning. When the work was done they would combine their fabric scraps and start a new one. Contentedly, they carried the serving dishes into the dining room and sat at the table.

Luke and Joseph ate and talked of the new school the Chernock's were building behind the current building. Joseph was pleased to be involved in creating a better place for his children to attend daily. Grace proposed a donation of books to the new school house.

"We cannot give of Papa's books!" Lily protested.

"Mayhap we shall make a gift of new books," Grace reassured her.

Lily scowled and looked down at the spoon in her hand. She continued eating the fish chowder as Grace and Colleen discussed the children's books. Mrs. Whitley placed a basket of fresh bread and a tray of venison on the table. Quietly, she slipped back down the hall to the kitchen.

"Where is Timothy?" Lily asked suddenly.

"He did depart for Boston this morn," Grace reminded her. "You did utter farewell afore he did go."

"How shall he take leave and I am left to my own?" she demanded.

"Lily…" Grace began as Lily stood up. She grabbed for the soup bowl and hurled it across the room. The china shattered, spraying chowder up the wall and across the ceiling. Clawing at her bare arms she fell back into the chair.

Stunned, Joseph grasped her hands to stop her scrabbling. As Grace and Colleen moved to comfort the frightened children, Luke and Joseph hurried to the kitchen with Lily. Joseph forced her down into a kitchen chair at the end of the table. Blood oozed from the deep scratches as Mrs. Whitley patted them with clean linens.

Luke gave Lily a heavy dose of Laudanum, followed by a cup of strong herbal tea and rum. He rinsed her arms with vinegar and applied a thick brown salve. She pouted as Joseph remained at her side still gripping her wrists.

When her arms were bandaged Luke began trimming her fingernails. They were pared as short as he could make them to prevent more of the scratching.

"What is to be done with her?" Joseph asked, staring up at Luke.

"Mayhap she shall be removed to the attic as Timothy does travel," Luke suggested.

"You mean to secret me away?" Lily asked in surprise.

"I cannot abide more of this," Luke responded angrily.

"I did naught!"

"Lily, you did heave the soup bowl!"

"Twas Joseph!" Lily insisted.

"Remove her to the attic or I shall take her across my knee," Luke told Joseph.

In the attic, Joseph built a fire in the Franklin stove while Lily dug through the old trunks there. She pulled out extravagant gowns and accessories that had belonged to Isannah. Mrs. Whitley made the bed with fresh bed linens and disappeared down the stairs again. Grace carried up a glass of mulled wine and several books and left them beside the bed.

"Sleep well," Grace whispered and kissed Lily's cheek.

"Mama, you shant be angry with Joseph," Lily told her. "Forgive that he did toss the soup dish."

Grace only shook her head and walked back down the steps with Joseph following close behind her. He locked the door and wandered down to the sitting room. Luke sat at his desk flipping through the pages of one of Phillip's journals. Joseph dropped into a chair beside the window and rubbed his temples.

"The Laudanum shall render her quiet through the night," Luke declared. "Did you provide the wine?"

"I did," Grace answered from the doorway. "I shall aid Colleen as she settles the children into their beds," she uttered as she walked up the stairs again.

A calm settled over the house at last. Late in the evening, Luke extinguished the lamps and made his way to the bedroom. He slipped into the bed beside Grace and draped his arm over her waist. Gently, he pulled her backward, against his body. He kissed her and inhaled the faint scent of perfume on her neck.

"Sleep well, my love," he whispered. He swept her hair back and brushed his lips along her shoulder.

"Luke, I beg of you, permit me to sleep."

"I do desire you greatly, beloved wife."

"Mayhap you shall desire me in the morn."

"Surely I shall, yet it shant alter my longing this night."

He continued feathering his lips up her neck to her jaw. Tenderly, he touched her chin and turned her head to kiss her lips. His hand slipped under the quilt and he began lifting her gown slowly. Reluctantly, she began responding to his enticement. At last she turned to face him and kissed him in return.

In the room above, a thundering of footsteps startled them. Luke pulled away and listened as he heard shouting in the hallway beyond the sitting room. Leaving Grace in the bedroom, he hurried out to the stairs. In the hall above, he saw a lamp burning and heard Joseph shouting angrily.

"Joseph!" he called as he reached the attic door and stomped up the flight of steps.

Lily stood at the far end of the room with her arms folded defiantly. Kneeling by the closest window, Joseph picked up a shard of glass and dropped it into a small wooden box. Luke looked around the room at the chests and boxes that had been turned over and the debris that littered the room.

"Joseph?" Luke called

"She did shatter the window in her rage! The trunks have been upturned as well!"

Luke wandered through the open space as he surveyed the damage. Beside the bed the wine glass had been spilled and the splatter stained the bedding. He looked at Lily and shook his head.

"What is to be done? Shall she be removed to the insane asylum?" Joseph demanded.

"I cannot," Luke murmured. "I cannot break your mother's heart."

"She is possessed of a demon!"

"You shall not speak so!" Luke shouted back. "Bring rope and bindings from the barn. She shall be bound in her bed through the night."

The fire in the attic stove was doused and Luke led her down to the bedroom she had shared with Timothy. Joseph brought in leather straps with buckles and coarse rope made of hemp. Her wrists and ankles were wrapped with fleece before she was bound and lashed to the bed frame. Luke draped the quilt over her and tucked it under her chin.

"On the morrow you shall be released," he advised her.

"How shall you handle me so!" Lily shouted indignantly.

"If you shall cry out again I shall muzzle you as well!" he countered.

She glared up at him but did not speak.

40

In the first week of July, Timothy returned at last. The repairs in the Gage house had been completed and the new furniture was quickly installed. Unenthusiastically, he readied for the move from Burghill House. Luke explained that Lily would need to be bound nightly to prevent her frenzied behavior.

The household staff was reassembled and the home was soon put back in order. Lily's chaos was removed from Burghill House and deposited in the fine old house of the Gage family.

As summer passed, several birthday parties were hosted at Burghill House. The guests marveled at the rich chocolate cake and blackberry ice cream made by Mrs. Whitley. Mac returned to East Grantham, for a week in July and enjoyed the chance to see Annie Stanton at Grace's party. The weekly Sunday dinners continued with the growing family in attendance.

In the fall, Colleen announced that she was pregnant with her third baby. Joseph was happy and confident that this child would be his second son. Luke and Grace looked forward to another child in the house.

Only days before Christmas, Grace played hostess at a spectacular party. The house was filled with family, friends and neighbors well into the night. Music and laughter floated through the rooms with the delicious aromas from the kitchen.

Lily remained in the rocking chair in a corner of the sitting room through the evening. As her opium addiction progressed with the extreme dosages of the Laudanum, she had become more reserved and even indifferent. With her rages controlled at last, Luke and Timothy saw no reason to lower the quantities of the drug.

Winter passed with only a few notable snowstorms. Into spring there was less snow accumulation than normal to markedly deter travel. One busy day blended into another and the gentle spring rains dissolved the last of the snow.

Cheerfully, Colleen looked forward to the birth of her third baby. She remained confident that, at last, she would bless Joseph with another son. At nearly seven year-old Azaria was excited about the idea of a new baby in the house. Daily, she hurried home from the school house, to tend to Thea and Clara.

In early May, strong southern winds blew into the region. The clouds drifted to the north, leaving a clear sky and brilliant sun. Temperatures climbed and the buzz of insects could be heard in the meadow beyond the lilac bushes. Grace and Mrs. Whitley opened the windows throughout the house and welcomed the fresh air.

Mrs. Whitley scrubbed tubs of laundry and helped Grace to carry them out to the back yard. Thea and Clara played under the big oak tree behind the house. Colleen wandered out to the clothesline and began hanging wet clothes. She tugged at heavy linens and Grace quickly scolded her for it.

Through the morning and into afternoon dry items were removed and Grace and Mrs. Whitley brought out another full basket. When they finished lunch, Colleen strode back out to begin folding more of the dry items. She lifted the heavy basket and moved across the yard toward the back door.

Near the back steps she dropped the hamper and fell to her knees. She gripped her belly and cried out as she rolled to her side. She tensed and held her breath until the sharp pains diminished again. Her water broke as she knelt there in the grass and she shouted for Grace.

Carefully, Grace and Mrs. Whitley helped her up and into the house. Slowly, they moved her up the stairs to the bedroom. Mrs. Whitley rode to summon Molly. They returned within the hour and Molly hurried upstairs to examine Colleen.

"She is resting well," Molly advised Grace, when she had finished with her assessment of Colleen. "If you shall sit with her I will begin brewing tea to aid with her travails."

Colleen progressed well into the evening and Joseph was permitted to sit with her for a few minutes. Molly anticipated that the new baby would arrive by morning if everything continued as it had been.

"Tis Joseph's son," Colleen announced proudly, as she touched her belly. In response, the baby kicked at her hand and she laughed.

Early in the morning Colleen had paled notably and began sweating profusely. Molly examined her again and discovered that she had begun bleeding heavily. While Molly tended to Colleen, Grace hurried downstairs to wake Luke and prepare a strong herbal tea.

Molly and Luke worked together to stop the blood flow and speed the delivery. Luke proposed sending Joseph to retrieve Ben Andrews. Molly agreed and Joseph rushed out the front door and along Kings Wood Road to Ben's house. Only fifteen minutes later they returned. Joseph ran to the kitchen to ready the surgical braziers, while Ben talked with Luke and Molly.

Ben opened his kit of surgical tools and prepared quickly. Luke stepped aside as Molly assessed Colleen again. The bleeding had worsened and Molly looked anxiously to Luke. He noted the pallid look of Colleen's face. Grace carried in more of the herbal tea and coaxed Colleen to sip it. The last of it trickled down her chin as she struggled to swallow the liquid. She coughed and moaned as she felt the pain increase again.

Molly placed her hands on Colleen's belly and felt for movement. She noted the relaxing of the muscles as the contraction passed but no other movement. Gently, she prodded in hopes of provoking a kick but there was no response.

Colleen cried out again and Molly announced that the head was crowning. She grasped the head and quickly rotated the shoulders as she pulled the infant up and away from Colleen. Hurriedly, she cleared the baby girl's mouth and slapped her bottom. Luke severed the umbilical cord and tied it as Molly moved away with the infant. Repeatedly, she attempted to stimulate the baby, but there was no movement. Worriedly, she watched as the tiny face varied from a pale bluish color, to a deeper grayish purple.

Luke and Ben labored over Colleen but could not stop the flow of blood. Colleen closed her eyes and her breathing slowed. As Joseph walked into the room with the brazier, Luke and Ben looked at him awkwardly. Joseph placed it on the table with Ben's implements. He looked to the other end of the room where Molly fretted over the baby. Without a word, he left the room and closed the door.

Grace approached Joseph in the hall as he stepped out of the bedroom. She looked into his face and held out her arms. He fell against her, nearly knocking her over. Desperately, he hugged her and cried. She dropped back onto the window seat and pulled him down beside her.

41

Joseph stood beside the casket that held his wife and lost child. The infant was named Daphne Rose Grenier and her name was added to the grave marker for Colleen. Joseph held the hands of his six and three year-old daughters as they fidgeted beside their mother's grave. Rev. Murray concluded the funeral service with an inspiring prayer but Joseph heard none of it. Teague and Azaria remained at Grace's side. When the burial concluded, the procession moved through the gates and onto the trail through the trees. The little girls walked ahead, tugging Joseph along.

In the days and weeks that followed, Joseph worked long hard days and spent his evenings with his children. He spoke little but appeared to listen well as they talked to him. Sundays, after church, he walked to the graveyard with them. He sat quietly beside Phillip's gravestone while the girls picked wildflowers. Teague sat by Naomi's stone while Thea and Clara decorated Colleen's grave with handfuls of colorful blooms.

In July Mac travelled north from Boston to East Grantham again for a week at home. As in the previous summers while he attended Harvard, a week was the most that could be allowed, with the travel time required. When he was not attending classes or studying in Cambridge, Massachusetts, he assisted several local doctors in a traineeship. The doctors and his professors were duly impressed with his natural ability to heal and the compassion he showed toward the patients.

During Mac's week at home he urged Grace to hold an outdoor party. He desperately wanted time with Annie Stanton. Until his education was complete, and he returned to East Grantham permanently, he could not begin his courtship. Without a courtship approved by Annie's father, Mac would not be permitted to call on her. Through his years of college, they communicated weekly by mail and saw each other only once a year.

Late in the day as the revelry continued, Mac led Annie along the trail behind Burghill House. With other couples serving as chaperones to one another, they found a short time to talk privately. Mac assured her that he would speak with her father the day he returned home to stay. In turn, she assured him that she would accept his proposal and they could be married soon thereafter.

"We shall live in the loft of my Father's barn if it be required," she whispered and squeezed his hand.

"I am to be a physician, Annie! You shant dwell in a barn. As I do return, you shall be made my wife and we shall live in a home finer than Burghill House," he insisted and stole a kiss from her.

Too soon, Mac departed again. He was greatly missed by his family as well as Annie. But they took comfort from the knowledge that Mac's gifts would not be wasted. He would possess skills and knowledge that Luke had not learned. Luke understood that his son would be an impressive healer like Phillip had been. He looked forward to working with him.

The governess, Alice Ramsey, remained in the Gage home, caring for Eddie, Faith, and Bon as Lily worsened. Lily's dependency on the opium had only increased. She grew painfully thin and rarely left her bedroom. She had lost all interest in her children and social life. During the night she endured strange and frightening dreams, waking often in tears. All Timothy could offer was soothing words and more Laudanum.

After a brutal heat wave through the last week of August, September was welcomed. The daytime temperatures rose into the low 80s but at night they dropped into the 40s. After several nights down into the 30s, the deep red leaves dotted the landscape. Slowly yellows and oranges were splashed here and there. The delightful smell of autumn was carried on the wind as the winter preparations began.

Emma went into labor late at night. Her three boys slept while she paced the floor in the kitchen and waited for Noah to return with Molly Andrews. With each painful contraction, she gripped the edge of the table and held her breath until is passed. She clenched her jaw to keep from crying out and waking her children.

At last, Molly arrived and aided by Noah's mother, she settled Emma into her bed. As the contractions grew stronger, she endured it well. Before the sun rose in the morning, Noah heard the cries from the bedroom. He waited patiently for his mother to carry another son from the bedroom. Emma had been certain this child would be a baby girl but he was confident that he knew better.

"Tis another son," his mother declared, as she held the swaddled bundle out to him.

"He does look as his brothers at their births," he declared proudly. "Tis a fine thing for his mother that he is not as stout," he chuckled.

"Emma did state, twas an undemanding birth."

"Might I speak with Emma?" he asked.

Mrs. Taylor opened the door a few inches and relayed Noah's request. Molly agreed and moved to the kitchen for a cup of tea.

"Tis a fine son," Noah told Emma and leaned to kiss her. He placed the infant in her arms and she smiled up at him.

"Mayhap you shall permit me a daughter with the next child."

"Mayhap I shall," he replied. "This boy shall be Lewis Joseph Taylor."

"Tis a fine name, husband," she told him and he kissed her again.

42

The first week of November a snowstorm delivered four feet of snow in two days. Fierce winds shook the trees and rattled the windows. As the temperature dropped, tiny pieces of ice fell with the snowflakes. Painfully they peppered any exposed skin, making travel unpleasant at best.

When the storm had finally passed to the north, a cloudless sky remained. Overnight the bitter air settled below zero and would remain there for the next week. Winter had come early and showed no sign of leaving again before spring.

The governess, Alice Ramsey spoke to Timothy about her concerns for Lily. Luke and Molly were both summoned to examine her. Luke observed the effects of the excessive consumption of alcohol and Laudanum. When Molly finished her assessment she announced that Lily was pregnant again.

"How shall she bear another child that she cannot attend to?" Timothy asked.

"She is too befuddled with the drink and opium," Luke stated. "If you shall give less of the tincture of opium and wine, she shall manage."

Molly only shook her hand and bid them farewell.

"If I shall lessen the Laudanum I do fear that she shall return to her capricious manner."

"Timothy, there has been no impulsive acts in near on two years now. Mayhap she has been healed in that time. End the dosing and mayhap you shall find that she has been cured at last," Luke suggested.

"Then there shall be no more of it. On the morrow I must depart for Portland and shant return afore a week has passed. I shall instruct the governess that she shall be dosed no more."

"I shall assess Lily in but a few days. Worry not as you do travel. Go with God," Luke told him and left the house.

Through the night Lily woke often and asked Timothy for more wine and Laudanum to aid her sleep. He refused and held her until her grumbling ceased. In the morning she begged him for a dose before he left but he continued to refuse it.

Timothy left Alice Ramsey to tend to Lily and the children, while the cook and housekeeper minded the household. Through the day Lily refused to eat and continued to demand the opium. Her withdrawals began the following day with symptoms like a simple head cold. Daily, her misery increased significantly.

Luke visited and advised the governess to provide a glass of mulled wine for Lily, only at bedtime. He instructed her to coax Lily into eating as well. Reluctantly, Alice agreed to comply.

Suffering flu-like symptoms, with vomiting, cramps and painfully aching muscles, Lily remained in bed and begged for the relief of the drug. After Timothy returned a week later, her misery continued. For another few days he waited as she agonized and pleaded for his help.

At last he could not endure watching her torture any longer. He relented and provided a dose of the Laudanum with a glass of wine. During the night he was awakened by Lily's first seizure. He lit the lamp and found her sweating profusely as another convulsion began. Hurriedly, he woke Alice and rode for Luke.

The following morning Lily was moved to Burghill House where Luke could watch her more closely. For weeks her misery continued and she begged for the opium. At last she began to improve physically. Her confusion diminished and she became quieter. Six weeks later Luke returned her to the Gage family home again and he pronounced her cured.

Timothy accepted Luke's decision and prayed that she would not relapse again. She began dressing appropriately again and ate with her family in the dining room. On Sunday morning she accompanied Timothy to church and occasionally even chatted with friends. At Burghill House she participated in the preparation of Sunday dinner and ate willingly. But she remained more reserved than she had been.

The first Sunday in February the family enjoyed an unseasonably warm day. As Mrs. Whitley carried in a tray of desserts, Laurent stood and tapped his knife against his wine goblet. He announced that Julia was expecting a fourth child. Wine glasses were raised and toasts made. Lily sat beside Julia at the table and she reached to hug her sincerely. Luke smiled and reached for Grace's hand.

In less than a week the winter weather returned with a vengeance as a storm blew inland from the ocean. Eddie and Faith remained home from school through most of the week. Alice Ramsey advised the children that their lessons would continue with her until the weather improved. But Lily ignored the instructions from the governess and took the children up to her bedroom.

Together Lily, Eddie, Faith, and Bon marched up into the attic. They dug through the boxes and trunks that were stored there. Piles of clothes, hats and other accessories were thrown down the stairs, where they piled up in the second floor hall. Giggling, they carried their treasures into the big bedroom and spent the morning playing dress-up.

The cook served pea soup, cornbread and smoked ham for lunch. Lily refused it and demanded that they be given cake and a hot chocolate drink instead. As the governess and cook protested, Lily lifted her fork and knife and began banging them against the table as she repeated her requested. With her encouragement Eddie, Faith, and Bon reached for their silverware and began hammering them and shouting as well.

Faith's knife slipped and shattered the china plate in front of her. Lily only laughed and continued her protest. The cook finally relented and the governess strode up the stairs in frustration. Cake and cups of hot chocolate were provided and the broken dish was removed. Lily leaned forward and bit into the cake leaving frosting on the tip of her nose. Giggling, the children ate theirs in the same manner. When the lunch was done they wiped their hands and faces on the white tablecloth and scurried up to the bedroom to play again.

When Timothy returned home in the evening, the governess complained about Lily's behavior. He tried to reason with Lily, but she insisted that the children had acted alone and promised that it would not happen again. Fearing what might come next he considered providing Laudanum for her. At last, he offered her a second glass of wine at dinner and dismissed the incident.

The next day they put on silk slippers and "skated" on the heavily polished floor of the great hall. When the cook announced a lunch of onion pie with chunks of bacon, Lily and the children went to the table as asked. Alice sat with them and corrected their manners through the meal.

Lily suggested that they return to their games in the hall as the governess proposed that Eddie and Faith work on their lessons. As the governess ordered the children to bring down their slates and primers, Lily stood and began clucking like a chicken. With her head bobbing and her arms flapping like wings, she circled the table. Quickly the children followed her, pretending to be chickens as well. Leading them, she waddled into the kitchen and demanded corn meal to feed her baby chicks.

"Mr. Gage, I can endure no more!" Alice announced as she greeted Timothy at the door early in the evening.

Timothy removed his hat and shrugged off his cloak. He stamped his boots and stepped into the parlor. Patiently, he listened as the governess related the events of the day. He shook his head slowly, poured a glass of whiskey and swallowed it.

"Tis naught I might do, Mrs. Ramsey," Timothy told her as he sat looking up at her.

"Your wife does hinder my work," she argued. "Mayhap you shall whip her soundly and correct her rightfully!" she snapped.

"You shall not instruct me regarding my household, woman!" he shouted as he rose from the chair. He glared down at her and she stepped back from him.

"I shall take my leave on the morrow," she stated and hurried out of the room.

43

Timothy sat on the bed beside Lily. She woke often with terrifying nightmares. He wiped away her tears and talked soothingly. With each passing day, he found it more difficult to calm her. Resignedly, he kissed her forehead and left the room.

When he returned, she was lying on her side clutching his pillow as she wept. He provided her a dose of the Laudanum. He waited until the opium took effect and she stilled again. She smiled and stared up at the canopy above the bed. Animatedly, she moved to kneel beside him and began kissing his face and neck. He offered a sip of wine and soon she calmed further. With the wine glass empty, he blew out the lamp. He fell asleep again as she rested her head on his chest and blissfully watched the clouds drift across the night sky.

In the morning he assured Mrs. Ramsey that Lily would no longer be a problem to her. Eddie and Faith would return to school and Lily would remain in her bedroom. She thanked him and agreed to stay.

Two months passed and the household remained calm and in order. With a slightly lower dose of the Laudanum, Lily was less vacant yet still controllable. In late April, Lily went into labor early in the afternoon. Mr. Dobbs rode for Molly, Timothy, and Grace.

Her labor progressed well and she complained little. Molly provided leaves for her to chew and teas to drink. Lily cooperated fully and Molly predicted that it would be a fast delivery. Shortly before midnight the tiny baby boy was delivered. Molly was shocked at how small he was as she held him in her hands. She became gravely concerned as the infant cried weakly.

The child passed early in the morning. Lily's dose of Laudanum was increased as she began grieving. As her lying-in continued, she soon forgot the boy and focused on the birds that lived in the tree outside her bedroom window.

Timothy named him Eugene Lloyd Gage and requested a simple, private burial in the family cemetery. Alone in the graveyard, he moved the last shovel full of dirt over the small grave. Penn Cooper would bring the stone marker and install it the following week.

Timothy dropped the shovel and sat on the low stone wall. He listened to the wind whispering through the trees. The late morning sun chased the shadows away from the three small graves that broke his heart. He considered his life with Lily and felt a heavy sensation in his chest. Alone in the quiet of the woods, he surrendered and the first tear rolled down his cheek.

44

In July, Mac returned for his week at home. The family put aside their problems for a day as they enjoyed the festive party behind Burghill House. Mac visited with family and friends as he waited for Annie to arrive. Late in the day he continued to watch the gate anxiously. As the sun slipped below the tree tops and the guests began leaving, he accepted that she would not be coming.

Mac sat beside the open window in his bedroom and watched the stars sparkling against the indigo sky. He pondered the promises he had exchanged with Annie in previous summers. He had been so sure that he would graduate and return to marry her. In her letters through the spring there had been no hint of a change in her thinking. He feared that her father had insisted that she begin courting someone else in his absence.

In a few days he would leave again for Cambridge to begin his year of medical lectures at Harvard Medical School. He had completed four years of college as Annie waited patiently for him. Uneasily, he realized for the first time that she might be required to marry before he could return again. Sadly, he moved to the bed but slept little through the night.

Mac presented his warm smile at the breakfast table in the morning but inside he felt miserable. He talked cheerfully with everyone but remained preoccupied with thoughts of Annie. His father suggested that he accompany him as he visited patients that day and was surprised when Mac declined his offer.

After breakfast Mac saddled a horse and rode to the Stanton home on Killock Road. He tied his horse to the post near the road. Disregarding social convention, he marched boldly to the front door and knocked loudly.

"Mackenzie Wallace," Mr. Stanton greeted him and extended his hand.

"Mr. Stanton, might we talk briefly?"

"Assuredly," he responded and opened the door wider. They moved to the parlor and Mr. Stanton closed the door. "What troubles you this day?"

"Sir, a celebration was hosted by Dr. and Mrs. Wallace yesterday, yet your family was not found among the revelers."

"Twas an invitation that Mrs. Wallace did extend and not a requirement," Mr. Stanton objected.

"Tis agreed, Sir. Yet I did take note of your absence. Might I query your reason as you did decline to attend?"

"Mr. Wallace, your words are most incongruous!"

"Sir, has your daughter, Annie begun courting?" Mac blurted out.

"She has not."

Mac exhaled loudly as relief washed over him. Mr. Stanton nodded and smiled as he stood to pour cordials. He offered one to Mac and sat again.

"Tis my daughter, Annie you do seek this morn."

Mac looked down, embarrassed as he spoke again. "In but a few days I must take leave. Tis a year of medical training yet to be done. I should like to ask your consent to court your daughter, when I do return in but a year."

"Tis rightful if Annie shall be found in agreement," Mr. Stanton declared as he opened the door to the parlor and called to her. Annie hurried into the room and stopped as she saw Mac. Her sleeves had been rolled up and soap suds dripped from her elbows. The front of her apron was stained with mashed pumpkin. A dusting of powdered chocolate was on her cheek and her hair was disheveled. Deeply embarrassed, she flushed bright red.

"Annie, Mr. Wallace shall think to court you," her father announced. Mac and Annie both stared at him. "Shall you consent to a courtship?"

"I-I, yes…" she stammered.

"Permit the man to speak," Mr. Stanton instructed her and gestured for her to sit across from Mac. Quietly he propped a chair against the parlor door to hold it open before he left the room.

"I did miss you greatly," Mac mumbled.

"Mother is sickly," Annie whispered and looked up at him. "Father would not permit that we attend a celebration as she does linger in her bed."

"Tis reasonable that he did state so."

"I am stupefied to find you in my father's house this day."

"I could not depart afore I did look upon you. Tis but one more year that I shall dwell in Cambridge and it shall all be done with," Mac declared. "Annie shall you await my return?"

"Tis not a thing you must ask of me, Mac Wallace. I did give my promise in years past and my heart shall not vary."

"Shall you accept this token of promise?" Mac asked as he opened his palm and revealed a delicate porcelain thimble decorated with violets and other flowers and a gold leaf border. "Twas purchased in Boston for you."

She dabbed at joyful tears as she touched it. "I shall," she uttered.

"Annie Stanton, I do mean to make you my wife when I return," he told her and flashed his charming smile.

"Shall I begin stitching a wedding quilt with my sisters?"

"Tis reasonable that you shall," he announced intrepidly. He looked to the doorway and leaned forward quickly to kiss her. With his heart thundering in his chest, he sat again, beaming at her.

Mr. Stanton allowed the young couple to sit and talk for nearly an hour before he advised Annie that she should return to her chores. He moved to the front door to permit them a private farewell. Mac kissed her again before she hurried back to the kitchen.

"As I do end my time in Cambridge I shall come again to talk of courting and a gift of land to you good Sir." Mac stated.

"Mr. Wallace, I have eleven children and seven are daughters. Tis little to offer in a dowry for Annie," he replied in earnest.

"I shall require no dowry afore I shall wed your beautiful daughter, Sir."

"Remain heedful in your travels," Mr. Stanton told him as he walked down the front steps. "Go with God."

Mac nodded and sprinted across the yard to his horse. Whistling happily, he rode back to Burghill House.

45

The first day of September, Julia gave birth to her fourth baby. The healthy boy was named Elmer James Morgan. Proudly, Laurent strode into the church the following Sunday with Reny, Rose, Bradford, and the new baby. Julia remained in her bed under Molly's watchful eye. When Laurent returned with the children, he brought Rev. Pender to repeat his sermon for his beloved wife. Julia smiled, delighted by his thoughtful efforts.

The week before Christmas, Noah's father suffered a heart attack as he tended the fire for the massive brick ovens. Noah rode for Luke Wallace as his workers moved the old man into the house. Before Mrs. Taylor was able to talk to him he had passed. His funeral would wait until the spring thaw. Noah moved his growing family from their small cottage to his father's house and his mother remained there with them.

Grace planned a small Christmas gathering as Noah mourned his father and Timothy struggled with Lily. The family celebrated the end of a difficult year as they welcomed the beginning of 1805.

Winter blended into spring and too soon the heat and humidity of July spread throughout the region. Mac returned, excited to begin his apprenticeship with his father. He strode through Burghill House greeting everyone before he carried his trunk up to his bedroom. He sat at the kitchen table and indulged Grace as she and Mrs. Whitley pushed food at him. As soon as Grace was distracted by the children for a moment, he slipped out the back door.

Holding his hat, Mac stood on the Stanton's doorstep. He rapped and waited nervously. Mrs. Stanton opened the door and welcomed him inside. Her family was seated at the table and she quickly offered Mac a place setting. Worried of offending the woman, he filled his plate and ate heartily, complimenting everything.

Through the meal Annie watched him and smiled. As he talked with her father about the growth of the town, he stole glimpses of her and fought to settle the butterflies in his stomach. When lunch was done, Mrs. Stanton and her daughters cleared away the dirty dishes while her brothers returned to their work on the family farm. Mr. Stanton led Mac into the parlor and closed the door.

"'Tis a fine thing that you did return," he announced as he reached to shake Mac's hand.

"I have come to declare my intentions toward your daughter, good Sir."

"How shall you do so afore you do move to court her?"

"Might you consent to the courtship?"

"I shall."

"Mr. Stanton, might you permit a union for Annie and me as fall does come upon us?"

"'Tis an unreasonably fleeting courtship you do suggest. There shall be talk of improprieties."

Mac sighed and thought of Annie. "I shall accept your consent to begin the courtship."

"As time does pass mayhap we shall talk of a marriage."

"Might I visit with Annie this day?"

"Annie does tend to her responsibilities. When the day is done you shall come again if you seek to talk with the girl."

"Thank you, Sir," Mac responded as he stood and extended his hand. Mr. Stanton walked him to the front door then returned to his work.

The courtship had begun at last and Mac quickly started his apprenticeship with Luke as well. Through the fall and winter Mac travelled often to sit with Annie in the family parlor. On Sundays, her father allowed one of her brother's to deliver her to Burghill House for the family dinner. Grace took her into the kitchen and welcomed her. Late in the day her brother returned to escort her home again.

46

During a snowstorm in January of 1806, Emma gave birth to a fifth baby boy. Noah named him Ephraim Jessup Taylor. Mrs. Taylor was delighted to have the distraction of a new baby in the house. Happy with another healthy son, Emma remained hopeful that the next baby would be a little girl.

As a late April snowstorm struck the area, the town waited for the coming of spring. The following Sunday the roads were passable again and the families travelled to church. Gathered at Burghill House after the service, the women worked busily in the kitchen. Emma, Julia, and Joanna carried the first of the serving dishes into the dining room and sat at the table. Grace hefted a tray of ham and turkey off the table and Molly brought out the tureen of pumpkin soup.

Grace hurried along the hallway as she chattered about plans to begin a new quilt for Mac and Annie. She heard the crash and turned as Molly dropped to the floor. Grace shouted for Luke and hurried back to Molly. She pushed the platter back on the kitchen table and knelt beside Molly where she lay.

Luke examined her and silently shook his head. Joseph and Mac moved her to the sitting room and placed her on a bed sheet there. Laurent rode for Jacob Frawley and Penn Cooper and they soon returned with a simple casket for her. The following morning she was moved back into the sitting room at Burghill House. Joanna sat beside the open coffin through the next two days.

Molly was laid to rest in the East Grantham Cemetery beside her late husband, Devin Andrews. Joanna struggled through crippling grief for the next month. Reluctantly, she agreed to attend a birth as the midwife in hopes it would make her feel a renewed purpose in her life again.

As the spring wore on, Mr. Stanton agreed to a marriage for Mac and Annie. Plans were begun for a church service followed by a reception in the meeting house. Annie suggested a July wedding and Mac readily agreed.

Through the year of his traineeship Mac had continually impressed Luke with his natural talent for healing. The week before the wedding, Luke announced that he was satisfied with Mac's skills and abilities. At last he would be able to call himself a physician. With a chaotic whirl of wedding plans going on around him, Mac remained calm and tended to his patients.

Dressed in the sable brown silk taffeta gown that her mother had worn on her wedding day, Annie stood beside Mac in front of the altar. Rev. Pender pronounced them husband and wife and Mac bent to kiss her cheek. Slowly the couple turned to face the congregation and the minister announced, "Dr. and Mrs. Mackenzie Wallace."

The reception continued late into the night before the bridal couple left for their first night as a married couple. Mac carried her into Botts' Tavern where a room had been rented. With her arms around his neck, he hurried up the stairs into a small room at the back of the building. Gently he lowered her onto the bed. He locked the door and began undressing quickly.

"Mac, shant you leave me to dress for our wedding night?" she asked, giggling.

"I shall not!" he responded with a chuckle. "Tis no reason to dress again and bid me remove it. Stand afore me and I shall aid as you do shed this enchanting gown."

"I do fear it shall be torn in your haste," she teased.

"Then I caution you stand quickly and tempt me no more," he declared as he grabbed her hands and tugged her forward.

With his large hands, he struggled to work the tiny pearl buttons. He winced as the first one popped off in his hand. Impatiently, he slipped several more through the silk loops before another dropped to the floor.

"Annie, shall you show compassion and permit me to tear this thing from you?" he pleaded.

"I cannot," she responded. "Tis the dress my mother did wear as she joined to my father."

"Surely Aunt Grace shall mend it," he implored as another button rolled on the floor.

Several more buttons worked loose and he wrestled with his growing impatience. At last, certain that the gown could be tugged over her slight hips with no more effort, he grabbed the sides and yanked it downward. A sharp tearing sound was followed by the pinging of a dozen tiny pearl buttons on the wood floor. Annie gasped and pulled away from him.

"Mackenzie, how could you think to do so?"

"Annie, forgive me," he apologized "It shall be mended well and your mother shall not be told."

She dropped to the floor and began collecting the buttons. He knelt beside her and worked furiously to untie and remove her corset. At last she stood again and the final layer of her undergarments was breeched. He stepped back and looked at her in amazement.

Tenderly, he placed her on the bed and began kissing her face. Passionately, his mouth covered hers and they felt the heat growing between them. Holding her in his arms, his lips trailed down her neck to her shoulders. She responded to his urgent desire and the dress was quickly forgotten.

47

Mac had promised a fine home of their own. But Annie understood when he moved her into Burghill House. With assurances that they would remain for only two years, she happily agreed. She found his family likable and they approved of her in return. A bond between Annie and Grace had already begun to flourish.

In December, Grace encouraged Joanna, Emma, Julia, and Annie to assist her with a spectacular Christmas Ball. Mac had been treating Lily through the fall and he hoped that she would be able to attend the great party and enjoy it too.

The first guests arrived before the musicians. Quickly, the last of the food was placed on the tables as Grace and Luke moved to the entryway. The house filled with revelers and the dining room was used for dancing as it had been since the year after Cherish passed.

Mac remained close to Lily through most of the evening. He was pleased that she was less detached as he had reduced her daily dose of Laudanum. He had added a unique botanical blend steeped in red wine and Lily had improved somewhat. But he still worried about the cautionary tales Luke and Timothy had related about her past behavior. He urged Timothy to draw his wife onto the dance floor. Even Joseph was coaxed out among the dancers with Millie Tanner on his arm.

At the end of the night, Grace was thrilled that she saw nothing but smiling faces as the last of the guests left the house. The last of the couples to leaves was Timothy who held Lily's hand as she walked at his side. Mac thanked Luke and Grace for the wonderful holiday party then scooped his beautiful bride up in his arms. She laughed as he marched up the stairs and carried her into their bedroom.

Luke and Joseph stoked the fireplaces and stoves then began extinguishing the candles that filled the chandeliers and the burning lamps. Luke poured a glass of wine for each of them and they settled in the sitting room. After the busy evening, a pleasant quiet fell over the house.

"I did note Millie Tanner on your arm much of the evening," Luke observed.

"It has been near on four years now since my Colleen did pass," Joseph commented.

"Tis fair and true. Shall you think to marry again?"

"I know not. Tis a fine thing that a man shall have a good woman to call his own. Mayhap in time I shall ponder a union."

"Tis good that you do smile with ease of late," Luke commented and sipped the last of his wine. "Sleep well," he declared as he stood and walked into the bedroom.

Grace lay on her side and appeared to be sleeping but he knew better. Quickly he undressed and slipped under the covers beside her. He kissed her neck and waited.

"Does he mean to wed Millie Tanner?"

Luke chuckled and brushed his lips against her neck again. "Yes, Mama, your wee one has found a lady."

"Why must you tease me so?" she asked.

"Grace, worry not. Joseph shall find his way," Luke whispered and gently turned her to face him. His lips pressed against hers and she felt his growing passion. She reached to touch his face and returned his heated kiss.

48

Joanna Pender accepted her role as midwife, believing that her work honored her mother's memory. Her thirteen year-old daughter, Margaretha, nicknamed Maggie, attended the births and assisted her. Proudly, she passed on the knowledge that traced back to her grandmother's aunt, Phoebe Bradford.

In July, 1807, Mac and Annie celebrated their first anniversary. At the family dinner the following Sunday, Mac proudly announced that a baby was due late in the fall. When the meal was done and the women moved to the kitchen, Grace stole quietly up the stairs to the attic.

The windows had been opened and a breeze blew through the space, but it remained unpleasantly warm. Grace dug through trunks and crates at the far end of the room. Sweating and dirty she found the item that she was seeking, buried under several elaborate gowns. Satisfied, she plodded back down to the first floor again.

"Annie," Grace called, wiping a smudge from her cheek. "This is the quilt I did stitch with Mac's mother, twenty-five years ago. On the day that Mac was delivered, Isannah did wrap him in it," Grace uttered as tears welled in her eyes.

Annie wiped away her own tears of joy as she accepted the special quilt. Grace hugged her tight and stepped into the vestibule to wash away the dusty remains from the attic. Quietly, Annie slipped into the sitting room. She took Mac's hand and led him out the front door. Hugging the quilt to her chest, she followed as he led her along the trail through the woods to the family cemetery.

Annie waited by the gate as Mac strode between the grave markers to his mother's stone. Under the warm July sun, he sat in the grass and talked to his mother of Annie and the coming of Isannah's second grandchild. He felt a deep sadness as he recalled that she had never known her first grandchild, Reny Luciern either. He forced a smile and reminded her of the special quilt that he had cherished as a child. Placidly he told her how Grace had gifted it to Annie for their baby.

At last the big man wiped his eyes and stood. He touched his lips to his palm and pressed it against the cold stone. "I do remember your smile well, Mama," he breathed. A beautiful yellow butterfly landed on the top of the gravestone and he chuckled as he moved back toward the cemetery gate. He grasped Annie's hand and walked slowly back to the trail with her.

In early November with a storm building over the Atlantic Ocean, the family finished Sunday dinner. Seated at the table, Annie felt her water break. Embarrassed, she stood and was escorted up the stairs by Grace and Joanna. She was quickly dressed in a simple white shift and made comfortable in the bed with a sheet of oil cloth beneath her.

Mac saddled his Morgan horse and rode to the Stanton farm to advise Annie's mother and sisters that her travails had begun. He returned and started pacing in the first floor hallway. Annie's mother, Ella and three of her sisters soon arrived and hurried up the stairs.

Into the night there were repeated trips down to the kitchen to steep teas and prepare concoctions that Joanna requested. Mac had ended his pacing and instead he rocked anxiously in the rocking chair. Luke sat at his desk talking of patients, in an attempt to distract Mac from his worrying. Joseph remained silent as unpleasant memories of Naomi and Colleen flooded his head. Millie Tanner sat beside him and touched his hand sympathetically.

At last, much of the house found a place to sleep as Annie's labor stalled and it became clear that the baby would not come quickly. Joanna dozed off and on, after encouraging Annie to sleep when she could.

As the sun rose in a garish pink sky, Joanna walked down to the kitchen to steep a special blend for Annie. While Mrs. Whitley prepared breakfast and strong coffee to serve, Joanna carried the tea pot up the stairs.

Annie accepted the tea and Joanna's assurances that the end of her labor was in sight. Less than an hour passed before her contractions strengthened again. The household woke and the men gathered in the dining room with the children. Mrs. Whitley served their breakfast and carried crocks of coffee and black tea up to the women attending to Annie.

Through the morning Grace watched over Annie while Joanna slept for a few hours. Joanna insisted that she be awakened if there was any sign of change in Annie's labor or her appearance. Near noon Grace woke her and asked that she assess Annie again.

Wind gusts tore at the trees, lashing them back and forth as the storm moved inland from the Atlantic. An icy rain pelted the windows. The fires throughout the house were built up to chase away the chill.

Mrs. Whitley served a thick rabbit stew as the men and children waited for lunch in the dining room. The tureen was passed and bowls were filled. She provided a basket of fresh warm bread and apple butter. The men talked and the children chattered noisily as they ate.

"Dr. Wallace," Grace called from the doorway as she entered the room. Both Luke and Mac looked up at her. "Dr. Mackenzie Wallace, tis your daughter," she announced as she held out the small bundle.

Mac stood, towering above Grace as he carefully lifted the baby from her arms. He marveled at the small head that barely filled his massive hand. Warily, he folded back the quilt and noted the thatch of black hair. The infant struggled and began to cry. Quickly, he tucked the quilt under her chin and passed her back to Grace.

"A healthy child?"

"The midwife is greatly pleased with her."

"What of Annie?" he asked and held his breath.

"She is well. Might you think to see her with your own eyes?"

"Yes," he replied urgently.

He followed Grace up the stairs. Near the door she stopped him and placed the new baby in the croak of his arm. He drew in a deep breath and stepped into the bedroom. Annie lay quietly with her eyes closed. Her mother and sisters were fussing over her but they stepped away as he entered.

"Annie," he whispered, worried he might wake her. She turned and smiled up at him.

"Shall you be dissatisfied with a daughter?" she asked.

"I shall not," he assured her. "She is a slight one, yet she does pull at my heart."

"Mayhap you shall provide a name for her," Annie prodded as he laid the baby in her arms.

"I do favor the moniker, Lydia Stanton Wallace."

"Tis a fine name for her," Annie responded as she stroked the baby's face with her finger.

"You must eat and rest now. Mrs. Whitley shall bring a bowl of stew."

Annie nodded and smiled as he walked proudly out of the room. Grace encouraged Annie's mother and sisters to go down to the dining room and eat. Joanna napped while Grace sat beside the bed and held the sleeping infant. Annie ate the stew to please her husband before she fell asleep.

49

Another year and a half passed before another baby was born in the family. In August of 1809 Emma delivered her sixth son, Peter Thomas Taylor. She was pleased to be blessed with another healthy boy but maintained the hope that she would eventually have a daughter as well.

Noah's brick business had grown. He looked forward to his boys working with him in the coming years. Their oldest son, Moses had stopped attending school at twelve years old and worked daily with his father. Ten year-old Jessup would finish one more year before he ended his education as well.

Emma remained in her bed for a month as her mother-in-law tended to the children and the household. Joanna suggested an additional two weeks but Emma insisted that there was too much work to be done and she could rest no more.

Luke had relinquished the care of Lily to Mac and under his care she had greatly improved. Along with the frequent doses of his special blend, he permitted a low dose of the Laudanum daily. Timothy was pleased that she had begun eating again and was no longer frighteningly thin. She could not tend to her children, but with the aid of the governess, Alice Ramsey they managed. Her days passed with few incidents.

Laurent Morgan expanded the livery as the town continued to grow and the demand increased with it. He purchased new horses and newer carriages. His wagoneers travelled throughout the region, making deliveries for the millinery and warehouse. Drivers were hired to provide coach service to Portland and Portsmouth. Monthly, one of his largest carriages travelled as far as Boston with passengers and mail.

While Julia worried over her children and tended to her home, Jacob Frawley managed the tavern. Daily, she prepared a pot of corn meal mush for breakfast, meat pies and stew for lunch and a single meal to be offered for supper from the kitchen of the tavern.

The widow, Kathleen Monahan, baked the bread and desserts for the tavern. Julia appreciated the help and knew that the young widow needed the coins to support her small children.

On a snowy morning in February of 1810, Annie gave birth to her second child. Mac welcomed a second daughter and named her Anna Elizabeth. He sat beside the bed with Lydia seated on his lap and Anna held in the crook of his arm.

"I could not be more pleased," he declared as he smiled at Annie. "Yet the next child shall be a son for me," he chuckled and kissed the babies forehead. Annie laughed and nodded sleepily.

50

After more than three years of courtship, Joseph finally proposed to Millie Tanner. A forty year-old widow with no living children, Millie had little to offer in the way of a dowry. She was a few years older than Joseph and she worried over him more than he liked. But he enjoyed her company and she was good to his daughters. He felt confident that the union would be good for both of them.

A small wedding ceremony was officiated over by Rev. Pender in the sitting room at Burghill House. Millie relinquished her job as seamstress at the millinery and her room above Botts' Tavern. As a hard worker and a naturally cheerful person, she was welcomed by the women of the house.

By June of 1810 when Teague Grenier celebrated his nineteenth birthday, he had been working at the millinery for four years already. On Teague's birthday a year earlier, Joseph had turned over control of the millinery and warehouse to him. Under his management the business was thriving. Shipments were flowing rapidly through the warehouse and fees incurred. Currently an expansion of the millinery was underway.

"What shall be done with the supplementary space aside the millinery?" Luke asked as he tasted the birthday cake.

"In cities to the south more foods are offered in markets alike the millinery. I do mean to make a common storehouse aside the millinery and bar the citizenry from pacing throughout the warehouse daily," Teague replied. "Wives shall be offered purchase of measured portions of dry goods and shant be forced to buy whole sacks and barrels any longer."

"Tis reasonable thinking," Luke replied.

More guests arrived for the birthday party and the noise level continued to rise. As Teague stood with his father and grandfather he noted several girls watching him and giggling. He shook his head and turned away, annoyed by their gushing.

"The young ladies do find you enchanting, Teague," Grace commented as she stopped in front of the men with a bowl of blackberry ice cream. She smiled as he rolled his eyes. She dipped the large spoon in and dropped a scoop onto Luke's plate.

"Gran, I have no time for such silliness," he responded as he pushed the cake aside and welcomed two scoops of the freshly made ice cream.

"Your handsome looks did pass from your father. You should be exceedingly proud," she chided. His dark hair was tied back from his remarkably attractive face. His dark brown eyes and strong masculine features charmed even the older ladies who visited the millinery. A closely trimmed beard covered his firm jaw line. With his moustache, only his full lower lip was exposed.

Grace did not add that his inherited looks had come from his handsome grandfather, Luke Wallace as well. Teague did not remember Phillip Grenier and would never think to question the similarity between Luke and Joseph if it was not pointed out to him.

As the musicians changed the tempo of the music from the slow, serene tunes to the Baroque dance music, young couples moved to the dance floor. Teague yielded quickly and approached the lovely Eliza Mayworth. When the dance was done he thanked her and moved on to Gennifer Wrathe. Through the afternoon the girls waited impatiently for a dance with the captivating Teague Grenier.

"I worry he shant be wed and there shall be no little ones if they do fawn so," Grace grumbled as she held Luke's arm.

"It shall come in good time," he replied and laughed. "Teague is a man of business. Tis rightful he shall attend to his work and the girls shall await him."

She frowned up at him and watched as Teague approached another of the young ladies waiting.

51

By late fall the Chernock's had finished the construction on the addition to the millinery. Teague quickly stocked the new area with the same foodstuffs that filled the storage area below the pantry at Burghill House. A smokehouse behind the store was filled with ham, bacon, fish, cheese and other goods that would be sold at his new "common storehouse" through the winter months. Most people were skeptical of such a venture but Teague remained confident that the business would succeed.

The first week of December a snowstorm dropped more than two feet of snow in a single day. A punishing north wind created blizzard conditions and the temperatures plummeted. It was an early start to a bitter winter with one storm after another.

The week before Christmas the roads were clear enough for local travel. Family, friends, and neighbors bundled against the cold and journeyed to Burghill House for the grand party. The celebration continued late into the night. Grace's oldest grandsons ruled over the dance floor as the young ladies competed for their attention. Luke smiled beside her as Teague Grenier, Reny Luciern, Eddie Gage, and Moses Taylor chose from the prettiest girls in town.

With a fine feast the family celebrated the arrival of 1811. When they had finished with dinner the women shared the kitchen chores. Grace noted that Emma was uncharacteristically tired and pale. Worriedly, she watched her while she prepared tea and portioned the desserts.

"Emma, are you well?" Grace asked quietly.

"Tis likely another child to come," Emma replied and forced a smile. "Mayhap I shall have a little girl of my own at last."

"Mayhap you shall ask that Joanna assess you this day."

"I shant burden Joanna. If there is to be a child she shant mind the delay of a week."

Grace nodded and pushed a cup across the table to her. Emma lowered her head and coughed.

"Mind that cough," Grace cautioned.

"You do worry so, Aunt Grace. A cup of linden tea and spoonful of honey shall remedy this quickly."

Grace returned her smile and lifted the tray of desserts for the men. She hurried along the hall to the sitting room and placed it on a table by the doors. They sat comfortably sipping their drinks and puffing on cigars and pipes. When she delivered the platter of treats, her grandsons rose quickly and moved toward it.

"Tis plenty for all," she assured. Contentedly, she climbed the stairs to look in on the babies in the nursery. She opened the door slowly and found fifteen year-old Azaria seated in the rocking chair. Annie's ten month-old baby, Anna slept serenely against Azaria's shoulder. Grace lifted a small quilt from the crib and draped it over the baby. She added another log to the Franklin stove in the corner and left quietly.

Only a few days later Moses Taylor came late at night to summon one of the doctors for his mother, Emma. Mac quickly volunteered to go. He saddled his horse and followed Moses back to the Taylor's home on River Road.

In a small bedroom on the second floor Emma was propped up on pillows in the bed. Mac listened to her cough. He placed his monaural stethoscope against her chest and tapped along her rib cage. Growing concerned, he moved it to her back and asked that she inhale deeply. He waited through her rattling coughs and listened again. Sadly, he noted the tiny droplets of blood on her bedding that had been expelled with her cough

"Tis the lung fever," he declared, as he diagnosed her pneumonia.

Mac prepared a thick mustard poultice and spread it over Emma's chest and covered it with a sheet of flannel. He fed her an onion syrup with lobelia for her cough and left her to sleep. In the parlor on the first floor he slept for a few hours then rose to check on Emma again.

As her condition worsened he removed the mustard plaster and applied an onion poultice. Again it was covered with flannel. She swallowed more of the onion syrup with a bit more lobelia added. He sent Moses for Luke and waited patiently near the bed.

Luke examined her carefully and agreed with Mac's diagnosis. Carefully, he listened as Mac described the treatment he had used. Luke nodded slowly.

"Tis no more that I might do," Luke stated. "You did serve her well. Watch over her now. Tis naught you might do but to bleed her."

"Emma is weak," Mac argued. "I cannot think to bleed her this day."

"If she shant be healed mayhap you shall in the coming hours."

Mac disagreed but did not argue with his father. Before Luke left he piled several heavy quilts over her, to sweat out her fever. When he had gone Mac removed all but one. He brought in a bowl filled with snow from outside. Quickly he packed the snow in small linen cloths and placed them on her forehead and against the bottom of her feet.

He continued the snow packs and linden tea but the fever could not be reduced. Another onion poultice was applied. The onion syrup had diminished the cough but he knew she was not improving.

Through the evening her fever spiked. She slipped into a dreamless sleep and did not wake again. Mac accepted that she had passed and gently tugged the bed cover up over her face. Mournfully he walked down to the kitchen where Noah and the boys sat around the breakfast table. Noah's mother, Mrs. Taylor stood near the hearth watching as Mac ducked to enter through the six foot high doorway.

"What of my wife?" Noah asked stoically.

"Tis no more I might do," Mac's deep voice rumbled as he spoke low.

"She is no more?" Noah pressed, struggling to keep his voice steady.

Mac slowly shook his head, looking down at the faces of Emma's six sons.

"How might I aid you?" Mac asked.

"Might you send the men from Botts' Tavern afore you shall go to your home?"

"I shall, Noah."

"Tell me of your fee and I shall make good the bill."

"Tis naught I should request of you. Emma is of my family as well. Speak not of coinage," Mac declared as he walked to the door. "Summon me if anything more might be required."

Mac stopped near the Botts' Livery and walked around to the scullery behind the tavern. He advised Jacob Frawley and Penn

159

Cooper that they would be needed at the home of Noah Taylor. Sorrowfully, he knocked at Laurent Morgan's door. He advised Julia that Emma had passed and accepted the dram of whiskey that Laurent offered.

Sadly, he rode on to the small house behind the church. He advised Joanna that Emma had passed on and asked that Rev. Pender go to speak with Noah and the boys. Michael agreed and Mac made his way back to Burghill House. In the kitchen, he sat with Grace and told her the tragic news. She hugged him and wept for her niece, Emma.

"Mac, might Noah permit that Emma be buried in the family cemetery with Mica and Abby?"

"I cannot know," he answered gently. "Mayhap Pa shall speak with him."

"Yes," Grace whispered. She wiped her eyes and struggled to collect herself.

"Afore my night shall be done, I will travel to talk with Timothy and Lily. I worry that Lily shall not accept the news well."

"Many thanks to you, Mackenzie. Go with God," Grace told him and kissed his cheek.

52

Mac sat with Timothy and Lily and related the news of Emma's passing. Lily wept, but handled the situation better than either man had anticipated. Mac waited until Lily slept soundly before he left the house. He reminded Timothy that he would be available through the night if Lily was in need.

At home for the night at last, Mac walked up the stairs quietly. He found Annie reading beside the hearth in their bedroom. She looked up as he entered the room. She stood and closed the book. Dressed in a delicate soft pink nightgown she stepped toward him. Slipping her arms around his waist, she rested her cheek against his chest.

"Emma did pass," he whispered and swallowed hard.

"Aunt Grace did tell it," Annie responded gently.

"I could not save her," he muttered. She felt the vibration as he spoke and she hugged him tighter.

"'Tis the decision of the Lord."

Mac bent to kiss the top of her head and hugged her in return. He stepped back and undressed as Annie climbed up onto the bed. He crawled in beside her and turned on his side facing her. His arm moved beneath her and he drew her against his body. Gently he pulled her up higher to kiss her soft lips. Lying with her in his arms he let go and cried for Emma. She felt him shiver and reached to interlace her fingers with his.

Eventually sleep drew his exhausted mind away and he slept. When she heard the change in his breathing, she wiggled out of his grasp and stepped down from the bed. She sat again by the fireplace and felt her heart tighten as she watched him sleep.

The winter dragged on with more snowstorms through the end of March. As the ground thawed in April, Emma was finally buried near her parents in the family cemetery. The family was surprised that Noah had agreed without a thought. After a simple graveyard service, family and friends travelled to the Taylor home. Noah's mother prepared food for the guests and neighbors brought in baskets as well.

Early in May, Grace removed the black crepe wreath from the front door and put it away in the attic again. She tucked her black mourning gowns in a trunk and drew out a pale lavender dress to be worn for church that morning. She tucked sprigs of lilacs in her hair.

When the morning service concluded, the family assembled at Burghill House. The meal was readied and served, but seven seats remained empty around the table. For the first time since Emma's death, Noah and their boys had not come for the Sunday dinner. Sorrowfully, Grace picked at the food on her plate but ate little.

Later in the evening, when the families had gone, Luke answered the front door and welcomed Noah inside. He showed him into the sitting room where Grace was seated. Noah accepted the small glass of rum that Luke offered and he removed his hat. He swallowed the drink and looked down at Grace.

"Aunt Grace, you did tend well to Emma after the deaths of her Mica and Abby Johnes. She did treasure you. You did train her up to be a fine wife to me and mother to my sons," he stopped and coughed, turning his hat over in his hands, uncomfortably.

"Noah, might you sit?" Grace urged as she watched him struggling.

"No, thank you, ma'am," he answered, shifting uneasily from one foot to the other. "I am to depart on the morrow."

"Where do you mean to go?"

"I shall travel to the State of Ohio with my cousin, Byron Taylor and his family. The brick furnace and house shall be left to my younger brother David. He shall tend to our mother."

"Noah, what of your children?" Grace cried as she jumped up from the chair.

"They shall accompany me."

"Peter is not yet two years! A mother is required for the smaller boys."

"Afore I shall go, the widow Charlotte Crane shall be made my wife. She has but one child and did agree to the journey as I bid that she marry me."

"Noah, how shall I know the children as they do grow? Twas but three months ago that Emma was taken from us. Must you take them from me as well?" Grace cried.

"Tis no affront to you, Aunt Grace. I cannot endure my life in this place without Emma. My sons do require their mother and I my wife, yet she lies in her grave. May you find it in your heart to forgive me as the years do pass."

Luke put his arm around Grace and whispered, "Tis rightful he must go. You shall pain him wrongfully if you do persist."

Grace choked back a sob and wiped her eyes. She looked up at Noah and forced a smile, "May you find only happiness and good will as you do travel. God go with you, Noah."

"Thank you," he replied softly and moved forward to hug her quickly. He shook Luke's hand and backed away, clearing his throat again. He nodded to them and hurried to the front door.

The door slammed closed and Grace dropped into her chair. Luke walked back to his desk and sat. "Tis dreadful that they shall take leave."

"Grace, he cannot bear to live with the ghost of Emma ever at his side. Charlotte Crane was a good wife and mother before the loss of her young husband, Wade and three small children. She shall love the boys and tend them well, as she does with her own baby, Cyrus. Worry not."

Grace stood and walked quietly into the bedroom. It was not a night for listening to reason. She felt the need for self-indulgent sobbing as she mourned the losses of too many loved ones. Luke understood and remained in the sitting room well after he was certain she had cried herself to sleep.

53

Through the spring the seventeen year-old cousins, Eddie Gage and Reny Luciern, both courted Rev. Murray's daughter, Norah. A pretty young woman, Norah had been sheltered in her parents' home and not permitted to accept suitors earlier. At eighteen, Norah had begun to worry that she might become a spinster. She enjoyed the attention they both gave to her, but favored Eddie Gage.

Eddie had plans to finish school and leave for college in Philadelphia. He would follow his father and the generations before him as lawyers. He felt confident he would eventually be a judge and would inherit the Gage family home. Eddie was very aware of his good looks. With blonde hair and beguiling blue eyes, he charmed the girls easily. Well aware of the way he affected young women, he had become a vain and cocky young man.

Reny Luciern had no aspirations of going on to college. He expected to remain in East Grantham and work with his family at the livery and tavern. His stepfather had instilled a love of hard work and loyalty toward family in him. With his father's fascinating golden brown eyes, dark hair, and remarkably good looks, he enchanted the girls as well. Yet he was far less aware of his natural attributes than Eddie was. Reny was a kindhearted and thoughtful young man with a devilish smile.

As the weather warmed in June, the First Parish Congregational Church of East Grantham held an ice cream social. A fiddler was seated on the front steps and he entertained the crowd with lively music. The young ladies gathered in the shade of the pines and giggled as they talked about the eligible young men. In kind, the young men mulled about in the afternoon sun and pretended not to notice the young women.

Large tables were set up in the shade provided by the building as the sun dropped lower into the sky. They were covered in cakes, pies, pastries, and iced tins of freshly made ice cream. Children ran and played, while the adults sat at on the tall benches that had been carried out from the church. Along the drive, several of the men gathered to discuss business and pass a jug of whiskey around.

A bonfire was built in front of the church with great stones that ringed the pile. Scrap wood from Somner Trail, rotted wood, and animal bones were dumped into the heap. Dry branches from fir trees were propped along the outside of the circle. As the sun slipped below the horizon, Jason Chernock splashed the wood with whale oil and ignited it. With a loud whoosh, the flames scaled the tall mound.

The heat of the day floated away with the clouds and the older people were the first to depart. Families with babies and small children soon gathered their carriage blankets and baskets and they left as well. Mac, Annie, Joseph, and Millie had volunteered to chaperone the young men and women who remained to enjoy the fire.

Venison sausage, cheese, bread, fruit compotes, and warm cakes were set out. Spiced apple cider and wine were provided as well. After he was bribed with a tankard of ale, the fiddler agreed to stay later into the evening.

Teague Grenier sat on one of the benches with three admirers seated close by. He ignored them and talked with friends. A makeshift dance floor was made from the roof of the paddock behind the church. It was set out on the grass and couples began dancing as the fiddler played on. Reluctantly, Teague reached for the hand of Mary Ward and followed several other couples.

Norah Murray sat on a bench with Eddie to her left and Reny to her right. She wanted to dance but felt uneasy about choosing one over the other publicly. When Eddie took her hand and pulled her up, she looked apologetically toward Reny and proceeded onto the dance floor. He whirled her around as her friends twirled nearby. She looked into Eddie's blue eyes and bit her lower lip as he held her fingertips and spun her.

Disappointed, Reny strode toward the table of food. He sampled the warm sausages and took a large slice of the chocolate cake. The fiddler began another lively tune and Eddie kept Norah out on the floor. Reny poured a glass of the wine and sipped as he moved to circle the fire. On the other side, Teague had returned to his bench. Celia Bailey walked to the table for a glass of wine and pastries for Teague. As she moved away, Reny dropped into her seat.

"Shant you dance, little cousin?" Teague asked.

"Eddie does dominate Norah's attention."

"Mayhap you shall interrupt him and ask that he forfeit her hand."

"If he shall not, then I shall be greatly discomfited."

"Mayhap it shall please Norah that you do ask," Teague encouraged.

Reluctantly, Reny stood and strode to the dance floor. He watched as the dancers moved in unison and laughed. Looking through the throng of people moving rapidly, he searched for the faces of Eddie and Norah. Several minutes passed and he walked along the far side of the platform. When he had circled it, he still saw no sign of either of them.

Frustrated and growing irritated, he walked back to his bench and sat alone there. He folded his arms and scowled at the dancers as he waited for Eddie and Norah to grow tired and return to their seats. He was determined to boldly ask her to step back onto the dance floor with him.

Fifteen year-old Azaria was seated between Joseph and Mac on a bench at the edge of the group. With her older brothers watching over her, none of the young men dared advance toward her. Dressed in an elegant white gown with primroses tucked into her dark hair, she sat frowning as she watched the other girls dancing freely.

"I shall be made a spinster if you shall not permit me liberty," Azaria complained to Joseph.

"Azaria, I have done naught to hinder the boys."

"Might I move to sit with Tabitha and Laurel Winthrop?"

"No, you shant," Joseph replied and stood to throw more wood on the fire. "Go to the bench where Teague does linger if it shall please you."

"Teague shall worry the boys further!" she argued. "None shall think to take my hand as he does scowl at them."

"Come, I shall caper among the dancers with you," he announced as he stood and offered his hand to her.

165

"Tease me not!" she grumbled, her dark blues eyes sparkling in the firelight.

"Tis no mockery, come," he grabbed her hand and pulled her forward. Grudgingly, she followed him onto the dance floor, trying to conceal her excited smile.

Reny sauntered back to the table and selected one of the pastries. Sarah Libbey offered him a cup of the spiced cider. He nodded, barely noticing her pretty face and warm smile. She filled a flint glass and brought it to him, staring up into his golden brown eyes. He thanked her politely and paced toward the fire again.

"Reny, take the hand of Miss Sarah Libbey and lead her to the center of the floor," Mac suggested and took another bite of cake from his plate.

"I do desire a waltz with Norah Murray. Yet Eddie shall deplete afore if he shant end their dance presently."

"Eddie is not found among the dancers," Mac stated as he watched the pirouettes. At 6'5" Mac was the tallest man there and could easily see over the heads of the young men spinning their partners. "Why should you think Eddie would be on the dance floor?"

"He did take Norah's hand and they did begin at this front edge some time ago."

Mac's face darkened and he ran around the far side of the church. He darted across the yard behind the building and found the opening to the path through the woods. Running as fast as he dared he headed to the right at the first fork on the trail. Approaching the end of the pathway he slowed. Ahead, the moon lit an open meadow and Norwich Pond beyond it.

He heard voices in the distance and moved slowly through the tall, dry grass. He steered around a cluster of blackberry bushes and saw two people seated on the ledge that hung out over the pond. Quietly he moved closer and circled around to come up behind them.

"Norah, you did speak your love for me," Eddie stated.

"Tis so."

"How shall you deny me if you hold a great love in your heart?"

"Eddie, I am a woman of virtue," she pleaded.

"If your heart be true it shant endanger your righteousness. I shant place you in peril, Norah."

Mac moved onto the rocks and climbed carefully up to the outcropping. He knelt there and watched the couple in silence.

"My love is true, yet I cannot, Eddie. It shall be my gift to you on our wedding night."

"Norah, I do crave you. It does pain me greatly that you shall deny me."

Mac leaned forward and pushed Eddie off into the water. Swiftly, he slipped an arm around Norah's waist and yanked her backward. He threw her over his shoulder and moved quickly back onto the path to the church. Near the end of the trail he lowered her to the ground again.

"Norah Murray, what should your father think of this thing? To permit Eddie Gage to spirit you away unchaperoned! You shall slide noiselessly along the side of the church and rejoin the revelry," he instructed as he glared down at her.

"Do you mean to tell it to Father?" she asked, as tears welled in her eyes.

"I shall not. Now go!"

Norah ran to the church building and Mac turned back to the path. He heard the sound of Eddie crashing through the brush along the trail. Quietly, he stepped aside and waited. When Eddie stepped off the path Mac grabbed him.

"Eiditch Gage, have you no morals?"

"Tis naught to you, Mac!"

"You shall ruin the girl with your wrongful acts. Tis no love for Norah within you. Take leave and dry your clothing afore you shall catch your death."

"Tend to your own, Dr. Wallace! You shant act a father to me," Eddie snapped as he stomped along the drive. He saddled his horse and rode down to the road as Mac returned to the bonfire.

Mac stopped at the table and poured a cup of wine. He watched as Reny led Norah toward the dance floor. He swallowed the drink in one big gulp. Watching Reny's face light up as he took Norah's hand and twirled her around, he shook his head.

54

With the expansion to the millinery well received, Teague began plans to improve the warehouse next. He had already implemented changes along the waterfront that made the area safer and more appealing to other businesses. As part of his scheme, he planned to draw more ships to the docks and justify the investment in new wharfs by the town.

Under his management, the revenue from both ventures had grown steadily. In early August he travelled to Boston to solicit two more seamstresses and a hat maker for the millinery. He visited shops and businesses throughout the city for ideas and inspiration to improve both the millinery and warehouse further.

While he cultivated new business relationships in and around Boston, the summer wore on. Eddie and Reny continued to court Norah under her father's watchful eye. The Rev. and Mrs. Murray had begun to favor Reny but Norah was clearly in love with Eddie. Confident that Eddie would soon propose marriage, Norah had begun stitching her trousseau. She recalled a magnificent Christmas Ball in the Gage family home years earlier and dreamed of living in the fine house.

August gave way to September with little notable change in the weather. A subtle breeze sighed through the trees under the warm afternoon sun. Mr. Dobbs walked up the drive beside the Gage home, leading the impressive Black Forest draft horse. The stallions black coat had been brushed to a fine sheen and the long white mane and tail hung loose. He stepped high as they approached the barn.

"Mr. Dobbs," Timothy called, as he stepped out the back door of the house. "'Tis a remarkable beast," he muttered as he stared up in awe at the massive size of it.

"That he is, Sir," Dobbs replied.

Timothy patted the glossy flank and took the leads. Mr. Dobbs hurried ahead to open the stable doors. The draft horse stepped forward on enormous hooves. Timothy walked into the garden behind the house and returned with a large carrot. He held it up and quickly pulled his fingers away, chuckling.

"A fantastic animal!" Timothy declared and stroked his muzzle with his open palm. "Might he be ridden?"

"I cannot say, Sir," Dobbs answered. "Mr. Morgan did only receive him this morn and knew little of his habits."

"Bring the milking stool. I do mean to trot along the trail with him."

"Into the wood, Sir?" Dobbs questioned. "He does seem outsized for the overgrown path."

"Tis a gentle nature about him," Timothy assured him as he stepped up onto the stool and mounted the horse.

Timothy made a loud chucking sound at the right side of his mouth and the stallion stepped forward again. He held the reins loosely as he passed along the side of the barn and down the slope beyond it to the woods. The horse hesitated at the opening to the path, but readily agreed and moved on.

Impressed by the comportment of the enormous animal, Timothy coaxed him along a bit faster. The horse raised his muzzle and shook his head but did not protest. Surefooted, he trotted forward between the close trees and bushes. Small animals scurried into the woods as he passed through.

The path widened and narrowed again as they neared Somner Trail. Timothy slowed to steer him around the branches hanging over the path. He circled Norwich Pond and picked up Somner Trail again on the backside. Too quickly, he was back on the trail headed home. Eagerly, he detoured onto a secondary trail that was seldom used. The beast slowed further, picking his way through the overgrowth.

The animal lifted his head high, sniffing the air and snorted forcefully. Before Timothy caught the scent of the dead animal ahead, the horse had already reacted. The great beast locked his legs with his ears up and eyes wide. Suddenly, birds flew out of the bushes, startling him further. His hind end dropped and he turned quickly to the left and right then reared up on his back legs. He bucked wildly and nickered in panic, trying to back up on the narrow path.

Timothy was thrown off and landed against the trunk of an ancient oak tree. Eventually, the horse turned sufficiently and crashed through a dense clump of cinnamon ferns and bayberry bushes. He thumped against several birch trees and bolted onto the main trail. Thundering along the trail in terror, he quickly broke out of the woods and up behind the barn.

Dobbs approached the horse warily and finally calmed him. He walked him into the stable and secured him there. Hurriedly, he saddled another horse and began searching for Timothy. A short time later he rode back to Botts' Livery to summon help. Hours later, Laurent Morgan found Timothy on the side trail. He retrieved a travois from his own barn and moved slowly back to the Gage family home with the broken body.

"It does appear that the fall did break his neck," Mac observed as he examined Timothy's remains. The body had been moved to the back of Jacob Frawley's new funeral coach. "Mercifully, he did not linger in agony."

"Where shall he be taken?" Jacob asked.

"When you've done with him, the casket shall be placed in the sitting room at Burghill House. Lily shant endure with it here in this house," Mac advised him.

Jacob and Penn Cooper secured the back doors of the glass sided wagon. They climbed onto the drivers' bench and rolled down the drive to the road.

Mac strode into the house and quickly found Luke sitting with Lily in the parlor. Rev. Pender sat at her side, patting her hand. Eddie returned from the school house with Faith and Bon. Luke and Michael moved to allow the girls to sit close to their mother. Lily stared straight ahead in silence as her daughters leaned close to her and wept.

Eddie rested against the doorframe and cleaned under his finger nails with a long hunting knife. He glanced up occasionally as the men spoke, but showed little interest in their conversation. He noted the glazed look in his mother's eyes and dropped his head again.

Grace arrived and enlisted the aid of Faith and Bon to pack a trunk for Lily. She insisted that Lily and the girls move to Burghill House at least until after the funeral was over. Worried for their mother, they quickly agreed. Eddie insisted that it would be best if he stayed at the Gage home instead. Reluctantly, Grace yielded.

Lily rode to Burghill House with Mac, while her daughters packed and readied to leave their home. Eddie carried their trunk down the stairs and out to the wagon. He reassured his grandmother, that all would be well and hugged her as she left the house. Grace remained apprehensive but she climbed up beside Luke without another word. As they proceeded from Killock Road onto Kings Wood, she heard her granddaughters sobbing behind her.

Dark settled over the Gage family home and Eddie lit several lamps. In the kitchen, Mrs. Quinn prepared a light supper for him. He ate in silence and marched up the stairs to his parents' bedroom. Leisurely, he opened drawers and cupboards, looking through the clothing and other items. He opened the chest where his mother's jewelry was stored and admired the colorful stones.

Late in the evening he walked quietly down the stairs again and stopped to listen. The only sound he heard was the steady tick-tock of the German tall case clock in the hall. Stealthily, he padded across the heavily polished parquet floor and into the kitchen. The fire in the hearth burned low and no light shone from under Mrs. Quinn's bedroom door.

He checked the locks on the back door and moved soundlessly through to the front entryway. Guardedly, he unlocked it and tripped the latch. Cagily, he slipped out into the chilly night air. The glow of the moon lit his way across the damp grass. He passed through a thicket of witch hazel bushes and yellow birch saplings. At the bottom of the slope, he skirted around a cockspur thorn bush and out onto Litchfield Road.

In the distance Eddie heard horses advancing and quickly ducked behind a scraggly pair of cat spruce trees. When they had passed, he stepped back out onto the road and hurried along. Spidery clouds crept across the indigo sky and hid the moon for several minutes. He slowed and waited until the clouds drifted to the north and the moonlight lit the area sufficiently again.

"Norah," he called as loud as he dared. Brashly, he cupped his hands at his temples and peered into the darkened room. In the deep shadows, he saw something move. He drew his knife from the sheath and tapped the blade against the glass. "Norah," he uttered again.

The window frame moaned as the sash inched upward. Norah knelt beside it and whispered, "Eiditch Gage, is your head befuddled? Father shall shoot you dead if he does find you at my window this night."

"Norah, my father did pass this day," he murmured sorrowfully.
"No, Eddie."
"Verily he did pass."
"Please accept my sincerest apologies."
"You've a good heart, Norah Murray."
"Eddie, we can speak no more. Father shall hear it."

"Come through the window, Norah," he whispered and touched her hand.

"I cannot," she protested weakly.

"Move hastily and your father shall not know of it. Norah, my heart does suffer so. Mother and my sisters did take leave of me and shall dwell at Burghill House. State that you shall not abandon me, as well, on the night of my father's death."

"Eddie, if father shall learn of it…"

"He shall not!" he hissed. "Norah, how shall you deny me as I do grieve so?"

She sighed, and stepped back from the window. In the dark room, she felt for her undergarments and began dressing quickly. At last she pulled a boiled wool cloak from the chest at the end of her bed and knelt at the window again. Eddie pushed it up further and helped her to climb through it, then closed it again as quietly as he could.

He hugged her briefly and took her hand as he led her back to his family's home. Swiftly, they stole in through the front door and Eddie locked it securely. Norah looked around at the great hall with the beautifully decorated ceiling. Eddie tugged at her arm and led her into the parlor.

"'Tis such a magnificent house," she sighed and looked toward the marble fireplace. Eddie smiled and poured two glasses of wine.

"If you were my wife, this would be my wedding gift unto you," he told her and passed one of the goblets to her.

"Eddie, are you sincere?" she asked, studying his sapphire blue eyes and captivating smile.

"I could not speak it if it were not truth, Norah. Could you be content to be titled Norah Gage?"

"Eddie, you shant say such a thing in jest."

"No, Norah, I would not. Mrs. Eiditch Gage," he breathed and moved to kiss her.

Entranced, she accepted his kiss and sipped the wine. Eddie stoked the fire, then tenderly removed her cloak.

"Shall there be children for us?" she asked, caught up in the fantasy he was spinning.

"Assuredly," he responded and kissed her again. "Many strong sons for me and daughters for you, dear Norah."

Her cheeks flushed and she sipped more of the wine. Eddie reached for the flagon and refilled her glass. She smiled sweetly and swallowed more of it.

"Shall I show you more of the house you shall dwell in?" he asked and drew her out into the hall. He escorted her through the dining room and into his father's library. Gently, he pressed a finger to her lips and pushed open the door to the kitchen. He looked toward Mrs. Quinn's bedroom door and saw no sign of light there.

Hastily, they left the kitchen and Eddie gestured toward the stairs. He climbed slowly, allowing time for her to admire the portraits hung along the wall that swept up to the second floor hall. As she sipped more of the wine, he began with the first door at the top of the staircase and showed her Bon's bedroom.

One by one he walked her through each room and encouraged her to look out at the view from the high windows. As they entered the largest and finest of the rooms at the far end, he took the empty glass from her hands.

"This shall be your bed chamber, Norah," he told her and opened his arms wide. "You shall slumber in this splendid bed and shall be given a glorious wardrobe to fill the armoires and trunks."

"Eddie, tis wondrous!" she exclaimed as she strode toward the dressing table. She lifted the silver handled comb and traced a finger along the filigree pattern.

"Tis none too fine for you, Norah," he breathed close to her neck. She moved to the window and looked out at the view of the town center. "By the light of day you shall see a delightful view of mountains far in the distance."

She stepped away from the window and stopped at the end of the bed. She touched the elaborately carved wood and sighed. "What of your mother, Eddie? As you do mean to make me your wife and gift me this remarkable room, where shall she reside?"

"Mother shall surely prefer to dwell within Burghill House with Faith and Bon."

"Eddie, forgive me!" she declared. "I do marvel at these fine things and indulge my head as you do grieve so. Tis horribly unkind of me."

"Tis reasonable, Norah," he spoke quietly. "Mayhap you shall offer comfort unto me in my time of great sorrow."

"Of course," she sympathized.

At his insistence, she sat in one of the silk covered Bergère chairs and waited as he hurried down to the parlor for the flagon of wine. He returned quickly and filled her goblet again. While she sipped, he opened a delicately carved chest in the far corner of the room. He pulled out a fern green gown of silk dupioni, pintucked into diamond shapes with tiny pearl accents and Alencon lace at the neck and sleeves.

"Tis the very dress my mother did wear on the day she wed my father. Mayhap you should like to costume yourself in it?" he suggested as he held it high.

"Eddie, tis such a lovely thing," she breathed, as she stood and walked toward him. "Shall your mother find it objectionable?"

"She would be greatly pleased. If you shall excuse me, I shall take leave as you do dress," he told her and kissed her quickly before he left the room.

Norah slipped her dress off and wiggled into the beautiful wedding gown. She hooked the clasps at the front of the bodice and turned to look into the mirror. Enchanted by the magnificence of the dress, she ran to the door and opened it. Eddie stood leaning against the balustrade.

"Tis the attire you should be draped in always," he told her and grinned.

She smiled and twirled in front of him. Without a word, he led her back into the bedroom and brushed his lips against her cheek.

"Might I wear such a dress on our wedding day?" she asked and giggled.

"Mayhap you shall wear this very gown," he declared.

"Oh, Eddie!" she cried and threw her arms around his neck. He kissed her passionately and she responded happily.

"I fear you shall mar it," he told her. "Let me aid you that it shant be spoilt before our wedding day."

Giggling, she sipped more of the wine and stepped toward him. He took the glass from her and gently began unhooking the closures on the bodice. He helped her out of the gown and carefully laid it out on a chair and reached to untie the front laces of her corset. He extinguished the lamp and removed his shirt. Standing near the windows, the moon cast a soft blue light over them.

Norah watched the movement of the muscles in his chest and upper arms. She felt a growing desire and as he kissed her she quickly responded. He slipped off his pants as she removed the last layers of her undergarments. Warmly, he led her to the big bed.

55

Early in the morning Eddie woke with Norah sleeping close beside him. He woke her gently and lit the lamp. "The morning light shall come soon. Dress quickly that I might see you home afore your father shall wake."

Norah hurried to collect her clothing. "Might you put out the light?" she asked, embarrassed as he sat on the bed watching her.

"I did know you, Norah. Tis no reason I shant delight in the sight of your body now."

"Tis a distressing thing," she pleaded.

"Norah, the sun shall rise and you shall be found missing," he chided. "Move to clothe yourself swiftly."

Reluctantly, she turned away from him and began layering the underclothes. She glanced up at Eddie and saw him watching her lewdly. She cringed and grabbed her dress. Eddie climbed slowly down from the bed and pulled on his pants without taking his eyes from her.

"Would that I might have time to take you again," he teased and tugged his shirt over his head. "You are made mine, Norah Murray. I shall know you when it does please me now."

"Eddie, twas wrongful that you did lay with me. We cannot do such things again afore we shall be wed," she disputed.

"Tis not so," he responded. His hand moved behind her neck and he kissed her roughly. "When a man does take a woman thusly, she shall be made his own. None other shall have her."

"Eddie, do you deem me to be lacking in virtue? Shall you think me ruined?" she implored.

"Certainly I do not, yet other men shall. Speak not of this night or you shall shame yourself and your family as well. Deny me not, Norah and I shant talk of it."

"Do you mean to make me your wife still?"

"Why should I think to marry if it shant be required of me? I shall enjoy you privately. Should that entitle you to public pronouncements?"

"I shall hear no more!" she cried and turned away.

"Turn not from me, Norah!" he snapped and spun her around to face him. "Refuse me and I shall disgrace you. None shall find you suitable for a respectable marriage. Heed my words, Norah."

Eddie led her down to the parlor and draped her cloak over her shoulders. Running through the bushes in the pre-dawn light she tripped several times and he dragged her painfully to her feet again. Behind her father's house he raised the window and boosted her up and into her bedroom.

"Norah," he grasped her bodice and pulled her face close to his. "Think not of time alone with Reny Luciern. You shall refuse him as he does come next. You are my woman alone, Norah," he whispered and pressed his mouth hard against hers.

As he stepped back, she lowered the window. She watched as he quickly disappeared into the trees behind the house as the sun inched toward the horizon. She sat on the edge of her bed and dropped her face into her hands. In the quiet of early morning she cried softly. Her head ached from the wine she had drunk the night before. But more painful was the agonizing ache in her chest.

Eddie ran back along Litchfield Road and up the path to the house. He walked in the front door and closed it softly. He locked it and hurried up the stairs. Carefully, he tucked the wedding dress back into the chest and closed it. He stripped away the soiled sheets and carried them back to his own bedroom. He shoved them under a pile of blankets in his trunk and flopped on the bed. As the bright yellow light spread upward from the horizon, Eddie slept soundly.

56

Timothy was buried near his parents and other members of the Gage family in the East Grantham Cemetery. Lily stood close to Mac, sobbing inconsolably, as Rev. Pender recited an inspiring prayer. Eddie stood between Faith and Bon as they wept.

"Now I know, in part, then I shall know fully, even as I am fully known. And now these three remain: faith, hope and love, but the greatest of these is love," Rev. Pender concluded and lowered his head.

Eddie realized that the service was nearing the end and he shook himself from distant thoughts. He had been contemplating his plans for college, and the apprenticeship with his father, which would not be possible now. He considered how soon he might assume ownership of his father's house and how much money he would inherit. If there was sufficient family money, he would not be required to work to support the family. Yet he did yearn for the prestige of being made a judge like his grandfather, Daniel Gage.

"Eddie!" Mac growled as he nudged his shoulder. "'Tis done and your mother shall require comfort from you this day. Eddie nodded, annoyed by Mac's brusque approach.

"I shall tend to my mother and sisters well," Eddie responded crossly.

"See that you do," Mac added. He stepped around Eddie and his sisters and walked slowly along the path with his arm around Lily.

"Mayhap she shall remain at Burghill House," Grace suggested.

"If it shall please her," Mac agreed.

Through the long afternoon, mourners visited the house with words of comfort and baskets of food. Lily heard little of their conversations. Grace and Luke spoke for her, offering thanks for the thoughtful gestures. Eddie, Faith, and Bon sat close by and nodded politely when they were addressed.

Mac provided a stronger brew of the herbal concoction that he steeped in wine for Lily. A small measure of the Laudanum was added and she was excused from any more of the social requirements. Mac walked her up the stairs with Grace close behind. Grace dressed her in a silk nightgown and put her to bed.

"Mama, how shall I endure without Timothy?" Lily asked in a low, sad voice.

"You shall persist for your children, Lily."

"I cannot," she whispered and closed her eyes.

As the weeks passed into months, Lily remained quiet but her state improved somewhat. Mac adjusted the brew to lower the dosage. Lily began attending family dinners again. She talked more and pondered questions of the future outloud.

"Shall you remain at Burghill House?" Grace asked gently, as they sat at the kitchen table peeling apples for apple butter.

"Tis rightful I shall return to my husband's home," Lily responded sorrowfully and cleared her throat. "Eddie, Faith, and Bon shall be wed and will fill the house with grandchildren for me. I shant be ever alone."

"Tis fair and true," Grace encouraged.

With the help of Luke and Joseph, the bills for the Gage household had been paid from Timothy's estate. Mr. Dobbs, Mrs. Quinn, and Mrs. Darby would remain to care for the home. Eddie was advised that he would not be given governing powers over the house or the financial resources of the family. He promptly decided to remain through the winter, then he would depart for Boston to attend college.

While Lily, Faith, and Bon remained at Burghill House, Eddie continued to spirit Norah into the house frequently at night. She tried to refuse him and protested vehemently on several occasions. Yet he made it clear to her that he would not hesitate to ruin her family name if she would not give in to him.

As Eddie had instructed her, she ended the courtship with Reny. Looking into his golden brown eyes she felt cruel sending him away. The relationship with Eddie had become nothing more than that of a man and his concubine. She knew he would not marry her and it was unlikely any other man would either.

November arrived with a frosty layer over the dead leaves outside the window. The harsh wind grabbed the trees and shook them fiercely. Norah stared out at a lonely squirrel scurrying along the fieldstone wall. It carried acorns to a storage place high in a tree just beyond the wood line. She wiped a tear from her cheek and hugged herself. In a few hours it would be dark and Eddie would come for her again. She shivered and realized that one way or another; this would be their last night of meeting like this.

She forced a smile and hurried into the kitchen to help her mother with supper. She was grateful for her mother's cheerful chatter that permitted her to sit quietly. When the bread was sliced she carried serving dishes to the table. With their heads bowed and hands joined Rev. Murray began to pray.

Supper was done and Norah stood at the slop sink washing dishes. She focused on the floral pattern that bordered the plates and refused to think of Eddie. When the kitchen was in order again she prepared a pot of tea and carried the tray into the small parlor. She poured cups for her parents and excused herself. Uneasily, she returned to her bedroom and sat by the window to wait.

Hours passed and she had fallen asleep in the chair before Eddie finally tapped at the window. She stood and tugged her cloak over her shoulders. In the frigid night air, the window sill squealed louder as she forced the sash up. She turned sideways and swung her legs out as Eddie lowered her to the ground. He reached to close the window again and grabbed her hand.

Without a word of greeting, he led her back to the house and up to his bedroom. After their first night together, he felt no need to romance her in the impressive bedroom that had belonged to his parents. He did not bother with wine and false promises. Callously, he walked into his bedroom, pulling her along behind him. He sat by the window and watched as she undressed. Her discomfort seemed to amuse him. When she stood naked before him with her arms covering herself, he laughed and stood to remove his shirt and trousers as well. He moved to the bed and extended his hand to her.

Norah climbed up onto the bed beside him and pulled the bedcovers up to her throat. She lay still and waited for him to move.

"Eddie, might we talk this night afore you shall begin it?"

"What troubles you so this night?" he asked as he trailed a finger along her jaw and down her neck.

"Tis a baby to come," she declared and turned to look at his face.

He sat up quickly and narrowed his eyes as he glared down at her. "No, Norah!"

"Tis so,"

"Did the midwife speak it?"

"She did not, yet I know tis a truth."

"How shall you correct this thing?" he demanded and swung his feet over the side of the bed.

"Tis naught I might do," she replied. "You shall be required to take me as your wife."

"Why should you think so?" he asked and laughed harshly.

"Eddie, it shall be known that you did father the child. It shant be my reputation alone that will be sullied. You shall be thought a scoundrel and a rascal!"

With a quick sweeping motion, he slapped her face. "You shant threaten me, Norah Murray!"

"Nor shall you strike a woman who is not your wife!" she shouted as she touched the hot spot on her cheek.

"Do not challenge me, woman! I am of the Gage family and you are but a lowly minister's daughter! If you shall think to speak of your bastard child, I shall deny that I did know you. There shall be unkind rumors that you did consort with the men of Wren's Tavern in the night. You shall be thought a filthy whore, Norah. What man shall have you then? Shall you threaten me further?"

"How might you treat me so cruelly?" she asked, as she clutched the quilt and cried. "Tis your child that does grow within me. If this be your son, shall you see him left to a dishonored life?"

"Tis no child I shall recognize, whatever it may be. Shall you spread your thighs for me this night afore I do put you out, my strumpet?"

"You shall not touch me again, Eddie Gage!" she asserted and moved to step down.

Eddie grabbed her arm and yanked her backward, striking her head against the headboard. "I shall do as I please with you! If tis my child you do hold within, then you shall not deny his father."

He held her back against the mattress and pressed his mouth hard against hers. His hand moved to her throat as he kissed her roughly and ignored her cries.

57

December loomed closer and Mr. Dobbs worried over the low woodpile. He had worked hard to make repairs, prepare for the coming of winter and chop the wood. Yet alone he had failed. At last approached Luke after the church service and confided his concerns. Luke assured him that it would be handled and sent him on his way.

Early the next morning Luke, Joseph, Mac, Teague, and Reny arrived with axes. Luke called Eddie outside to join them as they began splitting the logs and stacking them. Mr. Dobbs came out to assist them but Luke assured him they would manage the work while he tended to other chores.

"Did you aid Mr. Dobbs?" Luke asked Eddie when Dobbs had gone.

"'Tis not for me to assist the household help. He is well compensated for his work," Eddie snapped.

"In years past your father did work with Mr. Dobbs to ready the wood supply. Penn Cooper and others were solicited as well. How shall you expect the man to achieve it of his own."

"I am of the Gage family line and I shall not be thought a lowly handy man."

"'Tis wrongful thinking and it shall be your undoing," Luke told him and thrust a broad axe into his hands.

Mrs. Quinn served a feast for them early in the afternoon. They ate heartily and returned to finish the job. As the sun dropped behind the trees, Luke, Joseph, and Mac left to have supper with their families. Teague, Reny, and Eddie stayed to enjoy the turkey that Mrs. Quinn had prepared.

While she remained in the kitchen, washing dishes, they moved to the parlor. They ate thick wedges of apple pie and drank hot coffee as the fire warmed the room. Eddie rose and filled flint glasses with whiskey for each of them. He placed a jug on the small table and they sat talking late into the evening.

"Mayhap you shall think to court Celia Bailey, Teague," Eddie declared as they talked of future plans. "'Tis a fine thing that a man shall have a woman in his bed at night."

"I do prefer my work of late. As the business is built, I shall ready to take a wife. 'Tis not time for that yet," Teague reasoned.

"Shall you think to wed Norah Murray afore you depart for Boston?" Reny asked Eddie.

"I shall not! I will not be saddled with a woman such as Norah! 'Tis a respectable wife required of a man who shall be made a judge in years to come."

"How shall you state such a thing against Norah? She is a woman of virtue!" Reny shouted and jumped up from his chair.

"She does lift her skirts for men who shall ask it!" Eddie called back. Reny swung quickly, knocking Eddie over backward in his chair. Teague stood quickly and stepped between them.

"No more!" he yelled and pushed Reny back. "Why should you take issue with Eddie's words alone?"

"Tis a cruel thing that he did state!"

"Tis nothing cruel if it be the truth!" Eddie responded, as he stood and picked up the chair. He touched his fingers to his cheek bone and felt no blood. He turned toward the mirror above the mantle and noted the mark near his eye.

"Why should you think tis so of Norah?" Teague asked, as he remained between them.

"She did permit me liberties."

Reny pushed against Teague trying to get at Eddie again. Teague gripped his shoulder and shoved him roughly back against the tete-a-tete. "Do not rise, Reny!" Teague warned.

"Norah is ever at her mother's side. How shall you think to tell that she did lay with you?"

"In the night she does come to my door," Eddie announced. "We did sip wine and I did cede to her charms."

"Tis a fanciful tale," Teague declared and chuckled. "Yet tis wrongful to speak against a woman to puff up your braggary."

"Tis no braggary and no tall tales, Teague!" Eddie shouted.

"I see no truth in the story, Eddie. Let this be ended."

"You think it lies and swaggering?"

"I do," Teague replied.

"If it not be of truth then how shall Norah be with child?"

"Tis verity?" Teague pressed.

"Verily she did declare it to me a fortnight ago!"

"Do you mean to wed her?"

"If I shant think to court such a woman any longer, why should you think I would make her my wife?"

"Eddie, if it be your child tis your burden."

"She did submit willingly unto me, Teague! How should I think she would not lay with other men equally? I cannot sully my family name with such doings."

"And what of the child?"

"I know not of the father. Mayhap tis mine and mayhap tis that of another. Should you think to wed a woman lacking virtue who shall birth a child not of your blood?"

Teague turned away and Eddie sat in his chair again. He poured more of the whiskey and sipped it.

"You are a scoundrel Eiditch Gage!" Reny shouted. "If the child might be of you tis rightful that you shall wed her. If she shant be married afore the child is known she will be ruined. What respectable man shall have her when the child has come?"

"Tis naught to me," Eddie replied and waved a hand in the air. "That she shall be thought a harlot is not of my doing. The girl did offer her pantaloons of her own."

Reny looked up at Teague and back to Eddie. "You are a contemptible man, lacking of morals. What a lawyer you shall be!"

Reny stood and stomped out the front door, slamming it behind him.

"Shall you make to correct this thing?" Teague asked.

"No, I shall not," Eddie answered. "Speak of this afore the family and it shall only bring a swifter ruin for Norah. Mayhap her father shall remove her to the orphan asylum and the child shall be done with. If none do speak of it, mayhap she shall find a lowly husband yet."

Teague shook his head in disgust and strode to the front door. "Tis wrongful, Eiditch. May your conscience suffer for your misdeeds."

58

Teague raised his collar and jammed his hands into the pockets of his coat. He hurried around the side of the house to the barn for his horse. The door was ajar and Reny's horse was gone. Teague secured his saddle and mounted the mare. Slowly he rode on toward Burghill House. He considered stopping at Botts' Livery to speak with Reny but only continued on.

Reny led his horse through the dusting of snow beside the church. He tied the animal to the post under the shelter of the paddock. He buttoned his cloak and dashed across the yard to the pine trees on the other side. Picking his way through the dense boughs, he crossed through to the area behind Rev. Murray's home.

Standing in the cold, watching his breath as he exhaled, Reny considered the situation. He reached to tap lightly at the glass and waited. Impatiently, he rapped a bit harder and stamped his cold feet. Reaching to rap again, he heard the squeal of the wood as the sash inched upward. Norah's face appeared in the window and he inhaled quickly.

"Norah," he spoke and a plume of warm air rose between them.

"Reny," she cried and reached for the quilt from her bed.

"We must speak this night," he insisted.

"Reny, my father shall not approve. Take leave afore he does hear you. Come on the morrow and I shall receive you."

"No, Norah," he responded firmly. "Dress quickly and come out. I did talk with Eddie and I shant hear you refuse this request."

Norah turned away and closed the window. She felt an incredible sadness deep inside. Eddie had shared the story of her fall and Reny had come to demand liberties as well. She feared who might make demands of her next. As he stood waiting, she dressed and lifted the window. She knew she could not yield again. No matter what the threats might be she would refuse Reny. In the morning she would claim to be sick and stay behind when her mother left. Before her father returned late in the day, she would be miles away. It would be better if they missed her than for them to be told of the truth.

With Reny's help, she climbed out and he closed the window. He took her arm and led her back to the paddock. Inside, they were out of the wind and the horses provided some warmth.

"Norah, you must speak naught but the truth."

"Reny, I cannot acquiesce," she protested.

"Eddie did tell great tales and did state tis verity in his words. Did you go to him in the night and lay with him?"

"He did lure me from my window in the manner you did utilize."

"Are you with child?" he asked bluntly.

She covered her face and turned away from him. Angrily, he grabbed her sleeve and spun her around.

"You did turn me away and ended our courtship! Yet twas rightful in your eyes that you lift your skirt for Eiditch Gage?" he shouted.

"Eddie did require it of me. I did not will it!"

Reny pushed passed her and stepped outside. Shivering in the cold, he stamped his feet and looked up at the clear sky, dotted with a thousand sparkling stars. He approached his horse and stopped. He could not ride away and leave her alone and crying in the cold night.

Furiously, he walked back inside. She stood with her back to the corner, sobbing. He watched her and recalled Eddie's words. Her cries tugged at his heart, crushing the anger that had welled inside him.

"Do you love him?" he demanded.

"I do not. He did take me unwillingly. I pray you shall not demand it of me as well. On the morrow I do mean to depart from this place."

Reny moved toward her and realized that she was trembling in the cold as well. He pulled her close and drew her under the warmth of his cloak.

"Norah, how shall you think to take leave unaccompanied?" he inhaled the scent of floral perfume in her hair and felt her body pressing against him. His anger faded quickly and he held her close. "Shall you consent to be my wife?" he uttered impulsively.

"Reny, no," she argued, pulling away from him. "'Tis my burden to contend with."

"Norah, surely you do know that I love you. As you did end the courtship, it pained me greatly. I cannot see you go from this place. None shall know of your dalliance with my cousin."

"Eddie shall know it. He shant see me happy with you."

"Worry not of Eddie. Consent and your burdens shall be made mine. On the morrow you shall be my wife and shant depart from your parents. Your virtue shall be protected. I shant require that you do lay with me, Norah."

"Reny, you have no house of yourn. How shall we survive the coming winter?"

"Norah, state that you shall accept and fear not."

"I shall," she responded at last.

Reny hugged her tighter and lifted her chin to kiss her tenderly. "Return to the home of your father where you shall find warmth. I shant worry over a sickly wife," he chuckled. With their fingers interlaced they ran back to the house and he helped her through the window again.

59

Reny walked through the kitchen where his mother was preparing apple muffins for breakfast. He inhaled the warm scents of the coffee, apples, and cornmeal bubbling in the pot. Stepping outside in the cold morning air, he buttoned his coat and pulled on gloves.

"Pa!" he called to his stepfather as he neared the livery. "Might I speak?"

His younger brother, Bradford was mucking out the stalls. The boy perked up his ears, eager to hear what Reny wanted to talk about.

"Tell it as you do tend to your work," Laurent instructed.

"Mayhap I shall voice it in seclusion?" Reny asked and nodded toward Bradford.

Laurent chuckled and strolled out away from the livery. "Mind your chores!" he called back when Bradford started to follow. Frowning, the boy returned to the stall where he had been working. "What troubles you so?"

"Pa, this day I mean to wed Norah Murray. Shall you give consent?"

"Why should you think to do so?" he asked, eyeing Reny warily.

"I do love her deeply."

"'Tis more," Laurent observed. He folded his arms and leaned back against the far corner of the house.

"Shall you require that I tell it?"

"If 'tis not in you to reveal the truth, 'tis likely you do walk a wrongful path."

Reny inhaled the frigid air and considered the situation. He would need Laurent's help to resolve his problem and the aid would not be granted until he told him the whole story. He looked down at his boots and sighed, exhaling a small cloud of white.

"'Tis a child to come."

"Have you relinquished all morals?" Laurent demanded as he cocked his head and clenched his jaw.

"Pa, tis not of my doing. Eddie did compel her. She did tell it and he shant marry her for the child. Norah shall be ruined and her family shamed."

"Tis not for you to correct this thing," Laurent uttered and felt a twinge of guilt, remembering Albert.

"I do feel a great love for her."

Laurent nodded slowly and considered Reny's revelation. He touched his hand to his chin and rubbed the closely trimmed beard that covered his jaw. "Where shall you reside with a wife and child?" he asked patiently.

"I know not."

"You have yet to begin your apprenticeship with the Chernocks. How shall you think to provide for your own?"

"I cannot fail her. Might you think to aid me as I shall undertake this?"

"Tend to your chores and come to me when breakfast is done," Laurent stated and walked away.

When Reny and his younger brothers had finished their early morning jobs they hurried inside to the warmth of the fire. Julia ladled out bowls of steaming cornmeal mush and drizzled molasses over it. She placed the basket of warm muffins in the center and a dish of apple butter next to it. She poured hot coffee and sat next to Laurent at the table. He recited a prayer and they began eating.

Julia bundled her children, Rose, Bradford, and Elmer against the cold and sent them out for their walk to the school house. She draped her worn cloak over her shoulders and hurried to the tavern to prepare breakfast there. Laurent and Reny remained in the warm kitchen, sipping coffee near the hearth.

"Shall you rethink this scheme?" Laurent urged.

"I cannot."

"Tis unlawful that she did conceive afore a marriage. If you shall wed the girl there will be fines required of you." Reny looked down at his cup as he listened. "Afore your mother did wed to Ross Eastman, the millinery and warehouse were deeded to Joseph Grenier. Twas told that it should be returned unto you in years to come. Tis reasonable that you shall require it of him now."

"If he shall grant it, I shall work hard."

"What of Eddie Gage, Reny? Shall he protest that you mean to call his child your own?"

"He did refuse her! How shall he think to intercede as I do make her my wife?"

"That he did deny her does not end it with surety. If it shall be a healthy son and he does think to lay claim, her reputation shall yet be ruined. It shall bring scandal to your family, as well as her own."

"He cannot..." Reny faltered as he conceded that Eddie was a mean spirited man.

"A man shall shelter his own and keep them safe from harm. If you mean to make Norah your wife I shant oppose it. Yet tis not for me to right this thing. This day you shall confront Eddie with your plot and gain his accord."

"Pa, I did strike him as we argued. He shant find me favorable this day."

"Tis your botch, Reny. You are a man and shall mend this of your own."

"Might you accompany me?"

"I shall not! I did not take umbrage with him."

"I did tell Norah that we would marry this morn."

"Reny, tis not the play of a child you do purport! You shant think to be joined with her and believe that others shall make a way. To spare the good reverend, I shall tell the tale unto him privately. Yet I shall not aid you with Eddie."

"Might we reside in this house when the marriage is done?"

"You shall speak unto your mother and spill the truth. If she does consent, then I will agree."

"How shall I tell it to mama?" Reny asked and dropped his head onto the table.

"You'll find no sympathy in me, Reny. I shant see you hide such a scheme from your mother. You shall go to her with candor and trust in her heart," Laurent told him as he stood and threw another log on the fire. He refilled their cups and took another muffin from the basket.

"Pa, tis my desire to make Norah my wife and live out my life with her. I ask no more."

Laurent laughed heartily and popped the muffin into his mouth. "Your mother did make a gift of life to you. You shant be granted a blessed life, you shall go forth and earn it daily."

"Do you think me a fool as I mean to do this thing?"

"I do not. Yet you do embark upon a snaky path. Go to Eddie Gage and correct your gaffe. When you have done with him, you shall talk with Teague Grenier of the millinery and warehouse. I shall caution you, do not think to call upon Norah this day. Permit me to temper the state of Rev. Murray afore you shall beg his blessing."

"Yes, Sir," Reny replied, dazed by his new realization.

60

Laurent climbed the stairs of the church and opened one of the wide front doors. He stepped inside and whispered a simple prayer. "Rev. Murray?" he shouted, his deep voice echoing through the great open space.

At the back of the room he heard muffled footsteps as the minister hurried down the stairs from the upper chamber. The door at the corner of the room opened and he appeared, smiling cheerfully.

"Good morn, Brother Morgan!" he called jovially.

"Good morn, Rev. Murray," Laurent responded, and stepped forward with his hand extended. "Might I trouble you for your time this morn?"

"Assuredly, how might I serve you?"

"Mayhap we shall speak away from the church?"

"'Tis naught that shant be seen by the eyes of the Lord. Come up to sit by the stove," he motioned for Laurent to follow as he climbed the stairs to the sunny room above.

Seated at the massive table, Laurent accepted a cup of black tea. He cleared his throat and looked into the minister's eyes. "Rev. Murray, Reny did come before me greatly troubled this morn. Late into the night he did talk with his cousin, Eiditch Gage. Twas a confession made by Eddie of dalliances with your Norah."

"'Tis untrue!" Tomas protested.

Laurent held up his hand and continued to speak. "Eddie did compel your Norah to permit liberties. Twas not of her willful doing. Yet tis done and a child is to come. A scoundrel, Eddie shall not make right what he has done. Reny does love her deeply and shall make good for cousin's failings."

Rev. Murray sat staring into the far corner in stunned silence. Laurent waited patiently, drinking the tea as he waited for the minister to speak.

"Norah's mother did raise her up with virtue and righteousness," he uttered dejectedly.

"Your daughter is yet a fine woman and I shall be happy that she shall become my daughter as well. As Reny and Norah are joined, none shall know of this misfortune. Your family name shall be spared, good Sir."

"Why should Reny think to undertake such a thing? Shant Eiditch Gage be charged for his unlawful acts and be made to correct himself?"

"Tis rightful that you should summon Sheriff Mitchell and see that Eddie be arrested. Yet Norah shall be placed in chains as well. When the child is come, Norah shall be bound to the whipping post and given her lashes. The truth shall be made fodder for gossip and the child shall be known as a bastard. You and your wife would be disgraced. Shall Eddie's retribution make the consequence rightful?"

"It shall not," Tomas mumbled.

"Reny is a good man and shall make a fine husband for your daughter. The child shall be safeguarded and none shall know of the verity."

"How might I recompense your son as he does salvage the life of my only child?"

"Grant your blessing of the marriage and Reny shall be fully contented."

"I shall," he responded. "Yet I do fear this shall break my dear wife's heart."

"And mayhap my Julia as well. Yet tis done. For the betterment of all, the marriage must be made quickly."

"On the morrow it shall be done within this church," Rev. Murray declared and raised his cup to drink.

61

Reny knocked at the front door of the Gage home and waited anxiously. The housekeeper opened the door and ushered him into the library. Eddie sat behind the massive desk on the far side of the room with a book open in front of him. He looked up and scowled at Reny.

"Have you come to end me now?" Eddie asked, smirking. Reny noted Eddie's black eye, certainly the result of the punch he had received the night before.

"No," Reny told him and sat at the table. Eddie stood and strutted around the desk toward Reny. He sat across from him and rested one shoe against the polished surface.

"Mayhap you shall make your apology," Eddie provoked.

"Eddie, I do mean to make Norah my wife."

"'Tis folly!" Eddie laughed. "How shall you undertake such a woman?"

"Shall you oppose our union?"

"Why should I worry over such doings?"

"You did state that Norah's child is of you."

"'Twas the whiskey that did speak. 'Tis no child of mine! Mayhap you shall search the docks and discover the father among the drunken sailors there."

"Eddie, Norah is a woman of virtue," Reny protested, fighting hard to control his temper.

"If you mean to be her gull, I shant argue it."

"Might you make claim if it might be a fine son?" Reny asked and clenched his fists under the table.

"You have my word there shall be no such assertion, whatever it might be."

"Thanks unto you," Reny stood to leave, not trusting himself to remain.

"Shant you extend an invitation unto me?" Eddie prodded.

"Eiditch, might you attend the marriage between Norah and me?" Reny asked with his jaw tightened and his fists crammed into his pockets.

"I should be overjoyed to be in attendance," Eddie responded pompously. "May you enjoy a wondrous future with your delightful bride. You shall find her warmth in the night to be a stimulating thing."

"Good day," was all Reny could manage before he hurried out of the room.

Enraged by Eddie's manner and his statements, Reny marched through the kitchen and out into the cold again. He mounted his horse and rode at a full gallop along Kings Wood Road.

62

Over lunch at Botts' Tavern, Reny confided his plans. Teague listened without commenting, as he drank a tankard of ale and ordered second one. He looked down at the meat pie and took another bite as Reny talked.

"Eddie does act the fool and you shall move to make amends for his misdeeds," Teague commented at last.

"Teague, I do love Norah. I do not act to correct this thing for Eddie. Tis for Norah that I shall do it."

"Reny, tis not a child of your blood. Summon the sheriff and permit the law to right it."

"I cannot see Norah punished so."

"She did know him," Teague reminded him and swallowed more of the ale. "How shall you wed a tainted woman who did lay with another man?"

"Teague, twas not of her own doing," Reny argued.

"Reny, I caution you against this scheme."

"I cannot depart from her now. I did make a promise of marriage unto her."

"You shall join with a woman who does hold the child of another man within her, Reny. As you shall act wrongly, you do think to ask that I forfeit the millinery and warehouse unto you? I did strive to enlarge them and you do think it fair to reap the benefit of my work? Do you believe this to be a reasonable thing, Reny?" Teague asked angrily.

"How shall I sustain a wife and child?"

"Reny, I shant compensate you for the misfortune you do invite. No, I will not surrender it! Twas my labor that did increase the trade and I shant see it grabbed from me."

"Teague, how shall you refuse it?"

"If you mean to have it, then you shall earn it!" Teague demanded and slammed his fist against the table. "You shall rise with the sun and strike out for the warehouse all but Sunday morn. When you have done there, you shall travel to the millinery and see to the drudgery of it and the common storehouse beyond. Shall you agree?"

Reny looked at Teague and considered his words carefully. "If I shall relent, then you will forfeit it?"

"Reny, I will not reward your idiocy as you do this thing! I shall hand-off nothing, but shall apportion it reasonably when it has been duly earned. Shall you agree?"

"Tis a fair bargain," Reny responded and reached to shake Teague's hand.

As Teague left the tavern, Reny walked through the kitchen and out the back door. With flurries in the air, he rushed along the path to the house. Inside he found his mother standing at the table, scraping the seeds and pulp out from a large pumpkin. She looked up and smiled when he entered.

"Have you no work to be done?" she asked cheerfully.

"Mama, I mean to be wed on the morrow."

She stopped scraping the pulp from the pumpkin and stared at him disbelievingly. "How shall you think to marry? Who shall be your bride?" she stammered fretfully.

"Norah Murray shall be made my wife."

"Reny, she did end the courtship. How shall you believe such things?"

"Mama, tis a child to come," he spoke gently and looked into her eyes.

"No, Reny, you could not..." she faded and dropped heavily into the chair behind her.

"Eiditch did compel her, Mama. Twas not of her willful doing. If I shant move to join to Norah she shall be ruined. I do love her greatly and cannot bear to see her destroyed."

"Reny, tis to Eiditch to correct his transgressions. Rev. Murray shall summon the sheriff. I cannot have you thought an immoral man!"

"Mama, tis done. Eddie shant confess his sins. Norah alone shall suffer. Tis wrongful that she shall be pained so. My heart cannot bear it! On the morrow I shall speak my vows unto her. Teague shall impart gainful labors unto me. Mama, none shall know the verity of the fathering."

"'Tis mania!" she stood and grabbed for the large serving spoon again. Frantically, she gouged into the pumpkin.

"Mama, all shall be well. Norah is a good woman and she shall be made a fine wife."

"Reny, a respectable woman could not do so! You shall break my heart if you do this thing!"

"I beseech you do not forbid it," Reny implored as he watched her face.

"Speak no more of it," she demanded and hurried out of the room.

63

The snowfall gradually increased through the afternoon. A harsh wind blew in from the north, making the cold day unbearable. Bundled in her warmest cloak, Julia snugged the hood tight as she hurried along the path to the waiting carriage. She wiped at her cheeks with her gloved hand and scurried faster. Penn Cooper snapped the reins and the buggy lurched forward.

Desperately she banged the cast iron knocker and swallowed hard. Joanna opened the door and ushered her into the kitchen to warm by the fire. Worried by Julia's demeanor, she poured hot tea and sat with her.

"What troubles you, dear?" she asked.

"Joanna, my mind is muddled and I shant sort it."

"Talk of it," Joanna encouraged.

"My Reny does mean to wed Norah Murray on the morrow! A child is to come and tis no blood of my son!" she shrieked. "He did tell tis the issue of Eiditch Gage!"

"Why should Reny think to marry the girl if it be Eddie's child?" Joanna demanded.

"Eddie did rebuff the girl. Reny aims to save her reputation and shall be ruined for his efforts."

"'Tis wrongful! If the child be Eddie's, he shall be joined with her and shall confess unto the sheriff!" Joanna declared as she stood and stoked the fire.

"Joanna, Reny did state that Eddie does deny her. Reny does think her a woman of virtue yet tis not so. What woman shall conceive of one man and marry another?" she cried. "I cannot see him stain the name of his father!"

"Tis an emmanogogue brew, spoken of in my Grandmother's Aunt Phoebe's journal. If it shant be belated, mayhap it shall rid her of the wrongful child."

"Might you blend the brew that I shall end this thing?" Julia pleaded.

Quietly, Joanna opened a cupboard and began sorting through containers of herbs, leaves, barks, roots and tinctures. Nearly an hour passed before she finished with the process. She draped cheesecloth over the opening of a short, round crock and poured a deep purple liquid into it. She wrinkled her nose at the bitter scent and pushed a stopper into the neck of it.

"Tis a foul thing," she commented as she pushed the small jug across the table to Julia. She held up a little pouch made of burlap, attached to a thong of leather. "Add the drink to a strong wine and bid her drink four times each day for four days. The sachet must be worn round her neck night and day as well. Together they shall bring on her bleeding and the child shall be done with."

Joanna filled their cups with hot chocolate as a somber mood fell over the room. She stood and left the room, returning quickly with a small, milk glass jar. She handed it to Julia. "Place a bit of the Angelica Root above your doors afore she shall enter," she instructed.

"Many thanks unto you, Joanna. I cannot see my son left in ruins for the misdeeds of another. If he shall not relent, then the marriage shall be on the morrow. Tis naught I might do but to make done with the illegal child."

Joanna nodded sympathetically and sipped from her cup.

64

Julia walked angrily behind her husband as they entered the church. She and Laurent had argued late into the night. Tired of the discussion, he had finally forbidden her to object to the marriage or voice further objections outside their bedroom. Dutifully, she dressed in her best gown and proceeded to the church with her husband and son.

Norah waited beside her father in front of the altar. She stared down at the floor, her eyes puffy from a long night of tears. Her mother sat on the front pew sobbing into her handkerchief. Julia touched Aileen's shoulder sympathetically, and moved to sit on the pew across the aisle. The mood of a funeral hung in the chilly air.

The mothers wept through the ceremony as the fathers stood stoically with the young couple. Reny and Norah exchanged their vows as they studied the weathered grain of the old wood floor. Rev. Murray pronounced them man and wife and Reny brushed his lips against her cheek then stepped back again.

Rev. Murray stepped toward Aileen and took her hand. He urged her to stand and led her toward the front doors. Reny shook Laurent's hand and hurried on to his first day of work with Teague. Awkwardly, Julia walked beside Norah as they followed Laurent out to his carriage. They rode in silence to the house behind the tavern.

"Were you trained properly to tend to a home?" Julia asked as she began preparing the supper to be served at the tavern that evening.

"Yes, Ma'am," Norah responded politely. "My mother did guide me well."

"'Tis sewing to be done as I make a stew. Daily, the house shall be tended and meals readied for the tavern as well. You shant be a lay about under this roof," Julia chastised.

"No, Ma'am, I shant," Norah responded and moved to the end of the table where a sewing basket and several articles of clothing had been laid out.

Julia ignored Norah as they worked only a few feet apart. She hung the pot of stew on the hook above the fire and left the room. Norah wiped away a tear and worked the needle through the fabric. She could only hope that her new mother-in-law would warm to her when Reny returned.

Over the hiss and bubble from the hearth she heard the ticking of the mantle clock in the parlor. The chime startled her as it sounded in the quiet house. She counted the three bells and sighed, accepting that it would be long hours before Reny might come for supper. She missed her mother already and wished she could go home. Her poor mother had begun to cry inconsolably as soon as her father told her of the baby. Norah brushed away another tear and continued repairing a worn quilt.

When Reny finally returned in the evening, his family had already finished with supper. Norah stood at the slop sink scrubbing pots as he entered the kitchen. His mother ladled out a bowlful of stew and thumped it down on the table in front of him. She sliced a thick piece of bread and poured a tankard of beer for him. She scowled at him and glanced toward Norah. Without a word, she stomped out of the room.

Reny heard a sound and turned to look at Norah. She remained with her back to him, leaning against the sink. He strode toward her and stopped as he saw the apron pressed firmly against her mouth to muffle her cries. Shaken, he drew her into his arms and held her tight. She trembled with her face against his chest, trying to stop her sobbing.

"Shhhh," he whispered soothingly. Gently he walked her to the table and filled a teacup with whiskey for her. "Sip and it shall make you sleep."

"Your mother did provide a drink that shall permit me to slumber," she told him and lifted her apron to her face again.

"Shall you have me sleep in the room with Elmer and Bradford this night?" he asked. "I shant object if it does bring you comfort."

"I did vow afore God that I shall be a proper wife unto you, Reny. I shant bid you go."

As a quiet settled over the house, Reny stood in the hall and waited while Norah dressed in her nightgown. She opened the door to him and hurried to the bed. Quickly, she climbed up into it and pulled the quilt up under her chin. Reny threw another log into the stove and put out the lamp. He quickly undressed and readied for bed.

"Norah, I shant balk if you do bid me go," he declared.

"I shall not rebuff you, Reny," she told him and closed her eyes.

He stretched out on the bed and covered himself. Slowly he turned on his side and moved close to the edge. Norah rolled over and widened the gap between them. Lying in the dark, she felt fresh tears on her cheek. She swallowed hard and tried to remain quiet.

"Norah," Reny whispered. "Might I offer you comfort alone?"

When she did not respond, he moved to lay close behind her. He draped a protective arm over her and brushed her hair back from her face. Gently, he wiped away her tears and kissed her face. Still facing away from him, she relaxed in his arms and rested her head back against him. Gradually, her tears ended and she slipped into a deep sleep.

65

In the morning, when Reny had gone again, Norah sat at the kitchen table with the butter churn between her knees. Julia carried a glass of wine out from the pantry and placed it on the table in front of Norah. She nodded and gestured for her drink it.

"Tis a bitter blend," Norah mumbled. "I desire no more of it."

"You must," Julia demanded and pushed it closer to her.

Norah looked up into Julia's eyes and drew in a sharp breath. "Shall it rid me of this wrongful child?"

"Why should you think such a thing?" Julia cried, stunned by the question.

"Tis a distasteful blend that you do offer unto me. Tis no reasoning but to rid of this wicked babe."

Julia sat slowly and looked at Norah's sad face. It was obvious the woman had cried a great deal over the past few days. She did not act like a girl who had successfully tricked a man into marriage. She appeared to be a dreadfully unhappy girl.

"Do you love my son?" Julia asked, speaking softly as she watched Norah.

"He is a fine man with a kind heart. I did love Eiditch Gage, yet he did forsake me and pained me greatly. My love for him is done. In time, I shall come to love Reny well and shall be a dutiful wife to him."

"What of the child? Shall you cherish the progeny of Eiditch within you?"

"I cannot. I did mean to depart and leave the infant within the orphan asylum. If it shall be born with the look of him, I shant look upon it without weeping."

"Drink the infusion. Tis an emmenogogue to rid you of the child," Julia told her eagerly. She hurried back into the pantry and returned with the sachet. "Hang this about your neck and it shall heighten the power of the brew. Tis Angelica root above the doors as well. We shall be done with this child," Julia assured her.

"Mrs. Morgan, shall you bid me take leave from your house?"

"Tis the babe alone I shant abide. If you shall ensure my son a happy life then you shall have no battle with me."

Norah forced a smile and reached for the glass.

Late in the morning Joanna visited to assess Norah. When she was done, she left Norah to dress and returned to the kitchen.

"Do you believe the child is in peril?" Julia asked.

"Tis a healthy mother," Joanna observed. "As you dose her next with the amalgam it must be blended with an exceedingly strong coffee and not the wine. You shall add a nip of this," she told Julia as she passed a small silk pouch to her. Julia opened it and inhaled at the earthy smell of the ground bark.

Julia nodded and poured tea into three cups. When Norah entered the room Julia related Joanna's suggestion and reassured her again.

"Norah, you might upsurge the drink. Swallow quickly and you shall bear up with the bite of it. Eat bread or cake to foil the rising from your stomach as it shall work within."

The process continued for another four days. Julia blended the poison in stronger doses and stirred it into the robust coffee. Growing more desperate, Norah swallowed it and shivered at the horrible taste. She quickly bit into a slice of bread and fought the nausea each time she drank it. Julia remained confident that it would work and Norah trusted in her belief.

The following morning Norah rose in the morning, feeling queasy and uncomfortable. When she sat up in bed she felt a sharp pain in her lower back. She swung her legs over the side of the bed and another stabbing pain jabbed at her. As she stepped down to the floor, her stomach clenched and she began vomiting. Immediately she realized that the majority of the fluid that had come up was blood.

"Julia!" she cried and her stomach cramped fiercely again. The copper taste in her mouth brought on another wave of retching. "Julia!"

Reny opened the door, staring in horror when he saw the bright red splashed on the front of her white gown. "Mama!" he shouted toward the kitchen.

Julia rushed into the room and stopped abruptly. Norah's face was a ghastly shade of gray and the vomiting continued.

"Go for Dr. Wallace!" Julia demanded and Reny ran for the back door. "Rose, bring the wash tub and linens!" Julia called as she moved toward Norah.

Rose hurried into the room with the tin tub and Julia helped Norah to kneel beside it. Rose hurried back to the kitchen for a pitcher of water and porcelain basin. Julia sat on the floor beside Norah and quickly braided her hair back. She patted a cold wet cloth over her face and spoke soothingly.

Norah had begun sweating and her face flushed feverishly. Yet the unnerving gray tone of her skin remained. Her fingernails darkened to blue and she shivered with chills. She sat still for several minutes then arched her back, crying out in agony and rocked forward to retch again.

No more than fifteen minutes passed before Mac strode into the room. He ordered Reny out of the room and shut the door. Mac examined her quickly and prepared a list of items he would need from the apothecary. Reny left quickly to retrieve the medications and other items. Swiftly, he returned and Mac began preparing an unusual blend for Norah.

The vomiting had stopped at last, but she continued to experience dry heaves. Her stomach cramped painfully and the lower back pain had worsened. Julia and Rose worked to clean the room while Mac worried over Norah. With the cup of brew cooling on the bedside table, he helped her to stand. Quickly he realized that Norah was bleeding heavily.

"Are you with child?" Mac asked gently and studied her face.

Norah looked to Julia and she nodded. "Yes," Norah breathed.

"Summon the midwife," Mac barked as he lifted Norah and placed her on the oil cloth draped over the counterpane on the bed.

Through the morning Mac forced Norah to drink several cups of the mélange. Joanna arrived and assessed her before speaking privately with Mac. She confirmed that there had been a miscarriage, but made no mention of the emmanogogue she had provided.

Late into the night Mac remained, watching over Norah. He provided remedies to treat her fever and continued dosing her with the healing brew as well. Norah lay still in the bed, crying out occasionally when her stomach cramped excruciatingly and the muscles in her back tightened again.

The Rev. and Mrs. Murray were roused during the night when Mac began to worry whether Norah would survive the night. Tomas sat in a chair beside the bed praying while Aileen settled next to Norah on the bed. She wiped her daughter's face with the cold cloth and smoothed her hair.

Reny wandered in and out of the room in a strange dreamlike state. He knew the baby had been lost and accepted it well. But he could not grasp the idea that he might lose Norah. He loved her deeply and had only just begun his life with her. From the doorway he watched her sleeping restlessly with her parents sitting close. He felt a hand on his shoulder and turned to find Laurent there.

"Come," he uttered. "Let her be and eat the food your mother did cook."

Grudgingly, Reny followed Laurent back to the kitchen. He sat and stared at the bright orange flames as they crawled along the fat log. Julia placed a meat pie and tankard in front of him and encouraged him to eat. Outside the blustery wind gusted and freezing rain pattered against the glass. The sky had lightened from the inky blue to a murky gray. In an hour the sun would rise over the horizon, cloaked by leaden clouds.

In the early morning hours Mac left to sleep a few hours at Burghill House. He lay with the warmth of Annie's body against his. His hand rested on her full, round belly, feeling the baby kicking inside. He closed his eyes and slept.

Only two hours later he awoke with a start in the empty bed. He rose and dressed in the shadowy room. The December storm raged outside, shaking the trees fiercely. The sun had risen above the horizon but could not be seen.

"Mac?" Annie spoke softly as she entered the room.

"I must depart," he told her as he pulled on his boots.

"Where do you mean to go this stormy morn?"

"Norah Murray... Norah Luciern is gravely ill. I fear she shall pass this day if she did not expire already. Tis my duty," he told her and touched his lips to hers.

"I shall pray for her."

"Pray exceedingly," he kissed her forehead and left.

66

Mac walked his horse into the livery and removed the saddle. As he moved through the accumulation of fresh snow, he heard the sleigh approaching on the drive. He waited as Rev. Pender halted and moved to help his wife down. He tipped his hat to Mac and turned his team in a wide arc. Quickly, he disappeared again onto Kings Wood Road.

"Might we speak, midwife?" Mac addressed her forcefully.

"Such formal address, Mac?" Joanna questioned.

Mac nodded toward the livery and she followed him inside. He closed the door against the wind and leaned back against the wall. With his arms folded across his broad chest, he frowned down at Joanna.

"Do you know of the poison that Norah did take up?" Mac prompted.

Joanna's eyes darted left and right as she felt the panic rising inside. Butterflies danced in her stomach and she took a quick step back from him.

"Why should you think it so?" she probed.

"Twas a thought in my head as I did wake this morn. Joanna, if I am to preserve her life you must confess your transgression."

Joanna cringed and looked up from the floor again. "Twas an emmanogue to bring on her bleeding."

"To rid her of her child?" he barked angrily. "How should you think to do so? Tis your purpose to bring forth the living. Have you a muddled head?"

"Mac, the child is of an illegal conception. Tis unwanted by the mother and shant be accepted by the father."

"Who does know of this effort?"

"Tis but Julia, Norah and me."

"Tis a hangable offence!" he roared. "How shall your husband and children go on when you are done with so?"

"Do you mean to summon the sheriff?"

"I shall not if Norah be saved. You shall counter the poison and correct it."

Joanna nodded slowly and held out a silk pouch and small bottle. "Tis my fervent hope that this shall cure her."

"Talk of this thing to Julia Morgan and bind her tongue. If tis made known to Laurent or Reny, they shall not forgive such a misdeed," he told her and reached for the items she held out.

He left Joanna behind and hurried across the drive to the house. In the kitchen he accepted a hot cup of coffee from Julia and walked through to the bedroom. Reny slept in a chair just inside the bedroom door. Rev. Murray sat close to the lamp, reading aloud from the Bible while Aileen dozed beside her daughter.

"I must examine Norah," Mac declared. The low rumble of his voice woke Reny and Aileen both, but Norah slept on. Her color had faded to a deathly pale but the signs of the burning fever remained in her face. Worriedly, Aileen touched Norah's forehead and sighed as she pulled away from her.

Joanna entered the room as Tomas, Aileen, and Reny left. She closed the door and stepped back to wait for Mac to finish his examination.

"How shall the herbs be utilized?" he demanded.

"Pour the elixir into the dish and thicken it with the herbs. Force her to swallow it all and follow with a cup of mulled wine. Her breathing shall slow and her heart shall beat feebly yet she shall not pass. Tis an invocation that you shall speak."

"I shall have naught to do with such charms and bewitching, woman!" he boomed furiously. "Undertake the deed!" he told her and left, slamming the door behind him. In the kitchen he asked for a glass of strong wine for Norah and accepted another cup of hot coffee.

When he returned at last, Joanna sat beside the bed, holding Norah's hand. She accepted the goblet of wine from him and coaxed Norah to sip it. Norah's eyes fluttered open and she looked from Joanna to Mac.

"Is the child gone?" she whispered hoarsely.

"Tis so," Joanna responded gently.

A trace of a smile touched Norah's lips and she closed her eyes again. She quickly slipped into a deep sleep. Mac studied her and looked to Joanna.

"When might she progress?" he asked.

"If she shall survive, watch for her to wake in the night."

"If you mean to take leave, I shall look for you again when evening does come," he advised her.

"I shall come, Dr. Wallace," she stated flatly and turned to leave.

"Midwife," he cautioned. "Do not depart afore you shall warn Julia well. And pray arduously through the day as your very lives shall depend upon Norah's endurance."

She shut the door and returned to the kitchen. Rev. Murray had gone but Aileen sat at the table with Julia. The poor woman looked terrified as she sipped the tea and worried about her daughter. She was terrified to sleep for fear she might wake to find that Norah had passed.

Joanna drew Julia into one of the bedrooms and told her about the conversation with Mac. Julia slipped into a chair and dropped her face into her hands.

"Joanna, what have we done?" Julia choked back a sob. "The child is done with and Norah might pass as well. My family shall never absolve me of this thing. We shall be hung on the gallows for it."

"Julia, no!" Joanna snapped. "It shall not be! Speak naught of it. The cure shall correct her. Mac is a great healer and he shall salvage her yet. Put away your tears and stop this frenzy."

Julia drew in a sharp breath and shook her hands, struggling to calm herself again. She stood and paced rapidly. Quickly she dipped a hand into the pitcher beside the bed and touched her face. She pressed a linen cloth to her eyes and whispered a prayer.

"Comfort Aileen this day and I shall come again when supper is done," Joanna said and hugged her quickly.

Joanna passed through the kitchen with a few words of reassurance for Aileen. She scurried across the drive to the livery to ask Laurent for a ride home.

67

Late in the evening Joanna returned to the crowded house. Norah remained in the bedroom with her parents, husband, and

Mac watching over her. Together, Joanna and Julia walked into the room and looked around.

"Might I assess her?" Joanna asked gently. Mac nodded and herded everyone out to the parlor. Joanna opened her bag and pulled out a small leather pouch filled with mint leaves. She crushed a small handful and held them close to Norah's face. Norah turned her head to the side and her eyes fluttered. Joanna added penny royal to her palm and rubbed harder under Norah's nose.

"No," Norah breathed and brushed at Joanna's hand.

"Shall you wake that I might examine you?" Joanna asked calmly.

Norah bobbed her head slowly as her eyes drifted closed again. Joanna lifted the quilt from her and gave a quick appraisal. She covered her again and stepped back up to the head of the bed. Norah's color had improved from the ghastly white to a washed out roseate. Her fever had broken at last. Joanna sighed in relief that the worst of it appeared to have passed.

"Dr. Wallace," Joanna called from the doorway and he quickly strode into the room.

"Has she upturned?" he asked gruffly, as he closed the door.

"Her look has bettered and the fever is gone. The bleeding has slowed further as well."

Mac examined Norah and placed the stethoscope to her chest. "The beat of her heart is bolstered," he observed. "Mayhap she shall endure," he commented and smiled warmly.

"Tis a fine thing that your smile does return."

"You shant charm me with praise, Joanna. I am still cross with you and Julia. Twas a wrongful thing. Speak no more of it and pray it shall escape my head."

"I shall," she replied and walked out to the parlor to share the good news.

Mac assured the families that Norah had improved greatly. With his sureties the Rev. and Mrs. Murray left Norah to sleep and returned to their home. Reny slept in his clothes beside Norah that night. The exhausted family rested well at last.

The next morning Norah awoke and asked for breakfast. Encouraged by her appetite, Julia prepared a bowl of cornmeal mush boiled in milk. She topped it with honey and carried it in with a pot of weak tea. Reny sat beside Norah and spoon-fed her until she announced she was done.

"I did fear you would be lost," Reny told her. She looked at the haunted look in his eyes and the dark circles from his lack of sleep.

"All shall be well," she encouraged him.

"Did the midwife tell the child is gone from you?"

"She did speak it."

"Shall you endure the loss?"

"Reny, I cannot profess to be aggrieved. The child was not favored."

"Norah, twas your child," he murmured, stunned by her words. "Mayhap you shall repose. I believe your head may be jumbled from the great fever you did suffer."

"Mayhap," she replied.

"Mama shall watch over you this day as I do toil at the warehouse," he told her, studying her face as he stepped down from the bed.

When he had gone Julia talked with Norah about the emmanogogue and the consequences if anyone discovered the truth. Norah agreed to keep it a closely guarded secret. She knew what the reaction from her parents would be if they knew. Julia brought in soft foods and diluted wine through the day.

Reny returned and ate supper with his family. Norah was provided a light meal in bed. Julia helped Norah out of the bed and dressed her in a fresh nightgown. Soon she was settled in her bed again and Reny was allowed to enter the room.

The storm had blown to the southeast, out over the Atlantic Ocean. The moon took on a bluish hue in the cloudless sky. Only a light breeze remained to ruffle the boughs of the pines outside the window.

Reny extinguished the lamp and climbed into the bed beside Norah. Lying on his back, he looked up at the shadows on the ceiling, created by the flicker of the fire. He covered up with a separate quilt. Slowly he turned on his side and put his arm over Norah.

"No," she snapped and he yanked it back. "Tis painful still."

"Forgive my botch," he mumbled ruefully. "Mayhap I shall leave you to sleep alone this night."

"Mayhap you shall," she agreed.

He felt the sharp pang of rejection and sat up slowly. "Shall you bid me go, Norah?" he asked, hoping that she would ask him to stay. "I did think that you would benefit from my comfort this night."

"Reny, on the morrow I mean to travel to the home of my father," she declared.

"No, you cannot," he stammered anxiously. "Mac and Joanna shant permit it!"

"It shall aid my healing if I shall be consoled by my mother. Allow me to endure my lying-in in my father's house."

Reny felt a deep sadness inside. He was suddenly alone with her beside him on the bed. "Norah, might you permit me to remain this night afore you shall take leave?"

Norah lay still and quiet for a moment as she considered his request. She pushed back her quilt and reached for him. "Turn to your side and linger until morning."

He turned over and she grabbed his arm. She placed it just under her breasts. She offered part of the bedclothes to cover him as well. He closed his eyes and felt her warmth but did not feel the joy of the previous nights with her. He felt a lump in his throat and swallowed hard. The magic and hope he had experienced quickly withered and a hollow, empty feeling replaced it.

In the morning Reny woke facing away from Norah. He was partially uncovered and he felt the chill in the room. Quickly, he rose and built up the fire in the stove again. He dressed for work and hurried out to the kitchen.

The scents of coffee, cornmeal, cinnamon and apple butter swirled in the air. He sat quietly and poured a cup of the dark, bitter brew. He watched as Julia stirred the cornmeal into the pot hanging over the fire in the hearth.

"Mama, Norah shall journey to the home of her father this morn," he announced and sipped from the warm cup. "I shall send Penn Cooper for her. He shall deliver her in the closed Landau."

"Reny, why shall she think to depart? Tis her time of lying-in. She shall be imperiled if she shall be subjected to the cold."

"Tis Norah's desire that she shall be permitted the comfort of her mother. I shant deny her if she means to go."

"When her lying-in has ended she shall return," Julia reassured him.

"Mayhap she shall," he responded and walked out the back door.

An hour later Reny stomped back into the kitchen. Laurent looked up from his breakfast and raised an eyebrow. Reny nodded to him as he breezed through the room. He stopped in front of the bedroom door and tripped the latch.

"Norah!" he shouted angrily. Her eyes snapped open and she blinked at him.

"Reny?" she questioned and pulled herself up to sit against the headboard. She rubbed her eyes and yawned.

"Why shall you think to take leave this morn?" he demanded and slammed the door shut behind him.

"I did tell it last night. I do seek the comfort of my father's house as I do mend," she explained and extended her arms with palms up in a plaintive gesture.

"Why shant you seek the bolster of your husband?"

"Tis fair that I shall appreciate the company of my mother as I am restored. I shall suffer a time of grieving, Reny."

"Norah, you did assert your true nature last night. With verity, do you mean to depart from me this day and end our union?"

"No, Reny, I could not do so," she implored unconvincingly.

"The child is gone from you and you have no need for a husband. Mayhap you shall dissolve the marriage and return to your dalliances with Eddie?"

"How shall you think to speak so to me?" she screamed furiously as her face flushed.

"You did enchant me, Norah. I did give my heart fully unto you. In your time of need I did make you my wife! Yet you shant look upon me with any love in your eyes. As I do move to kiss you tis no response from you. You shant permit me any of the liberties of a husband. Do you think me ever the fool, Norah?"

"Reny, tis not so," she shook her head and scowled at him. "If you think me a devious wrongdoer then bid me go. I shant balk as you do end the marriage and see me gone from you."

"No, Norah," he spoke softly and smiled. "You shant take leave this day. Afore God and man you did vow to stand at my side unto your death or mine. You shant depart for the home of your father. If you do seek comfort it shall be given from your husband. You are no longer a child and I shant abide your petty entreaties."

"Shall you think to keep me against my will?" she shouted. "Am I yet your prisoner, Reny?"

"Norah, you are my wife and you shall feign it if there be no care for me in your heart!" he bellowed. "I am your husband and I do forbid that you take leave of this house. You shall remain in the bed as the midwife did order. Test me no more, my dear wife!" He left the room, slamming the door behind him.

In the kitchen Julia stood beside the table looking down as he entered the room. Laurent studied the residue in the bottom of his cup. Reny stopped by the hearth and strained to regain control of his temper.

"Mama, my wife does believe she shall travel to her father's home this day. She shall not depart from this house. I did forbid that she leave her bed and I shant be challenged further. I shall return to lunch with her. Good day!" he announced and left.

"Tis not the nature of my son," Julia observed, stunned by the change in his manner.

"A man shant tolerate being made the fool," Laurent commented. He stood and kissed Julia, shrugging into his coat before he stepped out into the frigid morning air.

68

Burghill House filled with happy guests for Grace's Christmas Party. The delightful smells of the delicious foods, fresh cut pine boughs and burning bayberry candles filled the house. Delightful music swirled in the air and the dancers spun around on the floor in the dining room.

Joanna had approved the end of Norah's brief lying-in period the morning of the grand event. Dressed in a gown borrowed from Julia, Norah entered the house on Reny's arm. She forced a smile and searched for her parents in the crowd of people on the first floor. At last she caught sight of her father in the kitchen.

"Reny, I should like to sit with my father and mother for a time."

He quickly released her hand and she disappeared among the throng of people in the hall. He strode back to the sitting room and poured a glass of whiskey. Teague stood near the fireplace and Reny moved to stand with him. He drew in a sharp breath when Eddie entered the room.

Eddie nodded toward Teague then to Reny. "Good Christmas, grandees," he called out and laughed. Reny smelled the alcohol on him and knew he had arrived drunk.

"Happy Christmas," Teague responded and raised his glass to him.

"Where is your lovely bride, Reny?" Eddie provoked and laughed wickedly.

"I shant speak of my wife afore you, Eddie."

"Tis but a social query," Eddie announced cheerfully and clapped Reny on the back.

"Mayhap you shall talk of the season and disremember my wife," Reny warned.

Eddie chuckled and moved to pour a glass of rum. He quickly gravitated toward the dance floor and began looking at the young ladies there. Flashing a confident smile, he reached for the hand of Cora Pender. She flushed bright red and hurried ahead of him into the dining room. As the musicians began to play again Eddie thoroughly charmed her.

When the music ended Eddie stretched out his hand to Belinda Lewis. She looked up into his sapphire blue eyes and quickly followed him. Sulking, Cora moved to stand beside her older sister Maggie. The melody concluded and he slipped by several young ladies waiting for him. He found his drink on a small table in the hall and stumbled toward the kitchen for a plate of food.

Standing near the pantry, he popped a piece of cheese into his mouth and swallowed more of the rum. He talked with Luke and Mac for a few minutes before sweeping along the table and filling his plate. Across the room he saw Norah and flashed a wicked smile at her. Quickly, she turned away from him.

Norah moved to the sink and complimented her aunt, Mrs. Whitley, on the great feast she had prepared. She felt him behind her as he approached slowly. His hand touched the small of her back and he leaned to beguile Mrs. Whitley as he spoke. "Dear lady, might I speak with my cousin's lovely wife for a moment?"

"Assuredly," she answered and bowed her head quickly.

"Norah, such a sensual creature you are," he breathed beside her ear. "I did hear tell that my child was lost from you."

"Mayhap you shant eavesdrop," she responded calmly.

"Shall you think to remain with Reny as you do desire me so?" he teased and touched the tip of his tongue to her earlobe. She shivered and stepped away from him. "Norah, I did know you and you cannot secret your moods from me. Tis a fire within you as you do feel me near."

"Eddie, take leave from me," she whispered.

"I cannot, Norah. Confess your craving and I shall captivate you as you do lie in my arms."

She remained beside him as her breathing quickened, her heart beat faster and a pink glow spread over her face. "I cannot," she protested weakly.

"I shall move to the front door and out to the loft of the barn. I shall await you there. Steal through the back unnoted and come to me there. You shant require a cloak as I shall make you warm beneath me," he laughed mischievously and walked away from her.

Norah stood breathless as her eyes darted around the room. Worried that someone had noticed their conversation she quickly turned around. She inched along the wall to the vestibule and pretended to look for something important on a high shelf. Lazily, she eased passed the sink and stopped casually to stare out the window. Slowly she reached for the door knob and felt a hand grip her arm.

"No," Reny growled as he clutched her arm and pulled it back. "Your father did depart. Why should you think to withdraw to the back yard, Norah?"

She glared up at him and yanked her arm away. "Unhand me," she hissed.

"Did Eddie tell it truly when he did state that you are naught but a common whore?"

"You are a detestable brute, Reny Luciern," she muttered quietly as guests moved closer, filling plates at the end of the long table.

"I do curse the day I did wed you as well, dear wife."

"Mayhap I shall pursue a gentleman who shall see me onto the dance floor."

"Norah, I shall caution you but once. I shant fault Eddie if there shall be a happening. He is known to be a toss and a scoundrel. You are perceived as a respectable wife and are yet the daughter of an honorable reverend. Mind yourself, dear one," he mouthed as she glowered and turned away.

69

On a snowy afternoon in early January, Annie delivered her third baby. Mac sat quietly beside the bed while Joanna tended to the birth. He had not forgotten Joanna's involvement in ridding Norah of her unwanted child and felt somewhat uneasy with her.

"A son at last!" Mac announced when he accepted the newborn from Joanna's hands. He smiled at Annie and bent to kiss her. Speaking as quietly as his deep voice would permit, he soothed the crying baby. "He shall be Orin Phillip Wallace."

Annie held out her arms and Mac passed the infant to her. She kissed his head and smiled at the thick dark hair. "'Tis a big boy alike his father," she commented.

"He is larger than his sisters at their births," Mac observed proudly.

Joanna finished the delivery and began the clean-up in the room. She hurried much faster than usual to escape Mac's watchful gaze. When it was all in order she measured out the herbs and tea blends that might be needed if an emergency occurred in the night. Leaving Annie in Mac's capable hands, she slipped down the stairs and into the sitting room. Impatiently, she waited for Joseph to harness the horses and take her home.

Lily and her daughters, Faith, and Bon had settled back into the Gage house with Eddie. Mac instructed Faith carefully in the distribution and monitoring of Lily's daily dosing. Eddie quickly declared himself the king of the castle. The self-proclaimed ruler met with no objections primarily because he was rarely in the house. Most evenings he could be found in one of the local taverns. He courted only the most available and receptive young ladies.

Faith Gage had the blonde hair and blue eyes from her father's family. There were a number of potential suitors seeking her attention, but she quickly settled on Glenn Alfray. At Christmas he declared his intentions and became the only young man who she would receive. At seventeen she was eager to marry. She was confident that the son of the Master of the Customs House would make a fine husband. Her mother and grandparents approved of him as well.

Sixteen year-old Azaria was finally permitted to receive gentleman callers. With dark hair, remarkable dark blue eyes and porcelain skin she attracted the attention of many of the local young men. She had inherited both her Grandmother Ruth's stunning beauty and her incredible charm. She enjoyed the attention of the numerous suitors but had no serious interest in any of them.

After little more than two months of marriage, Reny and Norah had come to despise one another. They slept in the same bed nightly but maintained a wide gap between them. Seated at opposite ends of the table, they ate their meals. During their short marriage there had only been a few kisses and the relationship had yet to be consummated.

Reny had grown tired of standing firmly against Norah. Nothing had been gained as she disliked him more each day. She remained unhappy and complained continually. He worked long hours to avoid her and ignored her when he was in her company. In early February he made the decision to end the discord.

On Sunday he readied a small sleigh to ride with Norah to her father's church. His family rode to Rev. Pender's church in a larger sleigh. While Norah waited outside for Reny, he hurried into the bedroom and packed her trunk. He carried it outside and loaded it onto the back of the sleigh. Norah watched him curiously as he climbed up into the sleigh.

"What do you mean to do with my trunk?" she demanded. He shook the reins and clucked his tongue against the roof of his mouth. The horse stepped forward and moved down to the road. "Reny, I did query you! How shall you think to remove my chest from the house. Tis rightful that you shall explain it!"

Reny sighed as they approached the town center. He steered the animal up along the drive and around behind the church. He jumped down and offered his hand to help her climb out. She pushed his hand away and slid down the side of the sleigh. He offered his arm as she approached the slippery steps but she turned away from him and marched toward the front of the building alone.

Near the front of the building she slipped on the ice and landed on her right side. She struck her hip against the frozen ground and fought to keep from crying out in pain. He stopped beside her and held his hand out to her. She took it, slipping and sliding on her high heeled shoes. Upright again, she pushed him away and proceeded slowly around the corner.

In the church Norah sashayed to the front pew and sat beside her mother. Reny remained standing at the back of the room near the doors. Rev. Murray delivered an inspiring sermon about the need for kindness and charity toward others. Reny agreed but the idea did not sway him.

When the final prayer concluded Reny waited in front of the tall doors for Rev. Murray. Tomas watched distractedly, as he approached his son-in-law. Reny extended his hand and the minister shook it.

"Norah shall return to your home this day, good Reverend," Reny stated.

"Might we speak of this when the congregation has departed?" Tomas asked awkwardly, as the parishioners approached along the aisle.

"Tis naught to speak of. I shall endure no more of her petty cruelty. Twas not consummated and I mean to seek annulment."

"Reny, might you reexamine your thinking with me in seclusion?"

"Forgive me reverend, but I cannot," Reny told him and walked down the front steps. He drove his sleigh the short distance from the church to the Murray's home. He tested the latch and found it unlocked, as usual. Hurriedly, he hefted the trunk out and carried it into the room that had been Norah's. He noted that her bed was still there for her.

Outside again, he jumped back up onto the drivers' bench and snapped the reins soundly. The horse trotted along the road passed the church again. He saw Rev. Murray on the front steps, shaking hands with the last of his congregation. With a heavy sigh of relief he rode on to Burghill House for dinner with his family.

Reny strode into the house and wandered through to the sitting room. He poured a glass of whiskey and sat in the rocking chair. He rocked slowly and sipped the amber liquid. For the first time in more than a month he felt a smile spread across his lips. He had expected to regret his decision but he felt nothing but happiness now that it was over at last.

When the dinner was done and the men settled in the sitting room, Reny sat near the doors and stretched his long legs. Eddie approached him and held out a glass of rum. Reny accepted it and Eddie sat beside him.

"Shall your wife be found with the good reverend and his wife this day?" Eddie prodded.

"That she is," Reny replied and smiled again as he sipped.

"You shant relish their company?"

"I did place her trunk in the home of her father this day."

"Have you done with the marriage?" Eddie asked in surprise.

"Tis done. I can endure no more of her petulant nature. The union shall be annulled."

"I did caution you against her," Eddie admonished.

"Shall you accept my apology for the clash in your home?" Reny asked sheepishly.

"I shall," Eddie chuckled.

"Do you mean to take up with Norah again?"

"No I shant. Tis unseemly to lay with your wife when you have only just ended all."

"Eddie, tis the reputation of a scoundrel that does follow you. How shall you think to assign moral confines to the woman now?" Reny asked and laughed.

"Afore I shall depart for Boston I must seek principles and mores regarding the women I do chance to know."

Reny took a sip and coughed hard as he laughed at Eddie's odd reasoning.

70

Rev. Murray collected his Bible and Hymnal and walked slowly along the aisle of the church. Aileen stood by the door with her arm around Norah's shoulders. She smiled and squeezed her daughter's hand, excited that she would be home again. Tomas pushed the door open and lowered his head as he walked down to the front path. He ignored their chatter as he made his way through the snow to his home.

Inside the house he removed his old cloak and hung it on the peg. He stoked the fire in the hearth and stuffed another log into the stove in the small parlor. Reluctantly, he poked his head into

Norah's bedroom and frowned at the big trunk near the window. Woefully, he moved back to the parlor and sat in the worn arm chair. He opened his Bible and began reading aloud.

"Father, shall you not welcome me openly?" Norah asked, bubbling with excitement.

"No my child, I cannot. Norah, your husband means to end the marriage."

"Tis reasonable, Father. I have no love for him and he has none for me."

"You did speak your vows before God, Norah. Tis not for love alone that you were to remain. Twas your duty to serve well as his wife."

"Father, I was made his wife wrongfully. Twas to Eiditch Gage I was meant to be wed. I cannot abide a marriage to Reny Luciern in his stead."

"Norah, do you believe any man shall make you his wife now? No, you shall be deemed an undesirable woman!"

"The marriage was not completed. If tis negated then I shant be a divorced woman. There shall be proper suitors to court me. I shall yet marry well."

"You did conceive illegally and your husband has done with you! What man shall think to make you his wife? Have you no sense, woman?" he shouted.

"Father, no," she uttered, grasping the weight of her situation for the first time. She sat slowly in a chair near the fire. Her face paled and she felt a tear rolled down her face. "What shall become of me?"

"You shall remain within my house. Mayhap work shall be found for you within the orphan asylum or one of the fine homes of Georges Falls."

"Father, you shall see me made a common housekeeper?" she demanded.

"Tis little more for you, Norah! Twas to you to enrich your marriage yet tis done with. When I have gone to my great reward there shall be none to provide for you, my child. There shall be naught but a life of toil for you, my dear," he lowered his head sadly.

"Tis wrongful that this shall fall upon me!" she shrieked.

Tomas rose and slipped quietly out through the front door with his Bible clutched at his chest.

71

After a month of harsh weather in March, April blew in with sunny skies and delightfully warm days. The snow quickly melted and fresh green hues colored the region. Windows were flung open and fresh air chased out the stale remains of the past several months. Buds sprouted from tree limbs and the first signs of flowers broke through the thawing ground. The gloom of winter was soon forgotten.

Only a week later, without warning, the wind shifted to blow in from the east. The clear blue skies grew dark and dense clouds chased away the sun. Through the morning a cold rain fell. As the temperatures plummeted, the rain chilled further and a messy slush blanketed the ground. Freezing rain tapped against the windows and the wind tugged at the thick pine boughs. Late into the afternoon huge snowflakes swirled in the air.

Luke and Joseph banked the fires before putting out the lamps and turning in for the night. Outside the wind howled mournfully. Luke snuggled close to Grace under the quilt and cherished the warmth of her body. He listened to the windows rattling as the storm raged, and hugged her tighter.

The clack of the door knocker echoed in the empty front hall and Luke squeezed his eyes closed. There could not be anyone out there. Surely the sound had been created by the storm. He tugged the quilt up higher and listened guardedly.

In the entry way a more urgent knocking sounded. Luke threw back the bed clothes and sighed with exasperation. He thrust his legs into his pants and hurried through the sitting room. At the top of the stairs Joseph and Mac stood waiting as Luke lifted the bar and unlocked it. He pulled it open and a blast of wind sprayed snow across the floor.

"Dr. Wallace!" a small boy cried as he clung to the door jam and turned his face away from the painful peppering of the icy flakes. "Grandpa is in need!"

"Who are you boy?" Luke asked as he grasped his shoulder and yanked him inside. He forced the door closed and looked down at the child.

"I am the grandson of Ben Andrews," the boy responded, shivering as the snow on his cheeks melted. He wiped at his cold, wet face and looked up the stairs at the lighted lamp.

"What has befallen Ben?" Luke asked anxiously.

"This day he took sick. He shant open his eyes," he cried.

"Joseph, ready the sleigh!" Luke called up the stairs.

"Pa, I shall go," Mac responded.

"Ben is an old friend," Luke answered. "I shall accompany you. Be quick!"

Mac hurried to dress and ran out to harness the horses. Quickly, he moved along the drive, stopping for Luke and the child near the front of the house. With their heads down, they rode through the blizzard to the Andrews' home.

Luke hurried into the house while Ben's grandson helped Mac to secure the sleigh inside the barn. Mac held the child close as they stumbled toward the back door and made their way into the chilly kitchen. The boy stood trembling as he removed his coat. His cheeks were red and his lips had chapped. Mac tossed another log on the fire, then followed the sound of the voices to an upstairs bedroom.

In the dim light of the bedroom, an old woman sat in a chair near the fire. Luke knelt beside her, talking softly. She raised a handkerchief to her mouth and closed her eyes. Mac cleared his throat as he entered the room. He looked toward the bed at the still figure lying beneath the bedding. Flecks of blood stained the area near the man's face. Mac moved closer and gently tugged the sheet up over his head.

"Mac, might you summon Jacob Frawley?" Luke asked as he stood slowly.

"Assuredly," Mac breathed and quietly left the room again.

By morning the worst of the storm had passed. The snowfall ended and the harsh wind diminished. Near noon Jacob and Penn Cooper returned with Ben Andrews' casket. In the Andrews' parlor, the lid was removed before they left. As the weather continued to improve, the word of Ben's death spread and family and friends quickly filled the house.

In two days, Jacob and Penn came again to retrieve the casket and move it to the crypt behind the tavern. The funeral would be delayed for several weeks as the ground continued to thaw. At last, Ben was laid to rest in the East Grantham Cemetery near the grave of his father, Samuel Andrews.

Luke sent an urgent message to Dr. Maynard Amcott of Boston. In his letter, he explained the sudden need for a skilled surgeon in the region. A fee would be paid to the good doctor for finding a suitable candidate.

Late in May, Luke received a response from Dr. Amcott. He recommended Mr. Nathan Stone, a fine young surgeon from Dorchester, Massachusetts. Mr. Stone had accepted the position and would arrive in East Grantham in early July.

In the spring, Glenn Alfray met with Eddie to ask for his consent to marry Faith. Eddie quickly agreed to the marriage and the dowry to be delivered to Glenn. Faith accepted Glenn's proposal and eagerly began planning for a July wedding. Lily's condition had deteriorated and she stayed in her bedroom alone most days. Grace took on Lily's role as she helped her granddaughter with the wedding arrangements.

At the millinery, Faith was measured for her wedding gown. She chose a bodiced petticoat of white crepe de chine and pale turquoise spencer jacket, made of velvet that covered the bodice. The slimmed leg 'o mutton sleeves added to the enchanting look of it. Alencon lace would be used for the veil, train, and elbow length gloves.

The wedding would take place at the First Parish Congregational Church of East Grantham and a reception would follow at the Meeting House. While Faith and Grace worked on their elaborate plans, Glenn Alfray readied his family home for Faith. Glenn inherited the house when his father had passed away only months ago. His mother and youngest brother would remain in the home.

Mac had promised Annie a house of her own before he married her. With three children Mac knew he owed it to Annie to fulfill his promise. He purchased the land across the road from Burghill House and the Chernock's began construction in the spring. They expected the house to be completed by the end of July.

With the beginning of the War of 1812 in June, shipping was disrupted and the arrival of Mr. Stone was delayed. On a rainy night in early July, two ships set sail from New Bedford,

Massachusetts with the surgeon aboard. As they moved north toward the Province of Maine both ships were heavily armed and manned by experienced crews.

Traveling under the flag of Spain, the first ship, *Mi Querida Charlotte* was piloted by Captain Henry. The companion ship, *Azul Cielo* followed close to assure the safe passage of the cargo and passengers aboard the *Mi Querida Charlotte*. The two had travelled together throughout the Caribbean and as far north as Nova Scotia for more than a year. Both crews remained fiercely loyal to their captain.

On an uncomfortably hot and humid afternoon the ships docked in East Grantham. Teague Grenier and Reny Luciern greeted Capt. Henry as he disembarked with his first mate. Both had heard of the brash young captain and were eager to meet him. Capt. Henry tipped his tricorn hat to them and strode confidently along the dock. A leviathan followed close behind him, eyeing both Teague and Reny warily.

"The valuable cargo shall be transported to the Customs House for assessment," Teague advised the captain and nodded toward the stone building beyond the warehouse.

"Kennelm, see to it," Capt. Henry advised his first mate in a low, even tone. The 6'7" giant nodded and boarded the ship again. "Shall we, gentlemen?" Henry asked, as they hurried along toward Wren's Tavern.

The young captain entered the tavern and looked around the large open space. The barkeep, Jim Tanner, leaned against the rough wooden bar, arguing with his plump, surly wife, Ivy. She heard the door creaking open and turned as the men entered. She noted Teague and Reny, then looked at the handsome stranger. Capt. Henry wore a white Tristan shirt with black breeches and thigh high boots folded over at the knee. A heavy red sash tied at his waist, held a double barreled pistol to the right, a sheathed French Sabre-Briquet sword and a razor sharp boarding axe at his left hip. An elaborately patterned, rust brown scarf, covered his forehead and tied at the back with his leather tricorn perched on his head. Colorful glass beads adorned the narrow braids scattered through his thick black hair.

"Good day, boys!" Ivy called out. "What shall ye be drinking this day?" She marched toward an empty table and waited as they sat. She stared into the captain's mesmerizing, dark brown eyes and touched her tongue to her upper lip. "Ain't you fetching!"

"Three ales, good lady," Capt. Henry declared, in his rich velvety tone. "Good Sirs, two passengers did come aboard my ship at New Bedford, Massachusetts. Might you tend to them?"

"Have you their names?" Teague asked.

"Mr. Nathan Stone and Miss Chloe Elkin," Henry responded as he glanced around the room at the few patrons seated there.

"I shall attend to it," Reny declared as he stood and offered his hand to the captain. Bill Henry stood and shook it, then sat again.

Teague and the captain ate and ordered a second round of ale while they talked. Teague offered him cargo that would be ready the following morning and the captain quickly accepted.

"Mr. Grenier, might you know of Dr. Luke Wallace?" Henry asked.

"Dr. Wallace is my father's uncle. Why should you seek him?"

"'Tis a private matter, Sir. Might I speak with him afore I do depart on the morrow?"

"If you shall sup with my family at Burghill House this night, you shall meet him there."

"'Tis a kindly invitation. I shall be greatly pleased to accompany you. A number of years have passed since I did last enjoy a family dinner."

72

"We shall require three additional settings at the table this night," Grace advised Mrs. Whitley.

"Shall dear Lily and her daughters be seated among you?"

"No, the surgeon, Nathan Stone has come from Boston at last. The new school teacher, Miss Chloe Elkin shall join us as well. Teague did extend an invitation to a ship's captain this morn. If the men shall bring more dinner guests, mayhap Azaria shall yet find one acceptable."

"She is but sixteen years," Mrs. Whitley smiled. "A beauty such as Azaria shall bide her time and choose well."

"Mayhap I do worry over her more than is reasonable," Grace acknowledged, as she sliced the blueberry bread.

In the hall, the front door banged shut and Grace leaned to look along the hallway. She watched as Teague hung their hats and strode toward the kitchen with his guest.

"Gran, tis my guest, Captain Bill Henry of the ship, *Mi Querida Charlotte*," Teague announced. He removed two glasses from the shelf and filled them with warm mulled wine.

Grace smiled as the captain reached for her hand and bowed slightly. "Tis an honor to meet such a fine lady. Your grandson does speak well of you."

"So young to captain a ship, Sir," Grace responded.

"Tis so," he smiled in return and accepted the glass from Teague.

"Teague, might you show your guest to the sitting room?" Grace asked politely.

"Mr. Stone and Miss Elkin," the captain bobbed his head at each as he entered the sitting room. "I did not anticipate our meeting again."

"Nor I," Stone replied as he eyed the captain warily.

"Capt. Bill Henry, tis Uncle Luke," Teague nodded toward Luke, seated behind his desk.

"Good, Sir!" Bill called, as he marched forward with his hand extended. "Your reputation does precede you."

"Tis a disadvantage that you are not known to me," Luke commented as he stood and they shook hands.

"I am the captain of the *Mi Querida Charlotte* and do own the *Azul Cielo* as well. They do sail proudly under the Spanish flag, yet we do maintain autonomy."

"Tis a perilous time to sail the seas," Luke observed.

"Mayhap, but adventurous seasons to tempt our hearts as well," Bill stated and flashed a brilliant smile.

"Shall I take leave that you gentlemen might speak?" Miss Elkins asked. Teague looked toward her, acknowledging her presence for the first time. He stared at her lively blue eyes and golden hair. A gentle smile touched her lips as she looked up into his handsome face.

"Tis no need, Miss Elkin," Luke announced. "We shall reserve the talk of men and move to the dining room. My dear wife shall provide a fine repast for all."

In the dining room Luke filled the wine glasses as Grace, Millie, Azaria, and Mrs. Whitley carried in platters, dishes, and baskets of food. The guests chatted happily as they ate and the wine continued to flow. When they had finished with the desserts, the men moved back into the sitting room.

Joseph and Millie escorted Mr. Stone and Miss Elkin to their temporary rooms over Botts' Tavern. In the morning, Miss Elkin would begin settling into the cottage beside the school house where she would become East Grantham's school teacher. Miss Elkin had been hired to replace Kathleen Sotton. Kathleen would be marrying John Larabee in a month and would no longer be permitted to teach in a public school. Mr. Stone would seek a house of his own there.

Teague poured whiskey and handed glasses to Luke, Mac, Nathan, and Bill. They sat discussing the recent declaration of war against Britain, by President James Madison. Mac passed the whiskey decanter and glasses were refilled. Joseph soon returned and joined in the conversation.

"Uncle Luke, Captain Henry did speak of a private matter he should like to talk of with you alone," Teague commented and sipped.

"The women have cleared the dining room. Mayhap we shall confer in there," Luke declared and moved across the hall with the captain following close behind. Luke closed the doors and they sat at the table. Luke sipped his whiskey and waited graciously for Bill to speak.

"You are Dr. Luke Wallace?" the captain questioned.

"That I am," Luke responded, watching Bill curiously.

"In your travels did you occasion to meet Mr. Obediah Vyncent?" he asked and smiled.

"Tis a name I do recall," Luke offered, as he tilted his head and raised an eyebrow. "Why should you think to ask of the man?"

"From your response tis assured that you do remember the man well. Perhaps you did travel to meet him in his manse in the night?"

"I am a physician," Luke remarked, guardedly. "Tis often that I am summoned in the night to attend to the sick."

"Dr. Wallace, twas not to attend to the sick that you and your young son did visit the home of Mr. Vyncent and his lovely bride. Mayhap you did carry an infant to his home that night?"

Luke jumped up from his chair and stared down at Bill. "Who are you that you shall accuse me so?" he demanded.

The captain smiled daringly and drained the last of his drink. "I am the child you did deliver unto Charlotte Vyncent. Sir, I should like to ask who you might be to me."

"You cannot be..." Luke faltered and lowered himself into his chair again.

"Charlotte was a breathtakingly beautiful woman with a gentle nature. She did birth many children but none did survive. Twas to save her sanity that Obed Vyncent did seek a healthy infant for her. You did arrive in the night with a child of but one year. Charlotte did name the boy William Henry Vyncent. Obed made payment for the child and knew that you meant to make it a charitable gift at the home for orphans.

I did love Charlotte well. She did pass as she struggled to deliver another child when I was but five years. Obed near lost his saneness when she did go from him. He cared not for his work and could not bear the sight of me when she had gone. I was but a sorrowful reminder of his beloved Charlotte's demise.

Obed's partner, Phineas Drake did mind the monies as Obed drank himself into a stupor nightly. He did pass on my birthday only three years after Charlotte had been taken. Three years too many, as he did think it. Drake did quickly vend all in his name and it was secured for me.

A helpless orphaned boy, Drake did send me away to a school for boys. At my twelfth year, I did have my fill of the fiend who minded me and the beastly head master. In the night I did light out to make my own way. I hid aboard the Dutch ship, *Grote Blauwe Reiger*. The ship had scarcely cleared the mouth of the harbor before I was found by a deckhand. When my whipping was done with, the captain ordered me put to work with the crew.

Twas my aim to learn their language and master the ship. At fifteen I did return unto Mr. Drake for my inheritance. I did purchase the finest of ships in the Caribbean and did hire on a fine crew. Twas no painless task, yet I did prove myself worthy in battle among Barbary pirates." He stroked his closely trimmed black beard and felt two long scars hidden beneath it. "Tis my tale, Dr. Wallace. Now I shall implore you, tell me why you did spirit me away in the night."

Luke closed his eyes and shook his head nearly imperceptibly. "Tis not my tale to tell," he breathed.

"I shall caution you, good Sir," Capt. Henry warned. "Tis my intent to know of it. I am a man of great determination and I shant be shucked aside. If you shant speak it, then I shall seek the truth of my own."

Luke considered his words and felt his chest tighten. He did not question that Capt. Henry was a determined young man. Silently, he considered the ramifications if this young man began asking for information throughout the town.

"Do you mean to make a scandal of it?" Luke asked softly.

"I do not. Tis the truth I do seek, but I shant see you ruined. Unless, per chance, you did take me illegally and delivered me to Obed Vyncent for profit. Yet, I do not believe that shall be the verity of it."

"No, I did not," Luke responded calmly.

"Shall you tell it or might there be others within this house who shall recount more of it for me?"

Luke stood and opened the doors. "Gentlemen, might you join us?" Luke called across the hall. He turned toward the kitchen. "Grace, I shall ask that you come as well and bring the jug with you."

Joseph, Teague, Mac, and Grace sat around the table watching Luke curiously. Azaria, Millie, Annie, and the children had all gone to bed. Luke refilled the glasses and sat somberly, struggling to think of some way to tell the story.

"More than sixteen years ago, Lily did birth a healthy boy. Her Timothy did name the child Albert James Gage. Twas known to Timothy that the child was conceived in an illegal act of adultery with Lily and Laurent Morgan." Luke stopped and swallowed more of the drink.

"Lily did confide the tale and bid me be done with the boy. He did greatly favor Laurent and she could not bear the reminding and shame. Twas Judge Daniel Gage and I who did scheme to remove the child from Lily. Timothy had gone to Portsmouth as we did undertake it.

In this house we did speak of it and determined to be quick with it. As Lily did comprehend the meaning of our plan, her heart did soften. She did plead that we end our scheme. As she did beseech us, the boy was taken out from her hands. Twas not to harm Lily, but to salvage the child that we believed it rightful.

Judge Gage did remove Lily with Eddie and Faith in tow. Woefully I did press Mac to ride with me as we did deliver the child unto Charlotte Vyncent. A woman of such a loving manner, I did think the boy blessed with a splendid life.

Twas a funeral to bury Albert James Gage, yet the coffin held no child. The scheme was meant to end it. Just to end it all! We did seek to be done with the wrongful act of Lily and Morgan. To see the child gone from us and talk of him done. Yet it did serve only to separate mother from child and commence Lily's trail into madness.

Poor Charlotte did pass in childbirth and the child was left to an uncaring father who did succumb to the lure of drink. Twas no placid life given unto the boy. At his birth, Captain Bill Henry was given the name of Albert James Gage. He has returned for the truth of the mother of his birthing. Tis likely he shall greatly regret that he did seek it," Luke added and refilled his glass again.

"Tis not the tale I did imagine," Bill acknowledged. "Might you tell me who you are to me?" he asked as he turned to look at Grace.

"I am Lily's mother, your grandmother. This is my son, Joseph," he gestured toward Joseph, Teague, and Mac. "Joseph's son, Teague and my nephew Mac. Luke was previously married to my deceased sister Isannah and Mac is their son."

Bill Henry looked at the faces around the table. "Where shall my mother be found?"

"Your mother is not well," Mac spoke more gruffly than he intended.

"Twas not my question, good Sir," Bill commented.

"Forgive my abrupt manner," Mac stated. "I am Dr. Mackenzie Wallace and I do tend to your mother. She does suffer with a disordered mind. Her grandmother and aunt suffered a like mania. Lily does take leave of her bed chamber for Sunday service and the family dinner alone."

"I should like to meet the woman."

"Tis wrongful that you shall trouble her as she does suffer so," Mac objected.

"You shall accompany me, Dr. Wallace. I do trust that you shall tend to her if I shall over burden her."

"Tis late, Capt. Henry," Grace objected. "How shall you think to disturb her this night?"

"What is the hour to the senseless mind? It shall not concern her greatly."

"If you shall require it, I will go," Mac agreed reluctantly.

"And what of my father?" Bill prodded.

"It shall create discord for Laurent and his wife if you shall knock upon their door at this hour," Grace tried to dissuade him.

"Did my father know the truth of me?"

"He did learn of it long after you had gone from us," Luke replied.

"Then I shall not disrupt the order of his household. Permit me to speak with my mother alone and I shall be satisfied."

73

Mac opened Lily's bedroom door and stepped inside. Lily sat in a chair by the window reading. She was dressed in the gown that she had worn on her wedding day. As Bill followed through the door, she looked up and smiled.

"Tis a fine night," Mac commented and gestured toward the open windows.

"Uncle Luke did prohibit that I open them and I did not. Faith did push up the sashes," Lily advised him. "I did promise that I shant sit upon the window sill."

"I am greatly pleased," Mac assured her.

"Tis a remarkably handsome man who does follow you," Lily whispered conspiratorially.

"The man is Captain Bill Henry. He should like to speak to you if you might oblige."

"How should I refuse enchanting eyes such as his? Tis a beguiling look about him. Is he a man possessed of great magic?"

"No, Lily. He holds no magic," Mac assured her as he carried two chairs forward and placed them near her.

"Captain, why have you come to me this day?" she asked and turned to look out the window. "Night has fallen," she observed with surprise. "Tis a strange thing."

"Mac did tell of the beautiful Lily Gage and I did strive to meet you," Bill told her.

"Mac is a good man and does care well for me."

"Lily, do you recall your son, Albert?" Bill asked.

"Twas a beautiful boy," she declared. Leaning forward to speak confidentially, she whispered, "Twas not the child of my Timothy. The children of Timothy did take on the flaxen hair and icy eyes of his people. I did birth Albert with the face of his striking father."

"What is the name of Albert's father?"

"Twas Laurent Morgan. My Timothy did forgive the misdeed," she declared and sighed sadly. "Might you remove your hat and the band beneath it?" she asked, staring at him intriguingly.

Bill removed his hat and the scarf that covered his forehead. Lily tilted her head and studied his face. He shook out his long black hair and smiled as he looked into her eyes. She smiled sweetly in return.

"You have come home to me, Albert," she breathed as tears welled in her eyes. "You do ever favor dear Laurent. Shall you forgive me? I could not love you for the guilt and shame of it. Yet I did not bid you go from me. I did grieve so and my Timothy did seek to return you unto me."

"I am astounded that you do know me, dear lady," Bill responded as he stared at her pretty face.

"You are ever in my heart, Albert."

"Tis likely that you are found in mine as well."

"Mac, might you summon Bon and ask that she brew tea? My head does pain me and I should like to sleep."

Mac nodded and walked down to the kitchen to prepare it himself. He blended wine, herbs and Laudanum for Lily and poured two glasses of wine. Suddenly he felt bone weary. He padded slowly back up to the bedroom.

Lily sat talking quietly about Albert's first year of life. She remembered sitting in the dark with him in her arms as he nursed. She stood and walked to a chest in the corner of the room where her wedding dress had been stored. From the bottom of it, she lifted out a white infant's gown, elaborately embroidered with gold metallic thread. She carried it back and held it out to him.

"I did dress you in this the day before you were removed from me. When you had gone I did hold it in the night and inhaled your scent from it."

As the drug took effect, Lily quieted. Mac asked Faith and Bon to go in to remove the wedding gown and dress her for bed. He thanked them and left with Bill Henry. They rode in silence along the road to Burghill House. Mac remained in the barn with the horses while Bill walked around to the front door again.

He knocked and stepped back, waiting patiently. Teague opened the door and ushered him into the sitting room, where Luke sat behind his desk writing in his journal. He looked up and nodded to Bill as he entered the room and sat near the front window.

"You did speak with Lily?"

"I did," Bill responded cheerfully. "She did identify me as Albert."

"Lily did know you?" Luke asked in surprise.

"That she did. She did state the look did tell it. She does believe that I do favor my father."

"Tis truthful, you do have the look of Laurent Morgan."

"I should like to meet him."

"Capt. Henry, tis unreasonable that you shall think to wake the man's household in the night for to greet him."

"I shant ask that he be roused. On the morrow I shall speak with him, if you might accompany me."

Luke considered the request. "I shall. Mayhap Teague shall deliver you to the docks now."

"My ships shall sail on the morrow. Yet tis my desire to know my family. Mayhap I shall remain and await the return of my vessels."

"Mayhap it shall be noblest if you shall make your introduction to Laurent and depart from this place on the morrow," Luke advised him.

"Noblest?" Bill asked and chuckled. "Shall it be deemed dishonorable that I shall think to know my own people? Tis rightful a man shall know his blood kin. Shall my ship remain the only home of my heart?"

"Capt. Henry, the people of this town do know of the death of Albert. How shall it be explained if you shall remain?"

"Why should it worry me that your lie shall be unraveled?" Bill asked as he rose slowly from the chair. "Twas not my lie, Sir. I am the aggrieved and you shall think to be called the wounded one! I am not a predator come to do you in! Tis to know my family alone that I do ask of you. Shall you bid me take leave?"

"I must ask this, Capt. Henry. Tis not to punish you that I shall require it, but to safeguard my family."

"No, you shall not," Grace spoke softly as she entered the room. "Luke Wallace, I shant see you turn him away. You shant remove him from the house of my father yet again. I cannot bear it."

"Grace, you will not challenge me so. If you must speak of this thing, I shall hear it in the bed chamber," he declared as he stood and gestured toward the bedroom.

"He is the child of my daughter and I shant hear more of this thing. Phillip would not see him gone and I shant permit it of you."

Luke stood speechless as Grace looked up at him. He reached for her arm and she pulled it from his grasp. "Grace, I shall speak with you in seclusion," he ordered and stomped into the bedroom. She exhaled loudly and followed him.

"How shall you think to speak so to me afore another man?" he demanded when he had closed the door firmly.

"Luke, we cannot turn him out. He is your grandson! You shant put him out to save the standing of this family. The sins of the past shall be righted for him."

"Grace..." he began.

"Luke, you did deliver him unto Charlotte Vyncent that he should be given a better life. That Charlotte should be lost was not known to you. Yet Lily does suffer from a peculiar mind and could not mother him well. Tis rightful we shall acquiesce and disremember the pain of what was done."

"Grace, if the verity of this thing shall be made known, it shall undo us all. Shall you sacrifice Joseph, Teague, Mac, Reny, and Eddie for this young man?"

"Tis no certainty, Luke. Accept that he is of our family and trust that he shall show decorum."

"I cannot."

"I shall ask that you do this thing for me, Luke Wallace. Shall you deny me?"

Luke looked into her dark blue eyes. He bent low and touched his forehead to hers. "I shall trust in you, Grace." She kissed him and smiled.

Grace remained in the bedroom while Luke returned to the sitting room. He apologized to Bill Henry and asked him to stay. Grace stepped into the room just long enough to advise Bill that the bedroom at the far corner on the second floor had been readied for him. He thanked her and she returned to the bedroom.

Luke, Teague and Bill sat up late into the night drinking and talking. Bill had lived through many great adventures in his years at sea, with horrific scars to prove it. He enjoyed telling the stories and they appreciated hearing them.

74

"Kennelm!" Bill roared as he walked through the door of Wren's Tavern. The cool morning breeze stirred the air until he kicked the door closed behind him. "Kennelm!"

The giant man thumped down the back stairs, thrusting his arms into the sleeves of his shirt. He looked at Bill from across the room and squirmed apologetically. He stomped his feet into his boots as he hurried across the floor.

"Good morn, Captain," Kennelm mumbled.

"You shall be found in the bed of a whore when my ship is to be minded?" Bill shouted up at him. Kennelm walked passed him and felt the kick of Bill's boot on his backside as he pushed the door open.

They walked side by side along River Road to the warehouse. Along the docks they watched as the crew of *Mi Querida Charlotte* and *Azul Cielo* were busy loading the cargo. Bill boarded the larger of the two ships with Kennelm behind him. Bill greeted his crew cheerfully and strode down to his cabin.

"Kennelm, how am I to trust my First Mate if he does seek harlots firstly at every port?"

"MacEwen did mind your vessels in the night. Shant you trust the man to walk your decks?" the big man growled.

"The man is trusted well," Bill acknowledged, as he hurriedly packed a large leather sack.

"The cargo is bound for Boston," Kennelm grumbled. "It shant glean much profit. Mayhap we shall sail for the West Indies and the promise of fair monies."

"Kennelm, tis the promise of bare breasted women you do seek!" Bill declared and they both laughed. "You shall captain *Mi Querida Charlotte* as it does move to the south. MacEwen shall oversee *Azul Cielo*. If the winds be with you I shall watch for your return in but two months."

"You shall remain in this hamlet?" Kennelm puzzled.

"Tis a family matter I shall take in hand," Bill stated. Kennelm nodded, and stepped back. He knew better than to question his captain further. "Prepare to sail when the cargo is secured. I shall look for you in early September. Guard my vessels with your life."

"I shall, Captain," Kennelm assured him and moved back up to the deck with him.

Bill spoke with the crews of both ships and left. On a horse rented from the livery behind the warehouse, he rode for Burghill House.

As promised, Luke accompanied Bill to meet Laurent Morgan. The three men sat at a table in the back corner of Botts' Tavern. Laurent watched the young man curiously as they waited for tankards and meat pie to be delivered to the table. Jacob returned with the food and drink and quickly left them to talk.

"Laurent, Capt. Henry did ask that you speak this day," Luke told him and raised the pewter tankard to his lips.

"Is it a fine horse you do seek?" Laurent asked, as he looked at Bill.

"No, Sir," Bill responded. "I do seek my father."

"Capt. Henry was born to Lily Gage and given the name of Albert," Luke interjected.

The color drained from Laurent's face as he stared at the handsome young man. "Albert of the grave?" Laurent whispered.

"That I am," Bill answered and chuckled. "I did sit afore my mother last night. A dear lady with a pretty face, yet her mind is upset."

"No, Sir," Laurent argued. "The child did pass and I was in attendance for the funeral."

"Laurent, the baby was removed from Lily and given unto Obed and Charlotte Vyncent. He did not pass on. Twas the wrongful decision of Judge Gage and me. Yet he has returned unto us and Grace does bid us welcome him fully."

"Luke, is it a certainty that this is my son?" Laurent pleaded, as confusion clouded his eyes.

"'Tis so," Luke affirmed.

"Jacob!" Laurent shouted as a warm smile lit his face.

"No, Laurent," Luke warned. "This thing cannot be made known. It shall bring ruin unto the children of Burghill House. Bill shall be welcomed openly, yet the tale of his parentage cannot be told."

"Luke, I cannot secret this from Julia. I cannot!"

"If you shall tell it to Julia, then let it be Julia alone. 'Tis a private thing," Luke emphasized.

"Burghill House is a place of secrets," Laurent confided to Bill.

Jacob approached the table and Laurent asked that he summon Julia. In only a few minutes, Julia walked toward the corner where they sat. She carried a rose scented cake with boiled frosting on top and a bowl of wild strawberries.

"Bill Henry, this is my beautiful wife, Julia." Bill stood quickly and reached for her hand. He bobbed his head and flashed his dazzling smile. She blushed as he touched his lips to her fingers.

"Good, Sir," she responded.

"Julia, 'tis Albert," Laurent whispered. She pulled away from him and scowled up at her husband.

"Laurent, the boy did pass," she whispered. "'Tis a grave in the cemetery to mark it," she reminded him gently and looked sympathetically at Laurent.

"'Tis so," he insisted. "The child was removed from Lily by Judge Gage and Dr. Wallace. He has come again to live among us!" he declared excitedly.

Julia dropped into the empty chair and stared at Bill's face. She studied his mesmerizing dark eyes and captivating smile. Slowly, she turned to look again at Laurent. The resemblance was unmistakable. Stunned, she gazed at Bill as the realization showed on her face.

"Albert?" she muttered.

"'Twas the name at my birth," Bill replied. "Of late I am titled Capt. Bill Henry."

"No," Julia hissed and stood again. "No, this cannot be." Julia backed away from the table as Laurent stood and reached for her. She pulled her arm away and ran for the kitchen.

"Julia!" Laurent called out but did not follow her. He sat again and lowered his head. "'Twas a shameful thing that I did."

"Adultery is a wrongful deed," Bill stated as he looked at Laurent and took a bite of the meat pie. Bill dropped the fork on his plate and stood quickly. He stalked toward the kitchen, ignoring Luke and Laurent, as he hurried ahead to stop Julia in her path. Julia froze, looking up into his dark eyes. Behind them Luke and Laurent stood in the doorway of the kitchen. Luke held his arm across Laurent's chest, holding him back as they listened.

"I implore you, permit me to pass," Julia posed, anxiously.

"Dear lady Julia," Bill spoke warmly. "Shall you bid me go from this village?"

"The mere thought of Albert does call up dreadful memories of days past. I shant be pressed to think of them again."

"You shant be faulted for your ruminations," he murmured soothingly. "'Twas Laurent Morgan and Lily Gage alone who shall be condemned for their wrongful acts. I cannot bear to see you pained so by the recollections. My father shall ever be Obed Vyncent and Charlotte my mother. I have not come as an orphan in search of parentage, but a man who does trail his bloodline. The bitter secrets shall not be unraveled."

"Shall Albert be raised from the grave and my husband's name be stained?" she asked.

"Albert is done with and Captain William Henry does stand afore you. I shant see your tender heart wounded. Might you impart a smile to light your lovely face?" he prodded and touched a gloved finger to her chin.

She smiled, hypnotized by his voice. He moved slowly to touch her hand and lifted it to kiss her fingers again. She drew in a sharp breath and quickly pulled it back as her cheeks flushed. He displayed his devilish smile and stepped aside as she hurried on toward the house. He watched her go before turning back and following Luke and Laurent into the tavern.

"Barkeep, three drams of whiskey if you please!" Bill called out as he sat again.

75

Faith's wedding day arrived with brilliant sunshine and a light breeze to temper the July heat. Dressed in the delightful wedding dress with the watery turquoise Spencer jacket, Faith made a stunning bride. The color of her jacket beautifully accentuated her pale blonde hair and soft blue eyes as she stood beside Glenn Alray in his gray waist coat.

A tremendous reception had been planned in the Meeting House. The room quickly filled with guests. Tables of supper foods and rich desserts lined the far wall. The doors and windows hung open even as the volume swelled.

The talented musicians began with *The Sussex Waltz* and dancers moved out onto the floor. Glenn led Faith into the fray, holding her lace gloved hand. Around them, Mac and Annie, Joseph and Millie, and Laurent and Julia danced as well.

Teague, Reny, Eddie, and Bill stood near the door sipping the fine rum that Bill had provided. Across the room, a number of young ladies watched them and waited impatiently to be invited to dance. The prettiest of the young women present were Azaria Wallace and Bon Gage. They chatted and ignored the repeated appeals from the charming young men.

The new surgeon, Nathan Stone, quietly edged closer to Azaria with two wine goblets in his hands. He stood beside her and extended the glass. Slowly, she turned to look at him and stared into his vivid blue eyes. A smile touched her lips and she turned to accept the wine from him. She sipped and studied his Romanesque features.

"Might you think to accompany me?" he asked and held a hand out to her. She smiled at Bon and bit her lip as she accepted his hand and followed him out among the dancers. The musicians began the *Slow Waltz in Bb*. Azaria gasped as he drew her into an embrace, but she quickly realized that others moved in the same manner. Surprised at the public display, a number of couples left the floor and moved toward the tables of food.

"You are a breathtaking young woman, Miss Wallace," he breathed close to her ear. She felt butterflies taking flight inside and her heart began to beat rapidly. He gazed seductively into her dark blue eyes and smiled wickedly.

Teague noticed the new school teacher, Chloe Elkin, standing beside Grace. He tossed back the last of his rum and strode toward them. Chloe saw him approaching and smiled amiably. She admired his dark eyes and strong, masculine face.

"Might you accompany me among the revelers?" Teague asked, and nodded toward the dancing guests.

"Such a sway would be most improper for a school teacher, good Sir," she responded.

"Mayhap I shall linger as this melody does end," Teague told her and reached for a piece of blackberry cake with buttery icing.

In minutes, the musicians stopped again and quickly began to play the English reel, *The Rose Tree*. Teague grasped Chloe's hand and hurried forward. She giggled as he twirled her around, keeping her at arms-length throughout the dance. The late afternoon sun shone through the tall windows open on the back wall of the building. He marveled at the golden glow of her blonde hair in the sunlight. Amazed by the effect she had on him, he watched her whirl happily in front of him.

When Teague yielded to Chloe's request and walked back toward Grace with her, he saw his Aunt Lily there. She was dressed in a lemony yellow velvet gown with daisies braided into her hair. At thirty-six years old, the beauty of her youth had only just begun to fade. She beamed as her attractive nephew approached.

"Joseph," she declared and moved to hug him.

"No, Aunt Lily, tis your nephew, Teague," he gently reminded her. She studied his face and pondered his words. "I am the son of your brother, Joseph."

"The son of Joseph," she repeated and scowled as she considered the idea. "Shall you dance with me, son of Joseph?"

"I should be delighted," he answered sympathetically, and took her hand.

Through the evening, Nathan Stone drew Azaria back onto the dance floor repeatedly. Her usual aloof response to the young men faded away as she was quickly charmed by the young surgeon.

"Might I call upon you, Miss Wallace?" he whispered as he handed her a glass of dark red wine.

"I shant object if my father shall permit it," she responded winsomely.

"The sun has set and the moon shall soon be upon us. Might you consider a walk in the night with me?"

"Mr. Stone, tis a scandalous thing you do suggest. I shant take leave in your company without a proper escort."

"My sincerest apologies, Miss Wallace. Twas wrong that I did think so suggest it."

"Tis forgiven," she responded, and waved her hand. Gently, he touched her elbow and led her back out among the dancers as the musicians performed *The Linnet*.

Several of the guests had gone and the bridal couple soon prepared to leave as well. Glenn and Faith would travel the short distance to his family home where they would spend their wedding night. They quickly thanked the remaining guests and said their farewells. With Glenn's mother and young brother following close behind, they hurried down the steps and out to the waiting carriage.

The couple maintained a proper distance from each other as the buggy bumped along the road. At the house, they walked stoically up to their bedroom and waited for the house to quiet. Glenn took her in his arms and pressed his fingers to her mouth.

"Mother shant hear any sounds from this room, Faith," he advised her. "It would trouble her and I shant abide that."

Faith nodded and stood in silence as he charily removed the Spencer jacket and unbuttoned the back of her dress. She pulled a sheer gown from her trunk, a special gift from Grace. Glenn shook his head no and tossed it on a chair. He dug through the clothing until he found a modest, white cotton nightgown. He handed it to her and turned away.

When she had dressed and covered herself with the summer quilt, he looked her way again. She stared down at her hands as he undressed and readied for bed. He climbed into the bed and lay still beside her. Hesitantly, he rolled toward her and touched her face. Quickly, he pulled her head closer and touched his lips to hers. With swift pecking motions he kissed her repeatedly then stopped and drew back.

"Say not a word," he whispered harshly. "Not a sound," he added as he reached to yank her nightgown up to her waist. With one hand over her mouth, he roughly forced her legs apart with his knee. Surprised by his cold manner, she began to cry softly as she struggled to breath beneath him. Cruelly, he moved against her, disregarding her muffled cries. When he had finished at last he turned away from her. "If you shant quiet yourself, I bid you take leave and sit in the night air until you are composed," he murmured and turned away from her.

Faith swallowed hard and choked back her tears. She did not like the idea of wandering alone in the dark of night. From the next room she heard the old woman snoring. She watched the myriad of stars beyond the open window and prayed for sleep to take her away from her new home.

76

Long after Glenn and Faith had gone, the party continued in the Meeting House. The musicians entertained and the guests continued to eat and drink happily. The alcohol flowed and couples frolicked on the dance floor. Soon, the last of the couples with young children and the elderly revelers had gone.

"Mrs. Wallace, might you suggest a proper escort to see me home?" Chloe Elkin asked Grace.

"It would be my honor to usher you to your door," Teague offered.

"I should think it unseemly," Chloe replied sweetly.

"'Tis but a hop and a skip across Litchfield Road to your door. I should think it suitable," Grace assured her.

"I shall rely upon your discretion, Teague Grenier," Chloe responded and moved to hug Grace. On Teague's arm, she strolled across the room and down the front steps. They walked along the edge of the drive without speaking and slowly crossed the dirt road. In minutes, they strode through the damp grass and up onto the small porch at the front door of Chloe's small cottage. "Thank you, Mr. Grenier," she nodded politely.

"'Twas my pleasure to do so," he sighed and backed down to the stone path. "I bid you a fair night, Miss Elkin."

"And to you as well," she told him as she unlocked the door and lifted the latch.

Teague continued to back away and stumbled over a large rock. He caught his balance and turned to walk to the road. He stuffed his hands in his pockets and dropped his head as he thought of the glow of the sunlight on Chloe's hair. He ran up the hill to the Meeting House and stopped. Music from the hall filled the air and he closed his eyes, recalling the heavenly scent, as he had moved close to her during the evening. He looked toward the cottage with the soft light in the upstairs window and began to run.

He stood on the top step and pounded his fist against the door. Through the open window he heard the clack of her heels on the stairs. The glimmer of the lamp shone through the small square window panes above the door and he felt his heart stop. The latch rattled and she pulled the door open.

"Mr. Grenier," she uttered with surprise. "Was something forgotten?"

"Tis so," he mumbled and quickly leaned forward to kiss her soft lips.

"Mr. Grenier! Tis most improper," she protested.

"Twas not a thing I could restrain," he appealed, and stepped down off the porch again.

"It shall be forgiven," she stated, as a smile danced at the corners of her mouth.

"I mean to make you my wife, Miss Elkin," he announced boldly.

"I cannot entertain such suggestions, Mr. Grenier. I am a school teacher and am not permitted to marry," she explained kindly.

"Then you shall teach no more," Teague proclaimed and grinned up at her. "Sleep well, Miss Elkin," he called out as he hurried back to the Meeting House.

Reny, Eddie, and Bill stood huddled near the first table of food along the back wall. They had danced with many of the young ladies present but eventually gathered to talk apart from them again. They watched as Teague strutted across the floor, wearing a wide grin.

"What does please you so?" Eddie demanded.

"I did meet my wife this night," Teague announced.

"Tis the drink!" Eddie declared and they laughed.

"No, tis a beauty such as I have not seen afore," Teague spoke, as he stared up at the high windows, smiling as if he could see her up there.

"More drink is required afore he shall misstep and wed the woman!" Eddie proclaimed. Bill grabbed a jug of rum from the table and they marched out the front doors and around the back. Laughing rowdily, they followed the path through the woods behind the church and made their way to Norwich Pond. Under the luminous glow of the full moon, they perched on the ledge and passed the jug well into the early morning hours.

77

Nathan Stone approached Luke the following morning to ask for his permission to court Azaria. Luke quickly agreed and advised Grace of the wonderful news. A respectable suitor would be calling on Azaria and she would accept him. They were very pleased and the family welcomed Nathan wholeheartedly.

Stone had purchased the former home of Captain William Corey, built by him more than fifty years earlier. After Molly's death, the property had reverted to her younger brother Will Corey but he preferred to remain in his own house. He was pleased to sell it to the new surgeon. Will lived comfortably with his wife and three sons and was happy to gift the proceeds of the sale to his niece, Joanna Pender.

After purchasing the house, Nathan Stone hired the Chernock's to build an additional room at the side of the house. He planned to use the space to store his surgical tools and other supplies and to provide a room where surgery could be done.

The following week Eddie boarded a coach bound for Boston. He was excited about the prospect of college and escaping the confines of the small town where he had grown up. With a quick hug, he said good-bye to Lily. She told him to enjoy the trip to Portsmouth with the Judge. He just shook his head and left the room.

Faith had married and Eddie was departing for Boston, leaving Lily and Bon alone in the big house. Grace insisted that the Gage house be shuttered and they move into Burghill House. Teague, Bill, and Reny prepared the attic for them and delivered the furniture that Grace had ordered. When they had finished, it was transformed from a plain open space to an elegant room both with a sleeping and sitting area.

As Eddie finished his plans before departing, Lily and Bon were moved into Burghill House. Only Mr. Dobbs remained to tend to the Gage property.

Mac and Annie moved into their new house across the road from Burghill House. Annie was thrilled to have a home of her own at last. With three children and more likely to come, she delighted in the additional space. The cook from the Gage home, Mrs. Quinn, was hired to cook and assist with the housework. They enjoyed a happy household and looked forward to the weekly dinners with the family at Burghill House after the church service.

Bill waited for his ships to return in early September. Daily, he travelled to the waterfront but received no word from them. Through his days, he chopped wood at Burghill House and for Mac and Annie. He worked in the warehouse with Teague and Reny and helped Laurent in his livery. Daily, he sat with Azaria and enjoyed their talks as they ate breakfast and lunch. Nightly, he visited Wren's Tavern to talk with the sailors there, in hopes there might be news of his ships.

A single woman and school teacher, Chloe could not receive suitors. Grace invited her for supper several times each week and she was attended Sunday dinner as well. Teague seized the opportunity to court her in Burghill House, with proper chaperones, through summer and into the fall. When he contemplated proposing marriage, he learned that her father had died years earlier and no male relatives remained. Puzzled by the dilemma, he approached his father to ask his advice.

"For the mere formality of it, I should suggest that you ask Uncle Luke for consent on her behalf," Joseph advised him. "If he shall agree, then you might propose to her. Yet no dowry shall be required of her and no gift of land provided by you."

Luke readily agreed and Teague planned to ask Chloe after supper that evening. Anxiously, he watched her, waiting for the family to finish with dinner. When the dessert had been served, Luke took pity on him and permitted him to go into the sitting room with Chloe. Grace propped the doors open and returned to the dining room.

Chloe sat in the rocking chair and watched Teague as he paced the length of the room twice. He sat in the chair next to hers and looked at her. He extended his hands, palm up and looked at her expectantly. Slowly, he nodded his head as if she must certainly know what he was trying to convey to her. She raised her eyebrows and shook her head no.

"Tis no then," he declared as he jumped up from the chair.

"Teague, I cannot state no, as I know not why you do behave so this day," she told him and smiled sympathetically.

"Miss Elkin, I am greatly troubled and I plead that you shall aid me," he announced and sat again.

"How might I aid you?" she asked, slightly amused and even more puzzled.

He stood again and walked to the doorway. In the dining room, several chairs scraped the floor as they quickly looked away from the sitting room. Teague frowned, and turned to face Chloe again.

"Tis rightful you shall end your teaching," he declared as he stopped in front of her. He stared into her eyes, waiting for her answer.

She understood at last that he was proposing, but considered forcing him to speak the words before responding. As she looked into his handsome face, she lost her nerve and surrendered. She held out her hand and guided him back to the chair.

"Teague Grenier, I shall end my teaching," she replied and smiled.

He shot out of the chair and dropped to his knees in front of her. Holding her hands in his, he leaned to kiss her. "She did consent!" he shouted, and quickly kissed her again.

"Mr. Grenier you do enchant me so. How might I rebuff you?" she whispered, and responded as he kissed her a third time.

He stood and pulled her up from the chair. His arm slipped around her waist as they hurried back into the dining room. Joseph refilled the wine goblets before the toasts began. Azaria, Bon, and Faith chattered excitedly with Chloe about wedding plans and a trousseau.

"Joseph is to be married at last?" Lily asked as she sipped her wine.

"No, Lily, tis your nephew, Teague," Luke corrected, and reached to shake Teague's hand.

"Teague did pass when I was but a small child," Lily proclaimed and dipped a piece of chocolate cake into the wine before she popped it into her mouth.

"Mayhap we shall remove Mama afore she does degrade further this day," Bon announced. She walked Lily up the stairs while Glenn strode out to the barn for his carriage.

"Felicitations, Teague and Chloe," Glenn stated when he returned from the barn. He pressed his hand to Faith's elbow and she stood hesitantly.

Michael and Joanna congratulated Teague and Chloe and thanked Grace for dinner. They left with their daughters, Maggie and Cora, to walk home in the pleasant early September weather. Laurent, Julia, and their children quickly followed.

"Azaria, might you walk with me along the trail into the wood?" Bill asked.

Nathan Stone had travelled to Froid with Mac that morning to manage an amputation. "I should be delighted," Azaria responded eagerly. She hurried up the stairs to change the dress and shoes she had worn for church that morning.

"Oh, I um..." Grace hesitated.

"Grandmother, do you think I shant be trusted with dear Azaria?" he challenged.

"No, Bill, yet..." she struggled to explain.

"Be assured that Azaria shall never be safer than she shall be in my company," Bill declared, confidently. Quietly, he moved up the stairs.

"Luke?" Grace worried.

"He is a capable man and he does greatly favor Azaria. He shant permit any harm."

Silently, Bill returned to the dining room with the sash tied at his waist and his tricorn hat. The pistol had been readied and tucked securely at his right hip. On the left, his sword was sheathed beside his boarding axe.

"Have you practiced the use of your sword?" Grace asked worriedly.

"You do yet fear for Azaria," he observed with amusement. "Mayhap I shall reassure you."

"Tis not required," Luke stated as he scowled at Grace.

The swish of the sword and an odd f-f-fut sound was heard. The sword sang as he sheathed it again. Grace looked up at Bill and frowned as Luke and Joseph exchanged quizzical looks. Bill leaned forward and tapped the first lit candle and watched the top half of it topple into a dish of sauce. He moved along the table tapping the candles one by one as the cut portion of each tumbled forward.

"Shall I demonstrate my accuracy with my pistol as well?" he asked casually.

"No, you shall not," Luke responded firmly.

"I shall make purchase of beeswax candles for to replace the ruined, Grandmother."

"Thank you, Bill," Grace replied and stood to collect the eight candle pieces left on the table.

Azaria clomped down the stairs and Bill offered his arm before they strolled into the kitchen and out the back door.

78

Nathan Stone visited Azaria to propose. With her father's blessing, she excitedly accepted. After the Sunday dinner, the men moved to the sitting room while the women worked in the kitchen and discussed plans for both of the weddings. Chloe was content with a small wedding but Azaria chattered about a big elaborate ceremony and reception.

As September passed, Bill grew more concerned for his ships and crew. October arrived and he continued to visit the waterfront daily in hopes of any news that might come. He heard repeated tales of problems resulting from the war with Britain. Men from the region had gone to join in the fight. Bill considered the possibility that one or both of his ships had been lost at sea but dismissed it and continued to wait for word.

"Teague, I must travel to Wren's Tavern this night," Bill spoke privately after supper. "Shall you accompany me?"

"Mayhap we shall call for Reny as well," Teague responded.

They rode to the livery and talked with Reny first. "My father, Reynolds Luciern did die after a stabbing affront of the warehouse. My mother shall forbid it," Reny explained.

"Then we shant speak of it in her presence," Bill declared. "Shall you come?"

"I shall," Reny replied at last.

The three young men soon arrived at Wren's Tavern. The horses were stabled in the livery behind the warehouse and they proceeded into the tavern. While they sat at a corner table drinking beer and whiskey, Bill left to speak with several sailors he recognized.

"Heb je gezien *Mi Querida Charlotte* of *Azul Cielo* in uw overlijden? Mayhap u hebt gesproken Kennelm of MacEwen?" Bill spoke in Dutch, at the first and second tables. As he moved on to speak with a group of French sailors he asked, "Avez-vous vu le *Mi Querida Charlotte* ou *Azul Cielo* dans votre trépas? Peut-être bien vous avez parlé à Kennelm ou MacEwen?"

Frustrated, he returned to the table with no news. He swallowed a dram of whiskey and drank from the tankard of ale. They listened, mesmerized as Bill told stories of his travel to ports in Turkey, Greece, Portugal and Spain. He told of encounters with the Corsairs in the Mediterranean and the loss of a number of his crewmembers there. Leaning forward, he parted his beard and displayed the long, narrow scars along his jaw. He pulled his shirt off the shoulder and showed an ugly zig-zag scar that ran up from his collar bone to his left shoulder and another along the side of his neck.

"If not for Kennelm I would have gone to the bottom of the sea in my end there," Bill announced and gulped another shot of whiskey. "The big man did accept a musket bore through his arm to salvage me in that battle." He laughed heartily, and opened his shirt to show more scars from a gash across his stomach and an uneven slash from his ribs down to his right hip. He pulled his shirt down again and retied the sash that held his weapons.

"Mayhap you shall remain and work within the warehouse," Reny suggested. "Tis a perilous life you do endure at sea."

"When the sea does seep into your blood, you shant endure a life upon the land," Bill declared and called for another tankard of ale.

"Tis a late hour," Teague shouted over the raucous noise in the tavern. "Shall we take leave?"

"I shant depart," Bill responded.

"We cannot leave you behind when you've drunk so…" Teague faltered, as Bill jumped up from the table with his pistol drawn and aimed at a big, scruffy man seated at the next table.

"Relâcher les pièces de monnaie!" he thundered. "Release the coins!"

The room stilled and the coins clattered to the floor. To his left, an old man bent to pick them up. He stood and looked at Bill as he reached to push the double barrels downward.

"What was seen, friend?" the old man asked.

"He did sneak your coins as you turned away."

"Did you think to abscond with the coinage?" the old man demanded.

"Tis lies!" the scruffy man shouted

The largest man at the table grabbed the offender by his collar and dragged him up from his chair. As the old man pocketed his money, they pressed through the crowd and out into the night air. Quickly another group of sailors made their way back from the bar to the empty table and called for more tankards of ale. The noise level rose again and Bill turned back to his own table.

"Shall he be removed to the sheriff?" Reny asked.

Bill accepted his fresh tankard of ale from the barmaid and laughed. "They are shipmates. He shall be corrected in seclusion. Tis of no concern to the law of your hamlet."

"Shall we take leave now?" Teague asked again, eyeing Bill in disbelief.

"Depart if you will, I shall remain," he responded.

"Tis a perilous place to drink," Teague prodded.

Bill nodded toward a young barmaid collecting dirty dishes from another table and smiled lecherously. "I shall take a room for the night and tempt the harlot."

Teague shook his head and chuckled. "Remain vigilant," Teague shouted as they stood to leave. As he followed Reny out the door, he looked back to see another group of sailors seating themselves at Bill's table. Over the din, he heard Bill shouting a greeting in French as he stood and shook the hands with the leader of their party.

Carefully, they walked along River Road to the livery. Teague carried his pistol drawn and primed. Quickly, they saddled their horses, mounted them and rode for the town center.

79

At the end of the week, a letter was delivered for Capt. William Henry. He broke the seal on the envelope and braced for the worst possible news. The message had been sent by Kennelm in a port at Charleston, South Carolina. *Mi Querida Charlotte* had been fired upon by a British warship near Bergen Point, New Jersey. The *Azul Cielo* returned fire and heavily damaged the British vessel. At Charleston, the ships put into port for repairs. The trouble delayed their progress south to Tortuga in the Caribbean. The war was plaguing the east coast shipping traffic. Kennelm planned to decline the shipment of wood from the island and would return with rum instead.

With the news that his ships and crew were well in hand, Bill's positive nature returned. He knew it would be at least another six weeks before they returned. While he waited, he remained busy with whatever work was required. He worked with Jacob Frawley and Penn Cooper for a few days, digging graves and tending to the cemetery property. He hunted deer with Laurent and Reny and moose with Joseph, Mac, and Teague.

"Good morn, ladies," Bill announced, as he strutted into the kitchen, holding a fat Tom turkey by the feet. Mrs. Whitley accepted it from him and carried it to the slop sink to rinse it in salt water. Bill had already plucked and field dressed it.

"'Tis a fine bird," Grace declared, as she poured a cup of hot tea for him.

"Might there be coffee to drink?" he asked politely. She smiled and began brewing it.

Bill watched as she scraped the pulp and seeds out of a large pumpkin.

"What do you mean to do with it?" he queried.

"It shall be gutted, peeled, chopped and boiled," she responded and scraped out another full scoop from inside it.

"Might I aid you?"

"If you wish," she agreed and laughed, as she pushed it across the table to him. He stripped off his coat and pushed up his sleeves. Grace poured a cup of hot coffee for him and watched with amusement as he deftly worked with his boot knife. She moved on to other work leaving the pumpkins to him.

Nathan and Teague had little time for courting through the fall with so much work to be done. With the additional work load, everyone worked longer hours and hurried faster. This translated to more accidents requiring the attention of both the physicians and the surgeon.

In preparation for the wedding in June, Chloe had confided in the mayor and his wife. The mayor had already found a new school teacher who would arrive in the spring. When the replacement arrived, Chloe would need to vacate the cottage for him or her. She planned to take a room at Botts' Tavern until the wedding and hoped it would not be required until the end of May at the earliest.

Late in October Luke's nightmares worsened again. He paced the floors late into the night again, fighting sleep that would bring the terror. He woke in the night screaming frightfully. Grace worried as she watched him struggle with the demons of his past. She prayed that it would diminish again as it had years earlier.

"Mac, the nightmares are upon me yet again," Luke confided.

"Why should they come again now?" Mac asked, and studied his father's face.

"I know not," Luke responded and shuddered at the thought of the horrors from the night before.

"Mayhap you shall take a dram of whiskey and a small dose of Laudanum afore you do sleep."

"Mayhap," Luke agreed and stood to pace the floor again.

80

Early in December Bill found himself waiting and watching for his ships again. He looked to the skies and considered the possibility that his ships might not return to the north before spring. News of recent battles between the British and American naval forces troubled him. But he trusted Kennelm and MacEwen and could do nothing more than wait.

With supper done, Bill strode out to the barn and saddled the horse he had purchased from the Botts' Livery. He secured the barn doors and rode for the waterfront. The night air was frigid but the sky remained clear. A thousand stars sparkled against the inky darkness in the heavens above, with a half- moon glowing there.

Bill left the black stallion at the livery behind Wren's Tavern. With one hand on his pistol and the other on the hilt of his sword he walked confidently around to the front door. At the door he greeted three sailors he recognized and stopped to talk with them. They told him of a deckhand from the French ship *Reine Vengeur* who spoke of an encounter with the daunting ship, the *Azul Cielo*. Bill thanked them and stepped inside to find the young man.

Inside the bar he asked for the deckhand, Lasalle Ancar. The barkeep shook his head. "I shant require names as they do imbide!" he shouted over the noise.

Bill crossed the room, stopping to ask for the man at several tables. He glanced sideways at a young barmaid as she bent to retrieve empty tankards from a table. He smiled and raised an eyebrow as she stood again and turned to look at him.

"Bill Henry!" she yelled and scowled at him, but the trace of a smile quickly passed over her lips.

He flipped a coin into her hands and moved on. Suddenly, he stopped and stared straight ahead. At a table in the back of the room he noted several Canadian sailors he recognized, eating stew and drinking ale while they talked. Seated at their table he saw Nathan Stone with a young woman in his arms.

Bill tilted his chin up and walked forward. He stopped at the empty chair beside Nathan and drew a deep breath. The other men at the table watched him warily, but the woman blocked Nathan's view of him. Bill drew the saber from the sheath on his hip. With an artful sweep of his arm, the tip of the sword rested against Nathan's neck.

"Be gone, harlot!" Bill ordered.

She stood and stepped away from the table with her hands at her face. The room quieted as Bill placed a foot on the seat of the empty chair and lifted the blade slightly. A drop of blood colored the end of the saber and Nathan held his breath.

"Are you not promised to Azaria Wallace?" Bill demanded.

"Yes," Nathan whispered in terror.

"I shall warn but once, Nathan Stone. If you shall be found in the company of another yet again, I shall end you swiftly."

"Y-y-es," Nathan acknowledged.

"Be gone!" Bill thundered as he withdrew the sword and sheathed it again.

Nathan bounded out of the chair and hurried to the door. Behind him, the room erupted in laughter. Bill dropped into the chair that Nathan had vacated. He nodded to the Canadian sailors and ordered a round or whiskey for them.

81

Winter struck with a vengeance Christmas week. For days the storm wavered between snow and freezing rain, until the temperatures plummeted. A smooth layer of ice covered the snow and hindered traffic along the roads. Grace conceded and the plans for a grand Christmas party were cancelled.

A brutal season of bitter cold and record snowfall was endured throughout the region. In February, Faith announced her first pregnancy. She forced a smile, but inside she was unhappy with her new husband and his wretched mother. Glenn had already advised the old woman that a child would be coming in the summer. She accepted the news with a scowl and stomped up to her bedroom, slamming the door behind her. Faith dreaded bringing a baby into that house.

Luke had become accustomed to drinking two glasses of wine at dinner, followed by several drams of whiskey in the evening, in hopes of minimizing the nightmares. He added a large dose of Laudanum at bedtime and waited as he paced in the sitting room. Most nights the alcohol and opium worked, but there were still miserable nights of terror that nothing could prevent.

Grace noted that Luke ate little and drank more as the winter passed. His mood had soured and he had lost weight. Dark circles appeared under his eyes and he was easily agitated. Worriedly, she approached Mac to ask that he treat his father.

"Papa," Mac spoke low, as he stood beside Luke's desk in the sitting room. "Tis a sickness that does hold you."

"No, tis but the night terrors," Luke responded, and continued reviewing his ledger.

"The nightmares cannot be quelled with the drink. You have worsened as the months have passed. I fear for you."

"Tis of no concern," Luke responded, as he looked up at Mac.

"Where is the pain within you, Papa?"

"A great ache does grip my head."

Mac prepared an herbal tea and elixir for Luke to reduce the pain. Over the next month he tried a number of remedies as the headaches intensified. In early March Luke asked that Mac take over the care of his patients. Daily he remained in the sitting room through most of the day. Reluctantly, he admitted to Mac that his vision was failing as the headaches progressed. Grace fussed over him as her fears increased. She prepared his favorite foods and coaxed him to eat even a small amount.

Near the end of March another strong snowstorm blew in from the ocean with intense winds and heavy snowfall. Luke woke in the morning to the low whine of the gale force winds. One of the shutters banged against the side of the house and needed to be secured again. He sat up in the bed and squinted into the darkness of the chilly room. He shivered, and realized that the fire must have gone out during the night.

Quietly, he slipped his legs off the bed and stepped down to the icy floor. He felt his way around the end of the bed to the fireplace. He picked up the striker tin from the mantle and knelt to spark it. Immediately he felt the heat from the flames and heard the snap and sizzle of the resin inside the burning log. He dropped back onto the floor and fought the rising panic. His fingertips traced over his lips and he strained to see them in front of his eyes. He lowered his head as he acknowledged that his vision was gone.

"Grace!" he thundered. "Grace!"

He heard the footsteps in the hallway and the door as it banged open. "Luke?" she cried as she hurried around the bed and knelt beside him.

"Is it dark yet, Grace?" he demanded.

251

"No, tis morning, Luke," she told him and reached to touch his face.

"I cannot see the light, Grace!"

She helped him to stand and dress. Struggling to remain calm, she helped him out to the sitting room. He sat at his desk while she prepared his breakfast. She sat quietly beside him and lifted the fork to his lips. Carefully, she held the cup of hot tea as he sipped.

"Bill might you summon Mac?" she asked gently, forcing her voice to sound calm.

"Assuredly," he responded. He pulled on his coat and hurried out into the glacial cold. The wind grabbed his hat and he slid along the icy path trying to catch it.

Mac sent Bill to bring Nathan as well. While Bill rode for the town center, Mac sat with Luke. Grace cleared away the dishes and remained in the kitchen while Mac examined him.

"Does your head pain you greatly?" Mac asked.

"Tis persistent of late," Luke replied. He rested his head against the back of his chair and closed his eyes. "Permit me to rest, my son. Tis naught you might do for me."

Mac sat in the chair across from the desk. Disheartened by the latest change, Mac waited in hopes that Nathan still might be able to help his father.

An hour later, Nathan arrived with Bill. Azaria sat beside Luke in the sitting room, holding his hand and reading to him. Luke's face was tense as the headache pain steadily increased. Mac steered Nathan into the dining room and closed the doors. They discussed Luke's symptoms for some time before they finally walked out into the hall.

Nathan sat with Azaria and Luke while Mac strode into the kitchen. He melted skunk fat and added sage and cornmeal to it. When the mixture had cooled, Luke was put to bed and the salve was applied to his forehead. He was given a blended tea with lavender and feverfew to diminish his headache.

While Luke rested flat on his back, Nathan moved forward to examine him more closely. He performed an arteriotomy, opening the artery at his right temple and bleeding nearly sixteen ounces. Gently, he applied a light pressure to end the bleeding and bandaged it. Luke was given more of the red wine, boiled with herbs and left to sleep.

Over the next week, Nathan returned several times and bled another three pints of blood from him. Mac continued to provide boiled wine and herbal blends for him. He slept more and ate little as the headaches caused more nausea. To help soothe his headaches, a lavender scented herbal balm was reapplied to his forehead every few hours.

Sunday, the family sat near the front of the church as Rev. Pender preached. Seated between Grace and Joseph, Luke tilted his head back and kept his eyes closed. He feared the endless darkness that engulfed him. He dreaded the return of the nightmares that plagued him night and day in his new dark world. Grace held his hand and squeezed gently to reassure him.

"Thorns and snares are in the way of the froward: he that doth keep his soul shall be far from them. Train up a child in the way he should go: and when he is old, he will not depart from it. The rich ruleth over the poor, and the borrower is servant to the lend..." Rev. Pender paused as Luke jumped up from his seat.

"End this thing you foul beast!" Luke shrieked as he clutched his head.

Joseph stood quickly and gripped Luke's bad arm. Luke yanked away from him and moved to flee in the other direction. He tripped over Grace and Mac's legs and fell, striking his chin against the pew in front of them. Fighting in the dark he struggled to his feet again, pushing away the hands of those trying to help him as he panicked. He stumbled again and landed on Annie where she sat beyond Mac. Luke continued scrabbling as Mac closed his arms around him and pulled him backwards, holding him tight.

"Papa, tis Mac," he spoke soothingly in his low rumble. "You are ever safe with me."

"Mac, they have come for me," Luke pleaded in terror.

"They shant harm you!" he declared forcefully. "You are many with your family at your side. Rise cautiously and I shall see you securely to your home again. None shall impair you as you do walk aside me, Papa."

With Mac's help, Luke stood again and moved along the length of the pew. Mac nodded to Rev. Pender and the minister continued his sermon, speaking louder to draw attention away from Luke. Joseph and Bill followed Mac out the front door and down the steps.

"Joseph and Bill shall accompany us this day," Mac explained to Luke. "None shall threaten as we do accompany you."

Reassured, Luke stood straight and hurried along beside Mac. They climbed into one of the family sleighs and travelled the short distance along Kings Wood Road to Burghill House.

Over the next few weeks Nathan bled another three pints of blood from Luke. The headaches worsened despite their best efforts. He had begun to suffer from hallucinations and was occasionally delusional as well. When Grace tried to coerce him to eat, he accused her of trying to poison him and demanded that she leave him alone. Mac was the only person able to coax him to eat or drink as he regressed. As Luke slept less each night, Mac increased the dose of the strong herbal remedy intended to induce sleep.

By April he was declining more rapidly. He soon struggled to walk and stopped speaking. From that point it was only a matter of days before he passed away early in the morning. His body was quickly removed to the scullery behind the tavern. Resting in a heavily polished maple casket, he was returned to Burghill House.

The frozen ground had begun to thaw but not sufficiently for the digging of graves. Luke's body was stored in the crypt behind the tavern for a few weeks as spring took hold. He was laid to rest, at last in early May, in the family cemetery.

Grace mourned the death of Luke and relived the dreadful loss of Phillip. She dressed in drab mourning attire and walked daily to sit near the graves of the two men that she had loved so. The black crepe wreath hung on the front door again. For a month, Grace left the house only for the Sunday church service. But there were weddings to plan and she could not disappoint Azaria and Chloe. The following Sunday she pushed herself to attend the dinner with her family. As dessert was set out, she announced that she would put aside her troubles and the weddings would go on as planned.

"Mayhap I shall end my plans to marry and shall remain with you, Mama," Azaria suggested sympathetically, as they began to clear away the dirty dishes.

"You shall not," Grace responded gently. "Your Father did consent to the marriage and he shant see you quell your happiness for his passing."

"I shant see you left alone, Mama."

"At Burghill House, I shall never be left alone," Grace nodded her head toward the sitting room where Joseph, Teague, Bill, and Nathan were talking loudly about the ongoing war. In the kitchen Millie, Chloe, and Mrs. Whitley talked of wedding plans. She smiled and hugged Azaria and walked back to the kitchen with her.

82

Only two months after Luke's burial, Azaria stood at the altar in the church beside Nathan. Dressed in a stunning burgundy gown, adorned with French needlepoint lace Azaria wept through the entire ceremony. She struggled to force a slight smile as she spoke her vows. Nathan held her hand and tried to console her.

When Rev. Pender concluded the service, Azaria followed Nathan to the front doors. They walked out into the brilliant June sunshine and hurried down the steps. In Nathan's carriage, she leaned against him and sobbed. He wrapped his arm around her shoulder and talked soothingly, as they rode to Burghill House for the reception.

"Azaria, they shall think you are unhappy as my bride," Nathan murmured and kissed her tenderly.

"I do miss Papa so," she uttered and responded to his kiss.

"Luke would require that you be happy and celebrate well on your wedding day, my love."

"This day I must sit at his grave."

Reluctantly, Nathan agreed, as he halted the buggy near the barn. He jumped down and extended his hand up to her. "If you shall dry your tears, then I shall accompany you to the graveyard," he assured her.

He lifted her down and drew her into his arms. Quickly, he kissed her again and led her into the house. The first floor had been decorated with colorful crepe streamers and fragrant flowers. In the kitchen, tables were covered with delicious foods and beverages. The dining room had been cleared for dancing and musicians played lowly as the guests began filling the house.

Nathan and the rest of the family kept Azaria occupied through the late afternoon and into the evening. The diversions, combined with several glasses of wine, left her dancing happily with Nathan. The windows and doors hung open and the scent of lilacs blended with the blooms scenting the house.

"Might I dance with your lovely bride?" Bill asked Nathan, when the music stopped briefly.

"'Tis rightful," Nathan responded, and moved to take Grace's hand as he led her out onto the floor beside Bill and Azaria.

The musicians began to play music from Handel's *Water Suite*. A number of young couples swept into the room. Bon Gage and Joanna's daughters Maggie and Cora had begun receiving suitors. With their young men, they whirled onto the floor and danced freely as well.

When the music halted and another tune began, Nathan accepted Lily's hand and moved to the middle of the dining room with her. Near the doors, Bill took Azaria's hand and led her quickly through the kitchen and out the back door. Swiftly he pulled her around the back of the barn to the meadow beyond.

"Bill, I cannot breathe!" she shouted, giggling as she ran to keep up with him.

"'Tis magic afoot that I must share!" he responded and laughed.

The sun had gone and a radiant full moon replaced it, rising against the indigo sky. Stars twinkled behind the wispy clouds, pushed on by a teasing warm breeze. Bill stopped, standing in the tall grass, wet with dew. Holding her hand, he put a finger to his lips to silence her. She waited, taking in the fragrant air in great gulps. As the sky grew darker, she gripped his hand tighter and watched the slight sway of the wild flowers in the lea.

"Bill?" she whispered, growing impatient. In the distance the music from the house could be heard faintly.

"Shhh," he urged.

Suddenly, a scattering of fireflies flew up from the meadow. Their lights flickered brightly against the dark sky as they fluttered about. Azaria gasped and clapped her hands together.

"'Tis delightful, Bill!" she declared and moved forward with the enchanting feel of magic in the air. Bill remained behind her as she ran through the wildflowers, chasing the blinking lights as the mellifluous peel of her laughter fell over the field. Exhausted at last, she fell back into the damp grass.

"You shall spoil your fine dress, Azaria!" Bill called out to her.

"Take me to Papa's grave!" she exclaimed and struggled to stand in the heavy, damp dress.

Bill offered his arm to her and they moved behind the barn to the trail that led into the woods. He drew his pistol and primed it, then tapped the hilt of his sword as they proceeded deeper into the forest. Eventually, they reached the copse of birch and advanced toward the gate to the cemetery.

Bill opened the gate and waited as she stepped inside. Under the light of the moon and stars, she made her way to Luke's gravestone. She dropped to her knees on the ground beside it and moaned softly. Her tears began flowing and she was quickly reduced to sobbing, as she rested against the cold stone. Bill waited just inside the gate as she poured out her heart beside her father's grave.

"Papa, I do miss you so," she choked out, as her sobs diminished at last.

From the top of an ancient pine tree, an owl hooted. Small animals scurried around, under cover of darkness. A fox darted across the open area and into the woods again. In the distance, a wolf howled mournfully and two wolves responded.

Bill's concerns increased as the wolves heralded their approach. Quietly, he crossed the graveyard and gently touched her shoulder. She looked up and nodded as he reached for her hand. She held an embroidered handkerchief to her face as she followed him through the gates again and back to the birch trees.

"Thank you," she stammered, as her breath hitched in her chest.

"'Tis naught," he responded and hurried along the path, pulling her behind him.

With the next call of the wolf closer behind them, he began to run, nearly dragging her as they moved through the trees. She stumbled over a tree root and he twisted quickly to yank her up before she hit the ground. He gripped her arm and heaved her forward. When she tripped a second time, he placed his hands at her hips and threw her up over his shoulder. Hurriedly, he moved forward, disregarding the noises behind them.

With relief, he left the path and broke into the yard behind the house. Swiftly, he crossed the open space and into the barn. He lowered Azaria to the floor beside the ladder to the loft. A burning lamp hung there and she appreciated the comfort of the light. Bill placed his hands on his thighs and bent forward trying to catch his breath again. At last he stood and exhaled slowly.

"I shant see the bride be made a wolf's dinner on her wedding day," he chuckled.

"Twas frightening, yet exhilarating," she declared and smiled.

"Invigorating!" he announced with a wink and a smile.

"We must return to the house," she stated, resignedly. "Nathan and Mama shall miss me."

"Azaria, tis rightful you shall enjoy a blissful marriage. Yet I shall remind you in your father's absence, if there shall be trouble, I am at your beckon. You neaten your appearance afore we do enter the house," he told her and reached to remove dry grass from her hair.

"Why should there be any woe for me?" she asked, and tilted her head as she looked up into his dark eyes.

"Tis not reasonable that there shall be. Yet if it shall come to pass, I give my pledge unto you that you might call upon me to make it right."

Bill turned away, looking back at the horses stabled in the shadows, while she readjusted her dress. When she was ready, he took her arm and led her across the drive to the back door of the house. Laughing, they hurried through the kitchen and into the hall where Grace and Joseph stood talking anxiously.

"Azaria!" Grace shouted and rushed toward her. "What has become of you?" Grace stepped back, looking at the damp dress with dirt smeared on it.

"Bill did walk with me to Papa's grave. Mama, he does rest well this night," she told her and smiled.

"Come let me repair your undoing," Grace admonished, as she steered her up the stairs and passed the musicians seated in the upper hallway.

"Why should you think to remove her without a warning?" Joseph demanded angrily.

"Twas only to show her the fireflies this night that I did remove her. Yet she did bid me move on to the cemetery," he explained inoffensively.

"Did you not think it would worry her mother?"

"Regrettably, the thought did not enter my head. Tis my regret that I did trouble Grandmother," Bill assured him.

"Tis done with," Joseph responded and moved along the hall with him. "Did she find comfort at the grave?"

"I believe that she did.""

"Then twas rightful."

"Bill Henry!" Nathan shouted and marched toward him. "How should you think to remove my wife without my consent?"

"Stand off, Nathan Stone!" Bill commanded and stepped forward.

"Twas wrongful, Captain!"

"I shant allot a second warning," Bill spoke calmly, as he gripped the hilt of his saber.

Nathan turned and moved into the sitting room. Bill smiled and returned to the kitchen to clean away the last of the mud from his boots. He returned to the dining room and watched the couples twirling around. He touched Maggie Pender's hand and drew her out among the dancers.

83

Nathan and Azaria settled into married life in the former home of Capt. William Corey, near the town center. Over the month following their wedding, Chloe and the women of Burghill House continued preparations for her marriage to Teague. The new school teacher, Hattie Cummins, had come to East Grantham a month earlier. Chloe was excited about the idea of becoming Teague's wife and of leaving Botts' Tavern to live in a proper home again.

Late in June the heat and humidity of a New England summer settled over the town. Chloe had chosen a charming dress in cornflower blue silk charmeuse. The quilted corset was laced with white silk ribbon over cast pewter lacings. Le Puy lace decorated the collar and cuffs of the puffed sleeves. A modesty petticoat was paired with the corset for an elegant look.

The ceremony was performed in Rev. Pender's church with the pews full of cheerful guests. A spirited reception followed at Burghill House. The beautiful couple danced for hours with other dancers whirling around them. Early in the evening Teague slipped quietly up the stairs with Chloe behind him. From the lower hall Joseph and Bill watched them go. Teague shushed them and smiled, hurrying Chloe along faster.

In the bedroom above the kitchen, with the musicians in the hall outside the door, Teague ticked the lock. He laughed and pushed the heavy armoire along the wall to block the door. Lastly, he moved the bed up against the armoire. Chloe only shook her head and giggled.

With the soft glow of the moon, lighting the room, Teague gently swept blonde curls away from her face. His hands touched her face as he bent to kiss her seductively. With his lips pressed firmly against hers, he untied the ribbons and began loosening the stays at the front of her corset. When it remained snug around her, she giggled.

"Tis but adornment," she whispered. "The closure is found at the back," she told him and turned slowly.

His fingers moved into her hair as he began removing the pins and combs that held it securely in place. He turned to toss them on the dressing table as the curls fell over her shoulders and down her back. Eagerly, he swept her hair over her shoulder and leaned to feather kisses over the back of her neck as his fingers opened the back of the dress. The corset fell to the floor and he unhooked the back of her skirt. It puddled around her feet and he inhaled her scent.

His hands moved over her hips as he pushed the pantaloons down. She stepped out of them and started to turn, but he held her there. His warm lips trailed along her back and she shivered, laying her hands on his at her hips. He rose excruciatingly slow as his kisses traced up her spine to her neck again.

As his arms circled her waist, he turned her to face him, kissing her jaw and cheek as she twirled. She looked up into his dark eyes and stretched to put her arms around his neck. With his mouth pressed hard against hers, he unbuttoned his shirt and tore it off. He unbuttoned his pants and left them fall, quickly stepping out of them as he pulled her tight against his body.

Effortlessly he lifted her up and she held fast to his neck as he walked to the bed. He turned and fell back against the bed, landing with her on top of him.

"I do love you so, Chloe Grenier," he breathed against her ear and kissed a trail along her throat.

"And I you, Mr. Teague Grenier," she giggled, and squirmed in his arms.

"You shant escape, dear Lady," he teased. "Surrender unto me."

"How should I think to refuse one such as you," she replied, and relaxed against him.

"If you shall acquiesce, I mean to take you my love," he whispered, his deep voice growling and she trembled with excitement.

"I am yours, Teague Grenier. Do with me as you will."

Lying close beside her, he kissed along her shoulder.

84

Teague and Chloe remained at Burghill House. They talked of plans for a house of their own when children came but Teague argued against the need for a home of their own, early in their marriage. Chloe happily agreed and her belongings were delivered from Botts' Tavern to her new home.

While Teague worked long days at the millinery, common storehouse, and warehouse with Reny, Chloe toiled at Burghill House. Grace appreciated the additional help in the house and welcomed Chloe's cheerful personality.

On a staggeringly hot day in early August, Faith Gage Alray gave birth to her first baby. After two days of starts and stops, her contractions increased rapidly until she finally delivered her son, Richard Timothy Alray. Neither Lily nor Glenn's mother attended the birth. Joanna, Grace, Bon, and Millie were with her. She endured it well, given the intense heat and humidity. Grace passed the crying infant to Faith and she accepted him contentedly. But when Joanna reached to remove him again Faith gently refused.

"I shant surrender him yet. He is a great wonder," she stated and smiled.

Over the next six weeks she tended to him as much as she could during her lying-in period. In September, when Joanna approved her to return to daily chores, she carried the baby from room to room with her throughout the day. With the aid of the new housekeeper, she tended to the household and began preparing for the coming winter.

A month later, with the rich scent of fall in the air, the family travelled to the First Parish Congregational Church of East Grantham for another wedding. Joseph's oldest daughter, Thea stood in front of the altar. She was dressed in the gown that her mother, Colleen Grenier, had worn on her own wedding day, seventeen years earlier. Her groom, Leonard Mitchell, the County Jailer's son, stood proudly at her side.

"I do pronounce that you are made man and wife," Rev. Murray announced. The couple turned slowly to face the congregation. Joseph watched his pretty daughter, with her mother's strawberry blonde hair and blue eyes and felt his heart skip a beat.

Slowly, they moved along the aisle and out into the shadowy light of late day. The sun hung low over the trees and leaves scattered ahead of the wind. Leonard grasped her hand and tightened his grip before she could pull it away. He hurried along, tugging at her arm, as he climbed the stairs of the Meeting House. Thea frowned and struggled to keep up with him.

Inside, the fires had been stoked in both stoves and the worst of the chill had gone. A delightful feast was provided for the guests. A string quartet was seated in the far corner and music filled the room. Leonard pulled Thea out onto the polished floor and danced with her as the musicians played on. When she finally persuaded him to stop for a drink of mulled cider and a plate of food, she dropped into a chair against the wall.

Leonard prepared a plate with meat and sweet cakes and filled a cup for her. He placed them on the end of the table beside her chair and knelt in front of her. "Thea, you were made mine this day," he sighed as he looked into her eyes. "You shall be ever at my side, my wife. I shant see you dance with another. Am I well understood?"

"Leonard, tis naught to worry over. I shant desire any man but you," she assured him.

"Tis not a worry for you in my head, Thea. Tis the corrupt minds of other men that do burden my heart. You shant challenge my words. If there be another man about, you shant take leave of me and none shall touch you for to dance. Shall you dispute my word?"

"I shant think to rebel against you," she told him and shuddered at the change in him.

"Mayhap you have a chill," he observed. "Come and sit near the stove."

He carried her chair and plate across the room as she followed with her cup. She felt foolish sitting alone near the stove. Leonard knelt beside her and watched as she ate slowly. She tried to ignore him and watched friends dancing.

"Shant you think to eat as well? The sweet cakes are delightful."

"Mayhap I shall," he responded and stood slowly. He strode back to the tables of food and began filling a plate for himself. As he selected from the turkey, venison and other items on the largest platter, he glanced back at Thea frequently. She sat with the empty plate on her lap and watched Leonard worriedly.

Reny strode away from the dance floor and stopped to congratulate Thea on her marriage. She smiled and thanked him.

"Might I ask you to dance?" he asked and held his hand out to her. Quickly, Leonard appeared at her side.

"How shall you think to accost my wife as I do stand away from her?" Leonard demanded indignantly.

"Leonard," Thea whispered anxiously.

"I meant no affront," Reny assured him.

Leonard stepped forward with his hand against Reny's chest as he backed him against the wall. "Tis my wife!"

"She is of my family, Mitchell! No insult was intended!" Reny reassured, as he pushed back. Leonard took a step back, then steadied himself again.

Teague and Bill approached from the right as guests began watching the confrontation. Teague gripped Leonard's arm and walked him backwards as Bill moved between them and spoke quietly to Reny. Thea remained seated, embarrassed by her new husband's behavior.

Bill passed the plate and cup to Reny, then took Thea's hand as she stood. Behind him, Bill heard the scuffle and swung around to see Leonard struggling to break free of Teague's grip.

"Tis my wife! You shant handle her!" he shouted at Bill.

Bill whispered to Reny and strode toward Teague and Leonard. Reny walked Thea to the end of the tables where Joseph, Millie, and Grace were sitting. Across the room, Bill leaned close to Leonard and talked low.

"Good Sir, tis your wedding day and I shant distress your dear bride by spilling your blood here on the floor. Yet if you shant compose yourself I shall correct you afore all. Thea is a woman of virtue and you shant scandalize her with undeserved suspicions. Might you resolve your misdeed of your own or shall you require the aid of Teague and me behind this building?"

"How shall you think to threaten me so?" Leonard hissed.

"Thea shant be shamed on her wedding day! Correct yourself or you shall be removed to be thrashed in seclusion," Bill spoke slowly through clenched jaws.

"Tis done with," Leonard snapped and jerked away from Teague. He stomped back across the room to stand with Thea. Joseph looked up at him as he stood slowly.

"Mr. Mitchell, I shant abide another display such as this," Joseph warned. "If you cannot manage a degree of decorum, my daughter shall be removed to my home."

"Yes, Sir," Leonard responded and looked down to the floor. "Thea, might we take leave?"

"No," Joseph responded. She shall remain and you shall regulate your mood. Take your lovely wife and dance with her. She shall wear a smile this day. I trust you shall ensure it."

Leonard took her hand and moved slowly out among the dancers. As they twirled on the floor, he saw Bill dancing with Thea's sister, Clara. He glared at Bill and looked away. Bill chuckled, and moved away from the bridal couple to prevent agitating the groom further.

85

After a long talk with his father and Joseph the following morning, Leonard was determined to prevent another confrontation with them. He and Thea lived in his father's house with the large Mitchell family. He knew that his father would remain aware of his manner at home and at work.

The Mitchell family attended the church where Rev. Murray preached and Thea was obligated to attend with her new husband. Yet, after the weekly service, they journeyed to Burghill House for dinner with her family. To appease both his father and father-in-law, Leonard made peace with Thea's older brother, Teague and with Bill and Reny, as well. He was pardoned and was quickly welcomed into the circle in the sitting room.

In Rev. Murray's home, Sunday had become an especially pleasant day for the minister and his beloved wife, Aileen. Norah had gone to live and work in the orphan asylum at Georges Falls. Yet on Sundays she travelled to East Grantham to hear her father preach and to enjoy dinner with her parents.

A month earlier she had been accompanied by Paul Hanscom, as she journeyed to the church. He was a handyman in his late 30s who worked at the children's home as well. He sat with Rev. Murray and asked for permission to court Norah under the watchful eye of Mrs. Humboldt, who now managed the orphan's home.

Reluctantly, the minister agreed. But before he would permit the courtship, he told the man of Norah's past. He advised Hanscom that he would be permitted to withdraw his request and leave peaceably. The minister would return Norah to the home the following morning.

"Good Sir, I shall not think to change my heart. Tis Norah I do hold dear and I shall see her made my wife, if you shant speak an objection," Paul replied.

"Many thanks," Tomas declared, and stood to shake his hand.

After a fine meal, Paul suggested that he and Norah return before it was too late in the evening. She agreed, but Rev. Murray questioned their travel without a proper escort. With Hanscom's assurances, he hesitantly agreed, and they quickly left.

Only five miles from Rev. Murray's home, Paul stopped at Cleary's Tavern for the night. With Norah at his side, he stated that only one room would be needed for him and his wife. Norah only smiled and followed him up the stairs to a small bed chamber.

Azaria bubbled about her pregnancy as the men talked about the latest news regarding the war. She was certain that her baby would be a boy. Teague worried over lost shipments due to attacks by the British Navy. When they were done with the meal, the other women cleaned the kitchen and Azaria sat at the table holding Faith's baby. Faith hovered close and gushed over her sleeping infant. Azaria finally smiled and relented, as Faith scooped the baby up from her arms.

"'Tis a fine thing that you shall be blessed with another child, Aunt Sannah," Lily announced, as she sipped from the blended wine that Mac had given her after dinner.

"She is Azaria, not Isannah," Grace corrected. Lily turned to stare at the flames curling up from underneath the log and sipped from her glass.

86

December brought mild temperatures and only a dusting of snow. Grace quickly announced that they would be holding a grand Christmas ball at Burghill House. The family had grown and in spite of the loss of Luke the previous spring, she wanted the holiday to be wonderful. As they sat at the table discussing plans, the women quickly agreed with Grace, while the men grumbled.

In the kitchen after dinner, the women began making great plans for the Christmas party. Azaria, Faith, Thea, and Chloe soon drifted off to the side where they talked about babies and their young husbands. Grace listened to them and smiled at their innocence. She thought of the early years of her marriage with Phillip and the years with Luke. She lifted her Great Grandson from Faith's arms and returned to the talk of Christmas.

Another two weeks passed and the holidays drew closer. The excitement in the house was building and Grace remained confident that the calm weather would remain. She had feared that without Luke the house would be dreary and the holidays unbearable. But surrounded by her children, grandchildren, and great grandchildren, she felt great joy. She whispered a word of thanks to Luke for the family that he had given to her.

The family began gathering around the table and the trays, platters, dishes, and bowls were placed along the center. Wine glasses were filled and additional flagons were set out. Grace sat at last and they joined hands as Rev. Pender led them in prayer. Swiftly the food was passed around the table.

Bon sat beside her suitor, Riley Lawrence. When the food had been served and they began to eat, she nudged Riley and smiled. He inhaled deeply and stood. Heads slowly turned to look at him.

He cleared his throat and looked to Joseph. Amused, Joseph nodded and smiled back at him.

"I should like to share that I did propose a marriage to Bon and she did accept. Her brother, Eddie is in Boston and I did dispatch a missive to him. He did state that he shall agree, if Joseph shall permit the union."

Everyone looked to Joseph. "I did endorse the marriage," he declared.

Glasses were raised and the toasts began. Bon glowed as she looked at Riley and admired his deep brown eyes. His cheeks flushed with the sudden wave of attention. The son of the local silversmith, he came from a small family. With only one sibling, an older brother, he was amazed by the massive gatherings at Burghill House. He looked forward to marrying Bon and beginning a large family as well.

The door knocker clanked firmly against the door and Teague stood to answer it. Faith's husband, Glenn made a humorous toast and the room erupted in laughter. In the entryway Teague raised his voice and the dining room quieted as they listened. Joseph stepped toward the doorway and looked out at the open doorway.

"Tis not my doing, Sir!" the old woman shouted.

"Madam, why have you come to this house?" he demanded.

"I do seek Mr. Stone!"

"Does the child require a surgeon?" he asked, as he gingerly touched the filthy blanket and looked at the tiny infant's dirty face. He stepped back, cringing in disgust.

"Are ye daft?" she shrieked. "The babe was fathered by him and he shall take it in hand. The mother did light out for Boston this morn and I shant be left to tend it!"

Teague looked at her in surprise and stepped back further. Gripping the door frame, she climbed painfully up from the top step to the floor in the entryway. She pushed the baby toward Teague and he raised his hands as he moved away from her. Joseph stepped forward and hesitantly accepted the child from her.

"Stone!" he roared and leaned into the dining room. Nathan remained seated with his head down, as everyone at the table turned to look in his direction.

At the front door, Teague held out a coin for the old woman and sent her on her way. He slammed the door and marched into the dining room. He stopped at the head of the table beside his father.

"The old woman did state that the child is of your blood, Nathan Stone! The mother is a whore from the tavern! What do you mean to do with it?" Teague thundered, angrily. The infant woke and began to cry. Nathan looked up at Joseph and Teague. He opened his mouth to speak and faltered.

Azaria's face blazed bright red as she absorbed the intense humiliation of the disclosure in front of her entire family. She blinked and tears spilled from her eyes. She wiped at them as her vision blurred. The room appeared to spin and she touched her fingertips to her forehead. Her breathing increased and her heart boomed against her chest.

She heard her brother, Joseph speaking and saw something moving in his arms. Teague yelled and she struggled to understand his words. Someone was crying but the sound blended with the angry words. She turned her head and looked at her husband, seated beside her. He stared into her eyes and moved a hand toward her. He spoke but she could not hear him. Her world was moving in slow motion and she felt a wave of nausea as the baby kicked inside her belly.

Swiftly, she grabbed for the basket of bread and threw several slices down on her plate. Reeling, she looked to Nathan again. She gripped the edge of the pickle dish, spilling the juice on the tablecloth as she dumped the pickles onto her plate. Her head swam as she seized the large meat fork from the platter and stabbed it through Nathan's hand to the table beneath it.

Nathan screamed as the big, silver fork staked his hand to the table. Gasps were heard around the table and Mac rose quickly to move between Azaria and Nathan. Azaria stood slowly and walked toward Joseph, still wiping at her wet face.

"Bill Henry, shall you accompany me?" she called out, as she looked at the grubby baby blanket.

Bill stood and shrugged as he walked to the end of the table. He watched as Azaria took the infant from Joseph and turned to look at Nathan. She watched with satisfaction as, Mac yanked the fork out of his hand and blood dripped on his favorite pants. Mac wrapped a linen napkin around it to slow the bleeding.

"Annie, bring a bowl of vinegar," Mac called to his wife.

"I shall remove this child to the orphan's asylum as it has no mother and no fitting father!" Azaria announced, as she hurried along the hall to the kitchen with Bill close behind her. She waited in the barn while he harnessed a team and prepared the carriage. Seated beside him, she rode through the town center and on to Georges Falls.

They arrived at the orphan asylum and he helped her down. She walked to the front door and pounded with her fist. She stepped back, surprised when Norah opened it. Norah looked down and reached for the child.

"Tis a foundling that shant be claimed," Azaria advised her. "Good day," she stated and tromped back down to the walk. Bill waited at the carriage and assisted her as she climbed up again. In silence they rode back to Burghill House, as slow as the horse would walk.

87

When Azaria and Bill arrived at the house, Nathan had gone. With her first baby due in just two months, Azaria made the decision to remain in her family home. Silently, Grace climbed the stairs with her and helped her into a night gown. She sat in the bed, propped up on pillows, with Grace seated beside her. Shadows danced up the wall, as the fire flickered in the fireplace. Mrs. Whitley carried in a tray of food and Grace coaxed Azaria to eat.

"Mama, did he never love me?" she asked, when Mrs. Whitley had gone.

"I know not," Grace whispered. "Sup now and you shall sleep."

In the morning Nathan knocked at the front door, as dry leaves swirled around his feet. A layer of frost covered the ground and the scent of snow was in the air. He inhaled and coughed as he pulled the cloak tighter at his throat.

"Mr. Stone, you are not welcome in my house this day," Grace told him, as she held the door open and looked out at him.

"Tis my wife I have come for, Mrs. Wallace," Nathan responded respectfully.

"Twas a wakeful night for Azaria. She is yet in her bed and I shant think to wake her."

Nathan nodded slowly and turned to walk back along the walk. He mounted his horse and rode north on Kings Wood Road. He trotted up the drive beside the tavern and stopped outside the livery. Laurent Morgan stood in the doorway of the barn watching him. Nathan lifted a hand and shouted a greeting, but Laurent only turned away and moved back inside.

Gloomily, Nathan walked around to the front of the tavern and opened the door. Inside the large, open room, several patrons were seated at tables, eating, drinking, and chatting. He noted the greetings from neighbors and concluded that the incident at Burghill House, the day before, had been hushed. Relieved, he dropped into a chair and waited for a tankard of ale.

Penn Cooper delivered two bowls of cornmeal mush to the next table and stopped to speak with Nathan. Quickly, he strode back to the bar for a flagon of wine and the ale. Nathan saw Julia enter with a large basket of bread, cakes, and muffins. She stared at him for a moment, then slowly approached him.

"Mr. Stone, you are unwelcome in this tavern," she told him quietly.

"Tis a public inn, dear lady," Nathan responded calmly. "How shall you bid me take leave?"

"The tavern is of my family. You did greatly offend our Azaria and I have no desire to look upon you."

"Tis wrongful that you shall behave so, Julia Morgan," he replied, and glared up at her.

"Think as you like, yet I shall bid you go," she told him firmly.

He glanced toward the kitchen and saw Laurent filling the doorway. Agreeably, he pushed the chair back from the table, scraping it noisily as he moved. He stood and walked out into the cold day. He mounted his horse again and proceeded through the town center to River Road. With a growing irritation, he urged the horse to a gallop as he passed the jail. He could hear the clamor from the busy waterfront long before he could see it.

Behind Wren's Tavern, he left his horse in the livery and marched around the building to the front door. The building was filled with the chaos of dozens of raucous conversations, laughter, and the sound of the fiddle being played at the back of the room.

Nathan found an empty table and sat beside a group of French sailors, loudly discussing a recent encounter with a British warship.

A young barmaid approached Nathan's table and scowled. "Mr. Stone," she uttered bitterly.

"Erin, I knew not of the child," he assured her.

"'Tis a lie, Sir," she retorted.

"Bring me ale and bread, Erin," he told her and looked away.

"Nathan Stone!" a deep voice called out behind him. He turned slowly and shrank as he realized the utterance had come from Bill Henry. Bill stood and made his way through the maze of tables toward Nathan. Smiling menacingly, Bill pulled out a chair across from Nathan and sat.

"I have no quarrel with you, Capt. Henry," Nathan declared and held up his hands.

"Were you not warned?" Bill asked darkly. His sword sang gloriously as he withdrew it from the sheath and placed it on the table. He pulled out a piece of silk and began polishing the shiny surface, almost lovingly.

"Shall you think to end me this day afore a room of watchers?" Nathan demanded, as the fear spread slowly through his body and gripped his mind.

"Mayhap I shall," Bill replied and chuckled. Bill stood quickly, with his sword held high. "This man did wrong against a woman of my family and I do mean to end him here this day!" he called out and a riotous cheer filled the air.

"You cannot," Nathan stated, trying to sound forceful.

"Cet homme fait de mal contre ma famille et je ne pense à lui termine ici ce jour!" Bill shouted and another group shouted in agreement and applauded. "Deze man verkeerd heeft gedaan tegen mijn familie en ik denk dat hier een einde hem op deze dag!" he proclaimed and the Dutch sailors hooted as well.

Bill sat again and laughed wickedly as he returned to polishing his saber. Erin delivered the ale to Nathan and another dram of whiskey for Bill, before she quickly retreated to the bar. The barkeep watched them warily but did not move against Bill.

"Capt. Henry, if you shall murder me, you shall hang," Nathan warned.

Bill dropped his head back and laughed heartily. He swallowed the whiskey and banged the flint glass against the table. "You shant be the first man to meet his end on my sword. Threat of a hanging shant lessen my spirit. I did warn you away from the barmaid. Did you doubt my words?"

"I did not," Nathan murmured. "Twas not an intentional happening. I do regret greatly that my actions did harm Azaria."

"Speak not of Azaria!" Bill warned and stared savagely into Nathan's frightened eyes.

Bill raised a hand and gestured toward the bar. The barkeep nodded and Erin hurried toward the table. She looked down at Bill and smiled at his handsome face.

"Sir?" she asked softly.

"Did Stone order food from you?"

"He did request a bowl of boiled cornmeal."

"Bring the bowl to him. I shall require a meat pie and another dram."

"Tis no meat pie to be served this morn," she responded and took a step back.

"Fear not," he offered, reassuringly. "No harm shall come unto you with such a lovely face. Might you fry eggs for me and serve bread with apple butter?"

"Yes, Sir," she responded eagerly.

He nodded and winked, and she hurried back to the kitchen. His smile faded quickly as he looked back to Nathan. Slowly, he lifted his sword and slid it back into the leather sheath. The silk cloth disappeared as well. He placed his hands on the table and exhaled slowly.

"This day you shall ride to the home for orphans and make a gift of monies. Mayhap you shall take diapering goods to them as well. Tis rightful you shall provide for the infant you did sire."

"I shall," Nathan agreed quickly.

Erin returned with the food and they ate in silence. When they were done, Bill stood and gripped the back of his chair. Leaning forward, he stared into Nathan's eyes. "You shall grant an end to the marriage and trouble Azaria no more."

"Tis wrongful that you shall require that the union be ended. Azaria shall understand that I am sorrowful. It shall be mended. Tis an infant to come, Capt. Henry!"

"Azaria did believe the child in her belly to be your first child. Yet your first progeny does linger in the home for orphans. She shall require a divorce of you and you shall grant it. Take leave, Nathan Stone," Bill advised him.

Nathan stood and backed away from the table. Quickly, he left the tavern and hurried toward the livery. Warily, he rode to his house and secured his horse in the barn. Inside his house, he barred the doors and stoked the fires. Mrs. Slade kneaded bread dough at the kitchen table, watching him curiously as he scurried through the house.

"The bars shall not be removed from the doors, nor visitors permitted within this day. If any shall call for me, I must be summoned afore you shall think to sanction entry," he jabbered anxiously.

She nodded agreeably and frowned as he bounded up the stairs and slammed his bedroom door. She shook her head and continued working the bread dough.

88

Two weeks passed and Azaria's mood improved with the distraction of the Christmas party. The house was decorated with the fresh pine boughs, holly sprigs and pine cones that Azaria and Bill had gathered. Aromatic bayberry candles burned throughout the first floor. The delicious mingled aromas of chocolate, gingerbread, and roasting meats wafted out from the kitchen.

Azaria strode down the stairs dressed in a dazzling white, satin gown, richly embroidered in gold thread with sapphire blue glass beads. Her dark hair was pinned up with silky blue ribbons braided through it. On the bottom step she accepted a glass of wine from Teague and they wandered into the kitchen.

Grace entered the room wearing an elegant red dress. Red and white silk ribbons, narrow strips of lace and holly berries adorned her hair. She smiled proudly at the decorations and the array of food on the tables in the kitchen. She thought of Phillip and Luke and knew they would be pleased with the house filled with friends and family for Christmas again. Memories of her father swirled in her head and she felt a deep regret that he did not survive to know his grandchildren and enjoy grand holidays in his house.

The musicians arrived and settled in the upstairs hallway. Over the next hour, the noise level rose rapidly and guests wandered through the kitchen and sitting room. Laughter rang out from the dining room where the dancing had begun.

The front door opened and another family arrived. Joshua and Katie Chernock nudged their eight children in ahead of them. Close behind Joshua, Nathan Stone stepped into the entryway. He unbuttoned his cloak and slipped it off his shoulders. Unnoticed, he moved toward the kitchen with the flow of guests. Warily, he watched for Azaria and chatted distractedly with friends and neighbors. He poured a glass of mulled wine and ate one of the small glazed pumpkin cakes.

Leisurely, he wandered to the sitting room and stopped outside the doors. Joseph, Teague, and Mac stood near the fireplace laughing and sharing toasts. He steered away and edged closer to the dining room. Just inside the doorway, he saw Azaria standing with Grace and Lily. He acknowledged Rev. Murray's greeting and slipped passed him behind Azaria.

"I have missed you greatly," he whispered, close to her ear.

Startled, she turned quickly and stared up at him. "You should not be here."

"Azaria, I must speak to you. Your family did prevent it wrongfully. I am yet your husband, Azaria Stone," he murmured softly.

"Nathan Stone, you are not welcome in this house," Grace reminded him, discretely. "I must bid you take leave."

"Mrs. Wallace, I beseech you, permit me to speak unto my wife. Tis my child that she does hold within."

"Tis wrongful that you did enter deceptively," she scolded.

"I shall talk with him, Mama," Azaria agreed, and patted Grace's hand.

"Mayhap you shall move to my bedroom to speak in seclusion," Grace offered.

"No, Joseph, Mac, and Teague do linger in the sitting room afore your bed chamber," Nathan pleaded.

"We shall climb quietly up the stairs and shall not be seen," Azaria assured her. She hurried across the crowded hallway with Nathan behind her. Quickly, they rushed up to the bedroom that had become Azaria's.

From the hall below, Bill had seen them on the stairs and he stepped into the sitting room. Joseph and Mac walked quietly up the stairs followed by Teague, Bill, and Reny. Joseph nodded toward the musicians and gestured to them, indicating that they should continue to play. As the refrain ended, Joseph held up his hand and they sat still, waiting. Mac leaned close to the door and heard the low murmur of voices inside. Joseph shrugged and nodded to the musicians as they lifted their instruments and began to play again.

Another lively tune ended and Nathan continued to plead his case. Azaria watched the snow falling gently in the moonlight outside the window, as he paced and chattered behind her. Her hand caressed the satin fabric that covered her round belly. The baby kicked against her hand and she laughed.

"Tis nothing of amusement in my words!" he barked angrily.

"Nathan, I shall hear no more this night. Allow me to return to Mama's party."

"Azaria, permit me to remain at your side. When the ball is done with, come to my home this night."

"I cannot," she protested. "The marriage is done, Nathan. I do mean to end it when the child does come."

"No, Azaria! You shall not think to end the marriage. You did speak vows unto me and you shant relent. My wife, I do order that you be done with this jabber and return to the home of your husband!"

"I shant, Nathan!" she proclaimed as he grabbed her arm and turned her around to face him. He gripped her shoulders and shook her fiercely. Furiously, he pulled her close and held her tight as she fought to break away from him. "You do pain me! Release me, Nathan!" she shouted.

The energetic baroque music ended again outside the door.

"No, Azaria," Nathan breathed and dug his fingers into her arms as he pressed his mouth over hers. As she struggled harder, he slapped her face. Holding her right arm tighter, he fought to hold her as she tried to pull away. With his second slap, she screamed and tore free from his grip. She fell backward against the hearth mat and rolled to her side, clutching her belly.

The door flew open, shattering the horsehair plaster as the doorknob smashed against the wall. Mac reached the fireplace first and knelt beside her. Nathan leaned close to assess her and Mac's elbow struck his cheek bone as the massive arm swept him back against the wall. Nathan dropped to the floor in a heap as Mac gently moved Azaria to the bed.

"Get my bag!" Mac shouted in his great booming voice. Reny dashed down the stairs and across the road to Mac's house. He grabbed the heavy leather bag and ran back.

Nathan was removed to the hallway with a diagonal gash over his cheek bone. Joseph remained in front of Nathan as Teague and Bill glared at him. Joanna was summoned as Mac worried over Azaria. The musicians moved down to the first floor where they played more sedate music. The remaining guests ate and drank but the dancing and raucous chatter had ended as everyone worried about Azaria and her baby.

As the evening passed, more of the guests departed, leaving only the family in the house by midnight. While Joanna tended to Azaria, Mac stitched up the ragged tear on Nathan's cheek that continued to bleed. When he had finished, he ordered Nathan out of the house. Teague and Bill escorted him out to the barn and watched while he harnessed his horse and readied his carriage.

"Did you bring the carriage as you thought to remove Azaria this night?" Bill asked.

"I have naught to speak of with you," Nathan shouted, as he climbed up into the buggy and snapped the reins. More concerned with Azaria, Teague and Bill went back inside to wait for news.

During the night Joanna delivered a tiny, infant to Azaria. She held the premature baby girl who struggled to breathe. The child did not cry and moved little. Azaria was conscious when the infant was born. She held her briefly before Joanna took her away again. Mac offered a strong herbal drink, blended with Laudanum to allow her to sleep.

"What of the child?" Grace asked anxiously as Mac worked in the kitchen blending another drink for Azaria.

"Tis unknown, yet tis nearly a certainty that she shall perish afore morning."

Mac sent Annie up to the bed chamber at Joanna's request. Annie opened her bodice and settled close to the warmth of the fireplace. Swaddled and covered by a folded quilt, the baby slept against Annie. Gradually, Annie expressed a few drops of milk into the infant's mouth and coaxed her to swallow. The process continued through the night and into the morning when Faith arrived to take over while Annie slept.

With the heavy drapes drawn over the windows, the room remained murky through the day. Mac tended to Azaria and was pleased when she asked for a tray of lunch. A chaise was moved into the room and placed close to the fire to permit her to hold the baby while keeping her warm. Faith helped Azaria to secrete colostrum for her tiny infant. With a half dozen pillows, she was able to sleep, well propped against the curved side of the chaise, while holding the child securely against her.

Nathan returned repeatedly over the next week. He begged and pleaded to be permitted to see Azaria and the baby. Grace wavered, sympathizing with him and feeling that he should see his child before she passed. Yet she could not forget that her own daughter had suffered at his hands. Reluctantly, she turned him away again.

Sunday morning before the church service, Nathan came again. Joseph agreed to permit him to see the infant if Azaria would allow it. Nathan assented and followed Joseph up the stairs. The door remained open and Teague stood outside the room, leaning against the railing. Joseph sat near the window as Nathan approached the fireplace.

"Why have you come yet again, Nathan?" Azaria asked impatiently.

"To look upon my child," he responded.

"How shall this child be more to you than the baby you did discard?" she posed.

"Azaria, the harlot was naught to me. You are my beloved wife and this child is of my heart."

"Nathan Stone, you do sicken me," Azaria declared coldly. She felt the tiny body move against her and lowered her voice. "I do mean to end the marriage. If this child shall survive, I pray that she shall never know of the night of her birthing."

"Shant you think to forgive my transgressions?"

"In time, mayhap I shall forgive, yet I shant open my heart to bid you welcome again. Tis done, Nathan. You did cut me deep with your misdeeds and I shant delight in a life with you ever more."

"Azaria, I beseech you," he pleaded tearfully, as he dropped to his knees beside her.

"Do not discomfit me further with such pleadings. If you mean to look upon the child, have done with it and take your leave."

Nathan stood slowly and moved to stand close to Azaria. She lifted the edge of the quilt and pulled it back to reveal the tiny body.

"Tis a diminutive soul," he uttered as he reached to touch the small hand.

"Twas afore the time for her parturition," she told, and looked resentfully up into his eyes.

"Is there naught that I might utter to sway you?"

"I did give her the name of Victoria Wallace Stone. When she is gone from me, I shall see her laid to rest in my family's cemetery."

"Might we speak apart from Joseph?" he whispered.

Azaria looked passed him to Joseph and shook her head, "No, we shall not. Take leave, Nathan and trouble me no more."

"Tis not the end of it, Azaria. You are my wife and I shall not see you dissolve the marriage we did make."

"Nathan, twas your deeds that did bring ruin unto it all. Go!" she shouted, and the baby made weak squeaking noises in protest.

Joseph stood and moved across the floor with his boots thumping loudly against the wood. "Tis done, Stone," Joseph warned.

"Have you no respect for the authority of a husband over his wife?" Nathan pressed.

"You did forsake your wife. Must I remind you that she is my sister and this is my house? Advance to the door or I shall remove you bodily."

Nathan leaned to kiss Azaria and she turned away from him. Angrily, he stomped down the stairs and out the front door, slamming it behind him.

89

The wind howled through the trees, whirling snow in the night air. Dense clouds shrouded the moon and the stars dimmed. Nathan woke and shivered in the chill of the room. He sat up and looked at the fireplace. Low flames flickered around the wood and the embers glowed beneath the grate. He studied it and threw back the quilt, rising to stoke it again.

"Tis a frigid night, Stone," the deep voice asserted.

"Who is there?" Nathan demanded.

"You speak as though you do not know me."

"Take leave of this house!" he demanded.

Seated on the back of the arm chair, with his feet flat on the silk brocade cushion, Bill watched Nathan's shadow cross the room. He chuckled and enjoyed the scent of Nathan's fear in the air.

"Move to build up the fire and we shall talk more. Tis a frightfully cold night."

"You have trespassed into my home. Tis wrongful," Nathan cried as he realized that the intruder was Capt. Bill Henry. Slowly, Nathan knelt on the hearth mat. The flames quickly curled around the kindling and spread to the logs that he added. A flickering light played along the wall. Holding his breath, he turned to face Bill.

Nathan caught the glint of light reflected on the shiny surface of the long sword. Terrified, he padded back across the icy floor and sat on the bed.

"Azaria does wish to end the marriage," Bill stated.

"She is my wife," Nathan protested.

"My tolerance does wane."

"The child shall be lost. Shall you require that my wife be taken from me as well?"

"Tis not my bidding. The woman shall appeal for a divorce and you shall grant it agreeably."

"Yes, I shall," Nathan lied as he pulled the quilt up to his chin and closed his eyes tight.

"Sleep well," Bill told him, and chuckled again. "And heed my warnings."

Nathan opened his eyes again and looked around. He sat alone in the room, shivering from the cold and his fear. When he summoned the courage, he slipped out of the bed and searched the room but found no trace of anyone there. He opened the door and hurried down the stairs to the entryway where the bar remained on the door and the lock was in place. At the back door, there was also a board to secure it. In a panic, he ran through the house, checking the latches on the windows.

"Twas but a dream," Nathan declared, as he felt the touch of the cold metal against his neck.

"Nathan Stone, on the morrow you shall travel to the orphan's home as you were instructed," Bill whispered from behind him.

"Test me no more," he cautioned, as he tilted the blade and drew it across Nathan's throat. He chuckled and withdrew the sword as blood trickled from the cut. "Mayhap you shall see me out," Bill announced and strode boldly back to remove the bar from the front door.

90

With freezing rain tapping on the windows, a messenger rapped at the front door of Burghill House. Grace accepted the pounded leather envelope for Capt. Henry. She offered the young rider a hot cup of coffee by the fire, but he politely declined. He would deliver a second message to the Customs House and take a room at the tavern for the night.

Grace hurried up to Azaria's room where Bill sat near the window reading aloud to her. The baby, Victoria, had survived her first month. Azaria remained on the chaise near the fire with her, night and day. Bill, Clara ,and Millie took turns visiting with her and reading books to distract her from the long, boring winter days.

Bill opened the leather sleeve and pulled out a sealed envelope. The hard wax seal snapped in two as he bent it and pulled out a single sheet of parchment.

"Of the spring 1813, *Mi Querida Charlotte* did sustain great damage in a skirmish with the British frigate, *Junan.* We did retreat to the south and put into port at St Augustine, Florida. Repairs were done to permit our return to Tortuga. As we did proceed north again, storms and aggressive ships did hinder us.

In the month of September, we did chance upon an exchange between the *USS Enterprise* and *HMS Boxer* above Massachusetts. The American brig did force the surrender of the Brit's sloop. The Commanders of both vessels were lost in the battle and much of the crews as well. Again, we were forced south. When the winter does break, we shall push north yet again, to the port at East Grantham. We do pray that our Captain shall be found well and good at our arrival."

"Do you mean to take leave of us?" Azaria asked.

"When my ships shall return at last, I must go. We shall make for the southern islands and await the end of the war. I shall come again," Bill assured her.

"We shall miss you greatly," Grace told him and frowned.

"I shant go this day," Bill reminded them, and smiled.

February brought bleak days of freezing rain and unpleasant winds. Joanna ended Azaria's lying-in term. Both Mac and Joanna marveled at the infant who had survived. Her breathing was still worrisome but they held new hope for her. Through the bitter winter days, Azaria kept the baby against her bare skin under the heavy quilt for added warmth.

Norah returned to ask that her father officiate at her wedding. The following morning, Paul Hanscom and Norah stood in her father's church as they spoke their vows. The couple remained for only a few hours before travelling back to Georges Falls on icy roads. Rev. Murray felt a great wave of relief that his daughter had married again at last.

As the date for Bon's wedding neared in the spring, Lily was moved downstairs to the bedroom next to Grace's room. Lily's windows were bolted shut and a lock was installed on the outside of her door. Most days she was disoriented, but calm. Yet there were still occasional days when she demanded the return of her cat and she reacted badly when it could not be found.

91

With the arrival of the spring weather, Bill began anxiously watching for his ships on the waterfront again. Daily, he rode to the warehouse and paced along the docks. He knew he would miss the family when he was gone again, but he yearned to return to the sea.

"Bill, might I talk with you?" Reny asked, as he approached Bill's table in Wren's Tavern.

"Assuredly," Bill responded and pushed a chair back with the toe of his boot.

Reny sat and folded his hands to conceal his edginess. He looked at Bill and forced a smile. "When you make to leave, might you hire me onto your ship?"

"I do mean to sail for Rum Point in the Tortugas, Reny. I shant come to the north again afore this vile war has ended."

"Tis agreeable," Reny nodded. "I am but a shadow of Teague in this place. Tis rightful I shall depart and be thought a man at last."

"Shall your mother permit this thing?"

"Bill, I am a man and shant appeal to my mother afore I determine to depart."

"Reny, my mother and father did pass and a dreadful life did befall me. I could not desert my family with not a farewell to them. You must go to your mother and the father who did raise you up. Do not take leave of them with a bitter feeling in your wake."

Reny relented and left to talk with Laurent and Julia. Laurent accepted the news well but Julia was quickly reduced to tears. She considered forbidding it but remembered the debacle with Norah. Laurent took her hand and nodded slowly.

"Shall the good Captain agree to this scheme?" Laurent asked.

"He will," Reny answered.

"Tis to you to make your way as a man shall," Laurent advised him and offered his hand. Reny smiled and shook it firmly.

When Sunday dinner was finished and the desserts were carried in from the kitchen, Reny rose and cleared his throat. The random conversations quieted as they turned to look at him curiously.

"Capt. Henry's ships are soon to return and he shall depart from us. Let us toast to him afore he does go," Reny announced. Around the table the glasses clinked together and they wished him well. "And I shall sail with him," he added, as an uncomfortable silence settled over the table.

Laurent rose and lifted his glass high, "Reny shall serve well on your ship, Capt. Henry."

Bill smiled and bobbed his head in agreement. He raised his goblet high to salute Reny as well. Another round of toasts was made and the glasses refilled before the men finally left the dining room.

"Did you mean to speak with me of this scheme afore you did take leave?" Teague asked as he swallowed a second slug of whiskey.

"I did," Reny answered apologetically. "The business shall be left in able hands with no opines from me."

"Shall you think to reap the profit of my labor as you do voyage?"

"I do not. Tis left to you, Teague and you shall yield the gains."

"Then I shall wish you naught but calm seas," Teague announced and clapped Reny on the back as they laughed and moved to the dessert tray.

92

From the top of the tall pine tree, an owl hooted and spun his head, surveying the field below. He swooped down, grasped a field mouse and landed on the high branch again. The sky gradually changed from an inky blue to a dusky gray. Birds began singing to each other and hopping around busily, on the tree branches.

A tall man rode passed Burghill House and stopped in front of the church. The instructions he had been given were to look for the large home before the church. Growing annoyed with the search in the dim light, he turned the horse and trotted back along the road.

At the front door, he drew his pistol, primed it and raised the door knocker. He banged it firmly and listened intently for sounds from inside. Edgily, he lifted his fist and pounded against the wood hard enough to rattle the knocker. The sound echoed in the hall. He turned and watched the sky warily as a bright pink glow colored the horizon.

Inside the house, the light from an oil lamp bobbed down the stairs and stopped in the entryway. Teague raised the bar and opened the door. "The physician shall be found athwart the road!" he snapped.

"Tis Capt. Henry I do seek," the big man demanded.

Teague moved back to the bottom of the stairs. "Bill Henry!" he roared.

From the second floor he heard a baby cry. He placed the lamp on the small table in the hall and moved back to the doorway. Bill strode down the attic stairs and walked with Joseph to the first floor.

"Teague, that you have no babies yet to be wakened does not lessen the burden for others." Joseph growled, as he approached the front door. "Who does roust the house at this hour?"

"Kennelm!" Bill shouted, and ran to shake the giant's hand. Still holding his hand, he pulled him inside and shut the door. They hurried back to the kitchen and Kennelm ducked to enter the room. Bill pulled out the whiskey jug and sat talking with his first mate, as the sun rose.

Mrs. Whitley appeared in the kitchen and began preparing breakfast. The men accepted fresh coffee and bread with apple butter as they moved to the dining room. Kennelm talked of the troubles and profits from the past year. Slowly, the house woke around them and a hearty breakfast was served.

Under the early May sun, Bill and Kennelm rode for the waterfront. Excitedly, Bill boarded the *Mi Querida Charlotte* and began wandering around the deck. He beamed, listening to the calls of the crew, as they worked busily. He hurried below deck into his cabin, where Kennelm's belongings remained. Still smiling, he looked back to the door of the cabin where his first mate stood.

"It shall be cleared this day, Captain!" he declared, as he studied the grain of the wood on the floor.

"Have they emptied the hold?" Bill asked.

"Aye aye, Capt. Henry!"

"We shant depart afore the morrow," Bill announced. "'Tis work yet to be finished, and then we shall sail for the Mediterranean under the Spanish flag. O'er the Atlantic we shall lower colors of Spain and shall raise the French tricolor."

"You mean to fly the French flag?" Kennelm prodded.

"Shall you think to voice objection?" Bill asked, as he looked up at him.

"No, Sir," Kennelm responded, and took a step back.

"My cousin, Reny Luciern shall sail with us. He shall depart as a decky, yet he shall return as a seasoned jack tar!" Bill declared.

"Aye aye, Captain," Kennelm responded, and rolled his eyes.

Late in the day Bill returned to Burghill House for the big family meal that Grace had arranged. He and Reny spent the evening with family and friends, sharing the venison, turkey, and Mrs. Whitley's fine desserts. The wine glasses were refilled and everyone remained in the dining room far later than usual.

As the men moved into the sitting room at last, Bill stopped Azaria in the hallway. "Has Stone agreed to the divorce at last?" he asked gently.

"He has not yet done with it, Bill. I fear he means to ruin me. I shall be ever bound to the man or publicly shamed as I do relate the sordid tale to the court," she whispered anxiously and shifted Victoria in her arms.

"Fear not," he told her and wiped a single tear from her cheek. "You shall not face ruin through his tenacity. You shall be freed from his wrongful grasp and shall be blessed with a happy life for you and your daughter."

Azaria hugged him quickly and smiled. "Go with God, Capt. Henry," she told him and kissed his cheek.

He nodded and winked before he turned and strode into the sitting room. The men talked and toasted Reny's first voyage. The women broke with tradition and joined them. Joseph poured cordials for the women and they were welcomed.

"When might you permit me to sail upon your great ship, Capt. Henry?" Azaria teased.

"No woman shall voyage on my ships," he replied apologetically. "'Tis sure to bring misfortune if a ship shall put to sea with a woman aboard."

Late in the evening Bill stood and gestured to Reny. They began the long round of farewells and finally made their way out the door. Under a clear, star filled sky, they rode to Wren's Tavern to meet with Kennelm and MacEwen. When the introductions had been made, they sat at a table and Bill ordered a tankard of ale and dram of whiskey for each of them. Bill gave Kennelm and MacEwen their instructions and asked Kennelm to step outside with him.

"'Tis a substance to ensure he does sleep well," Bill told him as he passed him a small tin of powder he had received from Mac. "Blend with his ale and when he has drunk it, carry him back to the ship. I shall board afore dawn and we shall sail promptly."

"Aye aye, Capt. Henry," Kennelm responded.

"I shall return in the night and shall require your aid as I do board," Bill advised him, and hurried around the building to the livery.

Bill trotted along the dark road to the town center. He passed dark businesses and homes, yet did not encounter any other people. When he turned onto Litchfield Farms Road he slipped off the horse and walked him along the side of the school house. He strolled around the back of the old barn beside it and tied the animal to a tree there. Moving in the shadows, he made his way to the back of the house.

In only a few minutes he was inside the home. Silently, he crept across the floor and along the hall to the staircase. He drew his pistol and primed it, then withdrew his sword. Noiselessly, he tripped the latch and opened the bedroom door. He heard the soft snoring to his left, and smiled.

Standing beside the bed, he stopped. "Mr. Stone, shall you rouse and speak with me?" he asked, cheerfully.

Startled awake, Nathan sat up quickly. He squinted into the dark but could not make out the shape among the shadows. "Why have you come?" he demanded angrily.

"Nathan Stone, did you grant the end to the union that Azaria did seek?"

"Bill Henry, take leave of my house!" he ordered.

"You... were... warned," he stated slowly. Bill twisted the blade to reflect the dim light from the moon and stars. He heard Nathan's gasp in the dark. "I cannot depart and leave you to trouble Azaria. You shant be permitted to ruin her happy, young life."

"I shall grant it to her," Nathan stammered. "Ride with me to Burghill House and I shall agree this night. In the morn we shall go to the esquire and I shall approve it."

"How shall I trust that you shall keep to your promise? No, I cannot. Tis but one solution left to me."

"No!" Nathan shouted. "Tis sinful! You shall linger ever more in the fires of hell, Bill Henry!"

"You do provoke me so," Bill uttered, rapidly growing tired of the exchange. Quickly, he moved at the edge of the bed and pressed his knee into Nathan's abdomen. He tied the man's wrists securely together. A silk scarf was pushed into his mouth and another one was wrapped over his mouth and tied at the back of his head. "Oblige me or face my blade."

Nathan stopped struggling and swung his legs over the side of the bed as he sat up. He stood and walked slowly in front of Bill, with the cold tip of the sword lightly grazing the back of his neck.

Quietly, they slipped out into the dark and moved in the shadows to Bill's horse. Bill boosted Nathan up to lie over the saddle. He grabbed the reins and ran along River Road toward the waterfront, with the horse beside him. As he neared the jail, he crossed the road and moved through the trees. Soon he heard the noise of the tavern in the distance. There were fewer patrons than there had been earlier but men still staggered out periodically. Further along the road, a night-watchmen made his rounds.

Bill led the horse into the line of trees behind the tavern. Quietly, he urged the animal forward. Nathan began to struggle and tried to call out. Bill grabbed his feet and pulled him backward, letting him fall to the ground. He knelt beside him and punched his jaw, then his temple. Nathan stilled and Bill fought to shove him back up over the saddle again.

Bill reached the livery beyond the warehouse at last. Standing behind the building, he grabbed Nathan's ankle and yanked it, stepping back as the man slid down again and landed in the dirt. He tied his ankles together and left him there as he walked the mare to the front and secured her inside. He hurried to the docks and ran up the gangway onto his ship. Kennelm and two other sailors waited on deck for him.

"Where shall Reny be found?" he asked.

"He does sleep soundly below deck," Kennelm responded.

Bill nodded and thanked him. "Follow me," he ordered, and rushed back to the livery. Kennelm threw Nathan over his right shoulder and darted back to his ship. Nathan was carried down to the hold and chained there.

"Shall we sally?" Kennelm asked as he followed Bill back to the stern. Bill nodded once and Kennelm began shouting orders. The crew on deck scrambled and the ship quickly began gliding along the dock. As they slid out into deeper water, the ship began turning into the current. Behind them the *Azul Cielo* followed.

The wind was with them and the sails were quickly unfurled. Bill held his hands behind his back, watching the shimmering wake in the dark water. He inhaled deeply and smiled. They moved rapidly to the south, skirting around slight bends in the channel. Traveling swiftly, they approached the mouth of the waterway several hours later. They veered southeast and floated out into the Atlantic Ocean.

Bill waited another hour before he called for the ropes and pulleys to be prepared. Kennelm relayed the orders to crew members and stipulated that the ropes should run from the port side to the starboard.

"No!" Bill shouted, and the crew froze. "You shall run it from stem to stern!"

"Stem to stern?" Kennelm asked. "'Tis certain death for the man, Captain."

"Challenge me not, Kennelm. It shall flow stem to stern," Bill told him.

Nathan was dragged up to the deck and dropped at the bow of the ship. The ship's doctor crushed peppermint leaves to revive Nathan and the silk cloth was removed from his mouth.

"Nathan Stone!" Bill shouted into the wind, as he gripped Nathan's hair and pulled his head up. "You are aboard the *Mi Querida Charlotte*!"

"Why have you taken me?" Nathan mumbled.

"Stone, you did aggrieve my family. Azaria was disgraced when the old woman delivered the child to her family home. As you did strike your wife, her baby did come early and shall ever suffer for it. She did plead for an ending to the union and you did refuse her. 'Tis a surety that you care not for your wife nor the children that you did father."

"Return to the shore and I shall make good for it," Stone pleaded, shakily.

"Do you think me a fool?" Bill asked, staring down into Nathan's eyes, wide with terror.

"I shant speak your name and I shall right my transgressions!"

"Nathan Stone, you shall be keelhauled for your many misdeeds!" Bill declared. "Be done with it!" he ordered and turned away.

Nathan was quickly stripped, then tied securely to ensure that he could not swim. A weight was attached to his legs as well. Two of the sailors hauled him to the bow of the ship and tied him to the ropes there. Three men stood at the far end of the ship waiting with ropes in hand. Nathan stood at the bow, struggling wildly in panic.

"Cease your tussle, Stone!" Bill called to him. "'Tis your rightful end come to you!"

The sailors wrestled him up and over the bowrail. They released him and he was quickly drawn under the ship when he hit the water.

"Pull!" Kennelm ordered repeatedly, as the three sailors at the stern drew the taught rope along the length of the keel from stem to stern beneath the ship. As they pulled the rope, Nathan's bare body was drawn across the razor sharp barnacles that had attached themselves to the bottom of the ship.

Eventually, his body appeared at the back of the ship and was hauled up and over the railing. The ropes were removed and he was untied before his bloody body was tossed back into the ocean. A young deckhand drew up buckets to wash away the blood from the stern. The ropes were quickly coiled and the sailors, not on watch, strode down to their quarters to sleep.

Bill remained at the wheel, waiting for dawn, as he smiled with satisfaction. Nathan Stone would trouble his family no more. He inhaled the salty sea air and relaxed, home again, at last, over his beloved ocean.

93

Early in June, Norah delivered a healthy baby girl. Born only six months after the marriage of her parents, she was named Melinda Aileen Hanscom. Just days after her birth, the sheriff knocked on the door of the orphan asylum. He presented a warrant for the arrest of Paul Hanscom and asked to see the infant.

Mrs. Humboldt quickly produced the robust, full-term baby. The sheriff noted the size and condition of the child and demanded that Hanscom speak with him. Mrs. Humboldt advised him that she had no knowledge of her handyman's whereabouts. She consented to a thorough search of the house and barn, but Paul was not found.

Sheriff Mitchell and Mrs. Humboldt were unaware that Paul Hanscom had been in the kitchen when the sheriff entered the home. He heard the discussion of the warrant and slipped out the back door. Traveling south under the cover of the trees, he soon crossed the Scaffel River. By noon he felt confident in moving to walk along the edge of the road. He planned to make his way through New Hampshire to Portsmouth and continue on to Boston.

At the orphan asylum in Georges Falls, Norah slept through the afternoon with her baby in the cradle nearby. In the evening, the cook carried up a tray with supper. She sat with Norah and told her about the visit from the sheriff.

"Why should the sheriff seek him?" Norah cried.

"The sheriff has knowledge of the child, conceived afore the marriage."

"'Tis a fine to be paid alone. None shall be hanged or jailed for such in this time of enlightenment," Norah declared.

"If a husband shall consent, tis but a fine to be paid. Yet if he shall deny the woman, she shall face the whipping post," the cook advised her.

"I must speak with my husband. Shall you summon him unto me?"

"'Tis no sighting of Mr. Hanscom from this morning."

"Fear not, he shall come," Norah told her and wiped away the first tears.

A week passed and Paul Hanscom did not return. Mrs. Humboldt reminded Norah that he was responsible for the cost of her room and board during her lying-in. If he had indeed abandoned his wife and child, she would be expected to contact her father and request support. When the sheriff returned again, he agreed to deliver Mrs. Humboldt's message to Rev. Murray.

The next morning, the minister and his wife travelled to see Norah and their new grandchild. Norah had planned to conceal the child for several months before disclosing the birth to them. Embarrassed and regretful, she wept as her mother held the infant and her father scolded.

"I have no monies to pay for your outlays in this house. You shall return to my house and shall convalesce under your mother's care," he stated firmly.

Silently, Aileen packed the trunk with Norah's belongings and the few clothes she had for the baby. Norah walked slowly down the stairs, clutching her father's arm. She lay in the back of the borrowed wagon with Melinda in her arms. Rev. Murray paid Mrs.

Humboldt the money that Paul Hanscom owed. He jiggled the
reins and kept the horses at a slow pace as they rode from Georges
Falls into East Grantham again.

94

Bon Gage and Riley Lawrence stood at the altar as Rev. Pender
read from the book in his hands. Lily sat in the front pew between
Grace and Mac. He had prepared a calming blend and watched as
Lily sipped it before they journeyed to the church. He held Annie's
hand and smiled lovingly down on her. His other arm rested
behind Lily's shoulders in case he needed to cover her mouth
during the ceremony.

"Riley Lawrence wilt thou have this woman to be thy wedded
wife, to live together after God's ordinance in the holy estate of
Matrimony? Wilt thou love her, comfort her, honor and keep her
in sickness and in health; forsaking all other, keep thee only unto
her, so long as ye both shall live?"

"I will," Riley responded.

"Hephzibah Gage, wilt thou..."

"Hephzibah?" Riley asked puzzled.

"Shhh," Bon shushed him. "Rev. Pender?" she urged, as her
cheeks flushed.

"Hephzibah Gage, wilt thou have this man to be they wedded
husband, to live together after God's ordinance in the holy estate of
matrimony? Wilt thou obey him, serve him, love, honor, and keep
him in sickness and in health; and, forsaking all others, keep thee
only unto him, so long as ye both shall live?"

"I will," she answered quickly.

"Who giveth this woman to be married to this man?"

Her Uncle Joseph took Bon's right hand and placed Riley's hand
over hers.

Rev. Pender continued with the ceremony and Riley placed the
finely crafted silver ring on her finger as he uttered, "With this ring
I thee wed, with my body I thee worship, and with all my worldly
goods I thee endow: In the name of the Father, and of the Son, and
of the Holy Ghost. Amen."

They knelt as Rev. Pender began to recite the prayers. "O eternal God, Creator and Preserver of all mankind, Giver of all spiritual grace, the author of everlasting life; Send thy blessing upon these thy servants, the man and this woman, whom we bless in thy name; that, as Isaac and Rebecca lived faithfully together, so these persons may surely perform and keep the vow and covenant betwixt them made, whereof this ring given and received is a token and pledge, and may ever remain in perfect love and peace together, and live according to thy laws; through Jesus Christ our Lord. Amen.

Those whom God hath joined together let no man put asunder," Rev. Pender declared. He pronounced the couple man and wife. *Beati Omnes* Psalm 128 was read aloud. The minister continued with a number of lengthy prayers. At last he turned the couple to face the congregation and introduced them to their family and friends as Mr. and Mrs. Riley Lawrence.

Dressed in the beautiful gown that Lily had worn when she married Timothy Gage, Bon took Riley's arm and walked along the aisle to the front doors of the church. They crossed the grounds to the Meeting House and ran up the steps together. As they hurried inside, Riley yanked her back behind one of the open doors. He pulled her into his arms and kissed her tenderly. She giggled and kissed him in return.

Through the afternoon and into the evening they danced, ate and drank with family and friends. They began their farewells at last and soon rushed out the door to the waiting carriage. The Gage home had been reopened and prepared for occupancy. Lily had become troublesome yet again, and Riley had agreed to live in the Gage house with her. Bon planned to care for her mother there while they waited for Eddie to finish his education in Boston.

"Hephzibah?" Riley prodded when they were settled in the back of the carriage.

"Tis an embarrassment, Riley," she responded and laughed.

"Speak it my dear bride."

"My mother has ever suffered from melancholia. In one of her fits, she did name me for her prized barn cat," she told him and sighed.

"I pray that you shall never share this tale with my mother," he pleaded. He pulled her into his arms and kissed her passionately.

95

It would be two years before Capt. Bill Henry and Reny Luciern would return to East Grantham. Sailing under the French flag, they toured the Mediterranean for months before setting out for the Caribbean again. There the French flag was lowered and they sailed under the Spanish flag again.

The morning after Nathan Stone's disappearance, his housekeeper made his bed and cleaned his room. She assumed that he had been called out for a surgical emergency in the night and gave it little thought. The second day she began to wonder, but only supposed that he was tending to a patient after a surgery. He had been gone for as much as three days before with no word, so there was little cause for concern.

A week passed before the housekeeper became concerned and contacted Mac Wallace to ask if he knew where the surgeon might be. The following day the sheriff was notified. He advised the housekeeper that Nathan Stone had likely become the victim of highwaymen, as he travelled in the night. No horses were missing from the barn and the sheriff determined that someone had come to call for the surgeon in his own carriage.

After another two weeks, as the sheriff found no trace of Nathan or anyone who had called for him or seen him, he ended the search. He guessed that the remains would eventually be found deep in the woods by hunters and would be buried then. The house was shuttered and the housekeeper moved on.

While the sheriff contemplated the missing surgeon, he made time to travel to the home of Rev. Tomas Murray. The good reverend's only daughter was arrested and charged with the illegal conception of her baby before her marriage to Paul Hanscom. The two month-old infant remained with Aileen Murray while Tomas accompanied Norah to the jail.

Norah was taken to the whipping post at noon and restrained there. While neighbors and old friends watched, she received her six lashes from the jailer's whip. When her punishment had been delivered, she travelled home again with her father. Aileen treated the open wounds with a salve provided by Dr. Mac Wallace. The scars on her back would remain for the rest of her life.

When the sheriff told Azaria of Nathan's suspected demise, she had no desire to return to her husband's house, with or without him. She believed that he had gone south to Boston to find the mother of his healthy baby and hated him more for the sudden departure. Her baby Victoria remained a sickly infant, and she would never forgive Nathan for the premature delivery. She felt more secure in the family home and more at ease with her brother, Dr. Wallace, just across the road.

Reny and Bill were missed but life continued as the seasons passed. A new surgeon, George Franklin, arrived in August to replace Nathan Stone. He worked well with Mac and quickly settled into the community. He would eventually marry Maggie Pender, Joanna's oldest daughter and midwife apprentice.

During a bitter storm in January 1815, Faith Gage Alray delivered her second baby. Another healthy baby boy, he was named Leland Alray. With no assistance or cooperation from her mother-in-law or husband, Faith delivered the baby alone in her bedroom. Only hours later, Faith rose from her bed to begin preparing breakfast for the family and to care for nearly eighteen month-old Richard. Faith would conceive six more children through the coming years but this would be the last successful pregnancy for her.

In February 1815, the War of 1812 finally ended and shipping along the Atlantic Coast became safer again. News of the end of the war slowly spread to the farthest corner of the northeast. The number of ships delivering cargo to the docks at East Grantham soon increased.

March arrived with the first fresh taste of spring. An early thaw allowed the flowers to burst through the ground sooner than they usually did. The buds on the trees quickly adorned the branches. The snow melted rapidly and the first spring rains rinsed away the last traces of winter.

Annie Wallace delivered her fourth baby, another boy. Mac was delighted to have a second son and named him Caleb Benjamin. Leaving Annie in Joanna's capable hands, Mac traipsed his children off to church on Sunday morning. He showed them off proudly as Rev. Pender baptized the newest Wallace baby.

Only a few months later, in July, Chloe Grenier gave birth to Teague's first child. The baby girl arrived with a head of thick, dark hair and large blue eyes that would eventually darken. Teague named her Patrice Aoife Grenier and quickly declared that she was the prettiest baby he had seen. Relieved that her infant was healthy and strong, Chloe only smiled at his bragging.

Too soon 1815 had passed and spring had come again. Early in the month of May, 1816, the *Mi Querida Charlotte* and *Azul Cielo* docked in East Grantham. Kennelm took charge of the off-loading of both ships while Capt. Henry acquired two horses from the livery. He stopped at the warehouse to great Teague, but found that he had gone for the night. With a sweet baby who had begun to walk already and a happy wife, he no longer worked late into the evenings.

Bill and Reny rode from the waterfront to Botts' Tavern. They sat at a table and waited to be served the rabbit stew and tankards of ale. Jacob Frawley remained at the table to answer their questions about the changes over their two year-long absence. When they were up to date on the local news, Jacob hurried out the kitchen door to tell Julia and Laurent that Reny had returned.

"Reny!" Julia shouted, as she ran toward him with her arms open. Laurent walked in behind her, beaming.

Reny stood and braced himself against the table as his mother threw her arms around him. He extended a hand to Laurent and he shook it firmly. Slowly, they noted the odd way that Reny stood and the way he held his left hand in his pocket.

"Reny?" Julia prodded as she looked from him to Bill. Awkwardly, he turned slightly and sat again. "'Tis a fine thing that you have returned," she announced uneasily, and sat beside him.

Reny and Bill ate and drank while they talked about their voyage home. As he relaxed, Reny removed his hand from his pocket again. He chattered happily until he realized that his mother was staring at the leather glove.

"Bill I cannot..." Reny mumbled and looked down at the table.

"In a skirmish with Barbary Pirates, near on a year ago now, a number of my crew was lost," Bill declared.

"'Tis dreadful," Julia responded guardedly.

"The ship's surgeon did save four men through amputations. Reny did suffer greatly after the removal of his right leg. Yet he did recover and a mock limb of solid wood and sturdy leather does fill the space."

"Reny, no!" Julia cried. Laurent moved to stand behind her chair and touched her shoulders reassuringly.

"Mama, I am well," Reny confirmed. "Tis but a limp that does remain."

"What of the glove?" Laurent asked gently.

"At my first sailing three fingers were lost in a tangle ropes on the deck. I did learn quickly and shant err so again."

"Reny, you shant sail with Bill ever more," Julia protested.

"Tis the man's decision, Julia," Laurent admonished.

"I beg of you, Reny…"

"Julia, you shant speak so. Tis of Reny's own to determine his course."

"I shall take leave of you that you might enjoy Reny's return," Bill stated and stood quickly. "If you do mean to sail aboard my ships, you shall be welcome. We shall depart in but two days."

"Tis rightful I shall board afore you do go, if you shall have me," Reny answered. Bill nodded and smiled. He hurried out the front door and rode on to Burghill House.

Grace welcomed Bill and quickly began planning a great family feast. The following evening they gathered in the dining room to enjoy a delicious array of foods. Bill and Reny held the new babies and marveled at the growth of the little ones that they had last seen two years earlier.

"How does Victoria progress?" Bill asked Azaria, as he held the toddler on his lap.

"She is smaller than reasonable for her years and she remains sickly, yet she is a delightful child. Her laugh does charm the darkest heart," Azaria replied, and tickled her. Victoria giggled and moved to stand on Bill's lap. She turned to touch his trimmed beard and moustache. He kissed her forehead and she laughed.

"Have you received word of Nathan Stone?" Bill asked.

"I have not," she responded, curtly. "He shall soon be declared deceased and it shall be done with. William Redmond did approach Joseph and Mac to ask for consent to court me. They did agree to permit it when the proclamation of Nathan's death has been signed."

"Is Redmond a good man?" Bill posed.

"He is a good and kind man. Victoria does adore him. He does tempt my heart as well," she told him and smiled, sheepishly.

"I pray you shall be exceedingly happy with him, Azaria," Bill smiled, and turned his attention to Victoria again.

The men moved to the sitting room and talked late into the night. Bill brought in jugs of the finest rum. Grace wheeled in a cart with various desserts for them to enjoy and quickly closed the doors as she left the room. She smiled at the murmur of the deep voices from the room behind her. She recalled the days when Teague Johnes, Phillip and Luke talked behind those doors. Cheerfully, she returned to the kitchen to visit with the women and spoil the little children.

The following day the ships hold was loaded with cargo to be delivered in Virginia. Near midnight they set sail at last with promises that they would not be gone so long with this journey. Reny felt guilty as he left his mother in tears, but he felt the lure of the sea as strong as Bill and eagerly boarded the ship.

Bill's ships had arrived in Virginia and departed for Jamaica when Eddie arrived in East Grantham in July. After four years in Boston, Eddie was pleased to be home and anxious to begin his apprenticeship. Judge Malachi Sterling had agreed to take him into his office beside the Court of General Sessions.

Riley and Bon had cared for Lily in the old family home over the past year. Dobbs had remained and a new cook and housekeeper had been hired. Eddie returned to the bedroom he had lived in as he grew up in the house. Lily occupied one of the smaller bedrooms, remaining in bed most days. She left her room only to attend the weekly church service, followed by the Sunday dinner. She always dressed in her finest gowns before leaving the house.

96

Beneath a deep blue sky, tiny snowflakes floated lazily down to the frost covered ground. The wind had stilled and silence settled over the area. Grace stood on the back steps looking up at the sparkling stars, surrounded by the icy blue moon. She inhaled the cold, clear air and smiled. As the chill penetrated her black, wool cloak, she stepped inside again and closed the heavy door.

Quietly, she strode into the kitchen and hung a kettle of water over the fire. She poked at the logs and added some kindling. The flames climbed higher and caressed the bottom of the cast iron pot. She closed her eyes and listened to the crackle of the fire. The resin in the wood began to sizzle and pop. She pulled out a chair with a scrape across the weathered floor and sat.

"Mama, tis the dead of night," Joseph reminded her, as he walked into the kitchen.

"Tis a sleepless night," she responded. "Shall you sip tea with me?"

"I shall," he sat and looked at the steam rising from the kettle. "Mayhap a slice of pie shall be found in the pantry?"

"Tis so," she chuckled, and stood to walk to the pantry. She gripped the table and hesitated, as she touched her hand to her chest.

"What troubles you, Mama?" he asked worriedly.

"Tis naught but dyspepsia," she assured him. "Mayhap Mrs. Whitley shall minimize the spicing of her dishes."

She served the slice of the apple pie to him and poured two cups of tea. She retrieved a tin of ships biscuits from the pantry and sat again. Outside the window, the size of the snowflakes increased and they melted as they touched the glass.

"Is your sleep often disrupted in the night?" he pressed.

"Tis in the night that I do miss Phillip and Luke most," she admitted.

"Tis reasonable that you shall."

"Joseph, in but a month it shall be Christmas. On the morrow I shall begin planning the grand holiday ball of Burghill House."

"Tis your delight, Mama," Joseph sighed, and smiled as he shoveled another big bite of pie into his mouth.

Grace felt the warmth of the fire and sipped the hot tea. When Joseph had finished his pie and tea, he stood and moved to build up the fire in the hearth. He walked throughout the first floor, adding logs to the fireplaces and stoves. He tended those on the second floor next. Quietly, he slipped back into the big bed where Millie slept soundly. He put his arm over her waist and nestled against her warm body. She roused and tilted her head as he moved to kiss her.

"Tis a late hour," she murmured sleepily.

"My mother does not sleep. Tis worrisome."

"She is an old woman, Joseph. Tis a common happening."

"Mayhap," he whispered and pulled her tighter against him. "On the morrow I do mean to talk of it with Mac."

"Tis reasonable that you shall. Sleep now," she yawned.

Downstairs, Grace passed back through the sitting room, stopping in front of her father's book shelf. She closed her eyes and pictured his handsome face. She was certain she could smell the scent of lilacs in the air. From childhood, she had always associated the fragrance with him. Happily, she recalled walking along the drive, with her small hand lost in his, as they passed the lilac trees in bloom.

From the bookshelf she selected Voltaire's *Candide*. She sat in the rocking chair and pulled a small quilt over her lap. The snow whispered against the window sill as it slowly began to accumulate. She flipped through the pages of the first chapter, searching for a favorite passage.

Speaking softly she began to read it aloud. "Observe that noses were made to wear spectacles; and so we have spectacles. Legs were visibly instituted to be breeched, and we have breeches. Stones were formed to be quarried and to build castles; and My Lord has a very noble castle; the greatest Baron in the province should have the best house; and as pigs were made to be eaten, we eat pork all year round; consequently, those who have asserted all is well talk nonsense; they ought to have said that all is for the best…" she paused and looked up to see Phillip standing in the doorway.

Dressed in his finest dark blue coat, with the polished silver buttons and white breeches, he was incredibly handsome. The gray that had been at his temples in his last year was gone. She felt her heart pounding in her chest and butterflies flew crazily around in her stomach as he slowly approached.

"Phillip?" she breathed, completely infatuated by him.

"I have missed you greatly, my love," he told her and knelt beside her chair. He touched her hand and kissed it softly.

"I have missed you as well, Phillip" she whispered and smiled.

Holding her hands between his, he looked into her eyes and spoke quietly,

"O my Love's like a red, red rose
That's newly sprung in June;
O my Love's like the melody

That's sweetly played in tune.

As fair art thou, my bonnie lass,
 So deep in love am I;
And I will love thee still, my dear,
Till a' the seas gang dry:

Till a' the seas gang dry, my dear,
And the rocks melt wi' the sun;
I will love thee still, my dear,
While the sands o' life shall run.

And fare thee well, my only love,
And fare thee well awhile!
And I will come again, my Love,
Tho' it ware ten thousand mile," gently he touched her fingers to his lips.

"Phillip, did you come this night only to promise that you shall come again?" she asked sadly.

"No, Grace, tis to fulfill my promise unto you. On the night that I did make you my wife, as you slept in my arms, I did recite the words unto you. This night I shall make good my word."

"Shall it be this night that I shall be rejoined to you?"

"'Tis so."

"What of Luke?"

"'Twas known to him that you were ever mine and he shall relent once again. We shall be parted nevermore, Grace."

Grace closed her eyes and sighed as a brilliant smile lit up her face. She felt his lips brush against hers and smelled his seductive scent. He held her hand and she remembered their wedding day as he held her hand in the church. Slowly she drifted into a dreamless asleep and the book slid off her lap to land at her feet.

"'Tis none I could ever love more, Phillip," she murmured in her sleep.

97

The sun rose in a vivid pink sky the following morning. Millie discovered Grace slumped in the chair in the sitting room. She quickly woke Joseph and Teague. The snowfall had ended but a cold breeze blew as Teague crossed the road to summon Mac.

Through the morning Jacob Frawley and Penn Cooper arrived to take Grace's body away. Mrs. Whitley carried the black crepe down from the attic and hung it on the front door.

Late in the day, Grace's fine casket was delivered and placed in the sitting room with the lid removed. Family and friends filled the house and supported each other as they mourned her passing.

On the third day, the casket was removed and stored in the crypt behind Botts' Tavern, where it would remain until spring. As the dreary winter passed, dreadful storms followed one after another. The Sunday dinners continued in Grace's memory, but much of the magic had gone. It felt more obligation than celebration without Grace among them.

Late in January 1817, Mac's wife, Annie gave birth to her fifth baby, Ian Michael Wallace. Grace had attended the previous four deliveries and she was greatly missed at this one. Joanna and Millie managed, but the absence of Grace's strong spirit was notable. As the years passed, Annie would give Mac a total of eleven healthy children.

A month after Ian's birth, Joseph's daughter, Thea went into labor with the first of seven children to come. Her husband Leonard had become a fine husband. When Joanna announced that a son had come, Leonard quickly named him John David and hurried out the back door. He rode to the jailhouse where he worked with his father and brothers. Proudly he announced the news and accepted their good wishes. He galloped along Killock Road to the Chernock's wood shop to share the news with Joseph.

The first week of April heavy rains fell, as Chloe Grenier's labor pains intensified. For two days they continued and finally strengthened further. At last, her second daughter, Teagan Grace was born. Joanna declared the baby healthy and announced that hers was the loudest cry she had ever heard. Teague would be blessed with six children, four of which would be sons.

In the summer of 1817, Eddie had become an attorney at last. He remained a high-minded and arrogant man. His dreams were focused on becoming a judge and he would achieve it in the years to come. After his return, Norah approached him to plead for a second chance at a future, but he quickly and cruelly rejected her. Four months later he married Eliza Payne, the oldest daughter of Judge Byron Payne.

Faith cherished her sons Richard and Leland and consoled herself with them as she lost six children in eight years. She and her husband Glenn Alray grew more distant until he eventually moved to a separate bedroom. When his mother finally passed, he suggested buying a covered wagon and traveling to the Missouri territory. He would talk of this plan for the next fifteen years until his early death after a bout of pneumonia.

Bon and Riley remained in the Gage family home but were asked to give up the grandest bedroom after Eddie married Eliza. They agreed, and accepted the smaller, yet sizable room. Riley worked with his father as a silversmith until the old man passed. Riley and his younger brother continued the family business. Bon blessed him with six sons and three daughters. Eddie and Eliza remained childless.

Bill and Reny returned again in 1818, greatly saddened to find that Grace had passed away. They visited her grave, between Phillip's and Luke's in the family cemetery. With Laurent suffering from a long-term, debilitating illness, Reny decided to remain in East Grantham for his mother. Bill understood and set sail without him a few days later.

Four months after Reny's return, Laurent slipped into a coma and died the next day. Reny accepted responsibility for the livery and tavern. Six months later he married Cora Pender. They settled into the house behind the tavern and Julia remained there with them. A year later, Cora delivered the first of eight sons, who would all inherit Reynolds Garand's golden brown eyes. Reny had mastered his prosthetic leg and managed well even with his missing fingers.

Bill sailed for the Caribbean again, returning every other year until he finally gave up his beloved sea. He would make his home in East Grantham in 1834, as he neared his fortieth birthday. A year earlier, he had married a young French woman at St. Augustine, Florida and broke his biggest rule in permitting her aboard his ship to sail north with him. His wife, Daphne Adenais delivered two sons and a daughter before she died in childbirth after seven years of marriage.

In the winter of 1820 Rev. Tomas Murray and his wife Aileen both died. Norah was quickly advised that she would need to vacate the home when the new minister arrived. She moved to one of the rooms above Wren's Tavern with her six year-old daughter, Melinda. Norah worked in the tavern as a barmaid, while the child remained in her room upstairs. A year later, she married a highwayman and travelled south to Massachusetts with him and Melinda.

Joseph and Millie remained in Burghill House until their deaths, many years later. The Sunday dinners and Christmas parties continued out of respect for Grace. The walls between Grace's bedroom and the sitting room were removed to make the sitting room far larger. The room that had been added for Cherish became a fine library.

Joseph's second daughter, Clara, married a cobbler, Abraham Quince and worked with him in his small shop. They lived contentedly in the rooms above the shop. Through the years, she delivered three daughters and a son, but only the boy survived.

Lily's mental condition diminished further after Grace was gone. The doses required to keep her calm gradually increased until she eventually became bedridden. In her early forties she suffered seizures from the years of Laudanum use. As her symptoms became more painful, she overdosed on the drug and asphyxiated. Although many believed that her death was a suicide, Mac declared it accidental and she was interred with Timothy in the East Grantham Cemetery.

Burghill House passed from Joseph to Mac, as the last living grandchild of Tobias and Ruth Chernock Burghill. Mac sold the house he built and moved into the family home with Annie and their children. Teague, Chloe, and their children remained in the big house as well. When Mac eventually died, the house was deeded to Teague Grenier, the first of the great-grandchildren. Through the centuries the house would continue to be recognized the finest dwelling in the area. Time would pass and new generations inhabited the home, but Burghill House would always hold secrets.

ABOUT THE AUTHOR

Kim Scott (1962-present) was born on Charleston
Naval Base in South Carolina and grew up in
Pine Point in Scarborough, Maine. She has also
lived in Colorado and Michigan.
Currently she resides in Southern Maine.

Ruth Chernock Series.

Regarding Ruth
In Ruth's Memory
On Grace's Shoulders
Pink Sky & Mourning

Made in the USA
Middletown, DE
25 March 2019